KU-216-616

THE LOST METAL

BY BRANDON SANDERSON®

THE STORMLIGHT ARCHIVE®

The Way of Kings
Words of Radiance
Edgedancer (novella)
Oathbringer
Dawnshard (novella)
Rhythm of War

THE MISTBORN® SAGA

THE ORIGINAL TRILOGY
Mistborn
The Well of Ascension
The Hero of Ages
Mistborn: Secret History (novella)

THE WAX AND WAYNE SERIES
The Alloy of Law
Shadows of Self
The Bands of Mourning
The Lost Metal

Elantris
Warbreaker
Arcanum Unbounded:
The Cosmere® Collection

ALCATRAZ VS. THE EVIL LIBRARIANS

Alcatraz vs. the Evil Librarians
The Scrivener's Bones
The Knights of Crystallia
The Shattered Lens
The Dark Talent

WITH JANCI PATTERSON
Bastille vs. the Evil Librarians

THE RECKONERS®

Steelheart
Firefight
Calamity

SKYWARD

Skyward
Starsight
Cytonic

WITH JANCI PATTERSON
Skyward Flight: The Collection

The Rithmatist

THE
LOST METAL

A MISTBORN NOVEL

BRANDON SANDERSON

TOR

A TOM DOHERTY ASSOCIATES BOOK

NEW YORK

This is a work of fiction. All of the characters, organizations, and events
portrayed in this novel are either products of the author's imagination
or are used fictitiously.

THE LOST METAL

Copyright © 2022 by Dragonsteel Entertainment, LLC

Mistborn®, the Stormlight Archive®, Reckoners®, Cosmere®, and Brandon Sanderson®
are registered trademarks of Dragonsteel Entertainment, LLC.

All rights reserved.

Interior illustrations by Isaac Stewart and Ben McSweeney
© Dragonsteel Entertainment, LLC

A Tor Book
Published by Tom Doherty Associates
120 Broadway
New York, NY 10271

www.tor-forge.com

Tor® is a registered trademark of Macmillan Publishing Group, LLC.

Library of Congress Cataloging-in-Publication Data

Names: Sanderson, Brandon, author.
Title: The lost metal / Brandon Sanderson.
Description: First edition. | New York : Tor, A Tom Doherty Associates Book, 2022. |
Series: The Mistborn Saga ; 7 | Identifiers: LCCN 2022040588 (print) |
LCCN 2022040589 (ebook) | ISBN 9780765391193 (hardcover) |
ISBN 9781250880963 (international, sold outside the U.S.,
subject to rights availability) | ISBN 9780765391209 (ebook)
Classification: LCC PS3619.A533 L67 2022 (print) |
LCC PS3619.A533 (ebook) | DDC 813/.6—dc23
LC record available at https://lccn.loc.gov/2022040588
LC ebook record available at https://lccn.loc.gov/2022040589

Our books may be purchased in bulk for promotional, educational, or
business use. Please contact your local bookseller or the Macmillan Corporate
and Premium Sales Department at 1-800-221-7945, extension 5442,
or by email at MacmillanSpecialMarkets@macmillan.com.

First U.S. Edition: 2022
First International Edition: 2022

Printed in the United States of America

0 9 8 7 6 5 4 3 2 1

FOR ETHAN SKARSTEDT

Who is a man of Honor.

CONTENTS

ACKNOWLEDGMENTS

Sixteen years ago, sitting in a dim booth at a local steakhouse, I first pitched to my wife an audacious idea I'd been developing: taking an epic fantasy world, and then expanding it through different eras into the future. I'd seen mashups of fantasy and science fiction before, and I'd seen epic fantasy inch toward industrial technology. But I'd never seen an author develop a world in quite this way—giving an expansive view of a planet moving into the future, using the lore of earlier book series as the foundation of religion and myth.

It was a gamble. Readers tend to like their genres well delineated. Here, I was pitching something that broke apart those genre lines in ways that historically did not sell well. Yet I was convinced that the larger-scale project (the vision of a planet and its magic throughout various eras) was worth the risk. That brings us here, to the final book of Era Two of Mistborn and my grand experiment with genre.

Whether I've been successful or not so far is up to you, the reader. But I can say this: I certainly wouldn't have gotten where I am without the help of a large number of people. I know these acknowledgments are a bit of a blur of names, but I'm so grateful to each and every one of them. These are the people who, when I come up with some new audacious plan, don't roll their eyes—they instead roll up their sleeves and make it happen.

For this book, Joshua Bilmes did his usual excellent job as my agent. On his team, Susan Velazquez and Christina Zobel were also a great deal of help, managing all the different overseas contracts and subagents.

Speaking of across the pond, I had some extra-special help from Gillian Redfearn on this book—she's my UK editor, and took the lead on this book performing the line edit work that often is shouldered by the US publisher. She did a fantastic job, and I'm lucky to have her help. In addition, I'd like to thank Emad Akhtar and Brendan Durkin at Gollancz in the UK, as well as my UK agents, John Berlyne and Stevie Finegan at the Zeno Agency.

Over in the US, Devi Pillai was the lead editor on this project, offering her excellent editorial eye for story and character as she always does. Also at Tor, I'd like to thank Molly McGhee, Tessa Villanueva, Lucille Rettino, Eileen Lawrence, Alexis Saarela, Heather Saunders, Rafal Gibek, Felipe Cruz, Amelie Littell, and Hayley Jozwiak. The copyeditor was our long-time collaborator in that field, Terry McGarry.

As for the audiobook, the irreplaceable Michael Kramer is once again giving voice to my characters and making me sound good. I appreciate you, Michael. Thank you for all you do. At Macmillian Audio, I'd like to thank Steve Wagner, Samantha Edelson, and Drew Kilman.

Increasingly these days, my books take a ton of extra work in the art department. So we'll give these gunslingers their own section— even though some of them could overlap with other sections. For instance, Peter Lutjen is Tor's art director, and deserves a hearty thanks. Chris McGrath did our jacket illustration. My internal art director at Dragonsteel is IY<—the artist formerly known as Isaac Stewart. He did the maps, symbols, and a lot of the work (including the writing) on the broadsheets. Keep an eye out for books by IY< in the future. (Yes, I did just make up that whole symbol thing. I can do that. I have a literary license.) Our good friend and longtime collaborator Ben McSweeney did most of the art you find in the broadsheets. Rachael Lynn Buchanan was our art assistant, and Jennifer Neal provided some additional help in creating the broadsheets.

In my company, Dragonsteel, our in-house Editorial department is headed by the Insatiable Peter Ahlstrom, with Karen Ahlstrom running continuity and various additional editorial help being provided by Betsey Ahlstrom. And Kristy S. Gilbert has just come on as our Production Editor.

Dragonsteel's Fulfillment and Events team is headed by Kara Stewart, and that team includes Christi Jacobsen, Lex Willhite, Kellyn Neumann, Mem Grange, Michael Bateman, Joy Allen, Katy Ives, Richard Rubert, Sean VanBuskirk, Isabel Chrisman, Tori Mecham, Ally Reep, Jacob Chrisman, Alex Lyon, and Owen Knowlton.

Our in-house Publicity and Marketing team is headed by Adam Horne, with Jeremy Palmer as our marketing director. Our Operations team is headed by Mat "My name is actually Matt with two T's" Hatch, with Jane Horne, Emma Tan-Stoker, Kathleen Dorsey Sanderson, Makena Saluone, and Hazel Cummings.

And, of course, my wonderful wife, Emily Sanderson, is our COO at Dragonsteel. And is the cutest person on this list.

Less cute, but still very helpful, are the members of the writing group. On this book they include: Kaylynn ZoBell, Peter Ahlstrom, Karen Ahlstrom, Alan Layton, Eric James Stone, Darci Stone, Kathleen Dorsey Sanderson, Emily Sanderson, and Ben "Rick Stranger" Olsen. Also, of course, there is Ethan Skarstedt—to whom this book is dedicated. The real-life inspiration for Skar from Bridge Four, Ethan has been helping me get my soldiering and gunplay right for some twenty years now. Many thanks, Ethan, for helping me pretend I know what I'm talking about.

Mi'chelle Walker created our beta reader feedback database, which was super useful. The beta readers included Trae Cooper, Tim Challener, Ted Herman, Suzanne Musin, Sumejja Muratagić-Tadić, Paige Phillips, Shannon Nelson, Sean VanBuskirk, Ross Newberry, Rosemary Williams, Richard Fife, Rahul Pantula, Poonam Desai, Philip Vorwaller, Paige Vest, Mi'chelle Walker, Megan Kanne, Matt Wiens, Mark Axies Lindberg, Marnie Peterson, Lyndsey Luther, Linnea Lindstrom, Lauren McCaffrey, Kendra Wilson, Kendra Alexander, Kellyn Neumann, Kalyani Poluri, Joy Allen, Joshua Harkey, Jory "Chief Chicken Head Scratcher" Phillips, Jessie Lake, Jessica Ashcraft, Jennifer Neal, Ian McNatt, Chris "Gunner" McGrath, Gary Singer, Frankie Jerome, Evgeni "Argent" Kirilov, Erika Kuta Marler, Eric Lake, Drew McCaffrey, Deana Covel Whitney, David Fallon, David Behrens, Darci Cole, Craig Hanks, Christina Goodman, Christopher Cottingham, Chana Oshira Block, Brian T. Hill, Brandon Cole, Lingting "Botanica" Xu, Bob Kluttz, Ben Marrow, Becca Reppert, Bao Pham, Anthony Acker, Alyx Hoge, Alice Arneson, Alexis Horizon, Aaron Biggs, Joe Deardeuff, Rob West, and Jayden King.

Gamma readers included many of the above, plus Sam Baskin, Glen Vogelaar, Dale Wiens, Billy Todd, Ari Kufer, Matthew Sorensen, Ram Shoham, Eliyahu Berelowitz Levin, and Aaron Ford.

We got some detailed help from a particular group on this book, people who I have asked to keep an eye on my magic systems and offer feedback on where I might need more explanations or might be in danger of contradicting myself. We're calling them our Magic System Continuity team, but I'm officially dubbing them Arcanists going forward. They are Joshua Harkey, Eric Lake, Evgeni Kirilov, David Behrens, Ian McNatt, and Ben Marrow.

I would like to extend a special thanks to my good friends Kalyani and Rahul, longtime beta readers, who have been encouraging me for years to look into Indian mythology and lore for inspiration for fantasy storytelling. They provided excellent consultation in this book on a certain character who the three of us worked on together to try to expand the Cosmere a little bit in this direction.

Thank you to everyone on this list. And, of course, to the readers. Mistborn has been a strange journey these last sixteen years, and I feel it's about to get even stranger—as well as (with a little luck) even more incredible.

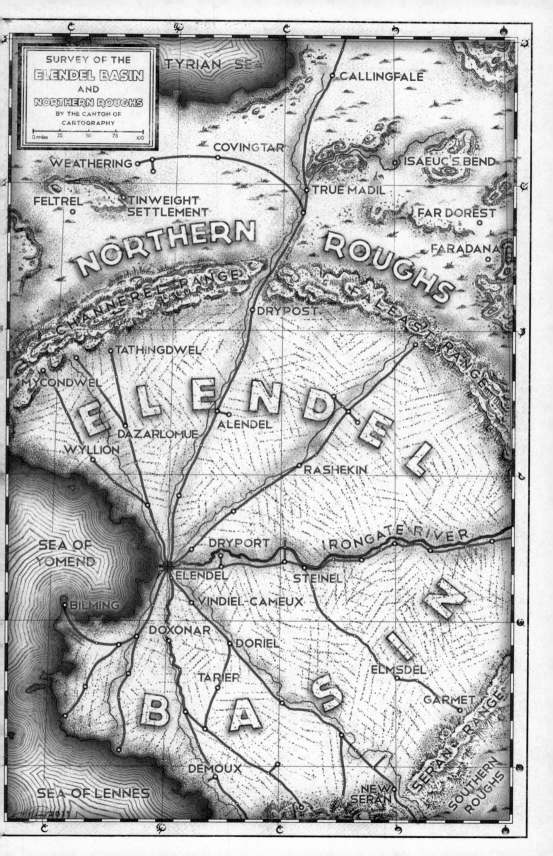

SURVEY OF THE
ELENDEL BASIN
AND
NORTHERN ROUGHS
BY THE CANTON OF
CARTOGRAPHY

0 miles 25   50   75   100

TYRIAN SEA

CALLINGFALE

COVINGTAR

ISAEUC'S BEND

WEATHERING

TRUE MADIL

FAR DOREST

FELTREL

TINWEIGHT
SETTLEMENT

FARADANA

NORTHERN

ROUGHS

CHANNEREL RANGE

FAR EAST RANGE

DRYPOST

TATHINGDWEL

ELENDEL

MYCONDWEL

ALENDEL

DAZARLOMUE

WYLLION

RASHEKIN

SEA OF
YOMEND

DRYPORT

IRONGATE RIVER

ELENDEL

STEINEL

BILMING

VINDIEL-CAMEUX

BASIN

DOXONAR

DORIEL

ELMSDEL

TARIER

GARMET

DEMOUX

SERAN RANGE

SEA OF LENNES

NEW
SERAN

SOUTHERN
ROUGHS

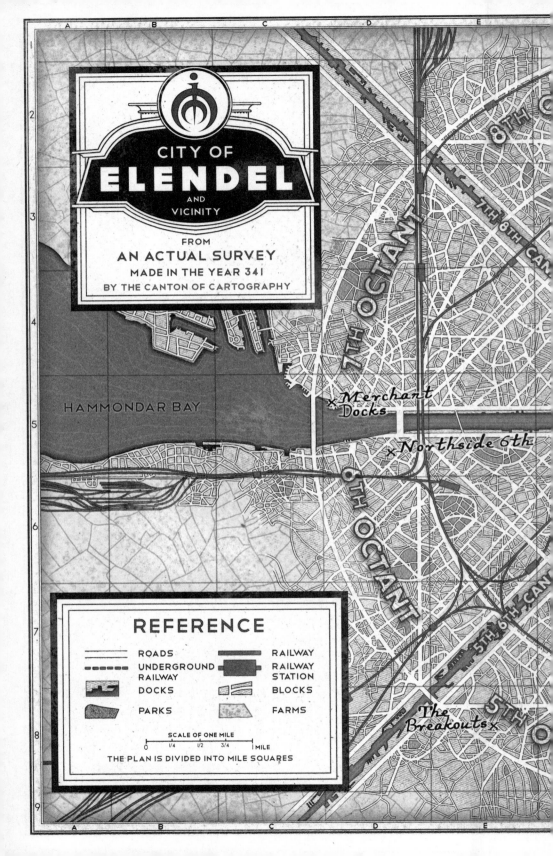

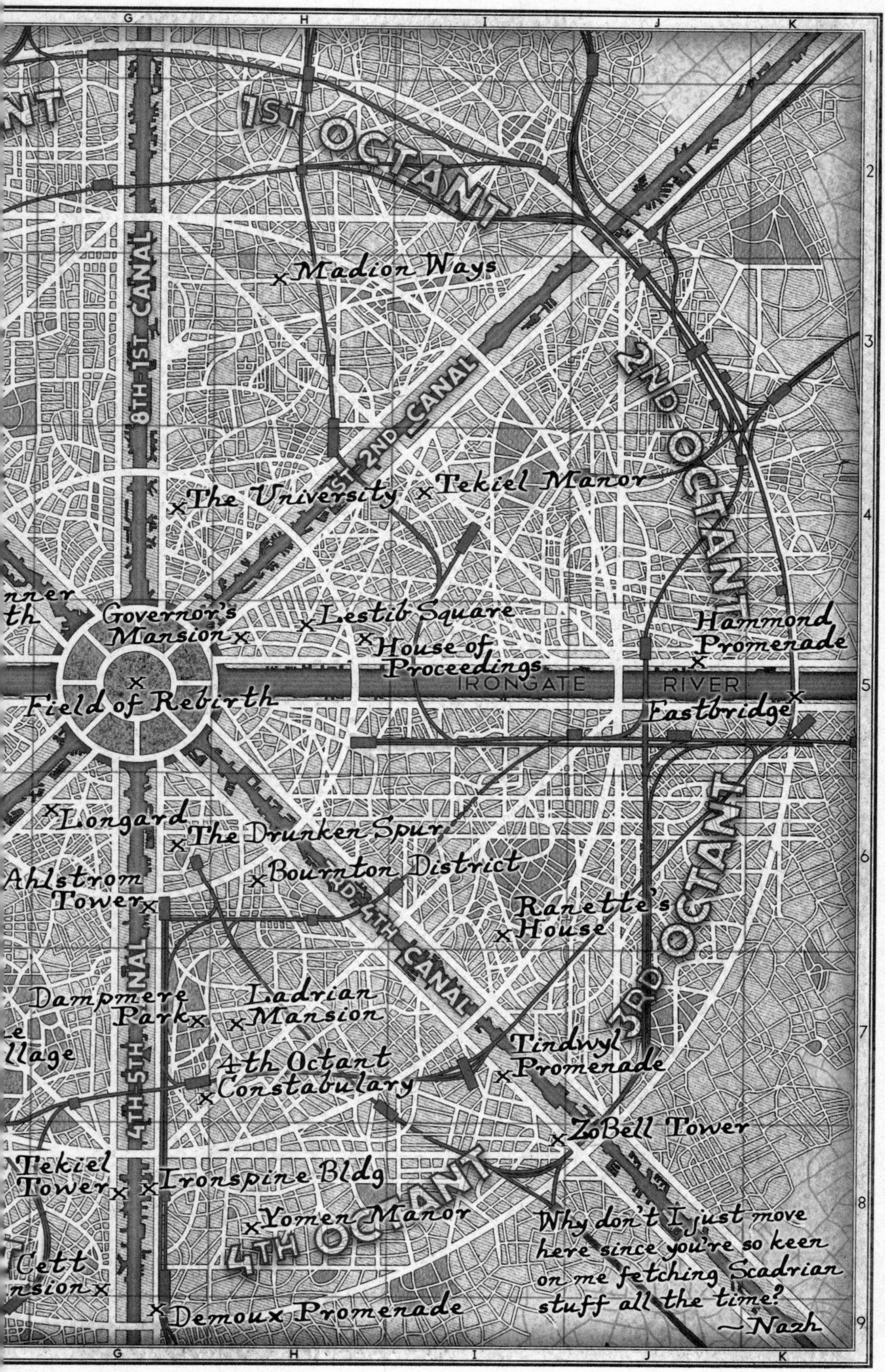

1ST OCTANT

2ND OCTANT

3RD OCTANT

4TH OCTANT

8TH-1ST CANAL

1ST 2ND CANAL

1ST 4TH CANAL

4TH 5TH CANAL

× Madion Ways

× The University × Tekiel Manor

Governor's
Mansion × ×   × Lestib Square
         × House of
           Proceedings.   Hammond
                                  Promenade ×

× Field of Rebirth

IRONGATE   RIVER

Eastbridge ×

× Longard

× The Drunken Spur.
  × Bournton District

Ahlstrom
Tower ×   Ranette's
                               × House

Dampmere   Ladrian
Park ×   × Mansion

llage   4th Octant
                     Constabulary   Tindwyl
                                          × Promenade

Tekiel
Tower × × Ironspine Bldg   × ZoBell Tower

         × Yomen Manor

Cett
nsion ×   Why don't I just move
                                        here since you're so keen
        × Demoux Promenade   on me fetching Scadrian
                                        stuff all the time?
                                                    —Nazh

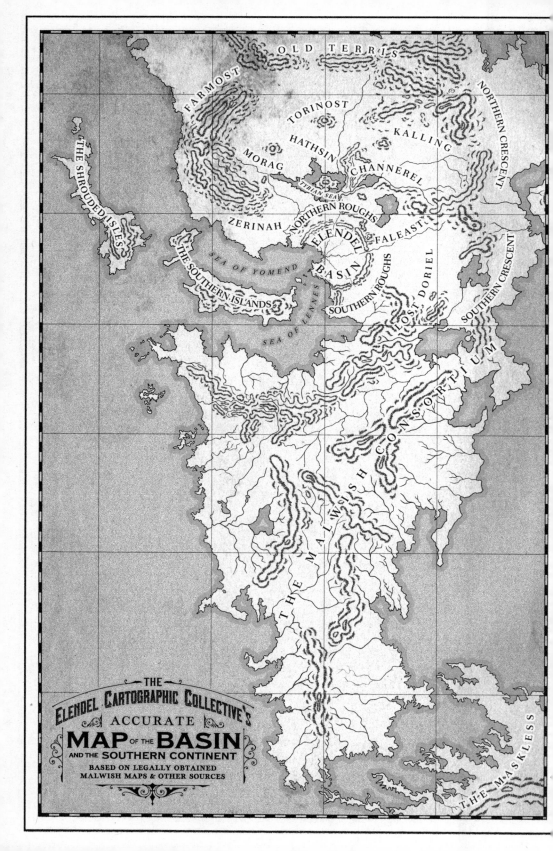

OLD TERRIS

FARMOST

"THE SHROUDED ISLES"

TORINOST

KALLING

NORTHERN CRESCENT

HATHSIN

MORAG

CHANNEREL

TYRIAN SEA

ZERINAH

NORTHERN ROUGHS

ELENDEL
BASIN

FALEAST

THE SOUTHERN ISLANDS

SEA OF YOMEND

SOUTHERN ROUGHS

LOST DORIEL

SOUTHERN CRESCENT

SEA OF LENNES

THE MALWISH CONSORTIUM

THE MASKLESS

THE ELENDEL CARTOGRAPHIC COLLECTIVE'S
ACCURATE
MAP OF THE BASIN
AND THE SOUTHERN CONTINENT
BASED ON LEGALLY OBTAINED
MALWISH MAPS & OTHER SOURCES

THE LOST METAL

PROLOGUE

Wayne knew about beds. Other kids in Tinweight Settlement had them. A bed sounded much better than a mat on the ground—especially one he had to share with his ma when the nights were cold, because they didn't have any coal.

Plus there were monsters under beds.

Yeah, he'd heard stories of mistwraiths. They'd hide unner your bed and steal the faces of people you knew. Which made beds soft and squishy on top, with someone underneath you could talk to. Sounded like rustin' heaven.

Other kids were scared of mistwraiths, but Wayne figured they just didn't know how to negotiate properly. He could make friends with something what lived unner a bed. You just had to give it something it wanted, like someone else to eat.

Anyway, no bed for him. And no proper chairs. They had a table, built by Uncle Gregr. Back before he got crushed by a billion rocks in a landslide and mushed into a pulp what couldn't hit people no more. Wayne kicked the table sometimes, in case Gregr's spirit was watching and was fond of it. Rusts knew there was nothing else in this one-window home Uncle Gregr had cared about.

Best Wayne had was a stool, so he sat on that and played with his cards—dealing hands and hiding cards up his sleeve—as he waited. This was a nervous time of day. Every evening he feared she wouldn't come home. Not because she didn't love him. Ma was a burst of sweet spring flowers in a sewage pit of a world. But because one day Pa hadn't come home. One day Uncle Gregr—Wayne kicked the table—hadn't come home. So Ma . . .

Don't think about it, Wayne thought, bungling his shuffle and spilling cards over the table and floor. *And don't look. Not until you see the light.*

He could feel the mine out there; nobody wanted to live nexta it, so Wayne and his ma did.

He thought of something else, on purpose. The pile of laundry by the wall that he'd finished washing earlier. That had been Ma's old job what didn't pay well enough. Now he did it while she pushed minecarts.

Wayne didn't mind the work. Got to try on all the different clothes—whether they were from old gramps or young women—and pretend to be them. His ma had caught him a few times and grown angry. Her exasperation still baffled him. Why *wouldn't* you try them all on? That's what clothes was for. It wasn't nothing weird.

Besides, sometimes folks left stuff in their pockets. Like decks of cards.

He fumbled the shuffle again, and as he gathered the cards up he did *not* look out the window, even though he could feel the mine. That gaping artery, like the hole in someone's neck, red from the inside and spurting out light like blood and fire. His ma had to go dig at the beast's insides, searchin' for metals, then escape its anger. You could only get lucky so many times.

Then he spotted it. Light. With relief, he glanced out the window and saw someone walking along the path, holding up a lantern to illuminate her way. Wayne scrambled to hide the cards under the mat, then lay on top, feigning sleep when the door opened. She'd have seen his light go out of course, but she appreciated the effort he put into pretending.

She settled on the stool, and Wayne cracked an eye. His ma wore trousers and a buttoned shirt, her hair up, her clothing and face smudged. She sat staring at the flame in the lantern, watching it flicker and dance, and her face seemed more hollow than it had been before. Like someone was taking a pickaxe to her cheeks.

That mine's eatin' her away, he thought. *It hasn't gobbled her up like it did Pa, but it's gnawing on her.*

Ma blinked, then fixated on something else. A card he'd left on the table. Aw, hell.

She picked it up, then looked right at him. He didn't pretend to be asleep no more. She'd dump water on him.

"Wayne," she said, "where did you get these cards?"

"Don't remember."

"Wayne . . ."

"Found 'em," he said.

She held out her hand, and he reluctantly pulled the deck out and handed it over. She tucked the card she'd found into the box. Damn. She'd spend a day searching Tinweight for whoever had "lost" them. Well, he wouldn't have her losing more sleep on account of him.

"Tark Vestingdow," Wayne mumbled. "They was inna pocket of his overalls."

"Thank you," she said softly.

"Ma, I've *gotta* learn cards. That way I can earn a good livin' and care for us."

"A good living?" she asked. "With cards?"

"Don't worry," he said quickly. "I'll cheat! Can't make a livin' if you don't win, see."

She sighed, rubbing her temples.

Wayne glanced at the cards in their stack. "Tark," he said. "He's Terris. Like Pa was."

"Yes."

"Terris people always do what they're told. So what's wrong with me?"

"Nothing's wrong with you, love," she said. "You just haven't got a good parent to guide you."

"Ma," he said, scrambling off the mat to take her arm. "Don't talk like that. You're a *great* ma."

She hugged him to her side, but he could feel her tension. "Wayne," she asked, "did you take Demmy's pocketknife?"

"He talked?" Wayne said. "Rust that rustin' bastard!"

"Wayne! Don't swear like that."

"Rust that rusting bastard!" he said in a railworker's accent instead.

He grinned at her innocently, and was rewarded with a smile she couldn't hide. Silly voices always made her happy. Pa had been good at them, but Wayne was better. Particularly now that Pa was dead and couldn't say them no more.

But then her smile faded. "You can't take things what don't belong to you, Wayne. That's somethin' thieves do."

"I don't wanna be a thief," Wayne said softly, putting the pocketknife on the table beside the cards. "I want to be a good boy. It just . . . happens."

She hugged him closer. "You *are* a good boy. You've *always* been a good boy."

When she said it, he believed it.

"Do you want a story, love?" she asked.

"I'm too old for stories," he lied, desperately wishing she'd tell one anyway. "I'm *eleven*. One more year and I can drink at the tavern."

"What? Who told you that!"

"Dug."

"Dug is *nine*."

"Dug knows stuff."

"*Dug* is *nine*."

"So you're sayin' I'll have to snitch booze for him next year, 'cuz he can't get it himself yet?" He met her eyes, then started snickering.

He helped her get dinner—cold oatmeal with some beans in it. At least it wasn't *only* beans. Then he snuggled into his blankets on the mat, pretending he was a child again to listen. It was easy to feign that. He still had the clothes after all.

"This is the tale," she said, "of Blatant Barm, the Unwashed Bandit."

"Oooh . . ." Wayne said. "A *new* one?"

His mother leaned forward, wagging her spoon toward him as she spoke. "He was the worst of them all, Wayne. Baddest, meanest, *stinkiest* bandit. He never bathed."

"'Cuz it takes too much work to get properly dirty?"

"No, because he . . . Wait, it's *work* to get dirty?"

"Gotta roll around in it, you see."

"Why in Harmony's name would you do that?"

"To think like the ground," Wayne said.

"To . . ." She smiled. "Oh, Wayne. You're so precious."

"Thanks," he said. "Why ain't you told me of this Blatant Barm before? If he was so bad wouldn't he be the first one you told stories about?"

"You were too young," she said, sitting back. "And the story too frightening."

Ooooh . . . This was going to be a *good* one. Wayne bounced up and down. "Who got 'im? Was it a lawman?"

"It was Allomancer Jak."

"Him?" Wayne said with a groan.

"I thought you liked him."

Well, all the kids did. Jak was new and interesting, and had been solving all kinds of tough crimes this last year. Least according to Dug.

"But Jak always brings the bad guys in," Wayne complained. "He never shoots a single one."

"Not this time," Ma said, digging into her oatmeal. "He knew Blatant Barm was the worst. Killer to the core. Even Barm's sidekicks—Gud the Killer and Noways Joe—were *ten* times worse than any other bandit that ever walked the Roughs."

"Ten *times*?" Wayne said.

"Yup."

"That's a lot! Almost double!"

His ma frowned for a moment, but then leaned forward again. "They'd robbed the payroll. Taking not just the money from the fat men in Elendel, but the wages of the common folk."

"Bastards!" Wayne said.

"Wayne!"

"Fine! Regular old turds then!"

Again she hesitated. "Do you . . . know what the word 'bastard' means?"

"It's a bad turd, the kind you get when you've *really* got to go, but you hold it in too long."

"You know that because . . ."

"Dug told me."

"Of course he did. Well, Jak, he wouldn't stand for stealing from the common folk of the Roughs. Being a bandit is one thing, but everyone knows you take the money what goes *toward* the city.

"Unfortunately, Blatant Barm, he knew the area real well. So he rode off into the most difficult land in the Roughs—and he left one of his two sidekicks to guard each of the key spots along the way. Fortunately, Jak was the bravest of men. And the strongest."

"If he was the bravest and strongest," Wayne said, "why was he a lawman? He could be a bandit, and nobody could stop him!"

"What's harder, love?" she asked. "Doing what's right or doing what's wrong?"

"Doing what's right."

"So who gets stronger?" Ma asked. "The fellow what does the easy thing, or what does the hard thing?"

Huh. He nodded. Yeah. Yeah, he could see that.

She moved the lantern closer to her face, making it shine as she spoke. "Jak's first test was the River Human, the vast waterway marking the border with what had once been koloss lands. The waters moved at the speed of a train; it was the fastest river in the whole world—and it was full of rocks. Gud the Killer had set up there, across the river, to watch for lawmen. He had such a good eye and steady hand that he could shoot a fly off a man at three hundred paces."

"Why'd you want to do that?" Wayne asked. "Better to shoot 'im right *in* the fly. That's gotta hurt something bad."

"Not that kind of fly, love," Ma said.

"So what did Jak do?" Wayne asked. "Did he sneak up? Not very lawman-like to sneak. I don't think they do that. I'll bet he didn't sneak."

"Well . . ." Ma said.

Wayne clutched his blanket, waiting.

"Jak was a *better* shot," she whispered. "When Gud the Killer sighted on him, Jak shot him first—clean across the river."

"How'd Gud die?" Wayne whispered.

"By bullet, love."

"Through the eye?" Wayne said.

"Suppose."

"And so Gud lined up a shot and Jak did likewise—but Jak shot first, hitting Gud *straight* through the sights into the eye! Right, Ma!"

"Yup."

"And his head exploded," Wayne said, "like a fruit—the crunchy kind, the shell all *tough* but it's gooey inside. Is that how it happened?"

"Absolutely."

"Dang, Ma," Wayne said. "That's gruesome. You sure you should be tellin' me this story?"

"Should I stop?"

"Hell no! How'd Jak get across the water?"

"He flew," Ma said. She set her bowl aside, oatmeal finished, and gave a flourish with both hands. "Using his Allomantic powers. Jak can fly, and talk to birds, and eat rocks."

"Wow. Eat *rocks*?"

"Yup. And so he flew over that river. But the next challenge was even worse. The Canyon of Death."

"Ooooh . . ." Wayne said. "Bet that place was pretty."

"Why do you say that?"

"'Cuz nobody's going to visit a place called 'Canyon of Death' unless it's pretty. But somebody visited it, 'cuz we know the name. So it must be pretty."

"Beautiful," Ma said. "A canyon carved through the middle of a bunch of crumbling rock spires—the broken peaks streaked with colors, like they was painted that way. But the place was as deadly as it was beautiful."

"Yeah," Wayne said. "Figures."

"Jak couldn't fly over this one, for the second of the bandits hid in the canyon. Noways Joe. He was a master of pistols, and could also fly, and turn into a dragon, and eat rocks. If Jak tried to sneak past, Joe would shoot him from behind."

"That's the smart way to shoot someone," Wayne said. "On account of them not bein' able to shoot back."

"True," Ma said. "So Jak didn't let that happen. He had to go into the canyon—but it was *filled* with *snakes*."

"Bloody hell!"

"Wayne . . ."

"Regular old boring hell, then! How many snakes?"

"A million snakes."

"Bloody hell!"

"But Jak, he was smart," Ma said. "So he'd thought to bring some snake food."

"A million bits of snake food?"

"Nah, only one," she said. "But he got the snakes to fight over it, so they mostly killed each other. And the one what was left was the strongest, naturally."

"Naturally."

"So Jak talked it into biting Noways Joe."

"And so Joe turned purple!" Wayne said. "And bled out his ears! And his bones melted, so the melty bone juice leaked out of his nose! And he collapsed into a puddle of deflated skin, all while hissing and blubbering 'cuz his teeth was melting!"

"Exactly."

"Dang, Ma. You tell the *best* stories."

"It gets better," she said softly, leaning down on the stool, their lantern burning low. "Because the ending has a surprise."

"What surprise?"

"Once Jak was through the canyon—what now smelled like dead snakes and melted bones—he spotted the final challenge: the Lone Mesa. A giant plateau in the center of an otherwise flat plain."

"That's not much of a challenge," Wayne said. "He could fly to the top."

"Well he tried to," she whispered. "But the mesa *was* Blatant Barm."

"*WHAT?*"

"That's right," Ma said. "Barm had joined up with the koloss—the ones that change into big monsters, not the normal ones like old Mrs. Nock. And *they* showed him how to turn into a monster of humongous size. So when Jak tried to land on it, the mesa done gobbled him up."

Wayne gasped. "And then," he said, "it mashed him beneath its teeth, crushing his bones like—"

"No," Ma said. "It tried to swallow him. But Jak, he wasn't only smart and a good shot. He was something else."

"What?"

"A big damn pain in the ass."

"Ma! That's swearin'."

"It's okay in stories," Ma said. "Listen, Jak was a pain. He was always going about doing good. Helping people. Making life tough for bad people. Asking questions. He knew exactly how to ruin a bandit's day.

"So as he was swallowed, Jak stretched out his arms and legs, then pushed—making himself a *lump* in Blatant Barm's throat, so the monster couldn't breathe. Monsters like that needs lotsa air, you know. And so, Allomancer Jak done *choked* Barm from the inside. Then, when the monster was dead on the ground, Jak sauntered out down its tongue—like it was some fancy mat set outside a carriage for a rich man."

Whoa. "That's a *good* story, Ma."

She smiled.

"Ma," he said. "Is the story . . . about the mine?"

"Well," she said, "I suppose we all gotta walk into the beast's mouth now and then. So . . . maybe, I guess."

"You're like the lawman then."

"Anyone can be," she said, blowing out the lantern.

"Even me?"

"Especially you." She kissed him on the forehead. "You are whatever you want to be, Wayne. You're the wind. You're the stars. You are all endless things."

It was a poem she liked. He liked it too. Because when she said it, he *believed* her. How could he not? Ma didn't lie. So, he snuggled deeper into his blankets and let himself drift off. A lot was wrong in the world, but a few things were right. And as long as she was around, stories meant something. They was real.

Until the next day, when there was another collapse at the mine. That night, his ma didn't come home.

PART ONE

1

TWENTY-NINE YEARS LATER

Marasi had never been in a sewer before, but it was exactly as awful as she'd imagined. The stench was incredible, of course. But worse was the way her booted feet would occasionally slip for a heart-stopping moment, threatening to plunge her down into the "mud" underneath.

At least she'd had the foresight to wear a uniform with trousers today, along with knee-high leather work boots. But there was no protection from the scent, the feel, or—unfortunately—the sound of it. When she took a step—map in one hand, rifle in the other—each boot would pull free with a *squelch* of mythical proportions. It would have been the worst sound ever, if not overmatched by Wayne's complaining.

"Wax never brought me into a rusting sewer," he muttered, raising the lantern.

"Are there sewers in the Roughs?"

"Well, no," he admitted. "Pastures smell almost as bad, and he did make me march through those. But Marasi, they didn't have *spiders*."

"They probably did," she said, angling the map toward his lantern. "You just couldn't see them."

"Suppose," he grumbled. "But it's worse when you can see the webs. Also there's, you know, the literal sewage."

Marasi nodded to a side tunnel and they started in that direction. "Do you want to talk about it?"

"What?" he demanded.

"Your mood."

"Nothing's wrong with my rusting mood," he said. "It's precisely the mood you're supposed to have when your partner forces you to stick your frontside into a buncha stuff that comes out of your backside."

"And last week?" she asked. "When we were investigating a *perfume shop*?"

"Rusting perfumers," Wayne said, his eyes narrowing. "Never can tell what they're hiding with those fancy smells. You can't trust a man what doesn't smell like a man should."

"Sweat and booze?"

"Sweat and *cheap* booze."

"Wayne, how can you complain about someone putting on airs? You put on a different personality every time you change hats."

"Does my smell change?"

"I suppose not."

"Argument won. There are literally no holes in it whatsoever. Conversation over."

They shared a look.

"I should get me some perfumes, eh?" Wayne said. "Someone might spot my disguises if I *always* smell like sweat and cheap booze."

"You're hopeless."

"What's hopeless," he said, "is my poor shoes."

"Could have worn boots like I suggested."

"Ain't got no boots," he said. "Wax stole them."

"Wax stole your boots. Really."

"Well, they're in his closet," Wayne said. "Instead of three pairs of his poshest shoes. Which somehow ended up in my closet, completely by happenstance." He glanced at her. "It was a fair trade. I liked those boots."

Marasi smiled. They'd been working together for almost six years now, since Wax's retirement following the discovery of the Bands of Mourning. Wayne was an official constable, not some barely-within-the-law deputized citizen. He even wore a uniform once in a while. And—

—and Marasi's boot slipped again. Rusting hell. If she fell, he would *never* stop laughing. But this did seem the best way. Construction on the citywide underground train tunnels was ongoing, and two days ago a demolitions man had filed a curious report. He didn't want to blast the next section, as seismic readings indicated they were near an unmapped cavern.

This area underneath the city of Elendel was peppered with ancient caves. And it was the same region where a local group of gang enforcers kept vanishing and reappearing. As if they had a hidden entrance into an unknown, unseen lair.

She consulted the map, marked with the construction notes—and older annotations indicating a nearby oddity that the sewer builders had found years ago, but which had never been properly investigated.

"I think MeLaan is going to break up with me," Wayne said softly. "That's why maybe I've been uncharacteristically downbeat in my general disposition as of late."

"What makes you think she's going to do that?"

"On account of her tellin' me, 'Wayne, I'm probably going to break up with you in a few weeks.'"

"Well, that's polite of her."

"I think she's got a new job from the big guy," Wayne said. "But it ain't right, how slow it's goin'. 'S not the proper way to break up with a fellow."

"And what *is* the proper way?"

"Throw something at his head," Wayne said. "Sell his stuff. Tell his mates he's a knob."

"You have had some interesting relationships."

"Nah, just mostly bad ones," he said. "I asked Jammi Walls what she thought I should do— You know her? She's at the tavern most nights."

"I know her," Marasi said. "She's a woman of . . . ill repute."

"What?" Wayne said. "Who's been saying that? Jammi has a *great* reputation. Of all the whores on the block, she gives the best—"

"I do not need to hear the next part. Thank you."

"Ill repute," he said, chuckling. "I'm gonna tell Jammi you said that, Marasi. She worked *hard* for her reputation. Gets to charge four times what anyone else does! Ill repute indeed."

"And what did she say?"

"She said MeLaan wanted me to try harder in the relationship," Wayne said. "But I think in this case Jammi was wrong. Because MeLaan don't play games. When she says things, she means them. So it's . . . you know . . ."

"I'm sorry, Wayne," Marasi said, tucking the map under her arm and resting her hand on his shoulder.

"I knew it couldn't last," he said. "Rustin' knew it, you know? She's like, what, a thousand years old?"

"Roughly two-thirds that," Marasi said.

"And I'm not quite forty," Wayne said. "More like sixteen if you take account of my spry youthful physique."

"And your sense of humor."

"Damn right," he said, then sighed. "Things have been . . . tough lately. With Wax gettin' all fancy and MeLaan being gone for months at a time. Feel like nobody wants me around. Maybe I belong in a sewer, you know?"

"You don't," she said. "You're the best partner I've ever had."

"Only partner."

"Only? Gorglen doesn't count?"

"Nope. He's not human. I gots papers what prove he's a giraffe in disguise." Then he smiled. "But . . . thanks for askin'. Thanks for carin'."

She nodded, then led the way onward. When she'd imagined her life as a top detective and lawwoman, she hadn't envisioned *this*. At least the smell was getting better—or she was getting used to it.

It was extremely gratifying to find, at the exact spot marked on the map, an old metal door set into the sewer wall. Wayne held up the lantern, and one didn't need a keen detective's eye to see the door had been used recently. Silvery scrapes on one side of the frame, the handle rubbed clean of the pervasive filth and cobwebs.

The people who had built the sewers had discovered it, and highlighted it as a site of potential historical significance. But the note had been lost due to bureaucratic nonsense.

"Nice," Wayne said, leaning in beside her. "Some first-rate detectivin', Marasi. How many old surveys did you have to read to find this?"

"Too many," she said. "People would be surprised how much of my time is spent in the documents library."

"They leave the research outta the stories."

"You did this sort of thing back in the Roughs?"

"Well, the Roughs variety of it," Wayne said. "Usually involved holdin' some bloke's face down in the trough until he remembered whose old prospectin' claim he'd been filchin', but it's the same principle. With more swearin'."

She handed him her rifle and investigated the door. He didn't like her to make a big deal out of it, but he could hold guns these days without his hands shaking. She'd never seen him fire one, but he said he could if he needed to.

The door was shut tight and had no lock on this side. But it seemed the people she was hunting had found it closed too—there were a bunch of marks along one edge. There was enough room to slip something between door and frame.

"I need a knife to get through this," she said.

"You can use my razor-sharp wit."

"Alas, Wayne, you aren't the type of tool I need at the moment."

"Ha!" he said. "I like that one."

He handed her a knife from his backpack where they kept supplies like rope, and extra metals in case they faced Metalborn. This kind of gang shouldn't have an Allomancer—they were your basic "shake down shopkeepers for protection money" types. Yet she had reports that made her wary, and she was increasingly sure this group was funded by the Set.

Years later, and she was still hunting answers to questions that had plagued her from the very start of her career as a lawwoman. The group known as the Set, once run by Wax's Uncle Edwarn, then revealed to involve his sister, Telsin, as well. A group that followed, or worshipped, or somehow furthered the machinations of a dark figure known as Trell. A god, she thought. From ancient times.

If she caught the right people, she might finally get the answers. But she perpetually fell short. The closest she'd gotten to answers had been six years ago, but then everyone they'd captured—including Wax's uncle— had been killed in an explosion. Leaving her to chase at shadows again, and the rest of Elendel's elite fully committed to ignoring the threat. Without evidence, she and Wax had been unable to prove that the Set even existed beyond Edwarn's lackeys.

Using the knife, she managed to undo the bar holding the door closed from the other side. The bar swung free with a soft clang, and she eased the door open to reveal a rough-hewn tunnel leading down-ward. One of the many that dotted this region, dating back to the ancient days before the Catacendre. To the time of myths and heroes, ashfalls and tyrants.

Together she and Wayne slipped inside, leaving the door as they'd found it. They dimmed their lantern as a precaution, then started into the depths.

2

"Cravat?" Steris said, reading from the list.

"Tied and pinned," Wax said, pulling it tight.

"Shoes?"

"Polished."

"First piece of evidence?"

Wax flipped a silvery medallion in the air, then caught it.

"Second piece of evidence?" Steris asked, making a mark on her list.

He pulled a small folded stack of papers from his pocket. "Right here."

"Third piece of evidence?"

Wax checked another pocket, then paused, looking around the small office—his senator's chamber in the House of Proceedings. Had he left them . . . "On the desk back home," he said, smacking his head.

"I brought a spare," Steris said, digging in her bag.

Wax grinned. "Of course you did."

"Two, actually," Steris said, handing over a sheet of paper, which he tucked away. Then she consulted her list again.

Little Maxillium stepped up beside his mother, looking very serious as he scanned his own list of scribbles. At five years old he knew his letters, but preferred to make up his own.

"Dog picture," Max said, as if reading from his list.

"I might need one of those," Wax said. "Quite useful."

Max solemnly presented it, then said, "Cat picture."

"Need one of those too."

"I'm bad at cats," Max said, handing him another sheet. "So it looks like a squirrel."

Wax hugged his son, then put the sheets away reverently with the others. The boy's sister—Tindwyl, as Steris liked traditional names—babbled in the corner, where Kath, the governess, was watching her.

Finally, Steris handed him his pistols one at a time. Long-barreled and weighty, they had been designed by Ranette to look menacing—but they had two safeties and were unloaded. It had been a while since he'd needed to shoot anyone, but he continued to make good use of his reputation as the "Lawman Senator of the Roughs." City folk, particularly politicians, were intimidated by small arms. They preferred to kill people with more modern weapons, like poverty and despair.

"Is a kiss for my wife on that list?" Wax asked.

"Actually, no," she said, surprised.

"A rare oversight," he said, then gave her a lingering kiss. "You should be the one going out there today, Steris. You did more preparation than I."

"You're the house lord."

"I could appoint you as a representative to speak for us."

"Please, no," she said. "You know how I am with people."

"You're good with the *right* people."

"And are politicians ever right about anything?"

"I hope so," he said, straightening his suit coat and turning toward the door. "Since I am one."

He pushed out of his chambers and walked down to the Senate floor. Steris would watch from her seat in the observation balcony—by now, everyone knew how particular she was about getting the same one.

As Wax stepped into the vast chamber—which buzzed with activity as senators returned from the short recess—he didn't go to his seat. Over the last few days, senators had debated the current bill, and his was the last speech in line. He had secured this spot with many promises and much trading, as he hoped it would give his arguments the advantage, give him the best chance to avert a terrible decision.

He stood to one side of the speakers' platform and waited for everyone to sit, his thumb hooked into his gunbelt, looming. You learned to put on a good loom in the Roughs when interrogating prisoners—and he was still shocked by how many of those skills worked here.

Governor Varlance didn't look at him. Instead the man adjusted his cravat, then checked his face powder—ghostly pale skin was fashionable these days, for some arcane reason. Then he laid out his medals on the desk, one at a time.

Rusts, I miss Aradel, Wax thought. It had been novel to have a competent governor. Like . . . eating hotel food and finding it wasn't awful, or spending time with Wayne and then discovering you still had a pocket watch.

However, the governor's job was the type that chewed up the good people but let the bad ones float blissfully along. Aradel had stepped down two years back. And it *had* made sense to choose a military man as the next governor, considering the tensions with the Southern Continent. Many people among the newly discovered countries there—with their airships and strange masks—were upset about how things had gone down six years ago. Specifically, that the Elendel Basin had kept the Bands of Mourning.

Right now, Elendel faced two primary problems. The first was the people on the Southern Continent, the foremost nation of which was known as the Malwish. They made constant noise about how small and weak the Basin was. Aggressive, militaristic posturing. Varlance had been a hedge against that, though Wax *did* question where he had earned all those medals. So far as Wax knew, the newly formed army hadn't seen any actual engagements.

The second problem was far closer to home. It was the parts of the Basin that were outside the capital, the people in what were collectively known as the Outer Cities. For years, maybe decades, tensions had been building between the city of Elendel and everyone else.

It was bad enough to be facing threats from another continent. But to Wax, that was a more distant danger. The immediate one, the one that gave him the most stress, was the prospect of a civil war among his own people. He and Steris had been working for years to prevent that.

Varlance finally nodded to his vice governor, a Terriswoman. She had curly dark hair and a traditional robe; Wax thought he'd known her in the Village, but it could have been her sister, and he'd never come up with a good way to ask. Regardless, it looked respectable to have a Terris person on staff. Most governors appointed one to a high position in their cabinet—almost as if the Terris were another medal to display.

Adawathwyn stood up and announced to the room, "The governor recognizes the senator from House Ladrian."

Though he'd been waiting for this, Wax took his time sauntering up onto the podium, which was lit from above by a massive electric spotlight. He made a slow rotation, inspecting the circular chamber. One side held the elected officials: senators who were voted into office to represent a guild, profession, or historical group. The other held the lords: senators who held their positions by benefit of birth.

"This bill," Wax declared to the room, loud and firm, his voice echoing, "is a fantastically *stupid* idea."

Once, earlier in his political career, talking so bluntly had earned him ire. Now he caught multiple members of the Senate smiling. They expected this from him—even appreciated it. They knew how many problems there were in the Basin and were glad someone among them was willing to call them out.

"Tensions with the Malwish are at an all-time high," Wax said. "This is a time for the Basin to unite, not a time to drive wedges between our cities!"

"This is *about* uniting!" another voice called. The dockworkers' senator, Melstrom. He was mostly a puppet for Hasting and Erikell, nobles who had consistently been a painful spike in Wax's side. "We need a single leader for the whole Basin. Officially!"

"Agreed," Wax said. "But *how* is elevating the Elendel governor—a position no one outside the city can vote on—going to unite people?"

"It will give them someone to look toward. A strong, capable leader."

And that, Wax thought, glancing at Varlance, *is a capable leader? We're lucky he pays attention in these meetings rather than going over his publicity schedule.* Varlance had, so far in the first two years of his tenure, rededicated seventeen parks in the city. He liked the flowers.

Wax kept to the plan, getting out his medallion and flipping it into the air. "Six years ago," he said, "I had a little adventure. You all know about it. Finding a wrecked Malwish airship, and thwarting a plot by the Outer Cities to use its secrets against Elendel. I stopped that. I brought the Bands of Mourning back to be stored safely."

"And almost started a war," someone muttered in the reaches of the room.

"You'd prefer I let the plot go forward?" Wax called back. When no response came, he flipped the medallion up and caught it again. It was one of the weight-affecting medallions the Malwish used to make their ships light enough to fly. "I dare anyone in this room to question my loyalty to Elendel. We can have a nice little duel. I'll even let you shoot first."

Silence. He'd earned that. A lot of the people in this room didn't like him, but they *did* respect him. And they knew he wasn't an agent for the Outer Cities.

He flipped the medallion and then Pushed it higher, all the way up toward the ceiling high above. It came streaking down again, glimmering in the light. As he snatched it, he glanced at Admiral Jonnes, current ambassador from the Malwish nation. She sat in a special place on the Senate floor, where visiting mayors from Outer Cities were given seats. None had come to this proceeding. A visible sign of their anger.

This bill, if approved, would elevate the Elendel governor above all Outer Cities mayors—allowing him or her to intervene in local disputes. To the point of *removing* a mayor and calling a special election, approving candidates. While Wax agreed that a central ruler would be an important step for uniting the Basin, this bill was an outright insult to all of their people living outside the capital.

"I know our position," Wax said, turning the medallion over in his fingers, "better than anyone. You want to make a show of force to the Malwish. Prove that we can make our own cities bend to our rules. So you introduce this bill.

"But this underlines *why* everyone outside Elendel is so frustrated with us! The revolutionaries in the other cities wouldn't have gotten so far without the support of their people. If the average person living outside Elendel weren't so *damned* angry about our trade policies and general arrogance, we wouldn't be in this position.

"This bill isn't going to placate them! It's not a 'show of force.' It's *specifically* designed to outrage the people. If we pass this law, we're *demanding* civil war."

He let that sink in. The others were so determined to appear strong to external enemies. But if left unchecked, they'd strong-arm themselves right into war over *internal* disputes. The Malwish problems were real, but not as immediate. Civil war, though, would be devastating.

The worst part was, someone was pushing for it in secret. Wax was certain the Set was again interfering in Elendel politics. His . . . sister was involved. He wasn't certain why they wanted a civil war, but they'd been trying for years now. And if he let this proceed, playing into the hands of their real enemies, both the elite around him now and the revolutionaries in the cities outside would have cause to mourn.

Wax pulled out the stack of papers in his left pocket. He tucked the dog and cat pictures at the back, then held the rest up to the room. "I have sixty letters from politicians in the Outer Cities here. They represent a large faction who *don't* want conflict. These are *reasonable* people. They are willing—eager—to work with Elendel. But they are also frightened about what their people will do if we continue to impose tyrannical, imperial policies on them.

"I propose that we vote down this bill and work on something better. Something that *actually* promotes peace and unity. A national assembly, with representation for each Outer City—and an elected supreme official elevated by *that* body."

He'd expected boos, and he got a few. But most of the chamber fell silent, watching him hold those letters aloft. They were afraid of letting power leave the capital. Afraid that Outer Cities politics would change their culture. They were cowards.

Maybe he was too, because the idea of the Set pulling strings terrified him. Who among those looking at him now were secretly their agents? Rusts, he didn't even understand their motives. They wanted war—as a way to gain power, certainly. But there was more.

They followed orders from something known as Trell.

Wax turned around slowly, still holding the letters, and felt a little spike of alarm as he turned his back on Melstrom. *He's going to shoot,* Wax thought.

"With all due respect, Lord Ladrian," Melstrom said. "You are a new parent, and obviously don't understand how to raise a child. You don't give in to their demands; you hold firm, knowing that your decisions are best for them. They will eventually see reason. As a father is to a son, Elendel is to the Outer Cities."

Right in the back, Wax thought, turning around.

He didn't respond immediately. You wanted to aim return fire carefully. He'd made these arguments before—mostly in private—to many of the senators in this room. He was making headway, but he needed more time. With these letters, he could return to each senator, the ones on the fence, and share the words. The ideas. Persuade.

His gut said that if the vote happened today, the bill would pass. So, he hadn't come here to repeat his arguments. He'd come with a bullet loaded in the chamber, ready to fire.

He folded up the letters and tucked them snugly into his pocket. Then he took the smaller stack—two sheets—from his other pocket. The ones that Steris had brought spares of in case he forgot. She'd probably made copies of the other stack too. And seven other things she knew he wouldn't need—but it made her feel better to have them in her bag just in case. Rusts, that woman was delightful.

Wax held up the sheets and made a show of getting just the right light to read. "'Dear Melstrom,'" he read out loud, "'we are pleased by your willingness to see reason and continue to enforce Elendel trade superiority in the Basin. This is a wise choice. We will deliver half a percent of our shipping revenues for the next three years in exchange for your personal support of this bill. From Houses Hasting and Erikell.'"

The room erupted into chaos. Wax settled in, hooking his finger into his gunbelt, waiting for the cries of outrage to run their course. He met Melstrom's eyes as the man sank back into his seat. The rusting idiot had just learned an important lesson: Don't leave a paper trail detailing your corruption when your political opponent is a trained detective. Idiot.

As the shouts finally died down, Wax spoke again, louder this time. "I *demand* we hold impropriety hearings to investigate Senator Melstrom's apparent sale of his vote in *blatant* violation of anti-corruption laws."

"And by so doing," the governor said, "delay the Elendel Supremacy Bill vote?"

"How could we vote on it," Wax said, "if we aren't sure the votes are being cast in good faith?"

More outrage. Wax weathered it as the governor consulted with his vice governor. She was a smart one. Anything Varlance accomplished that didn't involve cutting a ribbon or kissing a baby was probably her doing.

As the chamber calmed, the governor looked to Wax. "I trust you have proof of this letter's authenticity, Ladrian."

"I have affidavits from three separate handwriting experts to prove it's not a forgery," Wax said. "And you'll find my wife's detailed account of the letter's acquisition exhaustive and unimpugnable."

"Then I suggest impropriety hearings follow," the governor said. "*After* the vote on the Supremacy Bill."

"But—" Wax said.

"We will," the governor interrupted, "require Melstrom, Hasting, and Erikell to sit out the vote. *Assuring* that the vote is not corrupted."

Damn.

Damn, damn, *damn*.

Before he could counter that, the vice governor slammed her gavel. "Votes in favor of continuing?"

Most of the hands on the Senate floor went up. For a simple vote like this, a more straw poll method would do—unless the vote turned out to be very close. It wasn't.

The real vote, on the bill, would proceed.

"Have you any more explosions to detonate, Ladrian?" the governor said. "Or can we get on with this?"

"No more explosions, Your Honor," Wax said with a sigh. "They were my old partner's specialty anyway. Instead, I have a final plea to the chamber." His maneuver had failed. Now he had one last card to play. A request not from Waxillium Ladrian.

But one from Dawnshot, the lawman.

"You all know me," he said, turning around in a circle, meeting their eyes. "I'm a simple man from the Roughs. I don't do politics right, but I *do* understand angry people and the hard lives of working women and men.

"If we're going to take the role of parent, we should treat our children well. Give them a chance to speak for themselves. If we keep pretending they're toddlers, they're merely going to start ignoring us—at best. You want to send a message? Send the message that we care and are willing to listen."

He took his seat finally, next to Yancey Yaceczko, a good-natured and patient fellow—and one of the senators who'd actually listened to Wax.

"Good show, Wax," the man whispered, leaning in. "Good show indeed. It's always a pleasure."

Yancey would vote with him. In fact, a decent number of the nobles empathized with Wax. While a lot of the things Marasi had been saying recently made Wax uncomfortable about his hereditary position, in this instance the lords might turn out to be *slightly* less corrupt than their counterparts. The elected senators had to retain their seats, and voting for this bill was likely to improve the lives of their constituents.

That was the problem. According to the latest census, more people now lived *outside* the city than *inside* it. Most of the laws dated back to when there had been one city and a bunch of farming villages. Now that those villages had grown up into cities, their people wanted a stronger voice in Basin politics.

Elendel was no longer a scrappy settlement rebuilding after an apocalypse. They were a nation; even the Roughs were changing, growing, being modernized. Rusts, with all the land in the Roughs, he could imagine a time when more people lived there than in the Basin proper.

They needed to enfranchise those people, not ignore them. He still had hope. He and Steris and their allies had worked for *months* to erode support for the bill. Innumerable dinners, parties, and even—as he'd started doing for some of the city's elite—some training on the shooting range.

All in the name of changing the world. One vote at a time.

The governor called for the vote, and Lady Mi'chelle Yomen cast the first one—against the bill. As it proceeded, Wax sat, as anxious as he'd ever been before a confrontation with a bandit group. Rusts . . . this was somehow *worse*. Each vote was the crack of a bullet. *Lady Faula and Senator Vindel. How will they break? And Maraya? Was she persuaded, or . . .*

Two of them voted for the bill, along with multiple others that he'd been uncertain about. Wax felt a sinking feeling, worse than being shot, as the vote proceeded—and eventually landed at 122 for, 118 against.

The bill passed. His stomach fell further. If Wax was going to stop a civil war, he'd need to find another way.

MAREWILL 19, 348   Vol. 32, No. 247

THE TWO

BILMING

"No Two Seasons Are Alike,"

»› Handerwym Presents ‹«
NICKI SAVAGE
• and •
The COMPASS of Spirits

my last letter, the Haunted Man, my two Faceless Immortal npanions, and I saw the Coinshot Vila Mecant grab the mpass of Spirits and throw herself off a stone outcropping o the mists. The aluminum key that activated it, however, s still with me. Knowing Vila would be back, I entrusted key to the Haunted Man, who used his hellguns to launch nself to another outcropping, leaving me to convince my eless friends I had a plan… Which, of course, I *did*.

Chapter 8: "Flight of the Ornisaur"

KeSun rolled her eyes. "Exly *how* do you expect to low Vila and lure her out?" 'The aluminum bones lifted from the ornisaur arry," I said, patting baar's giant backpack. He groaned deep within his rpulent body. "Oh no…" 'You are incredible at imiion," I said encouragingly. Remember when you were uman the koloss in *A Hero All Ages*? You were master-! You can do this!" "He can't," said KeSun, folding her arms. "Not without me. n the one with experience npersonating birds." Turning to Tabaar, she id, "If you are willing to eld some control to me,

then we can carry Miss Sauvage across this abyss." "But the rest of my collection…" he said, the bag of bones shifting on his back. "We'll return for them," said KeSun, with a compassion in her voice she reserved only for Tabaar. "I promise." She raised an eyebrow at me. "Will you kindly look away?" she asked. "We'd rather you not see us when we…" "…*merge*," said Tabaar. What followed was one of the strangest things I've ever encountered, stranger even than the Beast of Belmon Couture or that time when I was Allomancer Jak's assistant.

(Continued below the fold!)

The Two Seasons would like to retract our dear editor Kyndlip Ternavyl's omments of two weeks ago, prior to her disappearance, when she comared our beloved mayor to "an irascible boar; no smarter, less attractive, nd unable to keep from rolling around in every mire he comes across."

ELENDEL SUP THREATENS I
UNITY OR DIVISION? PROGR

The Governor and Vice Governor

In a matter of days, Elendel's Senate will vote on what Bilming's top political mind, Professor Garven Munz, has called "the most monumental change to our government structure since the Words of Founding."

Days of speeches, debates, and posturing are planned leading up to the vote, and the eyes of the Outer Cities are focused on the so-called Lawman Senator of the Roughs, whose recent visits north of the Basin have solidified his stance with which many Outer City dwellers concur: Representation Before Supremacy.

Governor Varlance and his

cronies vehemently oppose this tack, their views summed up in Vice Governor Adawathwyn's bold opening remarks that "We'll need a strong, experienced leader when war comes to us from our masked Southern friends." Admiral Jonnes of the Malwish Nation looked visibly shaken and did not return after the Senate's following recess.

When Varlance was asked if he too thought the Basin might be headed toward war with the Malwish, he merely patted his chest where he'd conspicuously hung his military medals.

(Continued on back.)

ETTER TO THE EDITOR

nce again I must object to ur continued allowance of ds from Soonie Industries, anufacturers of the "Soonie up," who have also ignored y numerous letters regard-g their historically egregious

---

GUEST EDITORIAL
by Gemmes Millis, Interim Editor
ENFORCE NOSEBALL BAN!

We see them in every unsown field and vacant lot. Vagrants and layabouts, some of them even our own children, congregating in gangs and "playing"

The Man Who Electrifed Time!
The new novel by Bilmingborn working man Schrib Welfor. Available now in all fine bookshops!

HELP WANTED~Bendalloy Misting cook for new "quick eats" café. Will pay top boxing plus bonuses and bendalloy

---

Flight of the Ornisaur

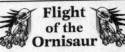

Though I desperately wanted to peek, my regard for my longtime companions compelled me to honor their request, even though the sound of their *merging* was

3

Marasi studied the footprints in the dust. They appeared to be a few weeks old, as they'd gathered dust themselves. She walked over to Wayne, who was inspecting the path farther down into the depths: an arduous-looking tunnel with a steep decline. He glanced at her.

"If they're slippin' in and out of the city fast," he said, "they musta found a different way out of here. They aren't makin' this hike regularly."

"Agreed," she said. "We should be stealthy anyway, in case they posted lookouts."

In response, he turned his lantern down and whispered, "You want to continue without backup?"

"For now. We want to scout and see what we find. I don't want to mobilize everyone for a dead end."

Together, the two of them struck forward through the tunnel. The difficulty of the path and its apparent lack of traffic encouraged her. If the enemy was down here but used a different route, then taking this path meant she and Wayne were less likely to be discovered.

They took the decline carefully. Rusts . . . thank goodness she had trousers on. If she was going to slip and break her skull, she could at least do it with dignity. Or as much dignity as a woman could manage after hiking through sewage for an hour.

She distracted herself by imagining that these caverns must be as old as the Ascendant Warrior—or even older. These tunnels had slumbered through the destruction of the world, through the Catacendre, through the rise and fall of the Final Empire. Had the stones they walked past broken loose from the ceiling during the days of the Ashmounts?

She couldn't help wondering if they would stumble across the mythical Survivor's Cradle—the Pits of Hathsin—though she knew that was foolish. Wax said he had been to them, and had found no magical metals of lore.

They eventually hit a particularly deep shaft down; it was essentially vertical, though with a lot of obstructions and clefts in the stone to climb on. Wayne brightened their lantern again, looking doubtful.

"We sure they came this way?" he asked in a whisper.

"Who else would have made the footprints?"

"Footprints?"

"In the dust? And near the opening, they were crusted over with sewage from boots? Seriously, Wayne, you can be remarkably oblivious for a detective."

"You and Wax are detectives," he said. "Not me."

"What are you then?"

"Bullet stopper," he said. "Skull knocker. Guy who occasionally gets exploded."

"We'll be doing nothing like that today," Marasi whispered. "We will peek in, see if I'm right, then get out for clearance and support."

"Guess we'll be comin' back up this way then," he said with a sigh, then dug the climbing rope out of his canvas backpack. He found a sturdy rock formation to tie it around, then tossed the other side down into the darkness.

He started down first, then Marasi followed, rifle slung across her back. The descent proved easier than she'd feared, as the rope had knots in it. Still, her arms were soon burning.

"So," Wayne said softly, dangling below, keeping pace with her instead of going on ahead, "wanna hear my list of ways how women break the laws of physics?"

"Depends," Marasi said. "How misogynistic is it? Can you give me a number on some kind of scale?"

"Uh . . . thirteen?"

"Out of what?"

"Seventeen?"

"What kind of insane scale is that?" she whispered, halting atop a boulder and glancing down at him. "Why in the world would you pick seventeen? Why not, at least, sixteen?"

"I don't know! You're the one what asked me for a scale. Look, this is good. Women. Break the laws of physics. I've been thinkin' on this forever. Couple days at least. You'll like it."

"I'm sure."

"Way one," he said, sliding to the next outcropping. "When they take off clothes, they get *hotter*. Strange, eh? Normal folks, they get colder when they take off—"

"Normal folks?" she repeated, following him. "By normal, you mean *men*?"

"Uh . . . I guess."

"So half the world is not normal? *Women* are not normal?"

"It sounds a little silly when you say it like that."

"You think?"

"Look, I just wanted to point out something interesting. Useful observationalizing 'bout the nature of the cosmere and the relationship between the genders."

"I think you thought of something that amused you, and wanted an excuse to say it." She landed on the little platform next to him, and below she could finally see the bottom. They were roughly halfway.

He met her eyes. "So . . . uh . . . fourteen then?" he said. "Outta seventeen."

"And rising. It's not even true, Wayne. Plenty of men get hotter when they take off clothing. Depends on the man."

He grinned. "What about Allik?"

"With Allik, it's more the mask."

"He raises the rusting thing so often, makes you wonder why he wears it in the first place."

"Moving the mask is like . . . emphasis to the Malwish. It's not *wrong* to let people see under the mask, though they pretend it's taboo—and maybe it was once upon a time. Now they like the way they can use it to express themselves."

He swung over the side and continued down. She gave him a little space, then followed.

"So . . ." he said. "Want to hear number two?"

"Actually . . . I kind of do."

"Ha! I thought so. Wax would have said no."

"Wax had years to get accustomed to the depths of your depravity, Wayne. To me, it's still *remarkable* how you manage to dig yourself deeper each and every time."

"Fair enough. Number two: Ask a woman how much she weighs. Then lift her. She'll have increased in weight. Feruchemists, every one."

"Wayne, that joke is so tired, it slept through breakfast."

"What. Really?"

"Absolutely. My father was making stupid cracks about women lying about their weight when I was a child."

"Damn. Old blustering Harms made that joke?" He looked up at her with wide eyes. "Oh, *hell*, Marasi. Am I getting old? Was that an *old man joke*?"

"I have no comment."

"Damn conners and their damn tight lips." He reached the bottom and dropped off the rope softly, with a rustle of cloth and boots on stone, then held the rope steady for her.

She climbed the rest of the way to join him. "So, what's number three on the list?"

"I don't got one yet."

"It's a list of two items, one of which was dumb?"

"*Two* of which was dumb," he said sullenly. "One was apparently also geriatric. Same jokes as Lord Harms. I'm losing my edge, I am." He met her eyes, then grinned. "Does this mean I get to be the grumpy old one in the partnership? You can be the young spunky one what swears all the time and makes bad life decisions."

She grinned. "Do I get a lucky hat?"

"Only if you treat it well," he said, his hand over his heart, "and take it off before somethin' unlucky happens, as to not break its lucky streak."

"I'll keep that in mind," she said, eyeing the tunnel that extended onward from the bottom of the shaft. "But let's cut the chatter—as much as I love learning whatever has metastasized in your brain lately, we can't afford to be overheard."

He dimmed the lantern again and they continued along the tunnel. People at the constabulary offices gave her sympathetic looks on occasion for putting up with Wayne—but the truth was, he could be a really good constable when he wanted to. And he usually *did* want to.

Case in point, at her request he kept his mouth closed and concentrated on the job. Wayne could lack decorum, and could be painfully un-self-aware at times, but he was a good partner. Even excellent. So long as you got past his bubble—not his Allomantic one, but his personal one. Wayne was a fort of a man, with outer walls and defenses. If you were one of the lucky few he let in, you had a friend for life. One who'd stand with you against *literal* gods.

We're going to find you, Trell, Marasi thought, creeping forward. She'd first heard that name uttered by a dying man, years ago—and she was increasingly certain Trell was a god of vast power like Harmony. *You can't hide forever. Not if you want to keep influencing the world.*

Wayne grabbed her arm, stopping her without a word. Then he pointed at a tiny light shining far along the tunnel ahead. They crept the final distance, then peeked around the corner and were rewarded by the exact sight she'd been hoping for: a pair of men in vests and hats only a few feet away, playing cards on an overturned box. A small lamp flickered on their improvised table.

Marasi nodded backward. She and Wayne crept away again, far enough to not be heard whispering. She looked to him in the darkness, wondering at his advice. Should they poke forward further, or was this enough of a confirmation to go get backup?

"Tragic," Wayne whispered.

"What?"

"Poor sod's got a great hand," Wayne whispered. "One in a million. And he's playin' against his broke buddy on guard duty? Rusting waste of a full-on Survivor's suite . . ."

Marasi rolled her eyes, then pointed to a small darkened side tunnel splitting off the main one. "Let's see where this goes."

Behind them, a cursed exclamation echoed in the tunnels; sounded like the fellow with the good hand had just revealed it. This smaller tunnel wound around to the right of the guard post, and they soon saw why it wasn't guarded; it hit a kind of dead end. Though some light did spill through a two-foot-wide hole in the rocks there.

They sidled up to it, then peeked through into a midsized cavern—roughly as big as a dock warehouse—full of men and women boxing goods or lounging on improvised furniture. The hole appeared to be part of the natural rock formations; dripping water from the ceiling had covered the wall with odd protrusions and knobs, covering up what might once have been a larger opening. Marasi and Wayne were maybe fifteen feet up.

She let out a long breath and surveyed the operation. It *was* here. Months of work. Months of promising Reddi her leads were good. Months of connecting theft records, witness accounts, and money trails. And here it was. A large-scale smuggling base set up directly underneath the city, funded by—best she could guess—a mix of Outer Cities interests and the Set.

It was actually here. By Harmony's True Name . . . she'd *done* it.

Wayne looked to her with a wide smile on his face, then nudged her in the shoulder. "Nice," he whispered. "*Real* nice."

"Thanks," she whispered.

"When you tell the constable-general about this," he said, "leave out the part where I whined because of the sewage."

"And the bad jokes?"

"Nah. Leave those in. You gotta give people what they expect, or they won't believe your lies when you tell them."

Marasi took in the sight. Thirty-seven people, counting the two guards, all armed. Even the menial workers wore holsters. Judging by the leads she'd been tracing, those boxes would be full of military supplies—with a frightening number of explosive components. The gang had tried to cover their tracks by making some more mundane thefts as well, but she was confident she knew what was really happening here.

Elendel had been squeezing the Outer Cities by refusing to let certain items—including weapons—be shipped out of Elendel, which was a central hub for all the train lines. This group was acting like an ordinary gang with their shakedowns and the like, but she was almost a hundred percent certain their purpose was to funnel weapons toward Bilming, current capital of Outer Cities interests.

She didn't like the Outer Cities being forced to work this way—but these gang members had killed innocent people on the streets. Plus, they were likely collaborating with some kind of evil god bent on the subjugation or destruction of the world.

"Right, then," Wayne whispered, pointing. "See that fellow near the back in the nice outfit? He's a Set member for certain. Maybe the new Cycle."

Marasi nodded. Cycle was the lowest level of real officer in the Set. They were local bosses that operated gangs of hired muscle. Miles Hundredlives had been a Cycle, reporting to the Suit above him. This man was dressed in an upscale way—visibly more decorated than the others in the cavern. He was also lean, muscular, and tall. As a Cycle, he might be Metalborn. So they'd best not underestimate him in a fight.

"You plug that fellow in the head with a nice rifle shot," Wayne said, "and I bet the entire group will fold to us."

"That isn't how things work in the real world, Wayne," Marasi whispered.

"Sure it is," Wayne said. "If that's the guy payin' them, those other sods got no reason to keep fightin'."

"Even if you were right—and I sincerely doubt you are—that's not how we're going to do this. Confirmation, coordination, backup, and proper authorization. Remember?"

"I try not to," he grumbled. "Can't we do this one my way? I got nothin' against some blokes just doin' their jobs, but I'd hate to hike through all that muck again, then return here and find this lot gone. Let's bring 'em in now."

"No," she said. "Your way involves too much chaos."

"That's a bad thing because . . ."

"Well, there's the whole *officers of the law* thing."

"Right, right," he said, then checked in his coat to reveal a shiny badge. It wasn't something they used in the city, preferring their paper credentials.

"Is that . . . Wax's old badge from the Roughs?" she asked.

"He traded it to me."

"For?"

"Half a meat-'n'-ale bun." Wayne grinned. "He'll find it eventually. They get *real* hard to ignore."

She shook her head, waving him back down the tunnel. They had to keep their lantern darkened though—and that made it difficult to see. So despite being careful, as they returned to the main tunnel they surprised a guard who had stepped that direction to relieve himself.

He glanced at them in the darkness, then shouted. Wayne had him down and knocked out half a second later, but cries of alarm sounded from the direction of the main cavern.

Still standing atop the body, Wayne looked to her and grinned again. "My way it is!"

4

There was no way for Marasi and Wayne to escape using the difficult route they'd taken to get here—not with the entire gang on their tails. Beyond that, she wanted to capture that Cycle, who would certainly vanish after this.

Unfortunately all of this meant Wayne was right. So much for protocol. It was time to do this his way.

They burst into the main tunnel, where the other guard had his gun pointed toward them. Wayne tossed up a speed bubble, giving him and Marasi time to step aside and flank the guard.

Once the speed bubble dropped, the gangster fired into now-open space. Wayne was on him a moment later, laying into him with dueling canes. Marasi left him to it, instead picking her spot. Beyond the card table was a wide tunnel presumably leading into the main warehouse cavern. She went to one knee and raised her rifle, sighting, calming herself, waiting . . .

She fired the moment someone appeared from that direction. Only her training on the range prevented her from immediately trying to cycle the bolt on her gun. This was a new semiautomatic Bastion rifle, and so she kept it shouldered and downed the next person who stumbled over the falling body. Those behind called a warning, and no one dared come barreling in after that.

Wayne wiped his brow, leaving an unconscious gangster on the floor. "You got the magic boxes?"

"They're not magic, Wayne," Marasi said. "Malwish technology is just different but—"

"Magic boxes from your boyfriend. How many?"

"I have three Allomantic grenades," she said. "All of the new design. And two flash-bangs. Wax charged one of the grenades for me before we left."

"Nifty," Wayne said. "Got a plan?"

"You hold the tunnel. I'll go back to that overlook and toss some Allomantic grenades to catch groups of enemies, then cover you as you move in. Once you're out of the line of fire, I'll follow."

"Good as done!" Wayne said, and they split, him heading toward the two people she'd dropped. There he picked up one of their handguns and fired it a bunch of times into the main chamber—not to hit, but to make those beyond take cover. His hand wobbled a little, and he tossed the weapon aside as soon as it was empty, but it was excellent progress. Not that he needed to be *more* deadly, she supposed.

She left him, rounding to the overlook, which made a decent sniper spot. She picked out several groups of gangsters behind nearby boxes, watching as Wayne fired a second gun.

Marasi carefully took a small metal box from the pouch on her belt. All her life she had suffered disappointment and even dismissal because of her useless Allomantic talent. She could slow time around herself, which was . . . well, not much use. It essentially froze her to the perspective of everyone around her—removing her from a fight, giving the advantage to her enemies.

She'd found occasional uses for it, but mostly she'd internalized the presumed truth that her abilities were weak.

Then she'd met Allik.

His people revered all Metalborn, Allomancers and Feruchemists alike. Though he'd been in awe of Wax and his flashy powers, Allik had been equally impressed with *her* abilities. She had one of the most useful Allomantic skills, he claimed. That had been difficult to accept, but the upshot was that if you had access to a little specialized technology, you could turn the world on its head.

Perhaps an inch and a half across, the Allomantic grenade hummed as she burned cadmium—and it absorbed her energy. She wasn't swallowed by a bubble of slowness; with these new designs, all the power went into the box. She'd charged it earlier, but that had been hours ago and she wanted to top it off.

Then, judging the distance carefully, she tossed it toward a group of enemies who had gathered behind some boxes for cover. Her months of practice paid off; she managed to land the device right in the center of the gangsters, who—focused on Wayne—barely noticed it rolling among them.

The grenade used ettmetal, which was tightly regulated by the Malwish, so she didn't blame the gangsters for not knowing what to do; even among the Malwish these were rare. If the men had heard of the devices—and they might have, since the Set was known to employ them—they had likely never seen one.

A second later, a bubble of slowed time popped up around the device, trapping about ten of the men and women. She quickly topped off, then threw, the second of her three grenades—this one aimed at a group of enemies farther along. Her aim was true, and she ensnared another eight.

Calls of "Metalborn!" echoed through the cavern as the rest of the gangsters noticed that over half their number were frozen. Those would move in turgid slow motion as they tried to escape the bubble—but the ten-minute charge on the grenade would run out before they managed it.

She unslung her rifle and laid down covering fire—even picking off two of those remaining—as Wayne slipped into the main chamber. He moved in a blur of speed for a moment, then popped out of his speed bubble and leaped over a cleft in the rock. It took a bit between uses for him to recover his talents and put up another bubble, but she swore that time was shrinking.

He avoided the trapped people; she and he would deal with them later. For now he took advantage of the confusion to get in close to a couple of enemies. They noticed him, but he became a blur again—then came in from above, dueling canes held high.

Their shouts of pain distracted the others, which let Marasi pick off two more. Then she dashed back around to the main tunnel. Here she glanced into the warehouse cavern, then ran in a low crouch—careful to avoid the faintly shimmering perimeter bubbles of the grenades. She knew all too well how it felt to be surrounded by that molasses air while everything around you moved like lightning.

Marasi found her own cover near some packing equipment, and as the remaining gangsters reoriented, gunfire began pounding the stone and metal around her. As a girl, she'd read all about Wax's exploits in the Roughs—and the more she practiced her trade, the more inaccuracies she spotted. Sure, the stories mentioned gunfire. But they usually left out how *loud* it was when bullets struck. With them pelting the equipment around her, it sounded like she'd given little Max a set of drumsticks and let him loose in a kitchenware shop.

A second later the sounds slowed—like a phonograph playing at a fraction of normal power. The air shimmered near her, and Wayne slumped up against the equipment, a grin on his face—and a bloody wound on his shoulder.

"Sloppy," she said, nodding to the wound.

"Hey now," he said. "Any fellow can accidentally get shot now and then. 'Specially if he's runnin' around with a pair of sticks in a room with lotsa guns."

"How much bendalloy do you have left?"

"Plenty."

"You sure?"

"Yup."

"Wayne, I'm proud of you," she said. "You're actually saving it, being frugal like I asked."

He shrugged like it was nothing, but she *was* legitimately proud of him. He received an allotment from the department, and during the early days of their partnership he'd always run out on missions. She'd been planning to talk to Captain Reddi about increasing the allotment, until she'd discovered that Wayne used his bendalloy for all *kinds* of non-combat, non-detective work. Playing pranks, changing costumes to delight children, the occasional casual thievery . . .

It was good to see him doing better.

"How many idiots left?" he asked.

"Eleven," she said.

"That's higher than I can count."

"Unless you're doing shots in a drinking contest," Marasi said.

"Damn right," he said.

Together they peeked out from around the equipment—which was for nailing lids to crates. Wayne immediately yanked her back under cover. A bullet moving in slow motion hit the perimeter of the speed bubble, then zipped through the air above them in a flash before hitting the other side and slowing again. Bullets behaved erratically when they hit speed bubbles, and you could never tell which way they'd turn when entering one.

"Guy in the suit is escaping out the back," Wayne said. "You want to grab him, or do you want to stay here and fight the rest of them?"

She bit her lip, considering. "We'll have to split up," she said. "You're better with groups. You think you can handle this lot?"

"Aren't most of these boxes full of stuff what goes boom?"

"Yes . . ."

"Sounds like fun to be had!"

"You should have another eight minutes or so on the grenades."

"Great," he said. "I'll see if I can take those sods alive. I can grab them one at a time from their slowness bubbles, using my bubbles to counteract. See, I've been practicing, been gettin' good at making mine bigger and smaller. Should be able to walk to the edge of one of your bubbles, put up mine in a way to overlap one person, then pull them out."

"Wayne!" she said. "That's amazing. Have you told Wax? It's really hard to control the size of your bubbles like that."

He shrugged. "You ready?"

She retrieved the flash-bangs from her pouch and handed one to him. Then she pulled the pin on the other to light the fuse. "Ready," she said. Even if he had "plenty," bendalloy was rare and expensive. They needed to be careful with it.

Wayne dropped the bubble, and she tossed the flash-bang. After it detonated, they scrambled out on opposite sides of the machine. Wayne went for the last group of gangsters while she dashed after the Cycle, who vanished through a reinforced metal door at the rear of the cavern. She reached it a moment later and picked the lock fairly easily. She spared a glance for Wayne—who was quickly being surrounded by enemies. He'd found cover behind a box marked EXPLOSIVES. He winked at her, then pulled the pin on his flash-bang and dropped it inside.

Delightful. Hopefully he knew what he was doing. Wayne's healing abilities were extraordinary—but it was still possible for him to take so much damage he couldn't heal. Any blast that separated his metalminds from the bulk of his body would leave Wayne dead, just like the Lord Ruler when he'd lost the Bands of Mourning centuries before.

Well, she couldn't monitor Wayne all the time. And *she* most certainly *couldn't* survive an explosion of . . . well, of any size. She slipped through the door and pulled it closed with a loud *thump*. The entire cavern complex shook a few moments later, but she focused on her task: heading into the dark cavern tunnel after the Cycle, who—among everyone in the cavern—was most likely to have answers for her.

5

Wax trudged across the floor of the Senate, and others gave him space. They seemed to not want to face him—even those who had voted with him. They turned away as he passed, stretching and chatting.

In the hall, he headed toward his chambers, crossing over inlaid floors and beneath a row of chandeliers. Crystal and marble. This was his life now. Everything he'd fled as a young man ornamented each footstep, and the shadows seemed darker now, despite the twinkling light from above.

He believed his accomplishments as a senator could far outshine his accomplishments as a lawman, in terms of the raw good done to help the most people possible. That meant his failures carried much higher stakes. In the Roughs you depended on your gun, your instincts, and your ability to ask the right questions. Here he had to depend on others to do the right thing. And so far there had been no greater test of his faith in humanity—serial killers included—than working with politicians.

He shoved into his chambers and found his family and Kath, the governess, there already. He tried not to let his displeasure show, but Max still sensed the mood, staying back with Kath and playing with his Soonie pup.

"Well," Wax snapped, throwing himself into his seat, "there goes over a year of work."

"We did everything we could," Steris said, settling down beside him.

"Did we?" Wax asked, glancing at her stack of notebooks. "I know you have *six* of those full of new ways to try to persuade individual senators. If we'd had more time . . ."

"We did everything it was *reasonable* for us to do," she said, "accounting for our other obligations." Then she hesitated. "Didn't we, Wax?"

He met her eyes, and saw she was trembling. Hell. This would be just as hard for her, wouldn't it? *Pay attention, you rusting idiot.* He took her hands and squeezed them.

"We did," he said. "We tried with everything we had, Steris. In the end though, it wasn't our decision."

He squeezed her hands tightly. Steris was incredibly stable—she'd been there for him ever since his return to Elendel, though he'd never imagined how much she would come to mean to him. In that moment though, he felt her shaking. And . . . rust him if he wasn't doing the same himself. They'd poured *so much* into stopping this bill. And every *single* rusting senator he'd talked to had said they needed more time. Now they voted like this? Now they—

No. It's done.

"We need to move forward," he said.

"Yes. Forward." She nodded, then looked around. "And maybe get out of this building for a while. Currently, all that's going through my mind are the various ways a convenient natural disaster could turn it to rubble."

Wax grunted, and helped Steris gather the rest of their things. As they did, Wax saw an envelope on the corner of his desk. That hadn't been there before, had it? Picking it up, he felt something heavy slide to the corner. A bullet?

No, he discovered after slipping it open. An earring. And with it a small note. *You'll need to make a second, once the proper metal arrives.*

He had no idea what that meant. And he didn't care. *Not today, Harmony,* he thought. *Leave me alone.*

"What's that?" Steris said.

"Something from Harmony," Wax said.

She paused, looking at him.

"So, likely," he added, "something useless."

Steris drew her lips to a line. She was a Survivorist, and didn't strictly worship Harmony, who was seen as the god of the Path—a distinct but complementary religion. Still, after all they'd done and the things he'd seen, Steris had adopted a somewhat . . . cross-denominational view of God. At any rate, she knew he'd once worshipped Harmony.

These days . . . Well, he and God had history. Wax felt he'd overcome his worst problems with Harmony, ever since their conversation directly before he'd donned the Bands of Mourning. But that didn't stop Wax from making the occasional snide remark. Today, he shoved the envelope in his back pocket and put it out of his mind.

They packed up their things—rusts, with kids there were so many *things* to cart around. Steris wanted another child, but Wax worried about that. He didn't fancy being outnumbered.

But then again . . . he couldn't help smiling as Max went running down the hall, making his Soonie pup leap between black squares of marble, avoiding the white ones. Wax didn't normally see the other senators with families; they claimed that having children in the building wasn't respectful. But if they respected the building so much, why had they made a mockery of it with that vote?

A good number did vote as you wanted, Wax had to remind himself. *And others are scared. Of being seen as weak. Of outside interests. They're not all slag for voting against you. Remember that. There are some good ones. Same as in every profession.* It was just . . . well, he didn't want to think about that right now.

Outside the building, fleets of motor carriages had arrived to pick up senators. They'd drive off to parties, or appearances, or informal get-togethers. Even those who worked with Wax rarely invited him along unless they wanted to strategize. It was like they thought he was above simple socializing. Or maybe he made them uncomfortable.

As his family gathered to wait for their driver, Max tugged on his suit coat. "Is ya sad, Pa?" he asked loudly. "I hates the sads. Right bad, they is."

The way he said it caused several nearby senators to turn their noses up and sniff. Wax cocked an eyebrow. "Has Uncle Wayne been teaching you accents again?"

"Yeah," Max said, softer. "Says I shouldn't tell you though, so you'd think I was a genius for doing it on my own." He smiled. "He told me to talk like that around the senators because it'll upset them. And they need to be upset today, don't they? Because they made you and Mother sad?"

Wax nodded, kneeling down. "You don't need to worry about that though."

"Know what makes me feel better when I'm sad?" Max asked.

"Hugging Tenny?" Wax said, patting the stuffed kandra on the head.

"Well, that," Max said, "and . . . um . . . flying?" He looked at Wax with big, hopeful eyes.

Nearby, their motorcar pulled up to the curb and Hoid, the driver, stepped out. "Your carriage, sir," he said, holding the passenger door. But rusts, who could deny a child when he looked at you like that?

"Thank you, Hoid," Wax said. "Please take my wife wherever she would like to go. Kath, you have the harness?"

"I do, m'lord," she said, handing Steris the baby, then digging into the enormous bag of extra clothing and washcloths. She tossed the harness to Wax, who gave her his coat and vest in exchange.

It gave him an impish stab of glee to pull on the leather harness and strap Max to his back in front of everyone. Then, with a fond kiss for Steris—and a promise to meet her at home—he dropped a bullet casing and turned toward the crowd.

"Don't none of you get jealous or nothin'!" Max shouted. "He can give you a ride fer cheap, if you ask real nice and stop being a pile o' bad turds!"

Yeah . . . maybe Wax should have a little talk with Wayne. But for now he waved to the crowd, then launched himself into the air, Max letting out a whoop of riotous glee.

6

The tunnel Marasi entered bore signs of ancient civilization: the remnants of brick walls covering up the rough natural stone. A smooth floor, chiseled and graded. Sconces on the walls, now pocked with rust as if suffering some terrible disease.

She took out the last of her grenades, the one Wax had charged for her. These newer ones could hold a charge for hours—though by now the effect wouldn't last long once activated. Three or four minutes at most. She still felt better holding it—and so, reluctantly, she set her rifle on the ground and instead drew her pistol. It also contained less metal than the rifle, making it a slightly better tool against a potential Allomancer. For the same reason, she left her pouch with extra metals, though she kept her belt with a few non-metal tools useful for fighting Allomancers.

Grenade and pistol in hand, she crept forward into the dim tunnel. The gang members had hooked some electric lights along the right wall, cords tied around the ancient sconces, but they flickered drowsily as if seconds from nodding off to sleep. She soon reached another vast open cavern but lingered at the entrance, crouching and inspecting the path ahead. The Cycle had come this way, and part of her wanted to scramble after him as fast as possible. The more careful part of her kept calm, watching for an ambush.

This particular cavern held a long, narrow rift running from her left to her right. An ancient stone bridge had spanned it, but it had fallen long ago—and instead a newer construction of boards and rope stretched across the perhaps sixteen-foot gap. About thirty feet of stone ground separated her from the chasm and bridge—and a tunnel in the wall on the other side continued the path forward.

She didn't go toward the bridge though. She hesitated, still at the mouth of the chamber. These brick walls were so old. Who had built them, centuries ago? Was this like the Originator Tomb in the heart of Elendel? Had people huddled in this cavern, their walls and bridge falling, as Harmony remade the world?

Regardless, she was worried. The Cycle had seen her; her instincts said he wouldn't just run off, his back exposed. He'd lay a trap. She looked carefully, and glimpsed a dark shape behind some rocks between her and the chasm. He was probably hoping she'd rush across the bridge, so he could shoot her from behind.

Unfortunately, as she spotted him, he rose and lifted a gun. Marasi activated the grenade—which she'd been holding close to her chest—by reflex. It let out a powerful Steelpush, ripping her pistol out of her hand and tossing it out in front of her. It fell straight into the chasm.

Her reaction had been just in time though, because the Cycle unloaded his pistol at her—and each shot missed, the bullets veering away and *snapping* into stone to either side of her. Marasi dashed straight at him, picking out his fine suit in the dim light. His features were more rugged than she'd expected. A thick neck, stubble on his chin.

She'd hoped he would be carrying metal, and her advance with the grenade would throw him off balance. Instead he merely lost his own pistol, which was Pushed across the chasm, hitting the wall on the other side and falling near the path over there.

Other than that, it appeared he—like Marasi—was wise enough not to keep much metal on his person.

"By the authority of the Fourth Octant Constabulary," she said, stopping ten feet or so from him, "you are under arrest for tariff avoidance, racketeering, and the illegal transport of weapons. You're unarmed and cornered. Do the smart thing and surrender."

Instead he grinned. Then began to grow.

His suit had buttons along the arms, which snapped open, giving more room as his muscles expanded to ridiculous proportions. His jacket stayed on, but also expanded through clever use of unsnapping wooden buttons along the sides.

Oh, hell. A Feruchemist. He didn't have the Terris look—but then, neither did Wayne. You couldn't always tell.

Marasi retreated. Getting into a fistfight with someone tapping strength was a quick road to a crushed face. Instead she switched off the grenade to conserve the rest of the charge, and ran for the bridge and the gun on the other side. The Cycle lunged forward and cut her off by placing himself directly in front of the bridge. There, with a laugh, he ripped apart the ropes holding it in place.

Okay. Feruchemists weren't like Allomancers. They couldn't just pop a new metal charge into their mouths and keep going. Maybe she could run him out of strength.

He dropped the rope, letting the whole wooden construct collapse. "Trell has wanted you in particular, lawwoman," he noted in a voice that seemed too high pitched for the enormous body. "So kind of you to deliver yourself to me."

Marasi turned and dashed for her rifle. Thumping footsteps chased her, gaining on her, forcing her to throw herself to the ground just before reaching the rifle. Her move let her narrowly dodge a grab.

She rolled as he punched, hitting the ground and grunting, then raising bloodied knuckles. Feruchemical strength could be dangerous—a lot of the Metallic Arts could hurt you. Her own included. She managed to dodge the next punches as well. Fortunately for her, the Cycle didn't seem practiced with his powers. Despite the prepared clothing, he obviously found it awkward to move and fight in this bulkier form.

What kind of Feruchemist didn't practice with their abilities? She scrambled for her rifle, getting to her knees and half lunging, half falling to grab it. He moved first, leaping over her with a powerful bound to snatch the gun. He then snapped it clean in half and hurled the barrel at her.

She barely activated the grenade in time, which bounced the barrel back at him—but she was holding the box awkwardly. It nearly slipped from her fingers at the jolt of force from the thrown object.

Steelpushes. Force transference. The Cycle wasn't the only one using powers they weren't practiced with.

She turned off the box as the Cycle dodged. The barrel of her rifle bounced against the rear wall and then rolled toward her. She reached for it, thinking to use it as a club.

Unfortunately, he lunged and seized her left arm, the one holding the box. His powerful grip squeezed her flesh, and *rusts,* it felt like he could crush her very bones. Cursing in pain, she scrambled at her belt and the sheath there. As her eyes started to water, she brought up a small glittering weapon and stabbed him straight through the arm.

He howled and dropped her, then yanked the bloody weapon free.

"Glass dagger," she said. "It's a classic."

He glared at her, then held up his arm. The bleeding wound began to heal.

Hell. Feruchemical healing? That proved it. She'd never met someone who naturally had two Feruchemical powers. He was using the forbidden art. Hemalurgy.

Marasi grabbed the rifle barrel and backed away, but their fight had positioned her so that she could only move toward the chasm. Each step took her farther from the doorway she'd come in through, where she might have been able to escape. Rusts.

She retreated, step by step, holding the barrel of her rifle in one hand, the grenade in the other. How much charge did it have left? In the chaos she hadn't tracked how much she'd used.

The Cycle followed, sticking her knife into his belt. Then, horribly, his eyes started to *glow* faintly red. "Trell is choosing hosts," he said. "Avatars, bestowed with his power. How would you like to be the accomplishment that proves I'm worthy of immortality, lawwoman? All you have to do is die."

She continued backward, her mind racing. He didn't seem worried he'd run out of strength anytime soon. Within moments, he had forced her up to the precipice of the chasm, near the clump of rocks he'd been hiding behind earlier. She put those between them, but they weren't very high.

A quick glance told her that the chasm now inches behind her was at least fifty feet deep. No escape in that direction.

"You've backed yourself up against a pit," he said, advancing. "Now what? Perhaps it's time to . . . what was it? Do the smart thing and surrender?"

Instead she set the grenade to go off on a few seconds' delay, then wedged it securely into a spot among the rocks. Then she gripped the barrel of her rifle under her arms and pressed it firmly against her chest.

He frowned. Then the grenade went off.

Force transference. Every Push creates an equal and opposite Push.

The grenade shoved the rifle barrel, which hurled her backward with enormous force—straight across the chasm.

She *smashed* back-first into the wall. That was enough to stun her, but then the grenade's charge gave out. She dropped to the ground. Safely across the chasm as she'd planned, but winded and dazed.

Through teary eyes, she saw the Cycle run and leap across the chasm. So she scrambled, half-blinded by pain, searching the dusty stone, looking desperately for the pistol . . .

There!

He loomed overhead, a terrible shadow, his arm raised to smash her skull. In response, she delivered three shots straight into his face. He dropped.

Oh hell, she thought, sitting up despite the pain. Wax did things like this all the time. Leaping off cliffs, jumping around and slamming into things. How on *Scadrial* was his body not horribly ruined by it all?

She prodded at her ribs, hoping nothing was broken. Her left shoulder protested the most, and she winced. The pain was so distracting that she had to force herself to focus. A shot to the head should stop a Bloodmaker from healing, but some part of her insisted she should check anyway.

She lurched over to inspect the corpse. And found the bullet wounds pulling closed on the man's head, the holes in the skull resealing.

Rusting *hell*.

She heaved the slumped-over body onto its back and scrambled to pull her knife from his belt. He was healing from bullets to the head? Something was very wrong here. She shot him again, but that would only be temporary.

Instead, she ripped aside his shirt—revealing four spikes pounded in deep between his ribs. As she had suspected. Knife in hand, she began the gruesome work of digging the spikes out. She dug faster as she realized at least one of them was made of a strange metal with dark red spots like rust. One they'd been searching for *forever*.

The Cycle's eyes snapped open, despite his broken jaw and the holes in his skull. Marasi cursed and worked faster, bloodied fingers straining to pry out the first of the four spikes, which was so tightly embedded between his ribs it was difficult to yank free.

Those eyes. They were glowing a vivid red now.

"The ash comes again," the man said through bloody lips, his voice strangely grating. "The world will fall to it. You will get what you deserve, and all will wither beneath a cloud of blackness and a blanket of burned bodies made ash."

Marasi gritted her teeth, working on the rusty-looking spike, slick with blood.

"Your end," the voice whispered. "Your end comes. Either in ash, or at the hands of the men of gold and red. *Gold and—*"

Marasi yanked the spike out. The red glow faded and the body slumped, the healing stopping. She felt at the throat anyway, and even when she found no pulse, she dug out the other three spikes.

Then she finally leaned against the wall, groaning softly. Wayne had better have found a way to deal with those other thieves—because Marasi doubted she had the strength to lift a gun at the moment. Instead she closed her eyes, and tried not to think about that terrible voice.

7

Max called for Wax to make each leap higher, faster. The boy's shouts of glee carried over the rushing wind and flapping clothing. And rusts if that wasn't infectious. Wax had been a solemn child, a trend that had continued into adulthood. But even he appreciated the rush that came from a well-executed Steelpush.

The sudden explosion of speed, the moment of stillness at the zenith. The lurch in the stomach as the plummet began. It wasn't like any other experience a man could have—at least, not and survive.

In the distance a Malwish trade ship hovered into the city, flying using their strange ettmetal devices, as the two of them bounded across the city, afforded a view that was somehow reductive and expansive at once. From up so high, you could see the octant divisions along major roadways. You could understand and feel the different neighborhoods, the crunched-up forced familiarity of the slums, the expansive yet isolated grounds of the manors.

Once, Wax had assumed this kind of experience—not just the height, but the motion while traversing the city from above—would always be reserved for Coinshots. Then the Malwish airships had taken that assumption and tossed it out a window from three thousand feet.

Regardless, something about this perspective felt like it belonged to him. This was *his* city. He'd returned to it, and had—over the years—come to love it. It represented the best that people could achieve: a monument to ingenuity, a home to thousands of different ideas, types of people, and experiences.

At Max's urging he took them higher, using skyscrapers as his anchors to Push upward, back and forth, until they landed near the top of one building in particular: Ahlstrom Tower. The penthouse was their home, and Wax had picked it specifically. It was tough getting to the peak of a too-tall building with Steelpushes as your anchors ran out below. Fortunately, this one had several tall skyscrapers unusually close, and that gave him anchors to Push himself inward.

Today Wax didn't stop at their penthouse. He took them to the roof, where there was a little built-in platform for a worker to latch on and lower window-cleaning devices. Wax settled onto it and Max unhooked, though he was still tethered to the harness by a strong cord. Wax wasn't worried about its reliability. Steris had designed it.

Max took out a pouch of twirly-seeds and began dropping them off the side of the building, watching them go spinning down toward the busy street below. Despite the height, Wax could hear cars honking on the roadway. Six years, and there was barely a horse-drawn carriage to be seen in the arteries below. Progress here was like a wrecking crew. You moved with it or you became rubble.

The platform faced north. To his left, the shimmering waters of Hammondar Bay were a vast highway toward . . . well, he didn't rightly know what. The people of the Basin weren't explorers. For all their love of stories about Wax in his young days, or worse that fool Jak, most were content to enjoy their city. That was a problem with Elendel: it had everything you thought you'd need, so why go looking elsewhere? They hadn't even realized there was an entire Southern Continent out there until an airship had sailed up to investigate the Basin.

Yes, there had been expeditions since then. But most people were content here, and he couldn't blame them. His best efforts at improving life had been focused on the Basin. He didn't know what to do about the Malwish. Six years, and he still found the suddenly expansive size of the world intimidating.

Max hopped up and down with glee, throwing out an entire handful of twirly-seeds. The boy's fascination with heights made Kath uncomfortable—but that was what happened when, from infancy, you were often strapped to a father who found ordinary means of transportation too time-consuming.

Wax looked north toward the Roughs. Toward wonder, mystery, and a life he'd loved. He felt . . .

Rusts. He didn't feel sad.

He blinked, cocking his head. Ever since his return, Elendel had felt like a duty to him. Adventure and comfort had both been outside the city, calling to him. Though things had improved over the years, he'd continued to feel it. That call. Until . . .

Until today. Today, he remembered the parts of his life he'd loved in the north—but he didn't want them back. He had a life here he loved equally. Maybe more, judging by the warmth he felt as Max laughed. This . . . *this* was where he belonged. More, this was where he *wanted* to belong.

It felt calming to realize these things. He'd . . . finally stopped grieving, hadn't he?

With a grin of his own, he scooped Max up and gave the child a powerful hug—though Max had been too wiggly, even as a baby, to stand that sort of thing for long. Soon, at the boy's urging, they were playing a game of fetch, a variety Max had invented a few months back. Max tossed a wicker ball with a tiny metal weight at its center, then Wax tried to launch it onto the top of a nearby building. The wicker would keep it from doing damage if it fell, but the metal let him aim it. Once it was in place on a roof, they would jump over and retrieve it.

Max threw, but Wax struggled to get the ball to go far enough. "Toss it higher," he suggested to Max once they'd recovered it.

"If I throw it up," Max complained, "it will come down on our heads. I want to go onto that building over there."

"Height first," Wax said. "Trust me. The higher you throw it, the farther I can get it to fly."

Max tried again. With more height to the throw, Wax was able to land the ball on the rooftop Max wanted. Then they leaped after it. He wondered what the people in the neighboring skyscrapers thought of the frequent sight of a senator shooting past their windows with a child strapped to his back.

Unfortunately, the fun of the game could only distract him for so long. They'd been playing for half an hour when he topped a building and was confronted by an awesome sight. The Malwish ship he'd seen earlier had come closer.

The wooden construction, moved by giant fans, loomed in the air over Elendel. Wax had seen Basin attempts to design their own airships using helium or hot air. But the size of the cabin those ships could lift—in the most optimistic of projections—was nothing compared to what the Malwish could field. Their ship soared, a fortress in the sky.

This was no trade ship as he'd thought earlier. It was a warship. A show of force, though not an overtly hostile one—as it was approaching slowly and low in the sky. It was meant to make a statement, not a threat.

So, with Max strapped securely back into place, Wax launched them into the air toward the vessel, intent on finding out what was going on.

8

Marasi eventually managed to find a service ladder to get her down into the chasm and back up the other side. Worn out, she approached the main chamber, shaken by what she'd heard and been forced to do. But she carried a small book of numbers and shipping dates she'd found on the corpse, and that looked promising.

She also carried something more dangerous. Four spikes. Curiously, the red-spotted one did not like touching the others—it pulled away from them if brought close. So she'd wrapped it in a bundle of cloth and kept them in separate pockets.

She stumbled through the reinforced metal door and found a scene of utter chaos. A large blast had set off several other explosions, judging by the scars on the ground. The cavern was littered with shrapnel, pieces of equipment, and an alarming number of bodies.

Wayne squatted in the center of it all, his clothes ripped, playing cards with a whole group of tied-up gangsters. He had their cards laid out on the floor in front of them—though their hands were tied behind their backs.

"You sure you want to lead with that one, mate?" Wayne asked, nodding at the card one of the men had tapped with his toe.

"It's the high card," the fellow said.

"Yeah, but are you *sure*," Wayne said, eyeing his own hand.

"Um . . . I think so."

"Damn," Wayne said, laying down his hand. "I play three eights on the back of the nines. You win."

"But . . ." another of the men said, "you know our hands . . . Why would you play it that way?"

"Gotta pretend I can't see your cards, friends," Wayne said. "Otherwise, where's the sport in it? Cheatin's one thing, but if I can just *see* what you're going to do, then . . . well, might as well be playin' with myself. And there are much funner ways to do that."

Marasi stumbled up. He had fifteen of them in various states of captivity. Exactly as he'd said, he'd been able to use his speed bubble to counteract her slowness bubble and grab them one at a time. His control over his powers was increasingly impressive.

She wasn't surprised he'd taken so many captive—Wayne preferred not to kill. It was something they agreed on. As for the card game, well . . . at this point his antics barely shocked her. She settled down on the remnant of a broken crate. "Wayne, I could have used your help."

"By the time I had these chaps all trussed up," Wayne said, "you already had that fellow in the suit down. I saw you restin', and it seemed best to give you some time."

She hadn't even noticed. Rusts, her shoulder still hurt. She grimaced, looking around the room.

"So, uh," Wayne said, "*damn.* Did you turn to cannibalism or something?"

Marasi looked down at her uniform, which was covered in blood. "Cannibalism? *That's* where your mind went?"

"One sees a lady covered in blood," Wayne said, "and it goes to a natural place: wonderin' if maybe she feasts on the livers of the people what she defeated. Not that I'm judging."

"Not judging?" Marasi said. "Wayne, that's *absolutely* something you *should* judge someone for."

"Right. Shame on you, then."

She sighed. "Here I was thinking that I was finally used to your Wayne-ness." She proffered the spikes, each six inches long with a thick head—save for the smallest, most interesting one, which was narrow and thin, barely four inches long. "I dug these out of the Cycle's body. He would have come back to life, healing himself, if I'd left them in."

"How?" he said. "It don't work that way."

"Did for him. This other spike might be why."

"Is that . . ."

"Trellium?" she said. "Yes. It has to be."

Wayne whistled softly. "We should celebrate. You save any liver for me?"

She gave him a flat stare, at which he just grinned. "We don't eat people," she said to the captives. "He's just joking."

"Aw, Marasi," Wayne said. "I've been workin' on my reputation with these blokes."

"We broke into their cavern," she said, "defeated their leader, blew up most of their goods, killed half of them and captured the rest. I think your reputation is fine." She narrowed her eyes, noticing that all of the captives were barefoot. "Dare I ask why you took off their shoes?"

"Shoelaces," Wayne said, and she glanced at their bound hands. "Old Roughs trick when you don't have enough rope." He nodded to the side, and the two of them stepped away to talk in private. "That's a lot of captives, Marasi, and shoelaces aren't going to hold them real well. Any moment now, one of them will pop out a knife I missed—or worse, a gun. So . . ."

"Instant Backup?" she asked.

"Rusts, I love that code name."

"As long as it gets me to a bath sooner, I'm for it. There should be a way up to the city through the door I used—and there's a ladder to the right, inside the chasm." She paused. "Check on the body for me? I have this terrible premonition that I missed a spike and he'll come looking for me."

"Got it," Wayne said. He surveyed the room. "Nice work."

"We blew the place up and killed the guy who had the most information."

"We survived," Wayne said, "stopped a gang of miscreants, protected the city, denied our enemies resources, and recovered some important metals. In my book we did a rustin' good job. You're too hard on yourself, Marasi."

Well . . . maybe she was. It was the sort of thing you learned, growing up as she had. So she nodded and let herself take the compliment, feeling some weight lift from her. Wayne jogged off, and she walked back to the tied-up gang of thugs, pistol held in a deliberately threatening way.

Judging by how they looked at her, she didn't need to do much to intimidate them. "You're the lucky ones," she said—mostly to distract them. "You're going to be treated fairly. So long as no one does anything stupid." She fished in her pocket, ignoring the book she'd taken from the Cycle for now, instead pulling out a notebook that was only *slightly* coated in blood. "I have a list of rights here I'm going to read to you. Listen carefully, so you know what options and legal protections will be available to you."

She opened the notebook and burned cadmium, tossing out a bubble of slowed time that covered them all. Hopefully they'd be distracted by her lecture, because if they were watching the perimeter they'd see the smoldering fires wink out too quickly.

That was probably the extent of the clues; there weren't as many tells in a cavern as there would be outside, where the motion of the sun, falling leaves, or passing bystanders would indicate exactly what was happening. As the minutes passed in slowed time for Marasi and the gangsters, Wayne would be jogging to the constabulary to get backup.

Marasi finished her recitation, then did a slow walk around the captives, pistol at the ready, metal burning within her. A few of them stilled as she passed; they'd been trying to work out the knots in their bindings. Wayne was right. This many captives presented a potentially volatile situation. Hopefully backup would come quickly.

For now though, she let herself think about the Cycle, whose dying words reminded her of what Miles Hundredlives had said when *he* had died. *One day, the men of gold and red, bearers of the final metal, will come to you. And you will be ruled by them.*

She touched the trellium spike in her pocket.

The ash comes again, the Cycle had said today.

That couldn't be true. The Catacendre had marked the death and rebirth of the world. Ashfalls were a thing of myths and old stories. Not something of these days, with their electric lights and petrol-powered autos. Right?

She shivered and glanced toward the door at the back of the cavern, eager to spot more constables. It was a relief when a blur indicated someone arriving. Marasi almost dropped the speed bubble, then paused as she saw it was only one person. Who was this? Wayne? The blurred figure zipped up to the perimeter of the bubble and stood there for a moment.

That gave Marasi just enough time—an eyeblink really—to pick out a female figure in dark clothing, a black cloth mask over her face. Not like a Malwish mask; more like one a thief might use, prowling in the night. She was slender, with straight black hair. Her eyes seemed to meet Marasi's, then she became a blur again.

Perhaps Marasi could have dropped the bubble, but it was over too quickly. Indeed, as she was still trying to sort through what had happened, a host of other blurs in constable brown entered the room. A second later, Wayne jumped into the slowness bubble. He activated his own powers and the two canceled each other out, creating a pocket of normal time around them.

Rust, could she get that good with her bubbles? Her schedule was so constrained that such experiments seemed impossible, but still . . . it was remarkable. And surreal, that she was now unaffected by her own slowness bubble. She turned back toward the frozen gangsters, one of whom had managed to untie himself and was trying to sneak away.

"You arrived just in time," Marasi said, noting the constables gathered around the bubble with nets and ropes. "Wayne . . . did you pass anyone on your way in?"

"No," he said, frowning. "Why? Your corpse is still out there, dead as when you deadified him."

"There was someone in here a moment ago," she said. "Maybe fifteen minutes ago regular time? She inspected us, then fled."

"Bizarre," he said. "You still have those spikes?"

She checked her uniform's pockets; three spikes on one side, one on the other, and they hadn't been disturbed. "Yes. Ready for the bubble to go down?"

He nodded and they dropped their bubbles, letting Marasi shout orders to the constables. They moved in methodically, taking the man who'd been about to escape, tightening the bonds on the others. Constable medics checked the dead just in case, and others moved in to gather evidence. Well, the evidence Wayne hadn't detonated.

"Come on," Wayne said. "They can handle this. We should show Wax what we found."

"Well, after some cleaning up," she said. "Judging by how you smell, Wayne, I don't want to *know* how *I* smell. But yes. We need to talk to Waxillium."

About more than just the spikes. About glowing red eyes, and cryptic deaths. *You will get what you deserve, and all will wither beneath a cloud of blackness and a blanket of burned bodies made ash.* She left the scene to the other constables, following Wayne as he led the way out.

9

A warship's arrival was certainly an event, but not an unprecedented one. They visited now and then, with permission.

Even its low altitude, unfortunately, was higher than Wax could reach with his Allomancy. He'd need a metal anchor of incredible size to Push himself that high—either that or he'd need . . . well, metals he no longer had access to.

There had been a time when he'd borne them all. A transcendent flash of incredible strength—as if he'd touched the Well of Ascension itself. But it was best not to dwell too long on his experience with the Bands of Mourning, lest he make all other moments seem dull by comparison.

Today, he made himself known by leaping up in a few high bounds near the ship. They sent a small skimmer down to collect him and Max, giving them medallions to decrease their weight, though Wax didn't need one. It intimidated the masked Malwish airmen when he handed his back—a reminder that he was Twinborn.

Of the five different nations that made up the Southern Continent, the Malwish—these people—were the ones Wax had interacted with the most. They were the only nation that had sent an ambassador to Elendel. And increasingly, all official interactions with the South went through them. From what he'd been able to gather, these last six years had shaken up Southern Continent politics even more than they had Basin politics. Once-tempestuous rivalries had stilled, and unity had been forged.

Why squabble with one another when there were actual *devils* to the north who might invade at any moment? Never mind that Wax's people couldn't even make airships yet.

A few minutes later the skimmer—which was shaped a little like an open-topped flying fishing boat—docked with the larger ship. Max was unstrapped by now and stood patiently, holding Wax's hand. Getting to board a real airship was so exciting that Wax could feel him trembling. Indeed, as they stepped onto the main ship—into a corridor made of dark wood, the walls bowing outward at the center like a tube—Max saluted the person waiting for them.

The man was the captain, judging by his intricate mask. Wooden, but carved and inlaid with six different metals in a pattern around the eyes. The man glanced at the child but made no move to salute back, as the constable officers cheekily did when Max saluted them. He didn't raise his mask either.

"Honored Metalborn," the captain said, nodding to Wax, "and . . . unless I miss my guess, Honored Once-Bearer of the Bands?"

"That's me," Wax said.

"And also taker of the Bands, which should have been restored to their rightful people."

"Also me. I delivered them to the kandra, as agreed—to be held so that no nation could control them or their power. If you need to be reminded."

They were silent for a few moments, staring at one another.

"I am Admiral Daal," the man said—sounding reluctant. "Welcome to my former ship, Blessed Thief."

"Former?" Wax asked.

"I've been chosen to be the new ambassador from the Malwish Consortium to your nation."

Malwish . . . Consortium? It seemed the unification of the South had been completed. "What about Jonnes?" Wax asked.

"She will be returning home," Daal said. "It has been determined that she has been too . . . familiar."

Wonderful. A political shift indeed. It was probably best not to say too much more than simple pleasantries, to avoid inflaming tensions by accident. "Then let me be the first senator to welcome you to the Basin," Wax said. "I look forward to continued peace and favorable trade between our nations."

"Favorable?" Daal said. "For you, perhaps."

"We've both benefited. You've had access to our Allomancers."

"*Limited* access," he said. "Far too limited compared to the rich accommodations you have received."

"Three skimmers?" Wax asked. "A handful of medallions? All essentially useless without the ability to maintain them on our own or create more."

"Surely you don't expect us to give up the *means* of our production? One sells the goods, not the *factory*."

Every time they tried to get more information on medallions from people in the know, they got stonewalled. Obviously these were Malwish trade secrets, which explained part of it, but interviewing Allik they were able to consistently pick out discrepancies in what he said and what they actually saw. Why weren't there Feruchemical soldiers in the Malwish army with extremely heightened strength, mental speed, or other dangerous Feruchemical talents? Why weren't there Allomancer medallions? The more they learned, the more certain Wax became that there was a secret there, indicating the medallions were not as effective or as versatile as the Malwish would like people to believe.

Right, Wax thought. *About not inflaming tensions by accident . . .* He was quiet, staring at the admiral. Air as tense as a midday duel.

Then Max tugged his sleeve. "Uh . . . Dad?"

"Yes?" Wax said, not looking down.

"I need the potty."

Wax sighed. Tense diplomatic situations were not improved by the presence of a five-year-old. But it could have been worse—he could have brought Wayne instead.

"Is there one available?" Wax asked Daal.

"He can wait."

"Do you have children, Ambassador?"

"No."

"Five-year-olds do not wait."

After another tense moment, the admiral sighed and spun on his heel, leading the way past masked sailors. Wax followed with his son. Years spent near Allik and others from the South had taught Wax to be comfortable around those masked faces. It was still hard to not feel intimidated by that line of shadowed eyes. Not a one speaking, not a one lifting their mask. Wax had laughed and drunk with Malwish in the past, but this crew seemed a different class entirely.

Daal presented the restroom with a gesture.

"Wow!" Max said, peeking in, the electric light flickering on inside. "It's so *small*. Like it's made for me!"

"Quickly, son," Wax said.

Max closed the door and hummed softly as he did his business. Wax stood with the admiral, feeling awkward. He actually found himself wishing for Wayne, who had a way of breaking tension like this—by creating a different variety of tension entirely. One which allowed you and your presumed antagonist to share a moment of mutual embarrassment, maybe even understanding.

I wonder if he does that on purpose, Wax thought. It was hard to tell with Wayne. At times he seemed deeply insightful. He inevitably ruined that impression. But you couldn't help wondering . . .

"The Bands of Mourning," Daal said. "They are safe, yah?"

"I assume so," Wax replied. "I haven't seen them since we delivered them."

"I passed the gun emplacements at the city perimeter," Daal said. "I've been told about those. The maximum range straight up is what, a thousand feet? Maybe two?"

Wax didn't respond. It was a little more than that, but . . . honestly not much, at least not straight upward, despite what propaganda would claim. And though the skimmers that had been delivered to the Basin had a maximum altitude of around fifteen hundred feet, he knew that some Malwish ships could sail so high that the air grew thin and men would die if they remained there too long.

"One wonders," Daal said, "what would have happened if our people had met during a more . . . warlike era. Why, one quick bombing campaign and your city would fold like an old flag."

"Fortunate," Wax said, "that we met now instead."

The admiral turned toward him, eyes peeking out through metal-encrusted holes. "What would you have done?" he asked. "If we had simply attacked?"

"I don't know," Wax said. "But I think you'd have had a harder time of it than you believe."

"Curious, how often your papers repeat the same lines," Daal said.

"Boasts about the kandra assassins and Allomancer soldiers. When I know that your demon immortals *can't* kill. And your Allomancers? Tell me, how did you reach this ship? By your own power, or . . . ?"

What a delightful individual.

"Of course," Daal said, "we don't live during such . . . brutal times. I am not here to start a war, Honored Twinborn. Do not look so offended. But I represent many among us who feel your people have taken advantage of our . . . lenient nature. In particular with the Bands of Mourning. They are ours, and should reside with us."

Wax wanted to leap to arguments. Explain the Bands had been found in *Basin* territory. That they'd been created by someone from the North, not the South. That a deal had been fairly agreed. But this man was baiting him, and—whatever he'd done in the past—Wax didn't speak for Elendel. He was only one representative out of many.

He refused to be goaded. "Then," he said, "that is a discussion you may have with the governor and our legislature. And perhaps with God."

The masked admiral regarded him, saying no more. But rusts, if tensions were getting worse . . .

This is the absolute worst time, Wax thought with frustration. With the Supremacy Bill passed, there was a real chance the Basin would crumble as a political entity. How would the South respond to that? Daal said he didn't want war, but what if the South saw the Basin as easy pickings?

Their initial encounters had wowed the Southerners. A northern land full of Metalborn and walking myths? But the longer they'd interacted, the more each side had recognized the ordinary nature of the other. Myths became men. And every society knew how to kill other men.

Max finally came out, holding up his wet hands to prove he'd washed them. Daal marched them back down the corridor, where Wax strapped his son into the harness again.

"It is good to meet you, Ladrian," the ambassador said. "Good for me, yah? It shows which stories I should believe."

"And which are those?"

"The true ones, of course," Daal said, and gestured for one of his airmen to open the doors, revealing the city below. "I trust my time here will be profitable. Good day, Senator."

With a sigh, Wax threw himself out of the airship—accompanied by a whoop from Max, who seemed to consider this encounter the highlight of an absolutely wonderful day.

Wax slowed them carefully with some Pushes, then sent them through a series of quick leaps back to Ahlstrom Tower. The penthouse had a landing platform, and moments later the two of them burst into their suite—Wax carefully locking the door behind them.

Steris was putting Tindwyl down for her nap, but walked out to the front room a short time later—to find Max playing with a puzzle while Wax mixed himself a drink.

"Mother!" Max said, looking up. "I got to *poop* on an *airship!*"

"Oh!" she said, with the enthusiasm for the topic only a mother could muster. "That's exciting!"

"I got some strange toilet paper!" he said, lifting it up. "It's white instead of brown! Traded for it just like Uncle Wayne says!"

"Oh. And what did you leave in exchange, dear?"

"Well," he said, "you know . . ."

"Right. Of course." Steris joined Wax behind the bar, slipping her hand around his waist. "What happened?"

"New ambassador," Wax said. "Doesn't much like us. Wants the Bands back. Made some vague threats."

"Delightful day for that," she said.

"You were right about the unification timetable," Wax said. "The ambassador will announce a new consortium of states under the Malwish banner."

"That won't help our work," Steris said. "The Elendel Senate will see today's bill as building a nation out of squabbling cities, a counterpoint to Malwish imperialism."

"Conquest by another name," Wax said, nursing his drink. He'd occasionaly disparaged Elendel whiskey . . . but the truth was, some of the stuff you could get here was fantastic. Strong flavored, smoky and complex. He'd come to like it better than Roughs varieties—and it was far, far better than whatever Jub Hending had made in his tub, which peeled off layers of skin as a punishment for drinking it. He did still miss good Roughs beers though.

"Well, I do have some potentially good news," Steris said, slipping a letter out of her pocket—she refused to wear skirts without them, no matter how fashionable they were. "It came while you were away."

He slipped the card out.

Meet us at the mansion at 3:00. Exciting news.

—*Marasi*

They shared a look.

"Do we bring Max or not?" Wax asked softly.

"How likely is it to involve explosions?" Steris asked.

"With us, you never can tell . . ."

"He stays here with Kath, then. His history tutor is coming anyway."

Wax nodded. "I'm going to wash up, and then we can leave."

10

Marasi felt about a thousand times better when she arrived at the Fourth Octant Constabulary headquarters, showered and cleaned up, wearing her preferred uniform of a vest and jacket over a calf-length skirt.

As a special detective, she technically wasn't required to be in uniform, but she usually wore one anyway. The uniform was a symbol. It meant she represented something bigger than herself: the people of the Basin and the good of all. The uniform comforted those who saw her—at least those who were happy to have a constable around. And if it gave warning to those who were up to something, then that was part of the reason for the law.

As she entered, younger constables in the main headquarters room lowered their reports and conversations hushed, all eyes turning to Marasi. Then came the applause.

Rusts, that always felt so weird. You weren't supposed to be *applauded* by your coworkers, were you? More than one new constable—most of them women—watched her with wide eyes as she passed. Marasi knew that she had specifically inspired both Wilhelmette and Gemdwyn to join up last year.

That left her conflicted. On one hand, she'd rather the broadsheets stop writing stories about her. On the other hand, if it was inspiring other women . . .

Either way, she was glad to stride into the back rooms, passing the offices of the higher-ranked constables. Even a few of these called out congratulations. She stopped and chatted with a few, asking after their own investigations. Though she just wanted to be on with her work, this was important too. You never knew when you'd need another constable's expertise.

Besides. It was *good* to have friends among her peers. Finally.

Eventually she neared Reddi's office. She passed Constable Gorglen on his way out—the tall man's head almost brushed the ceiling. He nodded to her and made way, and she found Reddi inside the large rear office, frowning at his desk. His drooping mustaches had greyed in recent years, and she knew the uniform of the constable-general weighed on him. He was more politician than officer these days, spending half his time in meetings with the city leaders.

"Constable Colms," he said, scratching his chin. "Can you make any sense of this?" He showed her the drawing, which proved to be a crude sketch of Constable Gorglen as a giraffe hiding in a constable's uniform. It said *Approved by Expert Types* at the bottom.

"I'll talk to Wayne," she promised.

Reddi sighed, then slipped the paper into a very large folder on the corner of his desk—the one where he kept complaints about Wayne. Reddi had evidently stopped returning it to the cabinet.

"I'm sorry, sir," she said.

"Sorry?" he asked. "Rusts, constable. *Sorry?* How many people did you two bring in today? At any rate, don't apologize for him—I've got a feeling if you weren't keeping Constable Wayne in check, this folder would be ten times as thick."

She smiled. "He does do best when channeled toward . . . productive activities."

Reddi grunted, picking up another folder. "Don't tell him this, but his imitation of me is amusing. Though you should know, those two men with the bowler hats were looking for him again."

"Any idea who they are?" she asked.

"Some accounting firm, probably their collections department," Reddi said. "It . . . seems Wayne owes money to some important people this time, Marasi. The kind of people that even I can't dissuade."

"I'll figure it out," she said with a sigh. Harmony's Bands . . . she hoped Wayne hadn't stolen something truly valuable.

"I'll leave that to you then." Reddi rapped the folder with his knuckles. "The governor has been breathing down my neck asking for evidence the Outer Cities were siphoning off weapons, and you provided it. Thank you, Marasi. Really."

"I hope to deliver even more, sir," she said. "I have a notebook from their leader, and it has some interesting shipping manifest information." She pulled the book out, then held it open to show him. "We'll want to make copies, get it through research and code cracking in case I've missed something, but I've already read some curious things."

She tapped a list near the front. "This," she said, "is a series of tests the Cycle was overseeing to determine what can be shipped into Elendel without being stopped by customs or raising red flags with inspection agents."

"Wait," Reddi said. "*Into* Elendel?"

"Exactly," Marasi said.

"It's not illegal to ship things into Elendel," he said. "This group was breaking the law by smuggling things *out*."

"Which is why this is so intriguing," she said. "The shipping list is all very mundane, too. Foodstuffs, lumber . . . but they've noted which ones were inspected, which package sizes were suspicious, all of that."

"I find this . . . vaguely unnerving," he said. "I don't have any idea what it means, and that's even worse."

"I'm going to dig into it," Marasi promised. "For now, I'll get some of these other pages copied by the scribes. They'll give you hard evidence that the explosives and weapons we found today were going to be smuggled to Bilming. That shipment *was* leaving the city, as have many others." She hesitated. "I've had an idea."

"Go on . . ."

"I'll need authorization to work outside the city for a while . . . and if possible, we need to keep this news from the press for a few days. That means quieting the other constables. I know it will be hard, but it will help me chase down the people these men were going to supply."

"What are you planning?"

"According to this book, someone in Bilming is expecting a shipment soon. Weapons, explosives, and . . . food."

"That matches what we found in the cavern," Reddi said, looking at the initial reports. "Lots of food."

That was curious. Why would they be smuggling dried foods to the Outer Cities? Were these soldier or sailor rations?

"Regardless," Marasi said, "the Set tends to run silent in times like this. I didn't see any radio equipment down there—they were deep enough that a signal couldn't get out anyway. So our enemies probably don't know their team has fallen. Which means . . ."

". . . *We* could send in the shipment," Reddi said. "And perhaps capture the people who are behind all of this."

"Or at least move one step farther up the chain."

"They'd be expecting to meet with one of their own," Reddi said, rubbing his chin. "We couldn't maintain the subterfuge for long."

"Well, sir," Marasi said, "we *do* have the Cycle's corpse."

"There are a lot of people who don't believe in this shadowy organization you're chasing, Colms," he said. "You know that, right?"

"What do you believe, sir?"

"All those people we interviewed six years ago were certainly up to something," he said. "I'm still not a hundred percent sure it wasn't merely an Outer Cities plot—and the idea of some kind of evil god doesn't sit well with me. But honestly, I've learned not to bet against you."

"You do have to admit," Marasi said, "at the very least, that Waxillium's uncle was involved in some kind of paramilitary group."

"Yes," Reddi said, "and *someone* assassinated him in prison—along with the others who followed him. If you say that was the Set, I believe you. But I need you to be aware—the governor and his people want our official focus to be on the Outer Cities and the threat they present to Elendel supremacy, not on some secret society that might be pulling their strings."

"Understood, sir," she said. "But I think this could accomplish both goals. Most of the people we caught were common street thugs—not actual Set members. I'll bet the only one down there who had any real contact with the Set was the man who had this book. It mandates radio silence from inside the city, to not be overheard, in the days leading up to a drop-off—so no one in Bilming is expecting to hear from him. I believe we can surprise them. Particularly since we have that corpse."

"Wait," Reddi said, "how does a corpse help us?"

"I figured I'd ask Harmony to lend us a kandra to imitate the dead man for the operation. Wayne could be a generic lackey, speaking with a Bilming accent, to help shore up the subterfuge."

"Oh. Um. Right." Reddi got uncomfortable when she implied she was close with Harmony—and doing so was a little cheeky on her part, since she'd never met him herself. She knew Death far better than she knew God.

Regardless, Reddi didn't like being involved with the kandra—Faceless Immortals had made him uncomfortable ever since the business with Bleeder. He'd probably prefer she did her thing and didn't mention how. But, well, she wanted everything to be on the up-and-up.

The department deserved to know how she got her results—she didn't accomplish them without things like Malwish tech on loan from Allik, or access to Faceless Immortals. She'd originally hoped that by making all this clear, her reputation would drop to more reasonable levels. She'd been wrong. Still, that had its advantages.

"My reform suggestions?" Marasi asked. "About how we police slums, and the proper training of constables? How is that going?"

"The other constables-general have agreed to the articles," he said. "All but Jamms, but I think after today he'll listen. Just need to get the governor to sign off on the ideas." He narrowed his eyes. "I like this shipment plan of yours. Get me a detailed proposal."

"Will do, sir. We'll need to move quickly."

"You will have the full support of the department," Reddi said. "The governor is going to be so pleased with today's results that I can all but guarantee you extra funding if your operation requires it. I'll wait for that proposal, but in the meantime I'll have some people get to work on replacing the supplies that were destroyed today."

"Thank you, sir," she said, taking a deep, satisfied breath.

"Something wrong, constable?" he asked.

"No, sir," she said. "Just . . . appreciating the path I've walked, and where it's led me."

"Appreciate it on your own time, constable!"

She eyed him, and he returned a rare grin.

"It's the sort of thing I'm supposed to say," he explained. "The governor likes it when I'm gruff. Fits his expectations better, I suppose. Oh, before I forget. Constable Matieu says you had something specific you wanted to show me? Something that's not in the reports. Was that the book?"

"That and a little more, sir," she said, taking the spikes from her shoulder bag. "I want you to turn these three in to the scientists at the university." She held up the thinner fourth one. "I'm going to keep this one for a bit though."

"Ruin . . ." Reddi whispered. "Is that . . . atium?"

"No, though it's nearly as mythical. We think it's trellium, a metal from offworld."

He eyed her. Talk of other worlds didn't sit right with him either, and she suspected he'd never fully accepted what she said about Trell.

"Isn't that the stuff they used to blow up the prison?" Reddi asked.

"I don't know if I believe that story," Marasi said. "There's no proof Wax's uncle had any of this on him."

"Still," Reddi said, "be careful with that. If it's half as bad as ettmetal . . ."

"I'll be careful," she said. "I plan to deliver it to Lord Ladrian for study."

Reddi grunted. "I thought he was retired."

"Depends," Marasi said, tucking the trellium spike back into her shoulder bag. "For this, you should consider him on the case."

"Well, I never revoked his constable privileges." Reddi wiped his brow with his handkerchief. "Just try to keep him from . . . causing any incidents. When he's involved, things tend to get . . . unsettling."

"I'll do what I can, sir."

"He doesn't have any other hidden apocalyptic family members or half-sane wives with mystical powers, does he?"

"If any show up, I'll have him file a report. And maybe move confrontations with them to next quarter, for budgetary reasons."

Reddi smiled. "I'm glad you're out there, Colms. Not just for my career. I'm glad there's someone rational around, to . . . you know, balance the insanity. Go. Chase your mysteries, and let me know what you need."

She nodded, feeling a deep satisfaction as she left his office and walked back down the hallway. She had achieved so much—both in life and in this case. She had done it; she'd *arrived*.

And is this all? She tucked that annoying thought away and hurried to the commissary, where she grabbed a sandwich and began stuffing it down. She didn't have long until her meeting with Wax. Still, Marasi was only halfway done when the cleaning lady came to take her tray.

"Actually, I still have half," Marasi said, holding up the rest of her sandwich.

"Thanks," the lady said, taking the sandwich from Marasi's hand and taking a bite. "I was hungry."

"Wayne," Marasi said with a sigh, looking closer at his face. "What are you doing?"

"Hidin' from those bean counters."

"The two men with the suits and bowlers?" Marasi said. "They bothered Captain Reddi about you again, Wayne. Who do you owe money to this time?"

"None of your business," he said around another bite of her sandwich. One might have thought he'd look silly in a serving woman's apron and cap, but—with the fake breasts—he wore it well. Wayne could never be accused of poor fashion sense. Just poor taste.

"I think it *is* my business," Marasi said.

"No, it *ain't*," Wayne said. "I'll make sure they don't bother old Reddi no more. You contacted Wax?"

"I sent him a note. Meeting at three o'clock."

"Then why are we wasting time playin' dress-up?" Wayne said. "We got work to do!"

11

Wax landed at the front doors to Ladrian Mansion, his ancestral home. Steris let go of his waist—as always, she'd clung to him with a death grip while flying, but had worn a gleeful grin the entire time.

They walked up the steps, and Wax undid the locks with a few Steel-pushes in a specific sequence, causing the door to swing open before them. Others could use a set of keys, but few occupied the place any longer. The staff had moved to the tower along with Wax and Steris. These days the place had a single tenant, who stayed there off and on.

Wax called out, "It's just us, Allik!"

Aside from giving the Malwish man a place to stay, the mansion had—over the years—undergone a small transformation. Space in the Ahlstrom Tower penthouse was tight, so Wax and Steris kept their projects and hobbies here.

Upstairs, Steris had *three* rooms for her ledgers, notebooks, and catalogues—which she liked to look through in her spare time. The things she thought they'd need—delivered these days via mail order—might have overwhelmed a lesser household. However, having repeatedly bene-fited from her preparations, Wax didn't feel he had reason to object.

Steris went to the washroom to fix her hair after the flight, but Wax paused next to the door, where a pair of long Roughs dusters hung on the wall. One was white, and the other—his old one—was sliced into two layers of thick ribbons. A mistcoat. Each coat had a Roughs hat on a peg above it. It wasn't quite a shrine. Because one of the people it represented wasn't dead; he'd just moved on to a different kind of adventure. Still, Wax paused, kissed his fingertips, then pressed them to the wood beneath Lessie's hat. Again, it wasn't quite a ritual. It was merely something he did.

A moment later, a masked head popped out above the banister on the second level. "Oh, hi!" Allik said. His current mask was bright red, with flakes of yellow paint radiating from the center. It always made him look eager, like his face was sweating sunlight. Then he raised it, and his toothy grin beamed even more brightly.

For all his short, spindly figure and somewhat embarrassing beard, Allik was a force to be reckoned with. At least when it came to his pastries.

"A new batch is almost done!" he called to Wax. "O Hungry One!"

"Don't start that again, Allik," Wax snapped. "And I didn't come here because I'm hungry."

"But you'll still eat, yah?"

"Yah," Wax admitted.

"Great!" He slammed his mask back down and disappeared into his room on the second floor, where he kept the fireplace running overtime. He'd had an oven installed as well, because the Malwish could never have too much heat. He was technically a "junior goodwill ambassador" to the Basin, a title he'd earned two years ago by being willing to take up semipermanent residence in Elendel. Wax had been glad to see it. Allik had been fooling no one with his constant "coincidental" trips up here to see Marasi.

Besides. His pastries were . . . well, they were *really* good.

Marasi and Wayne were apparently running late, so Wax went to brew some tea while Steris fetched "a few" of her ledgers from upstairs. She came wobbling back balancing some two dozen of them, then plopped down on a couch in the sitting room. Wax gave her a cup of tea, then—frowning—went looking for the source of an odd smell.

He'd just found half an old meat bun in the pocket of his mistcoat when a dog came trotting in through the front door. A large grey-and-white short-haired animal that almost reached Wax's waist.

"Hey," it said with a feminine voice. "Did you bring Max?"

"No," Wax said. "I wanted to run some experiments, and you know how those get."

"Explody?" the dog—MeLaan—asked. "Well, damn. I kept this body on for no good reason."

"Do you actually *like* playing fetch?" Wax asked, disposing of the moldy meat bun. "From what I can gather, most of you hate nonhuman bodies."

"Yeah, they're demeaning," MeLaan said, settling down on her haunches. "Except a body . . . influences you. It's hard to explain to mortals. Think of it like an outfit. If you're dressed up all fancy in a glittering gown, you want to dance and twirl. If you're wearing trousers with an axe over your shoulder, well, you're going to want to smash something. I only put bodies like this on when a mission requires it. But once I've got it on . . ." She shrugged, a gesture that looked distinctly odd in the dog's body. "But no fetch for me today. I'll go change."

She wandered off toward the room where Wax let her store her other bodies: bones, hair, nails. Most of the bones weren't real, fortunately. She much preferred what the kandra called True Bodies, made of stone, crystal, or metal.

He had joined Steris in the sitting room and was halfway through the latest broadsheet—a boy delivered some each day for Allik—when he heard Marasi and Wayne tromp into the foyer. Loud as a freight train, those two could be. He shook his head, sipping his tea.

"In here!" Steris called, and Wayne burst in a moment later. "Wayne. Could you *sometime* remember to brush your feet off before you track mud in? This isn't the Roughs."

"Be glad it's just mud," he said. "We been through the bowels of the earth today, Steris, and it was full o' stuff what's normally in bowels."

"A perfectly awful description," she said.

"Oh, stop complainin' at me," he said, hopping from one foot to the other. "We got news. We got news!"

Marasi strode up and pulled something long and thin from her pouch. A single delicate spike, like a long nail with a needle point. The otherwise silvery metal had reddish patches to it, especially visible when it caught the light.

Wax breathed in sharply. "You got one. How?"

"Remember that lead in the sewers I told you about?" Marasi said. "Found a member of the Set there, augmented with Hemalurgy, heading up a gang of ruffians."

"Fortunately," Wayne said, "he didn't have any use for the spike once Marasi was finished with him."

"Technically, he *did* still have a use for it," she said. "Which is why I had to remove it. Wax, he had four spikes. Isn't that supposed to give Harmony control over a person?"

"Supposedly," he said. That had been the whole issue with Lessie. Though the numbers varied by species, the principle was the same: spike yourself too many times, and Harmony could control you. It was an exploit to Hemalurgy that went back to the ancient days, when Ruin had directly controlled the Inquisitors, like Death himself.

But lately, Marasi had begun to encounter members of the Set with too many powers. Wax hadn't believed at first, but if she'd confirmed it . . .

"The limitation has been circumvented somehow," Wax said, inspecting the trellium spike. "Perhaps it has to do with the placement of this spike, as a linchpin?"

"Wax," Marasi said, "this group was packing supplies for Bilming. Weapons and field rations."

He shared a look with Steris. Rusts . . . the Outer Cities apparently thought war was inevitable. And with the vote today, it very well might be.

Still, to have another trellium spike after all these years . . . It reminded him of what had happened to Lessie, but he forced himself to hold it anyway. This wasn't from her body. They didn't know if her strange trellium spikes had influenced her madness. The kandra all said the spikes hadn't been to blame, but something had turned her against Harmony, sent her down a paranoid path. Something had taken the woman he loved and turned her into Bleeder. He refused to accept that she'd been fully in control of herself.

Those old pains were dead and buried these days, so he was able to pick up the spike and inspect it. This metal was a manifestation—presumably—of the body of a god. Much like harmonium, also called ettmetal. What could he learn from this new sample?

The door swung open, revealing MeLaan wearing stylish blue trousers and a buttoned shirt. She'd been going for an androgynous look these days, with very short blonde hair and almost no hint of breasts. For her friends, she often maintained relatively similar features. This face, for example, looked like her—just thinner, less overtly feminine.

As usual she had picked a tall, limber body—this one was at least six foot four. She was toweling off her hair—she liked to wash it after putting on a new body, to better style it and make sure she'd got the grain right.

"Hey!" she said, seeing the spike in Wax's fingers. "Is that what I think it is?"

"Yup," Wayne said. "Marasi turned some bloke into hamburger to get it."

"Nice!" MeLaan said.

"I did *not* turn anyone into hamburger," Marasi said.

"She's more a fan of liver," Wayne said, and earned a glare.

"Speaking of meat," Wax said, "did you leave a meat bun in the pocket of my *mistcoat*?"

"Uh . . ." Wayne said. "It was . . . um . . ."

"You realize I'll have to get that thing laundered," Wax said. "And you're going to pay."

"Hey," Wayne said. "You don't got no proof I did that."

Wax gave him a flat stare.

"You can't convict me on a hunch," Wayne said, folding his arms. "I know my rights. Marasi's always quoting them to people once we finish beating them up. I get a trial by my peers, I do."

"Yes," Steris said, "but where would we find so many slugs on short notice?"

Wayne spun toward her, then—after just a brief pause—grinned widely. Those two were getting along better these days, which Wax enjoyed seeing. For now, he kept inspecting the spike. What were its properties? Could it be melted? Could it . . .

He paused, then reached to his back pocket. There, nearly forgotten, was the envelope he'd found on his desk earlier. He opened it again and slid out the iron earring, a traditional accoutrement of the Pathian religion—and a means of communing with Harmony. Piercing your body with metal was a way to connect to God and give him some measure of influence over you.

He read the note again: *You'll need to make a second, once the proper metal arrives.*

Rusts. Why would Harmony tell him to make a second earring, presumably out of *Trell's* metal?

There was no explanation in the envelope, of course. Harmony knew Wax far too well. A mystery was a better way to get his attention than an explanation.

Damn him.

He tucked that envelope away again. "Nice work," he said to Marasi. "*Very* nice work."

"Thank you," she said. "We should have a chance at some more members of the Set soon. I'm planning a sting."

She turned toward MeLaan, who was leaning against the wall, arms folded. For someone who spent her life in subterfuge—imitating others and doing missions for God himself—she certainly did like to stand out. Today she had left her cheeks faintly transparent to allow the emerald of her skeleton to show through.

"I could use your help, MeLaan," Marasi said. "I have a corpse that needs to get up and walk around—just long enough to trick the Set."

MeLaan grimaced. "I would love to, but . . . I've got a *thing* . . ."

"We could work around your schedule," Marasi said.

"That might be hard," MeLaan said. "Since it's kind of on another planet . . ."

"Another *planet*?" Marasi said.

"Well, maybe between planets?" MeLaan said. "I'm not entirely sure. Harmony wants some of us to strike out, begin exploring, learning about the cosmere. It's become evident that the cosmere knows about *us*." She nodded toward the spike pinched between Wax's fingers.

"What's it like?" Marasi asked MeLaan, with a certain . . . hunger in her eyes. "Traveling out there. How . . . do you even do it?"

"It's difficult," she said. "Both to get to the other side—which is an inversion of the real world—and to travel while there. I'll be leaving soon, I'm afraid, but finding out what's happening with the Set is a priority for Harmony. I'll ask him to get you one of us to help on your mission, Marasi."

Wax glanced at Wayne. MeLaan was leaving. Soon? He'd have to corner his friend and ask how he felt about that.

At that moment however, Allik burst through the door bearing a tray full of steaming pastries. "Aha!" he said, mask up to show off his grin. "A full room. Who wants cinnamon puffs with hot chocolate for dipping! You are obviously planning to save the world again, with those concerned faces. This is an action that requires much choc, yah?"

Wax smiled, enjoying Allik's enthusiasm. He'd bounced back from the tragedy of losing so many friends to the Set years ago—tortured for information about airships. *People are elastic,* Wax thought. *We can keep reshaping ourselves. And if we're not quite the same as before, well, that's good. It means we can grow.*

Allik handed Marasi a mug of hot chocolate—almost comically large—with a wink. She took his hand and smiled, squeezing it. Four years of flirting and two years of formal dating, and those two still acted like schoolkids sometimes. Wax knew more about it than he really cared to, because Steris tended to take notes, then ask if she should be acting in equally ridiculous ways.

"There's one other thing, Wax," Marasi said. "I took a notebook from the Cycle I killed today. What do you make of this page?"

She handed it over and Wax settled back in his seat, Steris peeking over his shoulder as he read through dated entries in the notebook. "Looks like . . ." he said. "Annotated shipping records, into Elendel? 'Box one yard square, stamped with foodstuff labels, inspected four out of six times. Larger crate with warning labels, inspected and quarantined. Crate, two yards across, detained every time . . .'"

Steris frowned. "It looks like they're recording what gets inspected when shipped *into* the city."

"Which is odd, right?" Marasi said. "It's not hard to get shipments into Elendel. Only outgoing shipments are taxed for using our railway stations. That's the entire problem; the Outer Cities are tired of paying us to ship their goods to one another."

"Right," Wax said. "Why is the Set so interested in what they can get into the city?"

"Maybe they're planning to supply a rebel force inside it?" Steris said.

"But the whole point of their smuggling operation," Marasi said, "is to get weapons *out* of Elendel. They don't have *any* trouble giving weapons to the people inside Elendel."

They sat in silence, considering. Wax glanced at Steris, who shook her head. No thoughts at the moment. Finally, he returned the book to Marasi. As Allik continued distributing pastries, Wax went over to Wayne, who had uncharacteristically passed up a mug of chocolate. Allik handed it to Wax instead.

"Hey," Wax said to Wayne. "How much health do you have stored up? I might need your help with some experiments today."

"Sorry, mate," he said. "I gots an *appointment*."

"You're not going to get into trouble, are you?"

"The reverse," Wayne proclaimed, then checked his pocket watch. Which was one of Wax's. "Actually, I gotta get moving. I don't wanna get shot for arriving late."

"A moment, Wayne?" MeLaan said.

"I really—" he began.

"It's important. Very important."

Wayne wilted, then nodded, his eyes sorrowful. Wax gripped his shoulder, as if to impart some strength. This had been coming. MeLaan was a wanderer.

Wayne and MeLaan left, and Wax tried to focus on the wonderful gift Marasi had brought him. A whole trellium spike.

"I," he said, "am going to need my *goggles*."

12

Wayne sometimes pretended he was a hero. Some rusting old figure from the stories, off on some nonsense quest about slaying a monster or traveling to Death's domain.

Lately it was hard to wear that hat. Especially when the truth stared him in the face every time he looked in a mirror. He'd made a whole career out of pretending. People just thought it was a talent. They never asked what he was hiding from.

Today, he'd have given almost anything to be someone else. MeLaan, wearing that fetching body—they were all fetching, honestly—led him through the entry hall to a small private sitting room on the other side. He made a swipe for his lucky hat, hanging on the wall outside the room, as they passed. But he missed it.

Inside, she sat him down in an overstuffed chair that made him feel like a child. Didn't help that she was as tall as Wax was, in that body. Then she took his hand and crouched down, meeting his eyes.

"I'm sorry, Wayne," she said softly. "I need to leave you. Today. It's over. I tried to prepare you for this . . . but it was probably more painful to string it out, wasn't it?"

"Dunno," he said. "Never had my heart broke before. So I ain't got no experience."

She winced. "Wayne . . ."

"Sorry," he said. "You gotta do your thing. I know that. A fellow doesn't date an immortal agent of God himself without suspectin' that one day he'll take second place to the fellow what glows." Wayne frowned. "Does he glow?"

"I thought," she said, squeezing his hand, "that there would be fewer attachments with you."

"Where'd you get that idea?" he asked. "I get so attached, I wind up with all sorts of things what don't belong to me."

She grimaced.

"Was it . . . nothing to you, then?" he asked. "Six years?"

"It wasn't nothing," she said. "Just . . . not what it was to you. I know I should have expected that. TenSoon warned me, Ulaam warned me. Mortals see time differently. They *told* me. I'm sorry, Wayne."

"You ain't gotta apologize for somethin' you *don't* feel, MeLaan," Wayne said. "It ain't your fault."

It's mine.

"I . . . *asked* for this mission," she admitted. "Because I realized I was leading you on, and I knew the longer it went, the more painful it would be to break off. That's why I can't stay and help. I've got to go now. Before I lose my nerve."

"Would that . . . be so bad?"

"Yes," she said. "Because it's a lie, Wayne. I'd be staying because I didn't want to hurt you. Not because I actually wanted to stay."

He shouldn't want her to stay in those circumstances. But he did. Damn him, he did.

Still, he held his tongue. Sometimes you just had to stand there and get shot.

"It *is* an exciting mission," she said. "I get to cross the misted unknown, the dark vastness that Harmony calls 'Shadesmar.' I'll be the first kandra to go out there long-term, with an official mission.

"I get to explore the cosmere, Wayne. I get to go and see everything there is—worlds we can only *imagine*. I get to help those who need it—not one or two people, but entire *peoples*."

He nodded dully.

She stood, then leaned in to kiss him. He wanted to pull away, but . . . well, he would have regretted that. One long, last kiss, as could be delivered only by someone with a tongue that didn't confine itself to normal bounds of physiology.

"I did want to tell you something important," she whispered as she pulled away. "Something meaningful."

"Yeah?"

"You," she said, squeezing his hand one last time, "were a *really* good lay, Wayne."

"Really?"

"Really. To be honest, you were the best I've known."

"You're seven hundred years old," he said. "And *I* was the best?"

She nodded.

Well now, that was something. Something indeed.

"Thanks," he said. "That was sweet of you to tell me. It . . . helps."

"I thought it might," she said. "Goodbye, Wayne."

She let go of his hand and walked out. Knowing her, she'd send someone to box up the rest of her bodies. She'd picked the emerald today because it was one of her favorites—she'd probably take it and the aluminum one on her mission and leave the rest.

He sat staring at the door for a long time. He wasn't wearing a hat, which meant he had to just be himself. The true him, the one that knew this pain. They'd ridden together on many a dusty path. This pain had been his invisible friend since childhood.

The pain of knowing what he really was.

The pain of being worthless.

13

Wax led the way down to the basement, feet thumping on steps behind him as he was followed by Steris and Marasi. While the upper floors of the mansion were dedicated to Steris's hobbies and the various needs of his friends, the basement belonged to Wax. And he'd made some modifications.

He'd begun pursuing metallurgy in the Roughs, where the mining towns often had equipment to test metal purities and the like. He'd been surprised at how useful the hobby had turned out to be. For example, few criminals realized you could track their suppliers by testing bullet casings.

In Elendel, he'd expanded his curiosity tenfold. A basement full of metal samples, acids and solvents, burners, microscopes, and even a room with a forge and an anvil. It all reminded him of the Roughs in a good way. Of Lessie laughing when he made a breakthrough. Of evenings spent folding metal like he was some ancient warrior making a knife meant to kill a god—rather than a novice trying to make a dining implement.

Lately, he'd found electrolysis and plating *fascinating,* and his new electricity-powered spectrometer was absolutely brilliant. Together with the graphs representing the spectroscopic colors of various elements, it let him identify practically anything. How would trellium react to that? Or to his acids, or to the magnets?

The questions energized him. It was a kind of excitement he'd lost during his middle years. It was too pure. He hadn't been able to feel excitement about something so simple and enriching at a time when his life had been falling apart.

He strapped on his goggles. Steris followed, putting on her own, then got out her clipboard. She handed him an apron, and he relented—he was wearing one of his nicer vests, though he'd tossed the cravat aside somewhere. Her own apron was more enveloping and thick, almost a flak jacket. He'd only recently persuaded her that maybe she didn't need two pairs of goggles at once; she could just order an extra-thick pair.

They set up at one of the tables, where Wax inserted the spike into a clamp to hold it steady.

Marasi stopped in the doorway, then grinned. "You two," she said, "are *adorable*."

Wax shared a look with Steris. "I don't believe I've been called adorable since I was Max's age."

"She should get her eyesight checked," Steris said. "Marasi, dear? I have goggles with corrective lenses, arranged in the drawers to your right."

"I'm fine," Marasi said, stepping in.

Steris clicked her tongue and pointed at the sign just above the doorway. GOGGLES REQUIRED. It had an asterisk and a scrawled handwritten note below—in crayon—that said, "'Cept Wayne."

"It's a good rule," Wax said. "You know how things happen around us."

"Things?" Marasi said, selecting a pair of goggles. "You mean explosions?"

"Not just explosions," Steris said. "Acid spills. Fires. Accidental weapon discharges. Though I suppose that one is technically a subset of explosion. How's the hardness?"

"Hard," Wax said as he tested the spike with various substances. "Scratched by diamond, but barely marks corundum. Just above a nine."

"Noted," she said.

"It's brittle too," Wax said, carefully chiseling. "Not like harmonium at all, which is nearly as pliable as gold. Would you get one of the burners going?"

Steris lit a gas nozzle. Wax got a chip of trellium off and brought it over in a tungsten alloy bowl, then set it under the flame and watched carefully. The chip soon heated to white-hot, but did not liquefy.

"Melting point is extremely high," he said. "Over twenty-five hundred degrees."

"Similar to harmonium," Steris said. "Try the electric melter?"

He nodded. The melter ran a powerful electric current through the metal in order to heat it beyond what the burner could manage. He'd had some luck with harmonium using this process. Unfortunately, although the little bit of trellium again turned white-hot, it wouldn't even bend or stretch.

"Rusts," Wax said softly, using tinted goggles to stare at the glowing bit of metal. "This stuff is *hard.*" How was he going to make an earring out of it?

Was he actually considering that? At the thought, he realized he didn't know the envelope was from Him. Anyone could drop off something like that. He should talk to Harmony before doing anything foolish.

"TenSoon says that the metals are the bodies of divinities," Steris said. "So-called God Metals were the source of the mists back in anteverdant days."

"So why weren't everyone's lungs burned?" Wax said. "If I can heat this to over three thousand degrees without it liquefying, then it must be *extremely* hot when vaporized."

"Perhaps," Steris said, "these metals—unlike common ones—don't change states based on temperature, but on other factors."

Wax nodded in thought. Marasi leaned down beside the table, looking at the spike. "It's full of power," she said. "It's a Hemalurgic spike, so it's . . ."

"'Invested' is the term the kandra use," Wax said. "It has taken a part of a person's soul, through Hemalurgy, and stored it. Like a kind of . . . battery for life energy."

Marasi shivered visibly. "It's kind of like a corpse, then?"

"A murder weapon, at least," Steris agreed, turning off the burner.

"Wax," Marasi said, sounding reluctant, "when I was pulling this out of the Cycle, he started ranting. The way Miles did when he died."

Wax looked up from his experiment. "What did he say?"

"He talked about men of gold and red," Marasi said. "Like Miles. And then . . . he talked about starting the ashfalls again, as in the Catacendre. Restoring the days of darkness and ash."

"Impossible," Wax said. "The land just isn't set up that way anymore. The Ashmounts are either nonexistent or stilled. There isn't the tectonic activity to cause another ashfall."

"Are you sure?" Marasi asked.

He hesitated, then shook his head. "When Harmony showed me Trell's influence enveloping our planet, even he seemed baffled. Our world, and our god, are basically three and a half centuries old. There are things out there that are far, *far* more ancient. Far, *far* more crafty."

The lab fell silent, save for the *hum* of the electric current machine, which Wax flipped off.

"So we catch up," Steris said, rapping her pencil against the clipboard. "What's next?" Admittedly, *she* did look adorable in her oversized goggles and military-caliber vest over her tea gown. He also noticed his cravat sticking out of the pocket of her dress.

"Spectroscopy," Wax said in response to her question. "Let's burn some flakes."

"Wait," Marasi said. "You couldn't get it to melt—how are you going to *burn* it?"

He took a file to the clamped spike, catching the shavings on a piece of thick cardstock. "Most metals will burn, Marasi, if you can get the pieces small enough and can apply enough oxygen. We've managed it with harmonium, even though we couldn't melt it fully."

"That's . . . strange, isn't it?" she asked.

"Indeed," Wax said. "But we are, as has been noted, talking about the bodies of gods."

He set up the spectroscope and managed to burn some flakes, using the oxygen line, to take some readings. Then he heated a piece again to get it to emit light waves and took readings on that. The machine made a pen move on a piece of paper, like a seismograph—only here, the highs and lows represented frequencies of light. Those patterns of light corresponded to different elements.

In this case, strangely, he got a straight-across line—a full spectrum. Though at the end of the spectrum, in the red, the machine tried to send the line higher than the maximum. Which shouldn't have been possible, for all that he'd seen it once before.

He unscrewed the pin holding the arm in place on the paper and reran the machine. Again a full spectrum at maximum—into the red, where the pin on the arm swung out and off the paper with a jerk.

Wax breathed out. "Seems proof it's a God Metal."

"Indeed," Steris said, scribbling notes in the darkness.

"Someone tell the dumb conner what's happening," Marasi said. "How is this proof of anything?"

"It's complicated," Wax said. "Each element has a kind of signature, represented by the wavelengths it releases when heated. It's basically a way to identify elements and compounds. Like using fingerprints to identify a person."

"And this metal," Steris said, "somehow projects a *full spectrum,* as if it were made of pure white light. But it also has something strange happening in the red, as if it has a light beyond what the machine can calculate or read."

"I've only seen something like this once before," Wax said.

"From harmonium?" Marasi guessed.

"Yes." He tapped the table, then shook his head. "In dealing with these metals, so many things seem to break the laws of physics. I feel like I'm experimenting with something dangerously beyond our understanding."

"Should we move to the safe box?" Steris asked.

"Probably wise," Wax said. "Particularly since the next step is to put some of these shavings into acids."

The "safe box" was Steris's name for the small reinforced box they'd built into the back wall. Three feet square and three feet deep, it was made out of aluminum and steel, with a large safe-like door on the front. That door had a small plate of very thick glass at the top, so you could look in. This contraption could take a grenade without trouble, and had handled an ettmetal-water explosion before.

Harmonium—ettmetal—was highly unstable. You needed to keep it in oil, as it tended to react even to the *air*. Since they couldn't know how trellium would respond to his acids, Wax set everything up inside the box, then latched it closed. From there, he could use some thin arms on gears inside to tip a little bit of trellium into each of the ten flasks of acid—and two flasks of a base.

Harmonium wasn't affected by acids, but maybe this metal would be. Anything to give him more of a foothold, help him understand. As he worked, Marasi walked over to the wall where Steris and he had pinned ideas, experiments, and thoughts regarding harmonium. Rusts . . . the oldest of those were over five years old now. Wax found it depressing to realize how little progress they'd made.

"All of this," Marasi said, reading the notes. "I don't think I've looked at it closely before . . . You're trying to split it." She spun toward him. "You've been trying to *divide* harmonium into its base metals? You're trying to create atium!"

He looked back into his viewer, continuing to dump flakes into the acid.

"Not just atium . . ." Marasi said. "Lerasium too? That's the metal that . . . It *created* Mistborn! It's explained in the records left by Harmony. Allomancy entered the world because the Lord Ruler gave lerasium to some of his followers, who burned it and were changed. Those first mythical Mistborn—they held incredible power. You're trying to replicate that."

"No," Wax said. "I'm trying to see if it *can be* replicated."

"All these years," Marasi said, "and you never told me why you kept needing ettmetal? I thought you were trying to figure out how to make airships, like everyone else!"

"We've barely made any progress," Wax said, finishing with the acids and turning away from the safe box. "But Marasi, don't you see? The Set is devoted to restoring the ancient powers to people—they'll use eugenics, Hemalurgy, *anything*. So if it's possible to make lerasium again, *we* need to know about it."

"You still could have told me," she said.

"I wanted to have something useful to show first," Wax said. He walked over to join her, passing Steris, who was fiddling with the trellium spike. Beside Marasi, he looked up at the wall of pinned ideas again. Remembered how thrilling it had been when first working on harmonium.

Getting some trellium to play with had awakened that again. But now, staring at this board, he remembered the rest of the experience. The slow, steady realization that he wasn't going to crack this particular puzzle. He'd worked on enough hopeless cases to realize when one was growing cold.

He was a hobbyist, not an expert. He'd shared his notes with the people at the university, and they'd thanked him—but had plainly already made the same observations. If a breakthrough with ettmetal was going to happen, it would come from those dedicated scientists working to build Elendel its own airships, Allomantic grenades, and Feruchemical medallions.

He would probably have to turn the trellium spike over to them. He'd have his fun for a few days, but this was too important to keep from the real experts.

"Waxillium?" Steris said from behind. "You should come look at this."

"What?" he asked, turning.

"The trellium spike," she said, "is *reacting* to the harmonium."

14

Wayne ducked into the alley just in time. Those two fellows with the bowler hats passed by on the sidewalk a moment later. Wayne crouched there, heart pounding, and counted to a hundred before letting himself relax. Close call.

He'd mostly recovered from the meeting with MeLaan. In fact, he figured he'd handled it quite well. No*thing* was broken, no*body* was broken but him, and he'd only needed three shots of whiskey to get moving after. Plus, he'd realized what his day was going to be.

It was a rusting funeral.

You could take quests and flush them away. He was having a funeral today, and that was that. He had worn his nice jacket and a matching hat, all fancy and proper. He even had a flower in the lapel, which he'd *paid* for. With actual money. Fancy is as fancy does.

He rejoined the procession on the street outside. Yes, they all seemed to know it was a funeral day, they did. So many heads down rather than looking up at the sun. So many dull faces, like they were the dead, still up and moving because . . . well, in the city, there were jobs to do.

Did dead people think funerals were celebrations? Initiation parties? Reverse birthdays?

He kept his head down, acting like a member of the masses on the sidewalk. This city, it just had so many people. Floods of them on the streets in this part of the octant, the financial district, all in their funeral finest. It should have been easy for anyone to fit in since there was basically every sort of person you might want to meet. But somehow the financial district mashed people up into a similar ball of cravats and heels. You could almost not notice that some were Terris and others were koloss-blooded.

Hard to miss that rusting airship dominating the sky, but keeping your head down helped. Maybe today's funeral was for the city itself. Or at least its naiveté.

The Drunken Spur was on Feder Way, right on the corner of Seventy-Third. You couldn't miss it, what with the swinging wooden sign outside and the mannequins in Roughs gear in the window. Not a lot of upscale cafés used mannequins, but this place was special. Kind of like how a kid who ate mud was special. But Jaxy liked it, so one made accommodations. Wayne was an accommodating kind of person, he was.

He stepped inside and tried not to cringe *too* hard at what the serving staff was wearing. Roughs hats. Bright red shirts. Chaps? Oh, Ruin. He was going to gag. At least the greeter at the host's stand was in a proper suit.

"Your hat, sir?" the man said, and Wayne handed it over, then swiped the bell off the stand.

"Um, sir?" the greeter asked, looking at the bell.

"You'll get it back when you return my hat," Wayne said. "A man gots to have insurance."

"Uh . . ."

"Where's my table? It's got two pretty women at it, and one of them's nice, but the other probably threatened to shoot you when she was bein' seated."

The host pointed. Ah, there they were. Wayne nodded and stalked that direction. Rusting terrible attire for them to all wear on a day like this. You didn't go to a funeral in chaps unless you rode there on a horse. Or unless you were old Three-Tooth Dag, who liked that sort of thing.

Ranette was Ranette: curvaceous—though he wasn't supposed to talk about it—and wearing slacks. Jaxy was in a fine white dress, with short white-blonde hair in very tight curls, accented by diamond barrettes. She liked sparkles. He didn't blame her. Far too few sparkles in life. Adults was supposed to be able to wear what they wanted, so why did so few choose sparkles?

He sat down with Ranette and Jaxy, then thumped his forehead down on the table, making the silverware rattle.

"Oh, delightful," Ranette said in a dry voice. "Drama."

"Wayne?" Jaxy asked. "You all right?"

"Mumble mumble," he said into the tablecloth. "Mumble."

"Don't humor him," Ranette said.

"Yes, humor him," Wayne grumbled. "He needs it right now."

"What happened?" Jaxy asked.

"I am officially dumped," he said. "And my whiskey is wearing off. Stupid body. Metabolizing and neutralizing poisons as if I didn't dump 'em in there on purpose." He looked up. "You think I could cut out my liver and stay drunk forever?"

"I'll humor him on *that* one," Ranette said.

"I'm sorry, Wayne," Jaxy said, patting him on the hand.

"'S all right," he said. "At least you dressed up fer the funeral."

"The . . . ?" Jaxy asked.

"Ignore him," Ranette said. But then she softened her voice. "Hey. You'll live, Wayne. I've seen you get through worse."

"When?"

"That one time you *literally* got a cannonball through the stomach."

He looked up. "Oh yeah. That was something else."

Jaxy had gone pale. "Did it hurt?"

"Not as much as you'd think," he said. "Like, yeah, I got torn in half. But I think my body was just kinda confused, you know? Not every day you're in two pieces."

"Fortunately," Ranette said, "his metalminds were on the piece with his head. Otherwise . . ."

He forced himself to sit up, then sighed and put the bell on the table, then rang it. Then rang it again. Seriously, what was the point of these things if people didn't pay attention? The third ring finally got a server to step over.

"Vodka," Wayne said to her. "Worst you got. Closer to piss it tastes, the better."

"Wayne," Ranette said, "this is an upscale restaurant."

"Right," he said. "Putta olive in it or somethin'."

"Was that even our server?" Jaxy asked as the woman moved off.

"I try not to look too closely," Ranette said. "Given the awful outfits."

"I hear you," Wayne said. "Who thought a Roughs-themed restaurant was a good idea? Like, to be authentic you'd have to have only stew on the menu. Then when people ordered it, you'd be out of stew and just give them beans."

"I like it," Jaxy said. "It's amusing."

"It's insulting," Ranette said.

"Can we talk more about me?" Wayne said. "Because I'm still over here feeling like what's left of the grapes after the wine's been made."

"Poor dear," Jaxy said.

"You're too good to him, Jax," Ranette said.

"He's one of your oldest friends."

"Only because he can't die."

"Ranette . . ." Jaxy said.

"Fine," Ranette said, then put her hand on Wayne's shoulder. "You're strong, Wayne. You can get through this." She took the glass from the tray when the server came back, and handed it to him. "Look, here's your alcohol."

"Thanks, Ranette," he said, accepting it. "You really know how to make a fellow feel better."

"To be honest," she said, "I'm proud of you, Wayne. How you're handling this. It's relatively mature."

"This is mature?" he asked, then downed the vodka.

"Relatively."

"Suppose you gotta be an adult to get booze," Wayne admitted. "But . . . it's just . . ." He sighed and sat back. "I didn't think I'd ever meet someone who understood what it was like to have to be another person most of the time. And she did. She *did,* Ranette."

"You'll . . . uh, find someone else?" Ranette said. "Someone better? That's what I'm supposed to say, right? Even if it's probably not true, since I doubt there are many people who are better than a Faceless Immortal. And—"

"Oh, Ranette," Jaxy said, shaking her head.

"What?" she said. "I don't *do* comforting, all right?"

"Wayne," Jaxy said, "it will hurt. That's okay. Pain is just your body and your mind acknowledging that this is awful."

"Thanks," he mumbled. "You're a good friend, Jaxy. Even if you have terrible taste in women."

"Hey!" Ranette said. "*You* chased me for the better part of fifteen years."

"Yeah? And how's my taste, on average?"

"I . . ." Ranette said. "Damn. Stop aiming for the vital bits, Wayne. This is supposed to be a friendly meal."

"Sorry," he said, then put his elbows on the table, holding his head in his hands. They still hadn't seen their actual server, which made sense. This was a seriously fancy place; you could tell by their contempt for their customers.

"I meant it though, about being proud of you," Ranette told him. "You've grown, Wayne. A lot. We've been going to dinner for years now, and you haven't hit on me once."

"I promised. Besides, you're taken. I ain't a poacher." He slumped back in his seat. "This wouldn't be so bad if *that* day weren't coming up."

"The day . . ." Ranette said. "When you have to deliver payment to that girl?"

Wayne nodded. "Allriandre," he said. "She and her sisters don't have a daddy because of me." His day of trials was the worst day of the month, where he had to go face her. And admit what he'd done: murdering her daddy over twenty years ago.

You know you aren't forgiven.

I know.

You will never be forgiven.

I . . . I know.

Ranette leaned forward, tapping on the saltshaker with her fingernail. It was in the shape of a Roughs-style boot. So fancy that the awful decor somehow wrapped around to being tasteful.

"What if," Ranette said to him, "you *didn't* see her this month?"

"I've gotta," Wayne said.

"Why?"

"It's my punishment."

"Says who?"

"The cosmere," Wayne said. "I took her daddy from her, Ranette. I gotta remember. What I am. I gotta look her in the eyes and let her know I ain't forgotten."

The two women shared a look.

"Wayne," Jaxy said, "I've . . . wanted to talk to you about that. The way you treat that girl. I realize today might not be the best day . . ."

"Nah," he said. "Hit me, Jaxy. I'm mostly numb already. It's a good day to get punched."

"Why do you insist," Jaxy said, "on seeing her in person?"

"So she can punish me."

"Does she *want* to punish you?"

"She seems to enjoy it when it happens."

"Does she? Does she *really*, Wayne? Because the way you tell it, sounds like she asks you *not* to come see her."

"Because she's bein' too nice," Wayne explained. "But I don't deserve anyone bein' nice to me."

"I told you, Jax," Ranette said. "He's got the self-awareness of a half-eaten sandwich."

Wayne frowned. What was she on about?

"I've never met anyone," Jaxy said, "who can get inside the heads of other people as well as Wayne can. He'll understand."

"He gets in their heads when it suits him," Ranette said. "Not when it means seeing things he doesn't want to see."

Wayne looked away. Ranette said a lot of mean things, but they weren't . . . well, they weren't *actually* mean. He joked, and she joked. And sure, sometimes there was an edge of truth to it, but that's what friends was about. Making you look a little silly when you were together, so that you didn't look *really* stupid when you were apart.

But the way she said that last bit . . . it stung. He understood people, didn't he? Wax and Marasi, they were great at the investigating part. But they needed someone like Wayne who really *knew* the people who lived in the dirt—and counted themselves lucky, because at least it wasn't mud. Currently.

"Wayne," Jaxy said, "what do you imagine that girl wants? Can you think like her? Does she *really* want you to come remind her of her pain each month?"

"I . . . I want her to be happy. And beating up a fellow like me who made her unhappy . . . well, that's the best way."

"Is it?" Jaxy asked softly. "Or is it about you? Doing some kind of penance? Wayne, each time you ignore what that girl asks of you, you take a little joy from her and turn it into your own suffering."

He squeezed his eyes shut.

"You *can* see it," Jaxy said, patting his hand. "I know you can."

"I've lost my appetite," he said, shoving back from the table and stalking off through the restaurant.

From behind, Ranette's voice chased him. "I told you. He might not be as bad as I pretend, Jax. But he's not as good as you want to pretend either."

He traded the bell for his hat back, and only took one of the fellow's cufflinks in the exchange—a fair trade for them keeping his hat over some stupid bell that barely even worked. Outside, unfortunately, he all but collided with two men in bowler hats and vests.

Rust and Ruin! They'd found him.

"Sir," the taller of the two bean counters said, "we need to talk about your finances."

"Whataboutem?" Wayne said, shoving his hands in his pockets.

"You have *far* too much money," the shorter one said. "Please, sir. We *have* to talk about your investment strategy! Your current lack of diversification is a *crime*."

Well, to ashes with him, then. This day had actually found a way to get worse. He let them shove him into their hearse of a car, off to the mortuary. Or, well, the accounting firm that kept track of his wealth. Same difference.

In either case Wayne, as everybody knew him, was dead.

15

The trellium was moving.

Steris had been getting out a harmonium sample for study in conjunction with the trellium spike. And the trellium did *not* seem to like it.

Wax moved the small bead of harmonium—suspended in a vial of oil—toward the trellium. It again rolled away.

"Curious," Wax said. Then, on a hunch, he burned a little steel inside of him.

The trellium spike rolled away from him again. "I didn't Push," he said. "It responded to me *burning* steel."

"That's a result!" Steris said, scribbling furiously. "Wax, that's actually *useful*."

And . . . yes, it was, wasn't it? A way to test if someone was burning their metals? Seekers could do that, but having a mechanical way to accomplish it . . .

"Oh!" Marasi said. "I should have mentioned. That spike had a similar reaction to the other spikes I harvested."

"It's like Allomancy," Steris said. "Like the trellium spike is *using* Allomancy to Push."

"No," Wax said. "It's more like magnetism. The trellium spike responds to other sources of Investiture in the way one magnet responds to another one."

"It wants to stay apart from them," Steris said.

"More like it has the same charge," Wax said. "I doubt that it 'wants' anything." Though, as this was part of a god, who knew? Particularly since, so far as he was aware, other Invested items with a similar charge didn't repel one another.

A little experimenting showed him that the two metals—harmonium and trellium—repelled each other with increasing strength the more he tried to push them together. Again, like magnets. The response to harmonium was stronger than the response to him burning his metals.

Wax consulted a large chart on the wall; it displayed an extrapolation from a notebook that Death had given Marasi. Once upon a time, that event had been one of the most surreal Wax had ever heard described. These days it seemed almost commonplace.

The book detailed how to use Hemalurgy. He'd studied the notes in depth, and had created a chart of all the points on the body where spikes could be placed. A detailed list of the ways they worked, requiring linchpin spikes to coordinate and keep the network functioning.

The Set was experimenting further with Hemalurgy. And his sister, Telsin, was out there somewhere, high up in the leadership of the Set. Seven years ago, he'd thought she'd been kidnapped . . . but he should have seen. Telsin's incredible ambition fit perfectly with the Set's goals.

It had led her to spiking herself. Pinning pieces of souls to her own. It nauseated him to think of the people murdered for that purpose—to realize what Telsin and the Set were doing. In his fingers, he held not only a relic from a long-forgotten god; he held a tattered symbol of his sister's rejected humanity.

Rusts. He really was going to have to talk to Harmony, wasn't he? As little as Wax liked it, he was a part of this. He needed to finish what he'd begun all those years ago, when he'd fled Elendel—leaving his house to the machinations of his sister and uncle.

Footsteps on the stairs announced Allik, arriving with refreshments. Wax wasn't certain if the former airman did that so assiduously because he thought of this mansion as his home and wanted to entertain, or if he just enjoyed having people around to try his baking. Nevertheless, the sight of him—mask up, grinning widely and bearing two plates of chocolate biscuits—did lighten Wax's mood.

"You are being careful," Allik said to Wax, "never to put too much ettmetal in one place, yah?"

"I don't think I have enough to worry about."

"Still, always good to remember," Allik said. "One of the basic rules of handling it."

They had all kinds of odd rules about the metal, and Wax had trouble separating the superstitions from the science. Supposedly, you couldn't put a large concentration of ettmetal in one place, otherwise it caused strange reactions—though Allik didn't know specifics.

The perky Southerner marched up to Marasi with his offerings and held them out.

"Oh!" Marasi said, snatching a biscuit. "My favorite."

Wax took one too. He was accustomed to biscuits that could block a bullet in a pinch. It was the Basin way. Yet these were moist, even gooey. It was odd, but not unwelcome.

Marasi in particular seemed to be infatuated by the way Allik put sweetened chocolate in everything. "They're best when warm," she said, munching as Allik sat across from her. Wax *had* wiped off that lab table, hadn't he? "You know, you look more handsome when I'm eating choc. How curious."

"You just say that," Allik replied, "because you want me to make more."

"Of *course* that's why I say it," she replied, seizing a second biscuit.

Wax sat back on his stool, enjoying his biscuit, thinking about the metals laid out on the table in front of him. Harmonium and trellium. They repelled each other. More and more violently, the closer together they were . . .

I wonder . . .

He gathered up the materials and was setting up a new experiment in the safe box as another set of footsteps started down the steps. This made them all pause. Wax carefully slipped some bullets from his pouch, ready to Push them. Though when the door opened, it revealed a prim man in a brown suit. He had stark blond hair—perfectly styled—and spectacles with wire frames. The type of person whose entire bearing screamed, "I fact-check people's jokes."

"VenDell?" Wax guessed, putting his bullets away. The kandra was wearing a new body, but the creature's air was distinctive.

"Indeed, Lord Ladrian," VenDell said, entering the room and undoing his satchel. "You'll forgive me for letting myself in." He set a piece of paper on the table beside Marasi. "This is for you, Miss Colms."

"What is it?" she asked, wiping her fingers on a napkin that Steris materialized as if from nowhere.

"A note recovered from the site of your engagement with the Set," VenDell said. "LeeMar recovered it before the other investigating constables could notice it."

"Wait," Marasi said. "You have kandra among the constables I don't know about?"

"Several," VenDell said.

"Who?"

"Cassileux, for one. LeeMar took over her life about sixteen months ago, after the real woman died in that raid on the Nomad Gang."

Marasi's jaw dropped. "But . . . Cassileux and I had *lunch* last week!"

"Yes, she keeps an eye on you," VenDell said.

"She didn't tell me!"

"Should she have?" he asked absently, then sniffed at the biscuits that Allik offered him. "How horrible."

"Aw," Allik said, his shoulders slumping.

"I've told you, Master Allik," VenDell said. "I am a carrion feeder, and strictly carnivorous. These . . . creations . . . would not suit me. But if you are interested, I've been considering putting up good money for one of your masks."

"What?" Allik said, hand going to his mask, which was still up on the top of his head. "My mask?"

"There has been discussion among the kandra lately," he said, "about your masks. Many of us think they are as integral to your natures as hair or nails—virtually a part of your skeleton. As such, I have decided to start collecting them for future bodies. Do you have any for sale?"

"Uh . . ." Allik said. "You're an odd man, yah?"

"I'm not a man at all," VenDell said. "I'll leave you with an offer; let me know if you'd entertain some negotiations. I would only require the mask after your death, of course. If you persist in spending time with this group of people, that might not be far off."

He walked toward Wax next, then held out his hand. "May I see it, please?"

Wax sighed, then turned to the safe box where he'd been setting up his experiment. He took out the trellium spike and presented it to VenDell, who held it up toward the light.

"I thought you couldn't touch those," Steris said from the table beside Marasi.

"You are mistaken, Lady Ladrian," VenDell said. "This is not a kandra's spike, so touching it is not taboo."

"I'm not going to let you take this one," Wax warned. "It needs to be studied."

"Unfortunately," VenDell said, "I have no intention of recovering it, so we won't get to see if you could actually prevent me or not."

"You don't want it," Wax said, "because it's not a kandra spike? Unlike the ones that belonged to Lessie, which you stole from us."

"You gave those up willingly."

"I was not in an emotional state to do anything willingly," Wax said. "I still want to know how much that metal—trellium—had to do with what happened to her."

"The way Paalm . . . acted was a direct result of her decision to remove one of her spikes," VenDell said. "The trellium spikes may have exacerbated her ailment, but were not the root cause."

"Harmony implied otherwise to me."

VenDell turned the spike over in his fingers and didn't reply. Instead he nodded toward the safe box. "What are you doing here?"

"Electric current to soften some harmonium," Wax said, pointing at the equipment he'd set up: a system to deliver a powerful current through a tiny nugget of harmonium held at the center, coated in oil to prevent it from corroding. "That's the closest we ever came to dividing it."

"It cannot be divided," VenDell said. "Not so long as Harmony remains Harmony. I've explained this."

Steris trailed over with her clipboard, and they shared a look. It was true; harmonium wasn't actually an alloy. Yet Harmony held both Ruin and Preservation—so somehow this metal was both atium and lerasium, blended in a way that defied ordinary scientific explanation.

It seemed reasonable there would be a way to split it. Yet, acids for selective dissolution had failed. Different heating methods to get the components to self-separate while fluid had failed. Electrolysis had failed.

A dozen other ideas had failed as well. There was a reason he'd lost momentum on the project. But of all they'd tried, electric currents seemed to have come the closest. He activated the machine, and didn't bother closing the front of the safe box. He'd run this experiment often enough that he was comfortable doing it in the open.

The tiny bit of harmonium heated up. Marasi and Allik walked over, watching it glow with a powerful internal light. Then Wax activated the other component of the machine—which pulled the nugget apart.

Harmonium was pliable, more so when heated. When softened like this, it seemed to react differently to the air—no longer as volatile. As if . . . as if it were becoming something else.

This specialized machine continued to deliver electric current through the grips at the sides—but now those moved apart and *stretched* the metal. If he continued, he could divide it cleanly, making two pieces of harmonium. That itself wasn't remarkable. But the machine was set to pull only a few sixteenths of an inch, then stop. The result was two globs of harmonium at the sides, with a narrower stringy bit between.

"What is this supposed to do?" VenDell asked.

"Watch," Wax said. With his tinted goggles, it was probably easier to see—but after a few moments the metals started to *rearrange*. The glob of harmonium on the left side began to glow a blue-white. The one on the right adopted a stranger air, growing silvery and reflective. It *almost* seemed liquid, like mercury—the surface incredibly smooth.

"Is that . . . ?" Marasi asked.

"No," Wax said. "If you cut it in half right now, when the metals cool you'll just have two bits of harmonium. Yet in this state, the metals *almost* separate. You can see the left bit taking on aspects of lerasium. The bead on the right . . . that's how atium was described."

"It always looks like it *wants* to divide," Steris said. "That it's arranging itself to do so."

"Ruin and Preservation," Marasi whispered. "Atium and lerasium."

"I think that's the reason harmonium is so unstable," Wax explained. "Harmony has trouble acting, right? He's mentioned it before: his two aspects work against one another, leaving him indecisive, impotent."

"He's merely in equilibrium," VenDell said. "Equal parts the need to protect and the need to let things decay."

"Well," Wax said, "I'm increasingly certain we face a god who *isn't* hindered by that kind of equilibrium. I was skeptical at first, but Marasi convinced me."

"Trell is dangerous, VenDell," Marasi said, squinting against the bright light. "We have to do something. We can't wait for Harmony."

"Almost I am persuaded," VenDell said. "What did you think of the note?"

"It's confusing," Marasi said. "And vague."

Wax shot her a glance.

"I'll explain," she promised. "But first . . . are we going further with this?" She nodded toward the safe box they were all crowded around.

"Well," Wax said, taking the trellium spike back from VenDell, "we noticed that this metal repels all forms of Investiture—and it repels harmonium even harder. I thought . . . what if I stretched a nugget apart like this, then used trellium to try to split it? Might that repel the two sides harder, and actually separate out some atium and lerasium?"

He looked to the others in turn.

"What . . . are the chances that blows things up?" Allik asked.

"Considering harmonium is involved?" Steris said. "I'd say it's *incredibly* likely. But worth a try."

"That's why we have the safe box, right?" Wax said. "Plus, that's a very small bit of harmonium. How much energy could one piece of metal contain?"

The words hung in the air.

"So . . ." Allik said. "I think we should all go next door and be very far away when he does this, yah?"

"Yah," Marasi agreed.

Wax took a deep breath, then nodded. "I'll rig a timer," he said. "This basement is reinforced with enough concrete to pave a highway, so we should be fine upstairs."

"We could make the kandra do it," Marasi said. "They're basically indestructible."

"Basically," VenDell said, "is infinitely distant from 'completely,' Miss Colms. I have been instructed to help you with your little infiltration—I believe you have a corpse for me?—not to risk my life trying to accomplish the impossible."

"Timer it is," Wax said.

"I'll get a tiny sliver of trellium," Steris said, "so we don't have to use the entire spike."

"Good idea," Wax said. He should be able to repurpose his hydraulic punch . . .

It took a good half hour to set the whole thing up. All the while, Wax wondered. What if he *did* split harmonium? He'd have two metals, the bodies of gods, each capable of incredible things from ancient lore, like manipulating time or creating beings with mythological Mistborn abilities. What if he had that power? What would that change about him?

Nothing, he thought to himself. *I've held that power. And when I had it, I used it to save my friends.*

He finished the calibrations, leaving a machine on a timer set for five minutes. Once the time was up, it would press the tiny trellium shard forward into the center of the heated and stretched harmonium bead.

He closed the safe box tight, and together they all fled up the stairs and secured the thick metal door at the top. And then . . . Wax realized five minutes had probably been excessive.

"So . . ." he said as he pulled out his watch, "what about that note?"

"It was in one of the boxes in the cavern," VenDell explained. "One of the few that weren't destroyed in the explosions."

"During the mission earlier," Marasi said, "I spotted a masked figure in dark clothing. I had a slowness bubble up at the time, and she approached as a blur. I got barely a glance at her before she left, but I think this must be from her."

She turned the paper toward Wax, showing a simple message.

We are watching, Marasi, it read. *And we are impressed.*

It had a small symbol at the bottom, with three interlocking diamonds. It looked vaguely familiar to Wax, though he didn't think he'd ever seen the symbol before. More, the pattern reminded him of something.

"You ever seen this?" Wax asked VenDell.

"Uh . . ." he said, "that is a question I'm forbidden to answer. My apologies, Lord Ladrian."

"Forbidden?" Steris asked. "By whom?"

"Harmony himself, Lady Ladrian," VenDell said. For the first time that Wax could remember, the creature looked *uncomfortable*. "I suggest you speak to him directly."

"Great," Marasi said. "Nice to know we're working for the defense of the *planet itself* while God is acting like a child with a secret crush."

"False gods are like that," Allik said, and earned glares from all around the room. He just shrugged.

They all fell silent. *Why*, Wax thought, *does a few minutes feel like forever when you're waiting?*

"So," VenDell said. "Your bones, Lord Ladrian. Have you reconsidered—"

"Not for sale."

"But—"

"Not for sale."

"Ah well, then," VenDell said. "Can't blame a person for inquiring. Such a fine skeleton, and for it to go to waste . . ."

A sudden *blast* shook the entire building. Chandeliers rattled, the window to Wax's right cracked, and he heard dishes fall somewhere in the kitchen.

"Rusts," Marasi said. "They probably felt that in the next octant over. You . . . think the safe box held?"

"One way to find out," Wax said, walking toward the door to the basement.

"At least," Allik said to the others, "we planned for it this time, yah?"

"*Always* plan for an explosion around Wax," Steris said. "It saves a ton of effort."

Wax pulled the door open, then started down the steps.

16

Call and Son and Daughters Accounting and Estate might not have looked like a mortuary, but Wayne was absolutely certain it was one. Because you'd have to be dead to enjoy working in such a place.

Tall Boring Guy and Short Boring Guy sat him down and started embalming him right away. Not with the good stuff either. He'd have taken basically any kind of drink, but no, they had to use ink.

They dried his body out good first though.

"Your investments," Tall Boring Guy said, "are too high-risk, Master Wayne. We recommend a more balanced portfolio."

"How much money have I got?" he asked, sullen.

"Over twenty million at this point."

Well, damn. "I told you," he said, "to give it to people what don't have any houses!"

"Yes, and your affordable housing project was wildly successful," Short Boring Guy said, perking up and reaching for a ledger. "How you anticipated the impending subsidies is quite a stroke of—"

"And that girl?" Wayne said. "With the plugs in the walls?"

Tall Boring Guy smiled. "The revolutionary electric devices developed by Miss Tarcsel are at the forefront of your financial empire, Master Wayne! Profits are *astronomical*."

"Your real estate investments were wise," Short Boring Guy said, "but we need to liquidate some of your ownership in Tarcsel Electric and invest in other, newer companies, to provide a buffer against competition—which is beginning to pop up now that the initial patents are lapsing."

"You guys," Wayne said, "really need to get girlfriends or somethin'."

"Oh, we both are dating, Master Wayne," Short Boring Guy said. "Garisel is quite popular, I must say. And you have no idea how wild lady accountants can be! Why, the other night—"

"Shut it," Wayne grumbled. "Don't rub it in." Well, no use resisting. A man couldn't run from his own funeral. Mostly because his legs don't work when he's dead. "Fine. Give me one of those damn hats."

They looked at one another, but Wayne waved impatiently, so Tall Boring Guy finally took his bowler from the peg by the door and handed it over.

Wayne pulled it on, and his death was right and truly accomplished. Rust him all the way down to the bones. He eyed the ledgers, rubbing his thumb against the bottom of his chin. But that wasn't enough, so he absently took Short Boring Guy's spectacles from the man's vest pocket, then tucked them into his own pocket.

Still not enough. "Kindly fetch me," he said, "some honey tea with some lemon on the side and one tiny sprig of mint. Not too much, mind you, but enough to add some perk. You understand, don't you, Garisel? Good man, good man."

Soon he had it in hand while he surveyed the ledgers. They gave his last name as "Terrisborn," since he had no proper family name. He kept reading.

Yes, yes. Numbers. That was plenty of numbers, all right. Of the high sort, which accountants like him liked to see. Hardly any red to the ledger. Yes, hmm. Not enough honey in this tea.

There was no denying what the ledgers said. Wayne *was* dead. And in his place lived a fellow who was fancy. No, who was downright *opulent*.

"You at least," he said, "have my bendalloy?"

An aide fetched an enormous sack of it. Enough to buy two or three cars, if he'd wanted.

"Right, then," Wayne said. "Here's what we're going to do. You see this here?" He unfolded something from his inside pocket—a flyer recruiting boys for a local noseball league. "We shall give these chaps funding for equipment and will build for them a location in which to enjoy their engagements."

"Sir?" Short Boring Guy asked. "Why?"

"We'll include seating," Wayne explained, "and allow everyone to watch. See, right now everyone wants someone to yell at. And we, my friends, shall provide it for them. We shall create a large-scale noseball league, with a team from each octant. I've thought, gentlemen, for some time that the city needs a way to become drunken in a proper and controlled manner."

"I don't understand, sir," Tall Boring Guy said.

"A bar exists for a reason," Wayne said. "It is a controlled environment in which to drink. People are going to seek to partake in spirits, you see, and it is better for society that we plan for this.

"Currently, the octants are tense. The people are angry. The Outer Cities, why, they are riotous! We must allow *rage* to be experienced in a similar way to drunkenness—with a controlled outlet, with someone for everyone to dislike."

They looked at him blankly.

"We're gonna get a bunch of chaps to beat on one another," Wayne said in a lower-class accent. "Playin' for teams representin' the octants, so everyone can pick their favorite and hate all the other teams. In a right proper way."

"Ah!" Short Boring Guy said.

People these days, and their lowborn vernacular. Why, he suspected this pair didn't even know how to properly burnish a golden toilet! For fear!

"Yes . . ." Tall Boring Guy said. "I see. So, like the local clubs, but on a *citywide* scale."

"People love their local teams," Wayne explained. "We can do something good with that."

"Building arenas of the proper size will be expensive," Short Boring Guy said. "Even for you."

"We could charge people a bit to get in the door, then," Wayne said. "Everyone enjoys something more when they have a monetary stake in it."

"Yes . . ." Tall Boring Guy said. "Yes, this is *interesting*. Monetization of the rivalries—and the personal coding of interest—will be a seminal part of this activity . . ."

"That *is* my favorite part of *most* activities," Wayne noted.

Tall Boring Guy nodded. "This is excellent. We shall put our best people on it."

"Nah," Wayne said, "put your worst ones on it. They'll know more about loafing—the rapscallions—which shall serve me better in this particular situation. Now, let us discuss the beating of servants and how it's not really so bad for them."

Rusts, this hat. He pulled it off and wiped his brow. Stupid money and stupid rich hats. This one even had aluminum foil on the inside to protect from emotional Allomancy.

Well, surely *this* idea with the noseball would finally bankrupt him. It was, after all, his very worst idea—and he was an absolute idiot. He spun the hat on his finger and thought about it. What if Wax—or worse, *Marasi*—figured out he was rich? He'd never hear the rusting end of it.

Tall Boring Guy tugged at his collar. "Do you . . . actually want us to investigate using more corporal punishment on, um, some of your staff?"

"Nah," Wayne said. "Bein' in the army stinks."

"Sir," Short Boring Guy said, "what about the provisions in your trust? We'd like to talk about the more unusual ones you've made."

"Nope. Next."

"Your current housing situation—"

"Nope. Next."

"Have you yet confirmed with Waxillium that he understands he signed away likeness rights to you in that deal—"

"Nope. Next."

"Your fleet of cars?"

Those he liked. "What about them?"

"There's a new Victori," Short Boring Guy said, getting out a picture of it. It had *no top*. Like, so you could drive and spit into the wind, if you wanted.

"Damn, that's nice," Wayne said. "Get me one."

"Absolutely, sir," Short Boring Guy said. "How many shares in the company shall we buy?"

Wayne narrowed his eyes at him. "I see what you're doing."

They looked at him innocently.

"No more than a five percent stake," Wayne said, "and once these guys what play noseball get famous, have them drive the cars around so they get more popular and whatnot. Oh, and let's call it something other than noseball. Maybe change the long runner positions to let those two be Metalborn. Same with the goalie. That'll make things more interesting."

"As you wish, Master Wayne."

He spun the hat on his finger. *I've never met anyone who can get inside the heads of other people as well as Wayne can*. He could even get inside the heads of accountants.

Could he get inside the head of a girl who hated him?

To start, he had to remember what he'd done. He *deserved* that hurt.

Did *she*? He closed his eyes, thinking what it must be like to see him come slinking in each month. That man. That horrible man. Couldn't he just let her move on?

He'll understand . . .

What if he didn't want to?

Damn. Too late.

"Hey, Call," he said, opening his eyes and looking to Short Boring Guy. "I need you to set up a delivery for me. Some money to be paid to a young woman and her family. Um, every month. She has her own kid now, and needs the cash on time. It's a meeting I'm supposed to do in person, but I'm . . . getting so busy. Yes, too busy, you see . . ."

"Many of our clients have similar needs, Master Wayne," Short Boring Guy said. "Give us the address and we'll see it is handled with discretion."

Why'd they say it that way? Well, regardless, Jaxy had been right. If he was going to be dead, he could at least be the polite kind what didn't try to crawl out of the forest and eat you during thunderstorms.

Even corpses needed standards.

17

Steris had been doing a good job lately, she thought, of understanding other people. Once, she'd assumed they had the same worries she did, but hid their anxiety extremely well. As she'd grown older, she'd come to understand something more incredible. They just *didn't feel* that anxiety.

They didn't have a constant, hovering worry in the back of their brain, whispering they'd forgotten something important. They didn't spend hours thinking about the mistakes they'd made, and how they could have planned better. They lived in a perpetual state between blessed contentment and frightening ignorance.

Then she'd grown even older. She'd married Waxillium. She'd made friends—real ones—and had come to see more clearly. Everyone saw the world differently, and the Survivor had made people to complement one another. Metal and alloy. A Push for every Pull.

The others responded to the explosion below with a strange excitement and eagerness, practically racing one another to the door. But what if the steps were destabilized? Steris had a whole list of protocols to follow if there was an explosion in the lab—she'd spent three nights developing it.

She loved them. And so she wanted to cry out a warning, hold them back safe, forbid them from risking themselves. She also knew how extreme she got sometimes. That was the biggest revelation of recent years—helped by discussions with the women of her book group. Some of her preparations went beyond helpful. Understanding that line was vital to understanding herself.

And she had to admit, today the others showed *some* wisdom. They let VenDell go first, at her suggestion, since a fall wouldn't hurt him. Wax went next, since he could more or less fly if the steps collapsed. They hesitated at the bottom of the stairs—in case anything further was going to blow—before they opened the reinforced door.

"Wait!" Steris said, then dug in her handbag. "Masks."

She distributed the cloth masks to everyone, even Allik, since a wooden one wouldn't filter the air for him. They took the masks absently, or maybe even with a bit of an eye roll. All except Wax, who smiled at her as he put his on.

He liked her preparations. He found it endearing. But beyond that, he appreciated it. He thought she was useful, not persnickety.

"Anything on your watch list for explosions?" he asked.

She felt warm as she dug out her book of home emergencies. Yes, she knew she could be extreme. At the same time, making these was therapeutic. Her fears eased once she wrote them down. If she'd thought of something, catalogued it and considered it, then it stopped having power over her—she had power over *it*.

"Acids on the floor," she noted. "Those could mix to produce poisonous fumes. Glass shards. Secondary explosions—particularly from exposed harmonium. Those are my big fears."

He considered. "Marasi," he said as she pushed open the door, "I was testing with hydrochloric and hypochlorous acids."

"Which means?"

"Chlorine gas," he said.

VenDell grabbed Marasi's arm. Kandra had a *thing* about acids.

To Steris's surprise, they listened to her. Since the powerful ventilators installed in the basement weren't working, they let her fetch a room fan and set it up. Then they all returned up the steps and stood outside the mansion to allow the place to ventilate. When they went back down, everyone wore their masks without complaint and let her test the air with a kit. From there, they were careful where they stepped as they inspected the room.

The door to the safe box had taken a little jaunt across the room, and was now embedded deep into the thick concrete of the far wall. The steel of the box itself had been mangled beyond repair. And the rest of the room . . .

Well, it appeared that she'd have to put in an order for a new spectroscope. And a centrifuge. And some more flasks. And . . . um . . . new walls . . .

She resisted her urge to begin sweeping the glass to avert the hazard of stepping on it. Instead she stuck near to Waxillium. He might discover something interesting.

"Rusts," he said, walking over to the remnants of the safe box. "This thing survived harmonium detonations of up to three ounces. I used less than a *tenth* of that in this experiment."

He reached for the top of what remained of the box.

Steris wagged a glove in front of him.

"Right," he said, slipping it on, then feeling around the top of the broken steel box. His hand came away dusted with some black shavings—a fine metal powder. VenDell walked up beside them. Marasi was inspecting the safe box's door, while Allik had fetched a broom from above and was sweeping up the glass.

Steris had already liked him, of course, primarily because of how he treated her sister. But in that moment, her estimation of him went up another notch.

"We need to test these shavings," Wax said. "But . . . I don't think this is either atium or lerasium. It looks like remnants of iron from the equipment."

Steris gathered them in some specimen pouches anyway. Waxillium leaned into the broken box on the wall, then used a small file from his pocket to harvest something smoldering inside.

"Harmonium," he said as Steris dug out an extra vial of oil for him to put it into. "Plastered across the back of the box. I . . . think the experiment failed. It didn't divide."

"Actually," VenDell said, "I think you managed something far, far more dangerous." He took out a little notebook. "How much harmonium did you use in here? A few grams?"

"Around half a gram."

"This explosive force . . ." VenDell said. "This level of destruction . . . from such a small sample. It's possible, but only if . . ."

"What?" Wax said.

"This explosion was not caused by the division of the metals," VenDell said. "This level of energy release could happen *only* if some of the Investiture or the matter itself was transformed into energy."

He seemed to notice their confusion, so he continued. "I believe I've lectured you at length about the nature of Investiture. It is a particular study of mine. Along with my foremost expertise on skulls . . ."

"Not for sale," Wax reminded him.

"Mine is," Steris said.

Both looked at her.

"Why would I need it when I'm dead?" she asked. "Seems much better to have the money now."

"As I always say," VenDell replied. "Your impermanence is outlived by the beautiful internal shells you create—like sand medallions from the ocean, so are the bones of the human being. A lasting testimony of your presence on Scadrial. We shall discuss the terms of your sale at a later date, Lady Ladrian.

"For now, let me be brief. Everything in the cosmere is made up of one of three essences. The first is matter: the physical substances around you. Formed of axi, the smallest possible thing we know."

"There are things that . . . aren't matter?" Steris asked.

"Of course," he said. "There's energy." He waved to the ceiling, where two of the room's recessed and reinforced lights were still working. "Electricity, heat, light . . . Your kind has been harnessing it quite well lately. Good for you. Very modern."

"And the third?" Wax asked.

"Investiture," VenDell said. "The essence of the gods. Everything has an Invested component, normally inaccessible without certain abilities. When you burn metals, Lord Ladrian, you pull Investiture directly from the Spiritual Realm and use it to do work. Much like energy does work in those lights. But here is the key idea: Investiture, matter, and energy are all the *same*, fundamentally."

"I . . . felt that, once," Waxillium said, expression distant. "When I held the Bands. That all things were one substance."

"Indeed!" VenDell replied. "And states can change from one to the other. Energy can become Investiture. This is the soul of Feruchemy. Investiture can become matter. That is where harmonium comes from. And matter can *become* energy."

"And an example of that is . . ." Steris said.

VenDell nodded to the destroyed room. "We just witnessed it, I believe. There is an *incredible* amount of energy trapped inside matter. You managed to release some of it—only a small amount of what you put in that box, but still. If you found a way to release its full potential . . . Well, Harmony says the destructive power of it frightens him. Deeply."

"It should," Waxillium said. "Because this was easy to accomplish. Far too easy."

"Well," VenDell said, "it does require two very rare substances. And a great deal of energy, correct?"

"A great deal," he admitted. "For so small a sample. It would take quite a bit of electricity to scale this up. But the destructive potential . . ."

"Agreed." VenDell's skin had gone . . . not just pale, but actually translucent. "I . . . should report this. If you don't mind, I'll be upstairs communing with Harmony. Excuse me."

Waxillium shot Steris a look. "Worst case?" he asked.

She considered. What was the worst thing that could happen? It seemed obvious to her.

"What if the Set already knows about this?" she asked. "Marasi said the dying man mentioned returning ash to the Basin. Maybe they plan to use bombs?"

Wax nodded, grim. He'd considered the same thing.

"If the Set has discovered this interaction," she said, "then it was likely by accident—or through an experiment like ours. There might be a record of it."

"We could search for unexplained explosions in the Outer Cities," Wax said. "Smart. Ashes . . . What if an explosive like this were placed in one of the old Ashmounts? Could they be restarted?"

"That sounds appropriately terrifying," Steris said, feeling a deep nausea. How had she never considered that possibility? Looked like she had some planning to worry about. But first things first. "I'll order broadsheets from the Outer Cities from the library and have them delivered to the penthouse. We can start there."

Wax nodded. "With Marasi's authority, you should be able to access the constabulary records too."

It was an excellent suggestion. Steris walked to the back of the room, passing Allik—who had found some remnants of his biscuits splattered on the wall—and stepped up to Marasi. It had been . . . pleasant spending more time with her lately. Their childhood hadn't always encouraged sisterly affection. Their father—who was now retired to a country estate—

had been embarrassed by Marasi's illegitimate status. Steris had always worried Marasi would see it as a flaw in her*self* rather than in their *father.*

Marasi seemed lost in thought, though what she found fascinating about the broken door was beyond Steris. However, she stayed quiet, not wishing to interrupt. Silence didn't bother Steris. It was a purely neutral experience.

"The world is changing so fast," Marasi finally whispered. "I'm barely accustomed to electric lights, let alone the airships. Then there's this god . . . from another world. Now an explosive, a pinch of which can destroy a room . . ."

"I'm worried too," Steris said. "I wish recent events had been possible to anticipate."

"Makes me wonder," Marasi said, "why I'm spending my time on murder cases and basic crimes. I realize they are important . . . but there are people out there, Steris, who know about it all. Who are making moves that change the fates of planets. They have no oversight, so far as I can tell. They're probably *happy* to see us chasing down ordinary criminals and leaving them alone."

"That's why you hunt the Set," Steris said, nodding. "Why you've devoted so much to them, when most in the precinct think you're going a little overboard."

Marasi chuckled. "Runs in the family, I guess."

Steris smiled, then felt foolish, as Marasi wouldn't be able to see it behind her face mask. Before Steris could say something, however, Waxillium blew himself up.

It was a much smaller detonation, fortunately, but it was forceful enough to throw him back and drop him to the ground. Steris ran over, worried—and found him dazed, but relatively unharmed. He took her arm as he sat up, shaking his head, his nice vest—a Versuli, no less—ripped and charred. The apron she'd provided had protected it somewhat.

He brushed himself off. Though he didn't like to admit it, he *was* getting older. Being exploded when you were twenty was far different from being exploded when you were fifty.

"So," he said to her, "you mentioned something about secondary explosions?"

"It was on my list," she whispered.

"It's all right," he said, patting her hand. "I feel fine. I just did something stupid. I was gathering that harmonium plastered against the back of the safe box. It's too valuable to leave, and it must have reacted to the air or some liquid left from an earlier experiment—"

He sneezed, then smiled at her reassuringly. His mask was nowhere to be seen; it must have blown free in the explosion.

She hid her worry for him. Upon marrying Waxillium Ladrian, there was one thing she had vowed to herself: She wouldn't stop fretting about him, but she *would not* prevent him from being the person he wanted to be.

Each time he decided on an investigation, it terrified her. She did not let that control how she treated him. She would *not* be an obstacle. She loved him too much for that. Instead she did her best to be part of his world. It was far less frightening to be shot at than to sit at home wondering if *he* was being shot at.

It was to her eternal gratification that he, in turn, tried to be part of her world. Taking more interest in politics. Spending time with her doing the finances. They fit together, better than she'd ever dreamed they would. And she still felt warm every time they touched.

"Let's get some tea," Wax said, climbing to his feet with her help, "and talk this over."

18

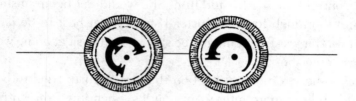

Marasi settled into the couch, her ears ringing from the second explosion. Allik sat beside her, mask down—he tended to lower it when he chewed gum, as he was doing now. Chewing visibly was a cultural taboo for him. Odd. If there was one thing it should be *normal* to lift a mask for, it was eating.

Still, she wrapped her arm around his and let him rest his head on her shoulder. Rusts, it was nice to have him around full-time these days. The early years of their relationship had been sixteen different varieties of frustrating.

While they waited for VenDell to finish his report to Harmony, Wax talked about meeting the airship—and the new ambassador. She felt Allik grow tense at the description.

"This is Daal the Primary," he explained to the rest of them. "He . . . is very well respected by the Hosts."

"I could tell he was important politically," Wax said.

"No, Wax," Marasi said. "Respected by the Hosts means he was successful in war."

"So his arrival *is* a threat," Steris said, nestled against Wax with her notebook out, shoes off, her stockinged feet up to the side in a posture that actually seemed *relaxed*.

She's changed so much, Marasi thought. She could remember a time w' n Steris wouldn't have dared take her shoes off in company. She'd have sat with perfect posture, trying to ensure she was holding her tea and saucer level.

Marasi had always loved her sister, even when resentment or forced distance had interfered, but she'd never considered Steris *pleasant*. Not until these recent years. Part of that had been Steris changing, but another part had been realizing that she and Steris had always felt the same burdens—that sense of entrapment.

"I wouldn't say it's a threat, Steris," Allik said. "Not specifically. But if it is true, and the Consortium has finally been achieved—the five nations agreeing to put a common face northward—then this is . . . a symbol? They send you their best. They want you to know it."

"Their best," Wax said, "and most stern, I assume? He is certainly more unyielding than his predecessor."

"Yes, Adjective Waxillium," Allik said, nodding. "They want you to know that they will not be bullied."

"He said," Wax told them, "that one of his goals was to bring the Bands of Mourning back to his people. Is that still a sore issue?"

"You have no idea," Allik said. "Us agreeing to leave the Bands here, it's like . . . like we left you with the body of our dead father, yah? A body that is also a powerful weapon. Nobody liked that decision.

"Sending him here, having him say he'll get the Bands back . . . this is a symbol, yah? A statement? They have been too lax with your people, and wish to indicate this laxness will end." He shifted in place, then lifted his mask. "Sorry."

"You didn't choose this, Allik."

"No," he said. "But I didn't *not* choose it."

"Dear, yes you did." Marasi squeezed his arm. "You don't have to take responsibility for *everything*."

He smiled at her, then put his mask down. Footsteps announced what she thought was VenDell returning, but then Wayne burst into the sitting room instead.

"Hey!" he said. "You all got blown up, and you didn't *wait for me*?"

"Waxillium got blown up," Steris said. "The rest of us merely witnessed it. I think he did it on purpose to annoy you."

"I'm rusting sure," Wayne said, narrowing his eyes at Wax. "You okay, mate?"

"My ears are ringing," Wax said, "and I've been reminded—quite profoundly—that I'm *at least* two decades past prime exploding age. But I should be fine."

"Glad you're back, Wayne," Marasi said, leaning forward. "Because we need to plan."

"Yup, glad to be back," he muttered. "Bein' the fifth in a room is what every feller wants, yes indeed." He stomped over to the small serving table and poured a cup of tea—then left the cup on the table and settled down in an easy chair with the *entire teapot*. "What?" he said to everyone's stares. "It's almost gone, an' I like the spigot part. Fun to drink outta."

He demonstrated, which made Steris put her hand to her face. Marasi sighed, but didn't say anything. If he was sitting then he was less likely to steal something. She did check her pocketbook just in case.

"All right," she said to the group. "I have the bones of a plan—imitating the Cycle to lead a local gang with a delivery scheduled to Bilming."

Wax leaned forward. "Are we sure that interrogating the current captives won't be enough?"

"They seemed like local flunkies," Marasi said.

"Who will barely know anything," Wax agreed. "So you'll want some constables on your sting, ready to capture any Metalborn."

"I keep telling Reddi we need a specialist team," Marasi said. "A squad *just* for dealing with Metalborn. He keeps resisting. I think . . . he considers *us* that squad."

As those words hung in the air, VenDell finally strode in, shaking his head. "I have," he said, "been re-ordered to avail myself to you, with much urgency, in your current plans."

"What did he say?" Marasi asked. "Does he know anything about the explosion?"

"Harmony is . . . worried." VenDell paused. "Trellium has a repulsing effect on other forms of Investiture. Merely touching it to harmonium is dangerous—but doing as you did, heating and stretching the harmonium first, created what he called 'an Invested matter-energy transference.' That's . . . very bad."

"Did the news surprise him?" Wax asked. "Did Harmony seem shocked we were able to do this? Or did he expect it?"

"I couldn't tell," VenDell said. "He only said what I've relayed. More than that . . . well, Harmony can be difficult to read. I suppose I don't need to tell you that. Did he send you a note, Lord Waxillium?"

"Yes," Wax said. "I think he implied that I should make an earring out of trellium."

"Whatever for?" Marasi said, frowning.

"I don't know," Wax replied. "I think he's trying to get me interested, since I've ignored his last couple of invitations to commune with him."

"This time it's different, Waxillium," VenDell said softly. "This time . . . Harmony is frightened."

The room fell silent, aside from Wayne slurping his tea through the nozzle of the teapot. Marasi thought she saw him adding something from his flask to it, and she tried not to let that make her nauseous. Who spiked *tea*?

He's hurting, she thought. *The breakup is final.* Rusts, despite everything else going on, she decided to find time to take him out to that noodle place he loved. Bring along a few of the other constables that he liked; remind him he had friends.

"My sting needs to happen soon," she said to the room. "The book says the next shipment to Bilming is to go out in three days, and I want to be ready."

"It's a good plan, Marasi," Wax said. "Steris and I have something we can work on while you're planning."

"Talking to Harmony?" she asked.

"Maybe," he said, seeming distant. "I haven't decided if I'm going to respond to him yet."

Curiously, he didn't indicate he wanted to be part of her mission. She'd have let him in, but she couldn't quite get a handle on Wax these days. The way he'd hung those Roughs coats in the entryway had an air of finality, like a shrine to his old life. That said, when his deputized status had come up for renewal last year, he'd asked Reddi to maintain his position.

Wax glanced at Steris, who was leaning against him as she scribbled notes. "We thought of something earlier," he said to Marasi. "It's vital that we know if the Set has discovered the explosive potential of mixing harmonium and trellium. We're going to do research to see what we can find."

"Sounds good," Marasi said, nodding.

Well, that confirmed it. A few years ago, she might have been happy to hear he was staying out of her investigation, but she'd quashed that feeling. She was proud of not letting his shadow—long though it was—

blot out her accomplishments. Besides, she'd had her chance to become the hero in Wax's place—she'd held the Bands of Mourning herself before turning them over to Wax. That simply wasn't who she was.

So today, she was sad to hear he wouldn't join her. Even worried, as she realized she'd assumed he would be there on this one. If she actually had a chance at high-level members of the Set . . . well, this could finally break the case open. And lead to answers.

But . . . she couldn't force him. Shouldn't force him. If he wasn't feeling as spry as he once had, then who was she to object?

"I'll go do some more listenin' to those fellows in prison," Wayne said. "VenDell, you want to come with? Maybe I could give you tips on your accent?"

"Master Wayne," he said, "I am an immortal kandra with *hundreds* of years' experience doing impersonations."

"And you always sound snide and upper class," Wayne said, "in every body I've seen you use. So . . . want some tips or not, mate?"

"I . . ." He sighed. "Harmony did *directly order* me to be about this. Ugh. Field work is so *distasteful*. But I suppose I can't say no."

Marasi glanced at Wax, who had settled back on the couch, thoughtful. Holding the envelope that Harmony had sent him.

"All right then," she said. "Let's get to it."

19

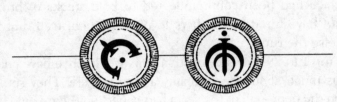

Three days later, Wax stood in his penthouse study, looking west toward Bilming. There was no mist tonight. Seemed like weeks since he'd seen any.

Preparations had gone well for Marasi's sting. The notebook had clear instructions on how to deliver the goods. Using intel from interrogations, Marasi had located the very trucks the captives had been planning to use. She had the exact outfits of the captives, and VenDell was playing the role of their leader. Wayne, in one of his finest disguises, was at his side to help sell the role. Even the boxes of goods were real.

They would leave sometime tonight. Wax wouldn't go to see them off, of course. He could be conspicuous, and Marasi had taken every conceivable step to make sure the enemy didn't spot the subterfuge.

They'll be safe, he told himself. *Their disguises are excellent, and she's extremely capable.*

This was the Basin, not some wayward town in the Roughs. Marasi had access to the finest constables in the city, along with resources in abundance. She didn't need an old Coinshot with an unloaded pistol who still felt the ache of having foolishly exploded his laboratory a few days ago.

Still, Wax lingered, looking through the wide picture windows of his small penthouse study. It had been exciting, these last years, watching the city grow electrified. He had evanotypes of the process, taken every few months from this high perspective. A grid of lights and streets, homes glowing with the calm light of progress, each adding another shimmering star to the Elendel constellation. Would the lights spread so far that eventually there wouldn't be any darkness at all?

Steris slipped over, then handed him a cup of tea. "With willow powder," she whispered. "For your aches."

"You think of everything," he said, taking a sip. "How are the kids?"

"Sleeping," she said. "We should be fine to go back to work."

Together they walked back into the living room, where practically every surface had been commandeered to hold stacks of broadsheets. They *could* have hired researchers to pick through it all, but why give someone else the fun?

And it *was* fun. Not of the sort that Wax would once have enjoyed, but fun was as much about the company as the activity. They settled down together on the floor—all of the seats had papers on them—and continued reading. Searching for any mentions of explosions in cities across the Basin.

To pass the time, they also looked for anything amusing.

"'Pickled Pachyderm Plays Piano,'" Steris said, holding one up. "Why do they always pick 'pachyderm' for these alliterative sentences?"

"Because it's a funny word?" Wax said, with a smile. "What's it pickled in?"

"Apparently it was sitting in a small swimming pool," Steris said. "I think that's a stretch."

He held up his own headline. "'Child Eats Tar. Mother Feeds Rat As Antidote.'"

"Oh, that *can't* be real," she said, taking the broadsheet from him. But it was a real story—and in a reputable paper as well. Turned out even the most highbrow of sources weren't above using a zinger to move copies on a slow news day. She grinned, setting it on her stack of amusing headlines.

For their true hunt, Steris had a system—because of course she did. They read only headlines at first, quickly skimming sheets for certain words in bold or large print. Anything that looked promising went into its own pile. But you didn't read the story, not yet. You'd want to read all of those together, to compare one against another and further winnow.

They were almost done with the most recent batch of broadsheets, delivered today. Wax enjoyed it, mostly for the time with his wife—though he seemed to still be suffering the aftereffects of the explosion. His vision kept behaving oddly, distorting at times for just a second or two. And his mind kept playing tricks on him, making him think he glimpsed blue Allomantic lines without burning metals.

He set aside worries over his health, and certainly did *not* say anything. He didn't want to concern Steris. He'd survived explosions before. His hand still ached from the mine detonation back in Dust's Beach . . .

"Here's one," Steris said, showing him a serious headline. "Explosion at a railway station."

Wax rubbed his chin as he read. "Sounds like a boiler malfunction. Not terribly suspicious."

"Perhaps it's covering something up?"

He shook his head. Seemed like an odd place to be running metallurgic experiments. Too many people nearby—but then again, *he'd* done his experiments in the basement of a mansion. So who knew?

Steris set it in the "maybe" pile, while he moved his current broadsheet—an account of a fire that was pretty obviously a lightning strike—into the "unlikely" pile. None of these felt right to him, which should have made him happy. Perhaps their enemies *hadn't* discovered the explosive interaction between harmonium and trellium.

Unfortunately, this sort of investigation could be frustrating for just that reason. He didn't *want* to find proof, because it would confirm his fears. Yet if they turned up nothing, they'd never know if it was because no proof existed, or because they had missed it.

"'Snake Sneaks Snoring Snails'?" Steris said, showing him one from her amusing pile. "I have to admire them for committing to the gimmick."

"Do snakes eat snails?" he asked.

"This one did, apparently." She smiled, and Preservation, he loved that smile. He found himself wishing this hunt were for lower stakes.

Ashes falling again, he thought, shivering. He'd often imagined what it would have been like to live in the mythical days before the Catacendre. When the Ascendant Warrior and Wax's own distant ancestor, the Counselor of Gods, had walked the land. When people had moved through stories like the sun behind clouds on a mostly overcast day.

In those days, the world had been dying. Ash had been its skin, flaking off as it disintegrated . . .

He sighed, rubbing his eyes—seeing those odd flashes of blue. Fortunately, the tea was beginning to work and his headache was at last retreating.

"Wax?" Steris asked softly. "Do you wish you'd gone with Marasi and Wayne?"

"They'll be fine," he said. "They don't need me."

"That isn't what I asked, love," she said softly.

He thought for a moment. Then shook his head. "I don't, Steris. I genuinely don't. I realized it the other day. I'm . . . past that stage of my life. I really feel like I'm done."

Except for one thing. The fact that his sister was involved. Still out there. Dangerous.

Most families had skeletons in the closet. And most of those were sensible enough to stay dead. His might be threatening the entire Basin. Ash falling again . . .

But he *did* feel done. Ready to move on. So, he showed Steris an account of a series of broken windows in the city of Demoux. It seemed to be the result of a small twister—a smaller cousin to the more terrifying ones that struck the Roughs. But maybe it was an indication of a sharp pressure change, like an explosion?

They put it in the "unlikely" pile. Unfortunately, after an hour of this, they neared the end of the stacks with no solid leads. Just a lot of very unlikely possibilities.

Steris watched him as she moved another broadsheet to the unlikely pile. He knew what she was thinking, but she didn't prod him.

"There is one thing," he admitted to her. "My sister. I should be the one to deal with her. But I have important work to do here in Elendel. Besides, I'm not that man anymore."

"Do you have to be *that* man or *this* man?" she asked.

"I have to make choices. Everyone does."

"And what about when you initially came back to Elendel?" she asked. "When you decided to hang up your guns the first time?"

"This is different," he explained. "Back then I was running from myself. I stopped running six years ago, in the mountains, Steris. *This* is what I want. *This* is who I want to be. I'm happy here."

She leaned into him, a steady warmth at his side. "So long as you know," she whispered, "that you don't have to be one or the other. You don't have to see yourself as two men, Wax, with two different lives. Those men are the same person. And he's the one I love."

He thought on that, considering those days when he'd come back to Elendel—determined to put his past in the Roughs behind him. Because it was what he thought he *should* do. And . . . well, because a part of him had been broken. A gouge that had eventually been ripped back open by Lessie's return.

Lying near death on a frozen mountaintop to the south had changed his perspective. When he'd returned to Elendel, he'd been able to *live* again. Growing, changing. And yet . . . did that mean the past him was no *longer* him? Were the inner rings in a tree less a part of it just because they were no longer exposed to the air?

"I'm worried about them," he admitted to Steris. "And . . . I'm worried about the safety of the Basin. I don't want to act like I don't trust Marasi and Wayne. But . . ." He reached into his pocket and took out the envelope with the earring. Which he still hadn't used. "Last year, when VenDell offered me a mission, it didn't have the same urgency. The same disquiet about it. I'm afraid that whatever is happening now has grown too big to ignore. Too dangerous to be stopped by detective work or police intervention, no matter how competent."

"Another god," Steris whispered.

He took out a second envelope. "I had this made," he said, shaking something out of it. Another earring. With a red tinge to the metal. It was nothing more than a stud, with the only trellium portion the bar in the middle, as the metal couldn't be melted to be forged.

"When I gave the trellium spike to the university for study," he explained, "I asked them to fabricate this for me. Because Harmony suggested I'd need it."

"Do you believe what Marasi said? About another ashfall? The return of those . . . dark days?"

"I don't know," he said. "But VenDell says Harmony is afraid. And *that* has me terrified."

Steris tapped her finger on the stack of broadsheets in her lap. "Let's identify our worst-case scenario. Consider: What's the worst thing you can imagine, in regards to our current hunt?"

"My worst fear?" he said, thinking. "It's that we're years behind. That the Set has known about this interaction between harmonium and trellium for a great deal longer than we assume—maybe since that first Malwish airship crashed here. My fear is that the Set is not *beginning* a plan. My fear is that we're in the *end stages* of said plan."

"Is there anything we could search for to prove this?" Steris asked.

Wax stood up, surveying the room full of broadsheets, each stack from a different city. "Rusts," he said. "We shouldn't be searching for *accidental* explosions. We should be searching for proof of *intentional* ones. And we're looking at too recent a batch of papers—if it happened, it could be five or six years old by now." He paused. "They'd want to test. It wouldn't be one explosion long ago. It would be a series of them . . . hidden somehow . . . because if they have this weapon, they'll want to develop it. Improve it."

"How?" Steris asked. "Should we search for records of harmonium busts?"

"I doubt that would show up in the broadsheets," Wax said, turning around the room. "The Set is good at hiding its resource movement, especially of contraband. Marasi's investigation proves that."

So what? Was there any way to find what he wanted? Evidence of tests . . . of explosions they'd keep hidden . . .

"Earthquakes," Wax whispered.

"What was that?"

"Earthquakes," he said, kneeling beside Steris. "They would test explosions underground, in the caverns. Where they'd be contained and hidden. But they can't fool the seismographs."

They dug into the headlines again—but this time with a different set of criteria. And admittedly, Wax broke format a little, peeking at the contents of the stories rather than just looking for headlines. Steris poked him in the side if he spent too long doing this, but he was curious. And excited.

The answers had to be in here somewhere.

The search took a solid three hours of work. But as midnight passed, Wax found it. A series of articles from an Elendel broadsheet about something happening in Bilming.

"A subway?" Steris asked, frowning.

"Reports," Wax explained, "of odd earthquakes in the city, starting years ago. Officials quickly explained that Bilming had decided to build a subterranean rail line like Elendel."

"That could be valid," Steris said, reading another broadsheet expanding on the story. "We used explosives to blast away rock and build the subway."

"But why would Bilming *need* a subway? They have that elevated rail they're so proud of. They *love* showing it off. Plus, these explosions have been going for four and a half years—and they don't have a single subway line up and running."

"Suspicious," Steris said, scanning the next article. "Very suspicious. A new initiative started seven months ago . . . Reports of buildings being rattled by large-scale detonations . . . They were detected all the way here in Elendel."

"They're calling it a financial scandal, with construction companies leeching away funds. But it's obviously more."

Steris nodded vigorously. The broadsheet that had uncovered this wasn't the most reputable source—it was the latest one to carry that fool Jak's outlandish stories—but there *was* something here, as confirmed by several other broadsheets, now that they knew what they were looking for.

Rusts, he thought. The Set were testing beneath populated areas? Why? Was that just where they could find the cavern space? This might be even bigger than he'd feared. Hadn't Bilming been building a navy?

Yes. Other articles talked about it. Ostensibly, the Bilming shipyards were creating a defense force for the Basin, in case of attack from the South. But they'd started *before* the arrival of the first Malwish airships—and they certainly liked to show off the capabilities of their guns.

Supposedly these ships were under Elendel's control. No one actually believed that though.

"Wax . . ." Steris said. "That list of shipments in Marasi's book. Where they were checking to see how tight customs was. How hard it would be to smuggle something *into* Elendel . . ."

A chill washed through Wax. What would they want to smuggle into Elendel?

A bomb.

"It looked like they were checking different cargo sizes," he said. "And how likely they were to be inspected when brought in via train or truck."

"And how big would this bomb be?" Steris said. "Theoretically."

"It's the generator that would be big," Wax explained. "If it works according to the mechanics we discovered, then they'd need a *great deal* of power. More than the simple lines to homes can carry, or even the lines to industrial locations. They'd likely have to build a very large housing for the device."

"Which explains why they were checking which sizes arouse suspicion and which don't. Wax, if you're right, then the broadsheets indicate they've been testing this for more than *four years*. Successfully. They might *have* the bomb already. They're just . . ."

". . . looking for a way to get it into the city."

Rusts. He looked to the side table, and the envelopes. Then, finally, he slipped the first earring out—the one Harmony had sent him. It had been six years. He'd grown increasingly reticent to have anything to do with Harmony. He no longer hated God, but still . . .

He looked to Steris, who nodded. So he put the earring in.

And was suddenly in another place.

Floating, seeing the entire world before him, and the dark vastness beyond. He spent a moment disoriented, though his feet felt like they were on solid ground. It was unnerving.

This didn't normally happen when he used an earring. But he *had* been here once before. On that frozen mountaintop.

Harmony stood in the distance. A serene figure in traditional Terris robes. Kindly eyes. Hesitant at first, Wax walked across the invisible floor toward Harmony. If he let his eyes unfocus, Harmony seemed as vast as the cosmere—two sweeping wings. One white, one black. Spinning together in the middle, the edges extending to infinity.

At the heart of it was that figure. Terris. Head shaved smooth. Rounded features, with an elongated face. The face of a legend, standing with hands clasped behind his back. Looking worried.

"Last time I was here," Wax noted, "I was dead."

"Dying," Harmony said. "On the very cusp of death. Sometimes I think that's where I reside. Always there, like a coin balanced on edge . . . a gulf on either side . . ."

"Where is the redness I saw last time?" Wax asked, nodding to the planet. Six years ago a red haze had been coming over the planet, as if to swallow it. "Did you drive it off?"

"No," Harmony said softly. "It Invested the planet. Invested . . . me. What you saw was a shroud, Waxillium. I responded too slowly. It is . . . a failing that grows more dangerous in me. By the time I realized what was happening, that shroud had come over me. It doesn't hurt, it merely dampens my ability to see."

"You mean . . ."

"I don't know what's happening," Harmony said softly, staring down at the planet. "What is Trell doing? What are they planning? They put that haze up as a kind of smoke screen. When I attacked it, the haze infected my ability to see the future. Temporarily. I will be rid of it in a few years. That's nothing on the timescale of gods. And yet . . ."

"And yet, the danger is right now."

"Yes," Harmony said. "Like a nearsighted person, I can see the danger now that it has come very close." He hesitated, then looked to Wax. "I can see you, hear you. We are Connected. And so, I know what you've discovered. I thought I had more time. I realize only now that I have been moving too slowly. Yet again, too slowly . . ."

Wax considered that, gave it due weight. These weren't matters or concepts one took lightly. God blinded. All of them years behind the enemy. A bomb being developed and a search for a way into the heart of his city.

One question rose to the surface. An old lawman's adage. If you wanted to stop a man, you needed to know what he wanted. Who he *was*.

"Harmony," he said, "who is Trell?"

"Trell is the god Autonomy," Harmony replied. "What we call a Shard of Adonalsium. Autonomy carries power like my own, a dangerous force for manipulating the very nature of reality and existence. Though Autonomy is held by a woman named Bavadin, her many different faces—or avatars—act with independence. Trell, a male god from the ancient records, can be considered one of these."

Wax blinked.

"You were not expecting so straightforward an answer?" Harmony asked.

"I've not always gotten them in the past."

"I'm trying to do better."

That was . . . somehow as unnerving as hearing that Harmony had been blinded. God should not *have* to get better.

"You rarely get to speak to Autonomy herself," Harmony continued. "As I've come to find, she speaks through avatars. Sometimes pieces of herself that she's allowed to gain a semblance of self-awareness, sometimes through chosen people she has given a portion of her power.

"Autonomy decided to destroy our world, as it is a dangerous threat to her. But I believe she has been persuaded to let it persist, so long as it can be . . . controlled. Autonomy offered me an ultimatum last year, as my blinding was taking effect and when she assumed I would be the most desperate. She demanded I give this world to her, then move to another.

"I rejected the demand—and one of the last things I saw was the person Autonomy has chosen. The same one who persuaded her that this world had value, and who presented a plan for its domination."

"My sister?"

Harmony nodded. "The leader of the Set. Invested by Autonomy. Avatar of a god on this world."

Wax exhaled softly. Telsin.

Thinking of her brought an immediate stab of betrayal. He remembered exactly how it had felt to realize, in one terrible moment, that she would shoot him. Despite his love, his attempts to help her, she'd been working against him all along.

That pain was acute, despite the years. And he realized that he hadn't left *everything* about his past behind. A thread lingered, a raw nerve exposed to the air.

Thinking of Telsin with the power of a deity in her hands . . . Rusts.

She'd spent her youth manipulating people. Getting her way. Telsin *always* got her way. It had been bad enough when she'd been able to persuade the adults she was sweet, obedient, and perfect—all the while sneaking out with her friends. It had become dangerous when she'd begun playing much higher-stakes games with the city's elite. And it had become deadly when she'd discovered the Set and started shaping world politics.

What would she do with *this*?

"You're only now telling me?" Wax demanded.

"I contacted you a year ago," Harmony said, "when I was first blinded. You . . . still did not want to speak with me. And I was trying to respect that."

Damn.

"But Wax," Harmony said softly, "it is time again. I need a sword."

A sword. That was what he'd been when he'd killed Lessie the second time. Cleaning up God's mess. Executing his rogue kandra driven mad by lack of spikes.

"I know you've changed," Harmony said. "I heard you earlier. I know you're happy. I know you want nothing more to do with my works."

"But my sister," Wax said, "has the power of a god. Rusts. Marasi and Wayne—does she know what they're planning with this sting? Are my friends in danger?"

"I wish I could say," Harmony replied. "So far as I know, the enemy knows nothing of their plan. But . . . I'm blind, and your sister is extremely dangerous. Wax, I have tried to handle this in other ways. I have failed. And so, I come back to the one weapon I've always been able to rely upon."

Wax took a deep breath. "Tell me what you know."

"Are you agreeing?"

"First tell me what you know. About my sister's plans, about this god. Anything relevant."

"I've shared most of it," Harmony said. "You should know, perhaps, that each of these powers—these Shards—has what we call an Intent. A driving motivation. I bear two: one driving me to preserve and protect, the other driving me to destroy.

"Autonomy is driven to divide off from the rest of us, go her own way. She pushes her followers to prove themselves, and she rewards those who are bold, who survive against the odds. She respects big plans and big accomplishments. I presume this is why your sister has persuaded Autonomy not to destroy our planet outright. Or at least to delay doing so."

"Telsin is still planning something catastrophic," Wax said. "She's trying to destroy Elendel. But what does that get her? The other cities will revolt against such a terrible act of destruction; she can't think they'll follow her if she kills so many."

"She's desperate," Harmony said. "Your sister has set up in Bilming. You'll find her there, building a new empire. She must know that her god is still eager to wage war on our people and annihilate them. So, she is trying what she can. If Telsin destroys Elendel, she can try to take control of the Basin and prove to Trell that she is capable of ruling this planet. I do not know if this is her true motive, but it is what seems most likely." Harmony glanced to him. "I'm sorry. I had not realized she would go this far."

Wax looked away, but it was difficult to blame Harmony. Wax himself had been blind to Telsin for years—and he didn't have the excuse of a divine shroud. He'd always assumed that he of all people knew the real her. Until he'd found himself just another pawn in her games, shown a false face. Made to feel an idiot. Why had he thought she would play everyone except him?

Because a part of him had loved his sister. Right up until the moment when she'd pulled the trigger and he'd known the truth. Family was nothing to her but a powerful cord with which to bind and manipulate.

"If what you have discovered is true," Harmony said, "we might not have much time for me to free myself from my shroud. Autonomy mobilizes an army from offworld to invade and destroy everyone on this planet. Telsin moves to circumvent that. Both plans are catastrophic to us, and both are in motion."

Damn. Wax took a deep breath. "You had me make a second earring. That's what finally convinced me to talk to you. Why?"

"I hoped that would work," Harmony said, a hint of a smile on his lips. "A good mystery is the best invitation."

"And? What do I do with it?"

"When Vin, the Ascendant Warrior, was resisting Ruin, she didn't realize that the little earring she wore linked her to him. It let him get inside her head, speak with her. Connect to her." He nodded to Wax's earring. "With a trellium spike, you will be Connected to Trell's avatar—much as you now are to me. She will be able to sense you, and you her."

"I don't know if that's a good idea," Wax said, shaking his head. "Whenever the two of us meet, she gets the better of me. I shouldn't try to play her games."

Harmony smiled. A faint smile, from one too burdened to be eager about the emotion. He actually seemed to do it on purpose, with effort. "As you wish. It is a tool for you to use. I've lost games over and over against Autonomy, but I still have help I can send you. Some do not realize I was behind their mobilization. Yet I did not know the urgency of our task. I did not know their bomb might be ready. I am caught flat-footed. That was their goal, I think. So I must ask. Will you be my sword again, Waxillium?"

"It is absolutely necessary?"

"That depends," he said, "on how you feel about the prospect of your sister taking my place as this planet's steward."

"That's . . . actually a possibility?"

"Yes."

"Damn."

"Disrupt Telsin's plan, and Autonomy will abandon her. That is our best bet."

"And the army Autonomy is bringing?"

"We will have to hope we have time to stop them after your sister's plan is subverted."

It didn't sound like much of a strategy. He looked to Harmony, and saw something different this time. Not the vastness of the powers, or even the figure of legend. But a man. Thrust into a war that none of them had been ready for, playing catch-up to learn powers that others had presumably spent millennia mastering.

He's doing his best, Wax thought. *And struggling to avoid being crushed by the opposing powers he holds. He needs help, and I'm all there is.*

When Wax had run to the Roughs, it had been to escape—but he'd *stayed* because people needed him.

He'd found peace in Elendel. He wouldn't return to the field because he wanted it or needed it. This time, he would go because he was *needed*.

"Final time?" Wax said.

"I promise," Harmony said. "Final time."

"All right," Wax said, and felt a weight settle onto him. "I'll stop Telsin. But you're going to have to deal with this Autonomy."

"Buy me time," Harmony said. "Time to recover. Time to build greater alliances in the years to come, so we can face her as a unified planet."

"I still don't know how bombing Elendel gets Telsin what she wants," he said. "It's too extreme. She's more rational than that. She's *got* to be planning to threaten us with it until we bend. Maybe she intends to . . . I don't know, detonate one in an Ashmount to cow us?"

"Perhaps. I do not know her ultimate plan. I'm sorry."

A mystery then. With terrible stakes. Wax met Harmony's eyes. "Is there anything you're not telling me?"

"Many things," Harmony admitted.

"Will any of them hurt, like what happened with Lessie?"

"Not on purpose," Harmony said. "But I cannot promise you will survive this. Or that if you do, it will be without pain. I can't promise much these days."

Wax made a fist.

"Do you trust me, Waxillium?" God asked.

"No," Wax said honestly. "But I trust her less. I've already said that I'll help. But I'm not only a sword, Harmony. I'm a lawman too. I'll find out what Telsin is doing. I'll answer the questions you cannot. I'll stop her that way."

"Thank you."

In a heartbeat, Wax was back in his penthouse. He'd never left, not physically. Steris knelt beside him, worried.

"He's been blinded," Wax said to her. "He didn't realize how urgent the problem was, and he's asked me to help. To intervene, and stop my sister." He took her by the arm. "I'm sorry. I need to go. I know you'll worry about me."

"Of course I will," she said. "But do you think I won't worry if you stay? If you're right about all of this . . ." She stood up. "It's not me or them, Wax. It's not politics or Allomancy. It's not me or Lessie. It's *never* been either/or. That part of your life isn't over merely because you didn't need it for a while. You need it now. We all do."

He stood up beside her. "I'll need to fetch my coat and my guns from the mansion."

"I have them here," she said, moving some stacks of broadsheets to uncover a cleaner's bag—from which she removed his mistcoat.

"I should have guessed that you'd have it laundered," he said. "Thank you for—"

There was a knock at the front door. They exchanged a look. Who was coming by at this hour of night, when even the servants had been dismissed? Wax walked to check, and outside—in the small hallway that led to the elevator foyer—he found a wrapped package.

He closed the door and showed the package to Steris. When unwrapped, it revealed a row of sixteen vials with—it appeared—a solution of alcohol and metal flakes inside. The last had a red-painted cork and a note. *Use the others instead of your normal vials. Use the last in an emergency only.*

Wax took these solemnly. Then, from the locked cabinet by the wall, he removed his strongbox—and from that two fully aluminum pistols, among Ranette's finest creations. Vindication II and the Steel Survivor.

The first was a powerful, large-caliber gun designed to hold hazekiller rounds in two extra chambers. Those rounds were oversized, the bullets designed with a secondary explosion for dealing with Hemalurgists. Ranette had come up with them to forcibly eject a spike from a person's body at close range. The second gun was a sleek mid-caliber pistol with an extra-long barrel for firing precision rounds. He generally loaded it with ordinary bullets that could be Pushed.

They slid into holsters that up until recently had held his unloaded guns. There was more in the box too. A gun bag, two feet long, holding something extra special, in several pieces that could be assembled. Ranette's most deadly design. He hesitated as he put a hand on it. Inside was a weapon not for a lawman, but for a soldier. Intent on destruction.

He put it back in the gun box. He wasn't going to need that. He was a lawman.

Steris bustled over with his large shoulder bag, extra wide and made of thick leather, for supplies. She packed his ammunition and extra metal vials—and, knowing her, a lunch—as he hurriedly gathered a few other things he thought he might need from the study. This included a belt with a pouch lined in aluminum, for holding metal vials. He could clip it closed, and the glass vials inside would be untouchable to enemy Allomancers. Into this he loaded half of the vials Harmony had sent.

When he returned, she held out his mistcoat for him. He took it in a two-handed grip.

"Steris," he said, "the Senate . . . I can't be in two places at once. Can you talk to the governor? This is a bad time for me to leave, with the new ambassador here. Hell . . . it might not be bad to prepare the governor for the worst, explaining about the potential for a bomb."

"I don't know if he will listen," Steris said. "The senators and the governor don't even listen to you—they'll outright ignore me."

"Still, we should try."

"We . . . could appoint someone to represent the house . . ."

"Steris," he said, "I stepped up to lead the house because of *your* dreams of what we could do. Your wonderful dreams. You saw in me someone who could do what needed to be done, and you were right." He took her gently by the shoulder. "I see in you the same person. A better one. I've been working on your ideas these last years. Your *genius*. You can lead as well as I can. Better, even."

"I'm not good with people," she whispered. "I'll ruin it. I've thought, and I've planned, and I always reach the same conclusion. I can't be trusted with something this important; we need someone more suitable."

"What if I think otherwise?" Wax said. "What if I think you're absolutely the *best* person to represent our house? War is building—and it's going to get worse if I do uncover a conspiracy in Bilming. We need someone to stop the hotheads. Someone meticulous, who has considered all the possibilities."

"I . . . I don't know. If I can do it."

"*I* believe in you, Steris. I will appoint someone else if you want. But I think you can do it best."

She met his eyes. Then, hesitantly, she nodded.

"Thank you," he said.

"If you *really* think this is best, then I will try. I am bad with people, but you are good with them. So it stands to reason that perhaps you are right. About me." She squeezed his arms. "Go. I will see to the Senate. Somehow."

He kissed her, still holding the mistcoat in one hand, wrapping his other arm around her. As he did, a small pair of hands gripped him and Steris around the legs.

"Max!" Steris said, breaking the embrace and looking down. "Why aren't you in bed?"

"Because I'm in here," he said.

She lifted him up as Wax stepped back and threw on his coat, then slung his heavy ammunition bag over his shoulder.

"You need to go fight monsters now?" Max asked.

"If I can find them," Wax said.

"You can," Max said. "You're the best detector that ever lived. Uncle Wayne told me. He said you can find any treasure there ever was to be found."

"I've already found the best treasures, Max," Wax said, turning— mistcoat tassels rustling in that old familiar way. Like whispers speaking an ancient tongue. "Now I just have to keep them safe."

He threw open the balcony doors and launched out into the sky toward the city of Bilming. Stars both above and beneath—with a highway lined in light pointing the way forward.

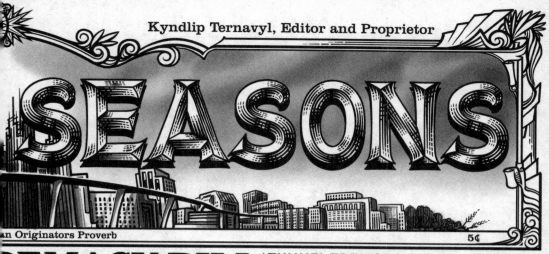

Kyndlip Ternavyl, Editor and Proprietor

SEASONS

an Originators Proverb — 5¢

REMACY BILL
ASIN UNITY
ESS OR PERNICIOUSNESS?

BELOVED EDITOR STILL MISSING

's been eight days since
editor's husband and
dren tearfully pled for
safe return. Since then,
reporters have combed
city, pestered the mayor,
followed each lead you
readers have submitted.
til further notice, and bar-
any urgent information,
daily updates will run
the back. Please continue
ding tips to our offices
the corner of 109th and
atten Way.

Kyndlip Ternavyl

TUNNEL TREMORS STOP ... FOR NOW

A sign the city is ready to abandon its underground rail?

It's every Bilminger's favorite gripe: when will construction crews finish the underground rail line? Initiated over four years ago with a bloated budget that rusts the metals of every Bilming taxpayer, the subway was to provide relief to the city's traffic problems. While little progress has been seen on the underground rail, in the same amount of time, the Bilming Transportation Authority has added more lines to the raised rail and more lanes to the highways. At this point, do we really need an underground railway, especially when its construction coincides with the small earthquakes that rattle our nerves every few months?

More coverage on back:
Owner of Soothing Parlor
Grateful for Public Agitation

ALLOMANCER JAK SETTLES WITH SIDEKICK

Allomancer Jak has reached a settlement with his former sidekick, Handerwym Terrisborn, who claims the famous media mogul skimmed Terrisborn's stakes in the company to invest in new media ventures, like the flash-in-the-pan evanoplays of several years ago. While Jak's adventures will continue in *The Sentinel of Truth*, "Handerwym Presents" will now be exclusive to our broadsheet in Bilming.

"This was my intention all along," said Jak to a crowd of eager fans, "to train dear Handerwym in the ways of greatness and then cut the apron strings, push him from the nest, and watch him sink or swim. Besides, now that I don't have to pay him, I can focus my time and money on writing my memoirs and exploring promising new forms of storytelling. Let me tell you what's next: vizbooks— they're stories you can read even if you don't know your letters!"

When asked for comment, Terrisborn just closed his eyes and sighed.

More details on back: Why
the judge let Jak keep the tiger

SPARKLE TONIC

BEWARE!
**COPYCATS CLAIM TO HAVE FOUND
THE SECRET FORMULA**

But these unscrupulous imitators only seek access to your pocketbook and will try to fool you into drinking less than the best. If your druggist says something else is "good enough," tell them:

**"I KNOW THE DIF
GIVE ME VIF"**
(Paid for by the **Vif Sparkle Co.**)

leeched her steel reserves.
Give me the compass," I
, "and we'll leave you at
next outcropping."
ila peered over her shoul-
at the approaching stone
re the Haunted Man
ed.
e glanced at me, her
ide no doubt realizing

PART TWO

20

Marasi got a few hours of sleep, nestled in the front seat of the truck as her convoy rolled toward Bilming. Fortunately they'd been able to recruit drivers from the constabulary night watch, so they were used to the hours. Hers wasn't the talkative type. The woman wore her jacket with the collar up, a cap on her head to shadow her face. The team had been told to maintain their disguises even while driving.

When Marasi had dozed off, they'd been traveling through the bleak darkness beyond Elendel. When she blinked awake, the sun was rising and they were passing the Bilming suburbs. Marasi had never been to the city, though it was only a few hours by train along the coast, but she had a good grasp on the politics of why this city was so important.

As traffic into the capital had grown overwhelming, Bilming had become an essential port and dockyard. Its seaside nature let it trade with other coastal towns, ignoring Elendel's railway monopoly. In addition, Bilming was a chief port for trade with the Southern Continent—where much commerce was being handled by traditional ocean shipping, not airship.

The discovery of those new lands had brought wealth into Bilming. And wealth meant power. Many in Elendel thought they had let the people of Bilming grow too independent—and in recent years, it had become the one city in the Basin that could legitimately rival Elendel.

Many in the capital spoke of Bilming snidely, pretending it was a rural outpost of half-educated sailors and drunken dockworkers. Marasi knew better. This wasn't a rural backwater; Bilming was a metropolis in the making.

She passed neatly laid-out suburbs—but even more swaths of land that had been set aside to eventually be filled. Many developments were mid-construction, houses being built, each in a different style, no two roofs matching one another. No two doorways in the same place. Yet there was a strange *symmetry* to it. One she couldn't quite pin down.

It was the same downtown, which—though still distant—she could see had half-finished pillars of skyscrapers growing up like the mythical spires of Kredik Shaw. A dominant building at the direct center was furthest along. It had to be a good seventy or eighty stories high, rivaling the tallest buildings in Elendel.

Each of the buildings—particularly the one at the center—had a strange aesthetic that mixed the feel of a fortress with modern sleek lines and steel finishings. As they drove closer, the roadway passed under a large elevated railway that ran in a circle around the city. Some sections were unfinished, but big swaths of it were already in operation.

Everything had a metallic feel to it, like burnished steel, enhanced by the skeletons of buildings rising up, their girders exposed. The finished buildings had metal roofs or siding—not always polished, and often with a patina. The overall effect gave the great variety of building shapes a cohesive theme.

She was impressed. Even half-finished, this was a city with a plan. The design screamed of industry, forward thinking, and accomplishment. They passed numerous billboards proclaiming the virtues of self-reliance and sovereignty. You didn't have to read far between the lines to see the tone those were setting. Independence from Elendel.

"You ever notice," her driver said, "how kids always draw houses the same way?"

Marasi frowned, glancing at her. The woman's voice was on the deeper side, but Marasi couldn't make out much about her. Marasi had chosen her truck at random, picking one that had boxes in the back, not constables—hoping that would help her sleep.

"I can't say that I've noticed," Marasi said.

"It's strange," the driver continued. "You can imagine the shape, of course. Square box. Triangular roof. Door right in the center. Two windows. Often a chimney, even though fewer and fewer homes have those these days. What house *actually* looks like that? Almost none. So why do kids draw them?"

"I guess it's easy," Marasi said.

"Perhaps," her driver said. "Or maybe they're not drawing a house. They're drawing someone else's *picture* of a house. What they've seen others make. An icon. A symbol."

Marasi narrowed her eyes. "That's an interesting observation, Constable . . . what was your name?"

"I go by Moonlight," the woman said. "We like code names. It's one of our things."

"I . . . have never heard that word before."

"You wouldn't have, since you have no moon here." The woman leaned back and stretched out her arm on the top of the steering wheel, causing her sleeve to inch back and reveal a red tattoo on her forearm, above the wrist. The same symbol that had been on the card left for her.

Slowly, cautiously, Marasi reached for the pistol in the holster under her arm.

"You won't need that," the woman said, her eyes still on the road. They'd been forced to slow considerably now that they were approaching the center of the city. Who would have guessed that an Outer City would have so much traffic?

"Where's the constable who should have been driving this truck?" Marasi asked. "What did you do to her?"

"Nothing," the woman said. "She's fine. But I find it amusing that's the first thing you ask. I mean, I understand—but maybe get your priorities straight, Marasi."

Marasi kept her fingers lightly on the grip of the handgun, but didn't draw it. "Was it you in the cavern? The person wearing a white mask?"

"It was black," the woman said, passing that little test. "Yes. That was me."

"And . . . are you human?"

"One hundred percent," the woman said. "I'm not a local though." She pulled off her cap, revealing straight black hair in a ponytail and uncommon features. A shape to the eyes Marasi had never seen, prominent cheekbones.

"Are you from the Southern Continent?" Marasi asked.

"No." Moonlight nodded to the city outside. "I've always hated Bilming. I should like the thought they put into design, yet the underlying message disturbs me. They're trying hard to make each building individual, but the way it comes together is too deliberate. It makes the artistry feel hollow."

"And why do you think that is?"

"Because of Trell's influence, obviously."

Marasi leaned forward. "Tell me. *Please.*"

Moonlight glanced at her for the first time. Such self-assured eyes, with a cocked half smile on her lips. This was a woman who had put herself at the very center of a group of constables and didn't seem the slightest bit worried.

"So hungry," Moonlight said. "We don't always share answers with outsiders, Marasi."

"I could have you arrested and interrogated."

"On what charges?"

"Interfering with constable business."

"Interfering? How? I was instructed to drive this truck."

"Don't play coy," Marasi said. "You're impersonating a constable—plus it's against the law to withhold information vital to an investigation."

The woman smiled, turning her eyes back to the road. "Strange how similar cops are, regardless of the planet."

Regardless of the *planet.* Rust and Ruin . . .

Marasi had known that there were other planets out there, of course. The kandra talked about it. But . . . rusts. It was still hard to accept.

They pulled to a halt as some traffic worked its way into the street ahead of them. As they did, a beggar came to Marasi's window. Per the notebook's instructions, Marasi unlatched the window and folded it down, then handed the beggar a few boxings. The dirty man slipped her a piece of paper.

"Can you get to Biggle Way?" Marasi asked, reading the note.

"Yeah," Moonlight said, turning them down the next street. "That's in the industrial district."

Marasi's truck pulled into the lead and the convoy followed her, all ten keeping in a tight double line. At the next corner, Wayne's truck came up beside them. She could make him out talking the ear off his driver—who turned out to be Hoid, Wax's coachman. How had *he* gotten involved in the sting?

"Can't tell these days," Moonlight said, "if I'm keeping watch on him, or if he's keeping watch on me. Realistically, we're both just keeping watch on the same third parties . . ."

"What. *Hoid?*" Marasi asked. "He's been in Wax's employ for years. He's an odd fellow, but . . ."

In the next truck, Hoid glanced at them—past Marasi—and nodded to Moonlight.

Damn. What in the world? How much of her time had she wasted on bank robberies or protection rackets, when *this* was going on?

Whatever *this* was.

"Has it ever struck you," Moonlight said, "how art is so destructive?"

"Art?" Marasi said, frowning. "Destructive?"

"Each new movement consumes the one that came before," Moonlight said, starting them forward as the traffic began to creep into motion again. "Chops it up and feeds on the corpse. Takes the bones, but drapes new skin on them. Each new piece of art is in some way a parody of what has come before."

"You sound like an artist yourself."

"I have certain talents," she said. "My experiences have given me an interest in the quirks of the artistic world—and its . . . *values,* you might say. Tell me. Let's say you had one of only sixteen extremely rare pieces of art by the same artist. What would you do to ensure yours becomes the most valuable?"

"If I play along," Marasi said, "will you tell me about Trell?"

"I'm trying to, right now."

Marasi frowned, considering. "I have one of sixteen pieces of art . . . and I must ensure mine is the most valuable?"

"Yup."

"I'd try to create an air of mystique around it," Marasi said. "I wouldn't show it off. I'd let the other fifteen become common by comparison—and the value of mine would increase as people shared the story. There *is* one more. One *no one* has seen."

"Clever," Moonlight said. "I'm impressed."

"And what would you do?" Marasi said.

"Steal the other fifteen," Moonlight said. "Then I'd be able to manipulate the market however I wanted."

"Ruthless."

"Not as ruthless as other options. These pieces of art exist, Marasi, and your planet's god holds two of them."

"Ruin and Preservation."

"Indeed. That makes Harmony the most valuable—the most Invested—being in the cosmere. One of the other sixteen decided the best way to improve *his* stock was to try to destroy all the others. He managed it in a few cases."

"And . . . is that Trell?"

Moonlight shook her head. "No, his name is Odium. Trell—Autonomy—had a different idea. You see these buildings? These houses? All pieces of a larger art installation. The grand creation is impressive, but it's not yours. This kind of pattern, and those straight lines, those reflective panels . . . that's from a Taldain movement known as brutalism.

"That's part of what I hate about Autonomy. She claims she wants everyone to be individual. Gives them each a little house that is distinctive from the others, but only in a way that fits *her* plan, *her* desires. It's fake individualism. A corporate uniqueness. Like an advertisement telling people to go their own way, be their own person—by buying this product like everyone else."

Marasi struggled to parse all of this. But what she understood reinforced what she had suspected. A being from another planet was leading this city, and had plans for the people of Marasi's world.

"What is Trell's goal, then?" Marasi asked. "If he doesn't want to destroy the other gods?"

"Trell is trying to edge out the others," Moonlight said. "She—he, they, it varies—doesn't like engaging other gods directly. We call them Shards, by the way. Autonomy is trying to outcompete the others by filling the cosmere with versions of herself. Crowd out the competition, so to speak. Like an extremely invasive plant moving into another ecosystem and strangling the local varieties."

Marasi frowned. "I . . . think I understand."

"Conversations about Autonomy can be confusing," Moonlight said, her eyes on the road. "Trellism is the remnants of an ancient religion on your world, originally founded by Autonomy long, long ago. A seed for when she decided to move in. Now, that time has come. Autonomy is looking for someone on this planet to fully take up that role, that identity."

"Wait, *take up* that role?"

"She wants to leave a god behind on this planet," Moonlight explained. "Someone who bears some of her power, who sees to her interests, and is—in many ways—a piece of her soul. She does this all around the cosmere. Some worlds have entire pantheons that are all versions of her, each of which has a distinct personality and identity."

"So . . . she's role-playing? With herself?"

"Yes," Moonlight said. "But Autonomy's Investiture has a life of its own, and so each version of her becomes its own thing over time. Sometimes they aren't a person but only power. Other times, if the situation needs more oversight, she picks someone to elevate."

"So . . ." Marasi said, "she's going to take our world by setting up a rival god and forcing Harmony out?"

"Basically," Moonlight said. "Your planet is a primary target for her, Marasi. Two Shards in residence, held by one person, frightens her. You had gunpowder weapons and electricity before any planet in the cosmere aside from her core homeworld. She sees you getting stronger, learning more and more. Getting close to real secrets. It makes you the biggest threat in the cosmere, at least to her."

"I don't see how this could defeat Harmony though."

"I don't either, honestly," Moonlight said. "I'm not sure any human can understand the full plan. But she knows Harmony has trouble acting, and so she has seen an opportunity."

Marasi sat back, breathing out, her hand slipping from her gun. Answers. *Actual* answers. She'd been searching for so long, hit so many dead ends. To finally get an explanation felt . . . wonderful.

"So Autonomy is looking for an avatar," Marasi said.

"She's likely found one. A woman named Telsin."

"Wax's *sister*?" Damn.

"Granted, there's rivalry among the ranks," Moonlight said. "There always is, with Autonomy. So Telsin will have to prove she's the strongest, the best. And, since creativity and individualism are Autonomy's stated intents, she'll reward grit, success, vision."

Moonlight nodded to the half-finished buildings they were passing. "This city is an example of that, all designed by one gifted architect Telsin promoted five years ago. His work is meant to impress Autonomy . . . but the individual homeowners? They don't get to design anything. They get a manufactured 'individual' house."

"Seems like a raw deal," Marasi said.

"Depends on what you want," Moonlight said. "Living under her can be safe if you keep your head down, don't stray into the dangerous regions where she demands that you test yourself. Autonomy is brutal, but also generous. If you impress her, you rise through her ranks. Even if you go *against* what you're told, and you are successful, you are rewarded."

"And if you fail?"

"It doesn't go well for you," Moonlight said. Her eyes grew distant. "She sickens me. But I do understand her . . . I think. It's taken a while."

Marasi sat back in her seat, thoughtful. Answers, finally. But at the same time . . . how much could she trust this woman? Was any of this true?

"Why explain this to me now?" Marasi asked.

"Because you've impressed my organization," Moonlight said. "We who defend Scadrial have to move very carefully; there are forces in this world—Harmony included—that might crush us, if we take the wrong step."

That gave Marasi pause. If they didn't work for Harmony, who *did* they work for?

Moonlight led the truck caravan off the highway at last, passing through the outskirts of the city on the northern edge.

"It's so . . . fabricated," Moonlight said. "Look at that sign. You see it?"

"The billboard?" Marasi said, glancing at the large posted drawing of a stylized version of Bilming, with light rising behind it. PRIDE IN PROGRESS, it said. OUTER CITIES SELF-RELIANCE MOVEMENT.

"Those are all over the city," Moonlight said. "Nights! The same exact piece of art, a hundred times over. Art that can be reproduced . . . is it really art at all?"

"Of course it is," Marasi said. "Why would it stop being art just because it's replicated?"

"It's crass."

"Said like an elitist," Marasi said. "If you truly were interested in the *beauty* of the art—instead of some tangential sense of control—you'd want everyone to be able to experience it. The more the better."

"Well argued," Moonlight said. "I'll admit that my distaste for Autonomy might taint my opinion."

They led the convoy onto Biggle Way, then drove slowly in a single-file line. Eventually someone fell into step alongside Marasi's truck, wearing a red jacket as the notebook said. She unlatched the window again.

"Ahead, across the Grand Motorway," he said. "Third building on the right."

She nodded and put the window back up. At the end of the street, they reached the Grand Motorway—a vast *six-lane* highway. Marasi had never seen a street so wide. "Are there really so many cars these days that such a thing is necessary?"

"They're planning," Moonlight said, "for a much larger city in the future."

Well, they might not need that many lanes yet, but there was still plenty of traffic on the Grand Motorway. They had to wait for traffic to slow and give them a chance to cross. Ahead she could see a line of large warehouses—the third one's cargo door was open. That was it, their drop-off.

"Are you going to interfere?" Marasi asked. "With our operation?"

"No," Moonlight said. "You have my word."

"Can I talk to you afterward?" Marasi asked.

"Yes," Moonlight said. "But Marasi, I can only say so much to an outsider. For now I'm just here to watch."

At a lull in the traffic, Moonlight pulled across—though the other nine trucks had to wait their turn.

"And what if bullets start flying?" Marasi asked. "You're going to sit here and watch?"

"I'm not a constable, as you pointed out," Moonlight said. "So yes. Consider me an external admirer of your work. Interested in the quirks of those who follow the law—and their . . . *value*."

She smiled in a knowing way, then pulled into the cavernous warehouse. As soon as all ten trucks arrived, the sting could begin.

21

Wayne nodded as the trucks ahead waited to cross the highway. "Well then, Hoid," he said to the coachman, "that's all I know about how to pickle vegetables."

". . . Thank you?" Hoid said.

"'S all right," Wayne said. "I'm a bastion of useful information, I am."

The truck ahead of them pulled forward, crossing the vast motorway filled with sixteens upon sixteens of cars. Hoid moved their truck up, next in line.

"Can I have my harmonica back now?" Hoid asked.

Wayne fished in his pocket and brought it out. "I traded you fair for this!"

"You did nothing of the sort."

"I did!" Wayne said. "The trade is in the glove box. You're always too watchy for me to slip things in your pocket. How'd you get so good at that, anyways? You're a rusting coachman."

"Practice," Hoid said solemnly. "A very *great* amount of practice." He opened the glove box, and a bright white creature with a long, hairless tail peeked out. "Wayne. A *live rat?*"

"I call him Sir Squeekins," Wayne said. "I wasn't gonna bring him, but he snuck into my pocket, he did. So I figure, 'That's the seventeenth time you've let him escape his cage, Wayne. Better give him to someone responsible.'"

"You are a uniquely bizarre individual," Hoid said, smiling as the rat crawled up his arm. "But . . . trade accepted, I guess?"

"Great, great," Wayne replied. "He likes strawberries and booze, but don't give him none of the booze, 'cuz he's a rat."

"Noted."

They waited at the edge of the wide roadway. And Wayne, he'd had this feeling all day today. Something was happening. Something important.

"You ever feel," Wayne said, "like you wish life was like the stories?"

"What do you mean?" Hoid asked.

"There's always a good ending in those stories. The ones my ma used to tell . . . they *meant* something. People, they were *worth* something."

"I think we live stories every day," Hoid replied. "Ones that we will remember, and tell, and shape like clay to be what we need them to be."

"The last story my ma told me," Wayne said, "was about a lawman. Funny, huh? That I'd end up becoming one. Except he was a hero. And I'm . . . well, I'm me."

"You do yourself a disservice, Master Wayne," Hoid said softly.

"Can't be no hero if you were a villain, Hoid."

"But in most of the stories, it is the villain who knows the hero best."

Wayne chewed on that, watching the flow of cars on the road ahead. And . . . found himself imagining that roadway as a river. Because a part of him wished that what Hoid said could be true.

Then he waited some more.

And some more.

Damn. Someone really ought to come up with a way to make it so cars that wanted to cross had a better chance. Maybe you could hire someone to stand at the corner and fire a gun in the air when too many cars were blocking the way, and frighten them to move faster? Anyway, that zooming of cars . . . that road could be a wide river. Yeah, a river of stone and steel. Faster than any other river in the world.

He smiled, remembering a calm, beautiful voice that had kept his world solid for so long.

Yeah, there's a bandit to be chased, he thought. *But it's still wrong. Where's the hero? He should be here, but he stayed behind.*

In a lull, Hoid gunned the truck and they scooted across—earning only three honks from cars that had to slow. Pretty good, considering. You could cross even the fastest river, full of the worst kinds of rocks, if you were in a bigger rock yourself. No need to fly, like Jak had in the story. This wasn't cheating. It was just a smarter way, it was.

Followed by the last of their convoy, they pulled into the dim warehouse lit by some unlatched windows up along the tops of the walls. Why put the windows up there, where nobody could see outta them?

Oh, right. Illegal stuff. Yeah, that made sense.

"Thanks for the ride, Hoid," Wayne said, pulling out his gangster hat—a worn wool cap traded off one of the thugs they'd caught. "You might wanna keep your head down if this next part gets shooty. Hope it won't though."

"Understood, Master Wayne," Hoid said. "Best of luck."

Wayne nodded, and it was time to become someone else. He scrunched up his face, squinting like Franis did—that was the guy he'd gotten the hat off of. A fellow Wayne's height and age, but more weathered. By time, by smokes, by the things he'd done. Wayne already wore a wig to change his hair color, along with a bit of rubber on his chin to square it out, and some makeup to sink his eyes. With the hat, he *was* Franis—missing only one thing.

He climbed out and swaggered. Franis sure knew how to swagger.

VenDell—wearing the Cycle's body, a man named Granks—met him outside the truck. The others waited quietly. All those dirty conners in the trucks would jump out only when they had someone important to catch. Someone more than a bunch of useless, low-level cretins.

Not that Franis was a cretin. He just needed work, you know? You started by taking a job at the docks, but work there grew tight. And the schedules were so bad. Then you heard your friend Vin had a job with someone who paid better, and all you had to do was move some boxes. Who could get into trouble for moving boxes? Even if you did have to keep a gun on you at all times, and be ready to shoot.

He swaggered in beside VenDell in his fancy suit and fancier body. "It's uncanny," the kandra said, "how you do that. You imitate a person nearly as well as one of my kin."

"Just gotta find someone what looks a little like you," Wayne said, "and make up the difference. Also, stay in character."

"Right, right," the kandra said. He wasn't half bad—considering what a fussy little thing he normally was. He wore Granks's body well. A gangster who had proven himself enough to be elevated. Given a title and some authority, while the rest of them were basically hired hands.

They crossed the vast chamber toward two fellows who emerged from the perimeter. Indeed, a lot of fellows began moving in. A good forty armed men. A local gang. That was . . . more people than the constables had.

We'll have surprise though, Wayne thought. And the trucks were armored, offering cover. It should be fine, with Wayne and Marasi—not to mention a Faceless Immortal—on their side. MeLaan was quite the fighter; VenDell should be handy in a scrap too.

The two fellows that stepped up to meet with them wore work clothing: suspenders, trousers, buttoned shirts. Not good enough. They needed at least a Suit—the rank that Granks would report to—and preferably a Sequence, or even a fully promoted Series. There were only a couple of those in the Set at a time though. And one leader. The Key.

Wayne/Franis didn't want any of those important jobs. He wasn't interested in wearing the fancy clothing and drawing the gunfire. Pay him his wages and let him pretend he wasn't doing nothing wrong.

"Cycle," said the stouter of the two men, nodding. He would *probably* be a fellow named Dip, according to the interrogations. Or . . . maybe he was one named Embrier.

Whoever he was, he glanced at Franis, but didn't say anything to him directly. "You can leave the trucks," he told VenDell. "Gather your men in the two vans outside and head home. Your success has been noted."

"Fine," VenDell grumbled—using a pretty good version of Granks's accent. "But I need to talk to the Sequence. There's an issue."

"The radio line isn't good enough?" maybe-Dip said, glancing at his companion.

"I have reason to believe the radios are compromised," VenDell said. "The Sequence is here, isn't he?"

That was Wayne's suggestion. The leader types, they *always* hung around and watched. Didn't trust good, honest(ish) thieves like Franis to do their job right. So yeah, a higher-level member of the Set would be here. Somewhere. Sure as Franis wasn't Franis right now, but was somebody kind of close—as close as someone could get, unless he could wear Franis's bones, which was cheatin' and that was that.

Anyway. Important negotiations. Life or death. Surrounded by forty armed men. Better pay attention.

"I will convey your message to the Sequence," maybe-Dip said.

"That won't be good enough," VenDell said. "There is a problem. A very large problem."

The two thugs looked at one another. Damn . . . they were suspicious.

Wayne glanced at the people at the perimeter, who would need only one offhand comment to start shooting. So he made a quick decision. The fellow wouldn't be the one named Dip. Because who would put a guy named Dip in charge of anything?

"Hey, Embrier," he said, using a slightly modified version of his own accent—dockworker, but overlaid with the kind of sniveling accent these thugs had all adopted. People what worked together, they started to pick up one another's ways of speaking. "Can we talk a spell?"

The stout man glanced at him, then nodded. "Yeah, Franis?"

Wayne waved him over, and they slipped to the side. VenDell started up a conversation with the other man, going over the inventory they'd been able to "acquire."

"What's up, Franis?" the thug said quietly, then thumbed over his shoulder. "The Cycle *never* cares about things like this. Just does what he's told."

"Brain like wet concrete," Wayne agreed softly. "Can you *believe* he's the one what got chosen?"

"I can believe it," Embrier said. "He never questions. Unlike you."

"Hey," Wayne said, "I only question when my paycheck is coming."

"Don't we all," Embrier said, then shot him a sideways glance. "You've been getting some sun."

Damn. The makeup hadn't been light enough. Could he get the man to ask after his father? Wayne had some good info from the real Franis on his father. "You know. Heavy work. Like Dad always said—best work is the kind you do with your arms and back."

"Yeah, but don't you live in a cavern?"

"I don't *live* in the rusting *cavern*," Wayne said. "What, you think I stay down there in the dark?"

Embrier grunted. "How's your sister?"

Sister? Aw, rusts. Wayne glanced at Embrier. That smile.

"You stay away from my damn sister," Wayne said.

"Just askin'," Embrier said, raising his hands. "Ruin. No need to come out swinging."

"Look," Wayne said softly, "Cycle isn't acting strange—he's worried. Saw some lady conner sniffing around our base. Dark hair. You know the one?"

The man cursed under his breath. "Why didn't you say so?"

"I just rusting did. But Cycle wants to report it. Thinks he'll get . . . you-know-who's attention. For spotting a conner what we *know* is likely to be around. Rusting idiot."

But Embrier had gone a little pale at the implication that the Cycle wanted to draw Trell's attention. Best to . . . ease away from that. Wayne threw his arm around the fellow's shoulder and walked them back toward the others.

"'Sides," he said to Embrier. "You can forget my sister. I've met this woman, she'd be great for you."

"Really?" Embrier asked.

"Sure. She thought *Yulip* was handsome."

"Yulip? The koloss-blooded who looks like a *frog*?"

"Same one," Wayne said, rejoining the others.

Embrier shook his head. "Insanity." He nodded to VenDell. "I'll go get the Sequence. You can start your men unloading."

VenDell turned, waving for the process to begin. Hopefully Marasi would keep her head down, like Wayne had told her. She was too damn obvious, that one. Needed to learn how to scrunch her face up and become someone she wasn't, once in a while. Really helped with the self-loathing.

Still shouldn't have crossed the river without the hero, Wayne thought as the two thugs jogged to the rear of the room and opened a door.

"Seriously," VenDell asked Wayne, "how do you *do* that? You don't even have their bones."

"Gotta have fewer sticks up your posterior, VenDell," Wayne said. "Yank one or two out, and you'll see."

"It's patently unfair," he said. "A mortal should *not* be able to stand beside one of the Bearers of the Contract and seem a fair match to their skill in imitation."

"Aw, jealousy," Wayne said. He breathed it in. "Smells like cherry blossoms. Also, stop breakin' character, ya sod."

Finally, two figures in nicer clothing stepped from a darkened room at the back of the warehouse. Perfect. That was what they'd wanted. Hopefully the waiting constables could—

Suddenly, the outer doors slammed open and figures in brown began flooding in, pointing guns at the thugs. "Drop your weapons!" a voice shouted. "This is a sting!"

"It's the heat!" Wayne said, slipping his gun out of his holster.

VenDell grabbed his arm.

"Oh yeah," Wayne said, letting his arm be lowered. "Right, right. I forget sometimes . . ."

But these weren't *their* people. What the hell? All around, the thugs were turning—but nobody fired, because more and more figures in brown were pouring in. At least a hundred constables. Wearing . . .

. . . the shield and tortoise, symbol of *Bilming*. These were local constables.

Marasi's sting had just been stung.

22

Marasi groaned and sat up in her seat, pulling off the hat she'd used to obscure her face.

Bilming city constables. Wonderful. She glanced at Moonlight, who shrugged.

"I had no idea," Moonlight said.

Marasi sighed. At least the locals knew to surround the Sequence and his flunky—a pack of at least twenty constables were holding weapons on him. They might not know about the Set, but they understood things like smuggling and gangsters. The rest of the newly arrived constables were rounding up thugs who had wisely decided not to shoot, as they were far outnumbered. They reluctantly dropped their weapons.

Marasi kicked open her door and hopped down. Immediately, several of the advancing constables turned weapons on her. She sighed and raised her hands. "I'm Elendel Constabulary!" she shouted at them. "Special Detective Marasi Colms!"

"What's this?" a voice demanded. A tall woman with short blonde hair—wearing a Bilming uniform—pushed through the constables. Marasi thought she knew the woman.

"Captain Blantach?" Marasi said. "We met at the intercity training event last year."

The woman looked Marasi up and down, then groaned. Nearby, some of Marasi's people were hesitantly climbing out of the backs of trucks—showing their credentials.

Captain Blantach put her palm to her forehead. "You're *kidding* me," she said. "You're running a sting *inside* my city?"

"I have jurisdiction in the entire Basin," Marasi said, fishing for the paperwork. "Constable-General Reddi authorized it under the oversight of the governor."

"You *claim* jurisdiction in the entire Basin!" Blantach said, waving the authorizations away. "Rusting Elenders. *Of course* you would pull an operation in my city and not even *send word*."

Marasi felt a little bad for the woman. Still, the Set had the Outer Cities under its thumb. Sending advance word to the local constables would have been far too risky; there were almost certainly Set agents within Blantach's organization.

Though . . . the fact that the constables were here seemed to disprove that theory.

"You're going to need to turn them over to us," Marasi said, waving at the gangsters.

"Like hell we are," Blantach said, folding her arms across her uniform jacket, stiff and buttoned tight.

"This is part of a much bigger network," Marasi said.

"Then we'll discover that during interrogation."

Marasi sighed, but took a deep breath. "Blantach," she said, "do we *have* to fight this fight?"

The taller woman eyed her, but said nothing.

"The politicians don't get along," Marasi said, "but that's their business. *Our* business is protecting the cities—all of them. Just a couple of conners with our hands full. Let's work together rather than squabble."

"Perhaps I can agree to that . . . if we do it on *my* terms."

"This thing I'm hunting," Marasi said, "it goes deep. Dangerously deep. And it has little tendrils of mist wrapping around all parts of society. Your city's leaders are *almost certainly* compromised."

"You said this wasn't about politics."

"I said we shouldn't worry about how divisive the politicians are being," Marasi said. "But everything touches on politics these days. The group I'm pursuing are deliberately stoking war between Elendel and the Outer Cities.

"If we get close to them, there are elements in *both* governments who are going to try to stop us. Which is why I couldn't warn you we were coming. I apologize for that, but most in my *own* government don't know about this operation."

Blantach waved away an aide who came trotting up, perhaps to deliver a count of enemies taken captive, and continued to regard Marasi. This situation was a bit like a political negotiation—but Marasi had an advantage over Steris and Wax. You never really could tell what senators wanted. But fellow constables?

You didn't take up this job for glory—or at least you didn't *stay* in this job for glory. Anyone who wanted glory quickly moved on to judgeships or attorney positions, promoted away from actual detective work as soon as possible. But Blantach was a career constable. She'd been in her job longer than Reddi.

"You're making me worried, Colms," Blantach said.

"How hard was this operation to organize?" Marasi asked. "Were those in your own government—higher members of the constabulary—working against you?"

"That's how everything is." Blantach shrugged. "You know red tape. It . . ." She trailed off, frowning. "There might have been a *tad* more on this mission."

"So why didn't they quash it entirely?" Marasi whispered. "Why'd they let you continue?"

"I was determined."

That wasn't it. If the Set had known about this mission, and had been intent on quashing it, they would have.

The weapons were being smuggled here to arm the forces in Bilming anyway, Marasi realized. *So it's fine if the government seizes them. They'll still go where they need to.* The Set had to run a delicate operation. They might be in control of Bilming, but most people didn't know that. So why tip their hand and prevent a raid, when all the Set needed to do was make sure the seized goods went to the right places in the city?

And what of the Sequence? Marasi glanced at the pile of constables surrounding him. He'd been bound, but maintained an air of confidence. He had a refined look, a stylish suit. Thick eyebrows and prominent lips. Her guess was that he had been aware of the sting and was playing along, knowing he'd be released later.

Then he saw Marasi. And he cocked his head, frowning. He stepped closer and had to be restrained by the constables—as if he'd forgotten about them. He stared at her, confused.

A moment later he smiled a broad, even excited smile. He flexed, then stretched his neck.

Rusts. What was she missing?

Oh *hell*. What better way to spark further controversy in the Basin than to suddenly find a bunch of Elendel constables interfering in local business? Particularly if . . .

"Blantach," Marasi said, grabbing her arm, "we have to sedate that man."

"What? *Sedate* him? Why?"

"Aren't you ready for Metalborn?" Marasi said.

"There aren't any Metalborn in this group," Blantach said. "I have it on good authority from—"

The Sequence chose that moment to let out an Allomantic Push of *incredible* strength.

23

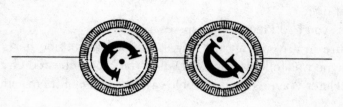

Marasi wore a breakaway gunbelt with metal pouches, so the Push didn't do more than strip away her equipment. The Bilming constables weren't so well prepared. They were tossed back by their own guns, handcuffs, and other accoutrements of their profession.

Blantach screamed as she was knocked off her feet, but she was lucky to suffer only a minor fall—many were tossed dozens of feet. *Trucks* rocked, and two even overturned. The doors at the sides of the building were blown free. Windows cracked and people cried out as guns were shoved across the floor and hit the walls—except for a few unaffected weapons that lay on the ground. Apparently some of the enemy had been given aluminum guns.

The Sequence casually scooped one of these up, now standing at the epicenter of a blast of power unlike any Marasi had experienced from an ordinary Coinshot. She stepped back, awed. That had been something like . . . like from the old stories. Like Harmony had recorded in the histories, detailing the power available to the Ascendant Warrior.

It was a horrible sign. Because Marasi realized why the Sequence was smiling. While he'd likely been planning to go along with his arrest, now that he'd found a chance to implicate Elendel in a scandal, he would want to cause as many casualties as possible.

While the others were recovering, Marasi dove for one of the aluminum guns. But the Sequence took aim and fired directly in front of her, driving her—still unarmed—into cover behind an overturned truck. The Allomantic Push had stopped for now, fortunately.

You've read about this, she thought. *It's one of the ancient powers available only to Mistborn.*

It was called duralumin, an arcane metal. Using it, an Allomancer could burn their entire metal reserve at once. Like detonating a keg of gunpowder instead of a single bullet, it released an enormous burst of Allomantic energy. At least . . . that was what she remembered. It hadn't been relevant in centuries, because no one could have two Allomantic powers at once.

Unless you had Hemalurgic spikes.

A figure in a wool cap and wig scrambled up beside her a moment later. Wayne was followed by VenDell in the broad-chested Cycle's body. A second later Wayne's speed bubble gave the three of them some breathing room.

"They were ready for us!" Wayne said. "They knew we was going to pull this sting!"

"No," Marasi said. "They knew about Blantach and *her* constables, but I think they didn't mind being captured. My guess is they were going to go along with *that* sting, and slip out of jail later."

"So what changed?" he asked.

"The Sequence just realized we're here from Elendel," Marasi said, "and decided to use our presence to create an incident—constables dead—and blame it on Elendel interference in a Bilming operation."

It was still merely a guess. The facts were clear though. The moment he saw Marasi, a man who had been about to go quietly had decided to fight. Which put everyone in danger.

She glanced out from behind the truck, now that she didn't have to worry about getting shot. The Sequence was casually pointing his gun toward Captain Blantach, who was climbing to her feet. At the perimeter of the room, constables and gangsters alike were picking themselves up off the ground, disoriented. Those who had recovered first were frozen in the act of scrambling for weapons.

"What's the plan?" Wayne asked.

"You distract that Sequence," Marasi said to him. "I'll organize our constables. The Set's forces seem surprised by that too—look at the shock on their faces. I really think they planned to be captured, then released by corrupt judges or prosecutors. We still have a chance to turn this around, if we can take advantage of their disorientation."

"This is *not* the plan!" VenDell said, peeking past her.

"Plans last until someone starts shootin', mate," Wayne said.

"So unruly," VenDell muttered. "All these beautiful bones are going to get crushed."

"Not if we can stop it," Marasi said. "Help Wayne with that Sequence and take down any armed enemies you see. Be careful of our drivers—they're out of uniform but all wearing white shoes."

"Um . . ." VenDell said. "My. Hmm . . . When you say, 'take down,' what precisely do you mean, Miss Colms?"

"Kill?" Marasi said. "Shoot? Maim? Eat? I'm not picky, VenDell."

"Ah, yes, er," he said. "You see, I am *not* much of a fighter. I'm a connoisseur. A good planner. A bearer of deep and important thoughts."

She glared at him.

"I follow the First Contract, Miss Colms," he said. "Like almost all kandra. I cannot kill, or even hurt, a living creature. *Particularly* not a human being."

"MeLaan never had that trouble," Wayne said.

"MeLaan is a miscreant!" VenDell said. "Why do you think she was assigned to you? Only she and TenSoon are capable fighters; the rest of us abhor it! I should, er, get away. And plan. Yes, plan how to respond."

Marasi glanced at Wayne, who was rolling his eyes.

"You're basically indestructible, right?" she said to VenDell. "Like MeLaan?"

"Well, technically. But you see, I—"

"Then get out there," Marasi said, "and draw some fire. Also, if you can manage it, toss me one of those aluminum guns."

"Very well," he said with a deep sigh. "This is the last time I let Harmony convince me—"

He broke off as a short woman rounded the back of the truck, somehow moving at their speed—and then she stepped *into* their speed bubble.

The stout woman wore a bowler hat and held a dueling cane in one hand. "'Ello, lovelies," she said. "What're we doin'? Havin' a meetin'? I like meetin' new folks. Killin' *them* breaks the monotony." She grinned, then leaped for Marasi.

It was such an incongruous experience—no one had *ever* violated one of Wayne's bubbles—that Marasi reacted with embarrassing slowness. Wayne wasn't so inhibited. He grabbed the woman by the arm as she swung, preventing the dueling cane from connecting with Marasi's head.

All three of them fell in a jumble. Wayne ended up with the dueling cane, but the woman scrambled away. She became a blur for a second as she hit the edge of the speed bubble—and then she was crossing the room at normal human speed. A moment later she froze in place, moving sluggishly.

"Damn!" Wayne said. "Another Slider!"

Of course. Someone with Wayne's same power—she could create her own speed bubbles. When she'd moved quickly for a moment, it was because her speed bubble had overlapped with Wayne's, doubling her speed for a split second. But she'd been forced to drop her bubble to keep moving through the room, as Sliders had to take brief breaks in using their powers.

"Wayne," Marasi said, "new plan. I'm going to try to grab my Allomantic grenades. They broke free during that blast earlier. You need to stop the strange version of yourself."

"What?" he demanded. "Because she's a Slider, she's a strange version of me?"

"I agree," VenDell said. "Wayne is already incredibly strange—so a strange version of him would be normal."

"It doesn't matter!" Marasi snapped. "Wayne, deal with the Slider. VenDell, distract the Coinshot. Ready?"

"Ready," Wayne said.

"Not ready!" VenDell said.

"Drop the bubble!" Marasi said, already leaping forward.

Wayne complied, and the sound of the room hit her in a cacophony. Men scrambling for weapons and starting to fire. Screams and shouts of pain. Constables trying to organize themselves—a dozen different voices giving conflicting orders.

Marasi tackled Captain Blantach—who had barely reached her feet—pushing her behind another of the trucks. The Sequence's shots hit the floor, tossing up chips of concrete, barely missing the woman.

Blantach scrambled to her feet in surprise, then nodded in thanks to Marasi, who already had her back to the truck. It was the one she'd ridden into the building—but Moonlight was nowhere to be seen.

Wayne tackled the Slider a moment later. VenDell hopped out from behind the fallen truck and began waving his hands. "Look at me! Defenseless! And a traitor! Ha! I'm going to tell the constables everything!"

He took a shot straight to the head.

"Rusts!" Captain Blantach shouted, finally putting it all together. "They have an *Allomancer*!"

Marasi sighed. "Can you organize a resistance, Captain!" she shouted over the increasing din. "The weapons at the top of each box in these trucks are real, and all of the vehicles are plated to provide cover!"

"Right, then," Blantach said, turning and waving toward the eastern wall of the room. "Constables! To me! We—"

The truck they were hiding behind lurched. Marasi barely leaped away in time as a *second* powerful Steelpush shook the room. The warehouse walls rattled, wood breaking and nails ripping free. Men and women who had found weapons were again shoved backward.

And the truck Marasi had been using for cover was *thrown* away like it had been drop-kicked. It crashed out onto the street, tumbling end over end, spilling boxes that shattered into weapons. Rusts!

It narrowly missed Blantach, who had already been on the move toward the snarl of constables and thugs. Many of them had been knocked to the ground.

Now that Marasi's cover was gone, she saw the Sequence shake an aluminum flask, then unscrew it and take a drink. *More metals,* Marasi realized. If she remembered correctly, every time the Sequence used duralumin he would need to restore his reserves.

As the Sequence finished drinking, a figure with a bullet hole in the forehead tackled him. VenDell was, at the very least, trying.

"Organize the constables!" Marasi shouted to Blantach, then ran for the gaping open front of the warehouse. Somewhere in the debris was her metals belt—with her grenades. Those had to be her best chance at stopping a superpowered Allomancer.

On her way, she passed an incredible sight: Wayne and the other Slider fighting.

Wayne leaped toward the Slider in a sudden burst of speed—but dropped his bubble in midair. She tossed hers up, catching them both, and the two became a blur of swinging dueling canes and frantic motion. The speed bubble dropped and they split apart, rounding each other— before speeding up and clashing again, so fast that Marasi couldn't even make out their blurs.

Rusts. *Stay focused,* Marasi thought. She dodged out of the front of the warehouse and scanned the debris—ignoring the sorry truck that lay upside down nearby, one tire spinning.

There, she thought, leaping to grab her metals belt, which was peeking from beneath a broken box. She yanked it out and fished inside a pouch, but the latch had broken open and two of the grenades had spilled free. She only had one.

A floppy body flew past and slammed into the overturned truck. It slumped and hit the ground, then rolled a mangled face toward her on a broken neck. "I have been defeated," VenDell said, words slurred by the broken jaw. "I am billing you for these bones."

"Don't be a baby," she said, and immediately started burning cadmium. The box buzzed in her fingers, charging up.

She dashed into the room to find that Blantach had gathered a group of constables—both Marasi's and her own—behind the cover of several overturned trucks. Many of the gangsters were grouped at the rear of the chamber near the Sequence. They were arming themselves with weapons from the back rooms, it seemed, and others were pulling out riot shields.

Wayne and his foe were still blurs. The Sequence had risen into the air, hovering on a Steelpush. Bullets bent around him, striking the wall, unable to hit directly. Rusts. If he could do that, he was far more experienced with his powers than the Cycle Marasi had fought. At least he couldn't do those mega-Pushes without harming his own people.

Marasi dashed in, low, and crouched up against one of the overturned trucks. She set the timer on her grenade and watched for a moment when the Sequence was turned. Hopefully he'd rely upon his powers to deflect bullets, and wouldn't see her grenade.

Unfortunately, the Sequence glanced in her direction as she hurled the grenade. He barely managed to Push it away, and it detonated near the far wall, not catching anyone. He caught her eye from up there, then shot a coin her direction. She barely ducked under cover in time. Rusts. He could move this truck at any moment.

No, she thought. *He'd need an anchor as heavy.* That was why the Sequence had been doing those powerful, all-direction Pushes. He could Push with equal force in every direction and stabilize himself. He couldn't move a specific truck unless he could Push *backward* against something equally heavy.

That was little comfort when a count of her people showed many bleeding as they hid behind cover. Several were down, immobile. Plus, their enemy was regrouping . . . it gave her a bad feeling. What kind of gangsters tried to *outgun* the constables?

The kind who are heavily armed, Marasi thought. *And think they can win. We shouldn't be fighting. Not this way.*

Gunshots echoed in the room, and bullets *banged* on metal and stone.

"We have to retreat," she said. She signaled to Kellen, one of her lieutenants. "We need to set up covering fire and organize a retreat! We're out through that opening."

"Retreat?" Kellen said, sliding closer. "But the enemy!"

"We're officers of the law," Marasi said, "not soldiers. I'm not going to perpetuate a full-on battle in the middle of a city! Mission is a bust. Time to get out."

Kellen thought for a moment, then nodded. "You're right," the woman said. "What do you want from me?"

"Gather the others and help the wounded. I'll coordinate with the Bilming group, then set up a distraction. Which truck has the real explosives?"

"Number six!"

"Wayne's? Who decided *that*?"

"Ruin, apparently," Kellen said. "Hadn't thought about it myself."

They broke. Marasi slipped her handgun from the holster on her metals belt, then dodged across the open space to truck number six, where Blantach was taking shelter. Remarkably it hadn't been toppled, though Marasi didn't think trying to drive out would be wise. Not when the Sequence had the power to overturn vehicles.

"We're going to retreat," Marasi said to Blantach. "You with us?"

"Rusts *yes*," Blantach said. "I feel like I opened a picnic basket and found a nest of hornets. Who *are* these people?"

"They're the ones trying to undermine our civilization," Marasi said. She slapped the truck. "We have explosives inside this one. I'm going to toss some at the enemy to cover our retreat."

"Give me a minute," Blantach said. "I'll get my people ready to join you. We have wounded."

"So do we," Marasi said. "Hopefully the explosion will give us enough time."

Marasi took a deep breath, then pulled open the door of the truck and scrambled inside. There she was able to open the panel between the cab and the cargo area and slip into the back. It was dark in here, but she knew the box with the explosives would be at the rear—ready to show off on delivery.

She located a few conventional grenades by touch inside the box. And what she hoped was a firebomb, which would be clay and liquid, immune to Pushes.

Worries chased her as she squeezed back into the cab, then ducked low, counting on the plating in the passenger door to protect her from gunfire. The more she considered it, the worse she liked their position.

If we run, he'll do another of those powerful all-out Pushes, she thought. *We'll be ducking out the doors while trucks roll over us.*

But what else could she do? She slipped out of the truck with her explosives. Kellen and Blantach nodded to her, ready for the retreat. The warehouse was alive with gunfire, but on their side it was only a few constables keeping the enemy distracted while the rest helped the wounded.

Time for—

The Sequence dropped from the air, landing directly in the middle of the four trucks they were using as cover. Then he Pushed—two trucks on each side—shoving the vehicles out of the way with an incredible Steelpush.

In an instant, their cover was gone. The collection of beleaguered constables found themselves completely exposed, hauling the wounded to their feet. At the other end of the room, the gangsters had built a little fortification out of sandbags—and now one of them snapped a large multi-barrel rotating machine gun onto a tripod. Military grade, liquid cooled and chain fed, with bullets longer than a person's palm. Those had been developed in case of a Malwish invasion, and were illegal to smuggle out of Elendel.

The full extent of how outgunned they were struck Marasi right then. The room fell strangely silent, though she thought she heard glass shatter somewhere. A part of her mind registered the sound, but she focused on that machine gun. She stood at the head of the constables, staring directly at the barrel. Realizing what was about to happen.

She'd brought barely armed police to a battlefield.

The machine gun started up with a ripping percussive sound, and spat a concentrated stream of bullets straight at Marasi and the others.

Then those bullets stopped in the air.

Then immediately went soaring *backward* toward the enemy fortification, hitting sandbags and shields and making the gangsters cry out in surprise. The machine gun cut off, and the warehouse fell silent for a moment. Unnerved, Marasi glanced over her shoulder—to find Waxillium Ladrian standing just behind her, mistcoat tassels flaring as he turned and aimed a pistol right over her shoulder. He fired with a single *crack* of gunpowder.

The shot drilled straight through the viewfinder on the machine gun and sent the man who had been firing it to the ground, a bullet through the eye.

"Sorry I'm late," Wax announced to the crowd. "Had to wait for gunfire to lead me to you. Shall we carry on, then?"

24

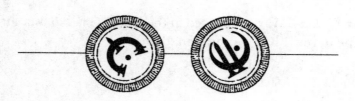

Fighting someone in a fair way was completely unfair, Wayne decided. He connected with his dueling cane—which made a nice resonant crack against the cheater's skull. She went down, but rolled and was back up in a second, grinning as the wound on her head healed—a little trickle of blood running down her now-pristine skin.

Of course they'd given her the ability to heal. Marvelous. Just rusting marvelous.

She became a blur, and he barely erected his own speed bubble in time to catch sight of her to the left. He crossed his canes to block her strike. Then he started swinging.

He pummeled her on one side as she did the same to him on the other side. Rusting Ruin and rusting hell! That *smarted.* And it made about as much sense as drinking the expensive whiskey once you were already drunk. Both of them backed off, wincing—but tapping their metalminds to heal.

"Harmony's holy missing bits, woman," he said, shaking his bruised arm. "You're annoying."

"You're annoying," she said. "You're . . . yoer . . ."

"Stop trying to get my accent!" Wayne snapped.

"Can you say 'my' again?" she asked, tossing her dueling cane up in a little spin and catching it.

Rusting.

Cheating.

Woman!

Wayne had gotten his powers the fair way. By being born with them through pure luck. She'd gone and stolen hers from other folks. That was *absolutely* cheating. Everybody knew there was things you could take and things you couldn't. Wax's unused pocket watch? Fair game. The watch Lessie had given him? Off-limits.

People's souls? *Way* off-limits.

The two circled one another, ignoring the rest of the chaos in the room. He did stop time as something hit near him—a bullet scraping the side of a truck—and he saw the sparks drop in slow motion. But Marasi and the conners would have to deal with the blokes with guns. Wayne had a very-much-not-at-all-clone-of-him to deal with.

She was grinning as he launched forward, swinging. Yes, she could heal if he hit her, but a person could only heal so many times before running out of stored health. He had to keep hitting and hope she ran out before he did.

She dodged away this time.

"Oi!" Wayne said. "Stand still."

"Oi . . ." she replied. "Oiiii . . ."

"Stop that!"

She danced back, smiling. "I've been waiting for this for years," she said—her accent fading away. "Planning, preparing. I was *built* for you, Wayne. Aren't you honored? I was *made* to kill *you!*"

"Ah! Do you hafta be *weird* too?"

"Once I kill you, I will wear your hat and carry your scent. It's all I'm lacking."

He stopped in place as she grinned at him. So. Rusting. Weird. She then turned, and her face fell. "What's *he* doing here?"

Wayne edged over to see what she had. And . . . rusts, *finally.* The hero had arrived. Wax stood there like Ruin himself, tassels swirling around him, protecting the constables and firing wantonly into the enemy ranks.

The cheater was as good as defeated, now that Wax was here. All was right in the world.

Course, Wax was busy at the moment, and would need help. So Wayne bull-rushed the cheater, rammed his elbow into her gut—and felt something sharp in her arm when he did. Her metalminds maybe? Or the spike? Well then. Now that Wax was here, they could do a Two-Faced Special. Except with only Wayne, because Wax needed to shoot some folks.

When the cheater tried to throw Wayne off, he twisted and let her lurch into position. Then he reached around from behind her, took his dueling cane in two hands, and pulled it up under her chin. With a grunt, she began battering at him, but that only threw her off balance.

In a moment Wayne had her on the ground, one knee against her back, dueling cane pulled up and choking her. He'd been in this situation himself, and it was not fun—feeling your metalminds bleed dry as you were forced to heal from suffocation.

She struggled in a frenzy. The world around them slowed and sped up in spurts as she panic-activated her powers. But for all her skill with the canes, she'd skipped basic wrestling techniques. Someone who knew what they were doing could have thrown him.

He shook his head, disappointed. "You can't skip wrestling holds, mate," he told her. "If you want to brawl properly, you've *got* to know how to win on the ground."

She responded with grunts, which was *much* better than before. He was lucky Wax had shown up. Wayne had been up against the wall before the hero arrived.

A figure in fine clothing dropped beside them. "Getruda," he said to the woman, "I'm disappointed in you." Then he pointed a gun at Wayne's head.

Right, then. Wayne let go and ducked away. He dodged into a roll—because who doesn't like a nice finishing roll—and came out of it with a speed bubble in place, sheltering him and Marasi, who had been seeing to one of the wounded.

"Hey," he said, puffing. "Things are looking up, eh?"

"We should still pull out," Marasi said. "This isn't what we're trained for."

"Shame to leave when we're winning though," Wayne said. He nodded behind him. The Sequence was pointing toward the way out—mid-order—and the cheater was on her feet, running in that direction.

"Are we?" Marasi said. She looked down at Mathingdaw—the wounded constable—who had her eyes shut tight, grimacing from the pain of a bullet hole in her leg.

"If Wax deals with that Coinshot we are," Wayne said. The enemy ranks were in chaos as their men tried to hide.

"They have at least a few aluminum bullets," Marasi said, pointing to the side. Indeed some bullets—moving ever so slowly through the air—were ignoring Wax's Pushes.

"Why so few though?" Wayne said. "Miles Hundredlives had tons of aluminum equipment."

"This group planned to be caught today," she said. "I'm convinced of it. They were going to let Blantach's constables take them, rather than raise suspicion by stopping the investigation."

"That's a leap in logic," Wayne said. "But you're often right about this sorta thing. They wouldn't want much aluminum to be taken. Departments have a habit of meltin' it down for the money."

Wayne glanced toward Wax, who stood out in front. Frozen as he pointed with three fingers at a passing bullet. He seemed to be . . . guiding it to the side.

Nah. That was a bit much, even for Wax.

"My gut says," Wayne replied, "that if we hold out this lot will scatter. See, they already got a newsworthy incident by fightin' us, and there's not much more to gain. But we have wounded, and it'd be tough to pull out."

Marasi nodded. "All right then. We hold position. So long as Wax chases off that Coinshot."

"Dropping the bubble."

"Go."

He dropped it. Wax continued his spin, and rusts . . . the bullet he'd been pointing at *seemed* to go straight for one of the gangsters trying to sneak up on the constables' position.

"Wax!" Marasi shouted. "We can handle these. But I need that Coinshot dealt with!"

Wax glanced at her, then nodded and fired at the Coinshot, who dodged into the air. The man launched straight up and smashed through the ceiling out into the city.

Wax followed, soaring through a broken skylight.

As the two vanished, the cheater ran out the front doors. The smarter gangsters realized what was up and ducked out any way they could. Wayne leaped out in front to draw fire, and Marasi scrambled to the side of the room. He wondered why until her grenade froze a small group of enemies.

The rest of this was cleanup; the real fight had moved to the sky. *Wait,* Wayne thought. He put up a speed bubble so two nearby wounded could crawl into the back of a truck for shelter. *Did anyone warn Wax that the Coinshot can do those crazy super-Pushes?*

Hmm. Well, Wayne supposed his friend would figure it out soon enough.

25

Wax darted into the air and felt a sudden moment of disconnect. He'd flown through Elendel so often that he expected to see its sights. This city—with its round layout, elevated train, and huge warships in the port—was disorienting. He had been here before, and knew about the strange design of the buildings, no two the same. But from up here, he could see they were arranged in an artistic pattern. Too orderly, too perfect, too balanced. Like a child's model of a city.

The enemy Coinshot bounded away toward the perimeter of the city, and Wax gave chase with a few Steelpushes. His opponent was talented, maybe even a true Coinshot, augmented by Hemalurgy. He expertly Pushed off the buildings they passed, when newer Coinshots always looked for anchors—like cars—directly beneath them, and forgot about those behind.

Still, Wax managed to gain on the man by anticipating where he would Push. Wax raised Vindication. He didn't want to kill the Coinshot—they needed answers—but perhaps a hit in the leg or arm would—

The man suddenly *blasted* into the air. The car below *crumpled* as if it had been stomped flat, and Wax winced for the poor people inside. The Coinshot launched high into the sky, swift as a bullet, difficult to track against the blinding sun.

Wax landed in a scramble on a nearby rooftop. Rusting *hell*. That had been . . .

Duralumin. Damn. It had only been a matter of time before he faced an enemy with this strength, but he'd merely read of those powers. Never faced them. This threw out Wax's every understanding of how to duel with another Coinshot. How did you fight someone who could launch himself a mile into the air with a single Push?

Same way you fight anyone, Wax thought. *With skill and wit.*

If Wax's memory was right, the man would need to drink a new vial each time he used the power. Wax made his way to another rooftop, where he'd stowed his pack before joining the fight. Here he grabbed an extra pouch of aluminum bullets and dropped the Steel Survivor, as it was loaded with conventional rounds. He raised Vindication, fully aluminum herself, and loaded with aluminum cartridges. The only other metals he had on him were the vials Harmony had sent, inside his belt sheath, which was also lined with aluminum.

He'll try to take me from above, Wax thought, scanning the sky. Sure enough, gunfire came from up there. The enemy had an aluminum weapon too, but Wax was able to leap over the side of the building to dodge. As he fell, he Pushed in through an upper window, landing in an apartment.

The room was empty. So if Wax could slide over to a window in another room, he could maybe trap the enemy by—

The entire apartment wall caved in, torn to pieces by the metal girders beneath the stonework. A wave of debris crashed into Wax and pushed him back against the far wall. He groaned, rubble tumbling around him, and caught sight of motion through the newly ripped-open wall.

The Coinshot bounded up, holding an aluminum flask for restoring metals, gun in his other hand. He'd caused a similar amount of destruction in the building across the street, which he'd used as an anchor for his terrible Push. A flask was clever; assuming he had it well saturated with his metals, he could take a swig each time he used duralumin.

Wax ducked behind some rubble as the man fired, the stone popping with sprays of white dust as bullets hit. Debris crunched underfoot and streamed off Wax's body as he took a few unaimed shots to drive the enemy away. It worked, but *Ruin.*

Wax shoved through the debris on shaky feet, stepping out into the hallway of the apartment building. He hid here for a moment, lightly burning steel to reveal sources of metal around him so he could judge the size of the rooms in the surrounding apartments. He quietly reloaded—and slipped a metal vial from his belt to quickly restore his reserves.

As aluminum had dropped in price—from extravagant to merely expensive—people had started to use it more and more. Like the sheath on Wax's belt. But that flask his enemy held, that was better. Wax's vials would be briefly vulnerable as he pulled them out to drink, whereas—

A bullet drilled through the wood of the wall and nearly hit Wax in the head. He dropped down, cursing, and waved away the confused bystanders who had begun peeking out of their apartments. Another bullet followed, again nearly hitting him. The Coinshot was firing them from outside, and Pushing them through the wood. But how was he seeing Wax? He should be invisible in here . . .

Idiot, Wax thought, extinguishing his steel. The enemy must have a spike that let him use bronze to sense when someone was using Allomancy nearby. Wax ducked a little farther along the hallway, and no more bullets came in through the wall. Perhaps the Coinshot would think him dead?

Assuming he's a natural Coinshot—which might be the case, given his skill—he's got one spike for bronze and one for duralumin. At least. A human body could hold up to three spikes without exposing it to Harmony's influence and direct control. But Marasi claimed the enemy had found a way to bypass that limit somehow. Perhaps it was Harmony's blindness.

People continued filling the hallway behind, despite Wax's urgings. Many gathered around the broken apartment, gawking. Too many civilians. Wax couldn't stay here. He reached the end of the hallway, opened the window with a solid kick, slipped out, and dropped—using his Feruchemy to decrease his weight so he wouldn't hit too hard.

Immediately, the enemy Coinshot appeared on a nearby roof and began shooting.

Wax scrambled around a corner and stopped filling his metalmind—which these days he wore embedded deep in his skin. A change he'd made, with the help of surgeons, after the events surrounding the Bands of Mourning. A person's body acted like aluminum, protecting things like metalminds from interference.

Then again, the stories said that with enough power, an Allomancer could ignore that. The Ascendant Warrior had done it. Rusts. At any rate, the man had appeared soon after Wax tapped a metalmind. He'd seen Wax's *Feruchemy* with his bronze, something only the very rarest of practitioners could do. How skilled was this man?

If he's watching for me to activate my abilities, Wax thought, *let's use that.*

He moved around the back of the building and found a drainage grate beside the street. Wax gave it a single flared Push, popping him up in the air, but immediately cut off to soar upward by momentum. As most Coinshots would sustain long Pushes as they flew, this single short one might make it appear that Wax was still on the ground.

The Push threw Wax up a good twenty feet, where he grabbed the side of the building just below the roof and clung to a stonework formation. He hung there, still hoping to take his opponent alive.

Feet scraped the rooftop above, and a shadow shifted. With a deep breath, Wax Pushed himself upward so he sprang up right in front of his enemy. A quick Push behind sent Wax slamming into the man, bringing them both down in a heap on the rooftop.

Using the element of surprise, Wax—kneeling on top of his enemy—punched the man's wrist to make him drop his pistol. Then he grabbed the fellow by the vest and raised his fist. By sticking close, he wouldn't have to worry about potential speed bubbles—and Wax had no Pushable metal on his person. It was possible the fellow had pewter for strength. A few punches across the face should be enough to determine that.

Wax pulled his enemy up and began laying into him. And damn, maybe he was excited to be fighting again, but the blows didn't seem to hurt Wax's knuckles as much as they once had.

The enemy scrambled for his gun in a panic, but Wax kept punching. There was a certain disorientation that struck the first time a fellow got punched, particularly in the head. It was a kind of disbelief, a stunned irreconcilability. Wax remembered his first time—the way his mind couldn't bridge its past experiences with its new painful, fist-to-face existence. The man's panic rose, and Wax realized his miscalculation a second later—as the enemy unleashed an explosive Steelpush downward, against the nails and iron rods in the rooftop.

Wax and the Coinshot were flung upward in a roar of wind and a sudden burst of g-forces. Wax managed to hang on to the Coinshot for the first part of the ride. But before they reached the peak of their ascent, the man put his hand to Wax's face, and Wax felt a sudden coldness.

His metal reserve vanished.

The Coinshot had another power. He was a Leecher, with the ability to drain other people's Allomancy. He smiled, meeting Wax's eyes—and Wax scrambled to grab a vial from the pouch on his metals belt. The Coinshot then grabbed Wax's metals belt in one hand and *kicked* the two of them apart. The belt, made to break away if someone Pushed on the metals inside, ripped free, and since Wax had his hand in it, the open latch meant the vials were flung out into the air.

But Wax had managed to grab one vial. His steel gone, a hundred feet in the air, he raised the vial to his lips—but only got the briefest taste of the liquid inside before the vial exploded. A shot from the enemy toward Wax's face barely missed—but hit the vial, shattering it.

Wax immediately increased his weight, and the strange way that affected his momentum meant his upward speed slowed to a crawl. The next shot passed through the air right over his head. A second after he crested his rise and started falling, he switched to filling his metalmind to instantly boost his downward speed—but made sure not to get so light that wind resistance would counteract that. More shots passed over his head as the Coinshot had trouble predicting his motion. Wax fell in a tumble, and despite the mayhem—despite the way his guts were in a knot and his mind dizzy from the sudden ejection—he realized one thing.

Without metals, he was dead. If he couldn't change his trajectory, the next bullets would strike him as the Coinshot adjusted his aim. Falling slowly wasn't enough. He reached for metals inside of him, and managed to find the faintest bit of steel from the sip. He used it to shove himself in the air, Pushing on the spire of a building, dodging the next shots from above.

Then it was gone. Nothing but rushing wind. Then he looked up and saw one of his vials tumbling downward, and he momentarily increased his weight once again to slow his fall and draw even with the vial. He stretched out his arm, reaching for it, but it was inches away, just beyond his fingertips . . .

Snap. The vial fell into his palm. Wax spun in the air, downing half the vial. Like a burst of light, his steelsight returned. He passed between buildings as he fell and Pushed himself, haphazardly, to the side. Bullets from above ripped through the air around him a moment later—the ground approaching at a frightening pace. At the last moment Wax threw the half-full vial beneath him and *Pushed.*

The vial hit the ground and exploded, but the metal inside was enough of an anchor. He slowed and hit the ground in a skid, mistcoat tassels flying around him. His heart thundering, he ripped his gun from its holster and pointed upward.

But the sky was empty. The man had decided to cut his losses and flee.

Wax had landed in a city square with decorative paving stones and a few impressive statues—designed in a strange chunky and blockish art style. His drop had drawn . . . well, more than a little attention. It seemed he had interrupted a dedication ceremony for a new building, for a journalist was there with an evanotype stand for taking pictures.

One flash of light later, and Wax had the sinking realization that he would be top-of-the-fold news in the afternoon broadsheets. Delightful. He stood up, calming himself, and took cover beneath an awning just in case. Then, as he was considering what to do next, a sleek black car rolled up and Hoid the coachman, of all people, popped out—wearing a chauffeur's cap and white gloves. What was *he* doing here?

"Your carriage, sir," Hoid said, gesturing.

"How on Scadrial did you find me?" Wax asked.

Hoid cocked an eyebrow at the gathering crowd. "Pardon, Lord Ladrian, but you *do* create quite a spectacle. It's not terribly difficult to track you."

Well, that was fair. As the crowd started chattering, Wax could see the appeal of slipping into the car and driving off. But the others were still fighting for their lives.

"Thanks, Hoid," he said. "But Wayne and Marasi need me." He launched into the air, drawing even more attention—and a second flash of light from the evanotype machine.

26

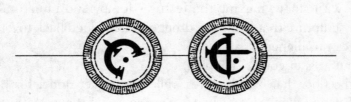

Marasi reluctantly agreed to let the local constables handle cleaning up the site—though she'd managed to retrieve two of her Allomantic grenades—and imprisoning the Set members they'd managed to capture. She disliked the idea, as it would possibly mean the captives ended up in the Set's hands. But there wasn't much she could do about that at the moment. Her wounded officers were a more pressing concern.

Beyond that . . . well, the moment Blantach and her people had arrived, the entire mission had become a huge mess. Which was how—three hours after rolling into Bilming—she found herself with Wayne, VenDell, and Wax in a room of the Bilming Constabulary headquarters. She'd seen to her people in the hospital, and was sitting with the casualty report.

Two dead constables. Rusts, it hurt to read their names. This was a disaster.

For now though, she tried to keep her mind on their predicament. "So you're saying," she said, "that Harmony is *blind*?"

Wax nodded, his eyes distant as he stood nearby, staring at the wall. "He said he'd send us what help he could. But he was frightened, Marasi. Legitimately frightened. And given what Steris and I uncovered . . . I worry our enemies are close to a weapon. Dangerously close."

He glanced at her, then fell silent. They didn't want to say too much, in case they were being observed. No one was at the door, but they could listen in on this little room in other ways. Wan yellow walls and a free-hanging light bulb gave the place an intentionally bleak air. She bet they used it for interrogations.

The Bilming officers hadn't locked the door—they wouldn't dare—but Wax and the others had been forced to surrender their weapons. And when they'd been dropped off in here, the implication had been clear: *Don't try anything.*

Though they had been given four chairs, only Marasi sat—at the back of the room. Wax paced in front of the door. VenDell sat on the floor by the wall, looking exhausted. He'd stitched up his bones, holding them in place with sinew, making the features lumpy and unnatural. Like a ceramic sculpture that had been dropped, then glued back together with the pieces misaligned.

Wayne was, of course, napping.

On the floor, hat over his eyes, rolled-up jacket under his head as a pillow. Rusting man. She wished it were so easy for her. With two dead, she felt her confidence crumbling. Cali Hatthew had been a constable for only two years—and had begged to come on this mission. That blood was on Marasi's hands. She thought she'd planned well, but . . .

Wax walked over and squatted down. "Hey," he said, "you all right?"

She shook her head, tapping the casualty report. "The two people who knew anything useful escaped, and I lost two good constables. At least a dozen others have serious wounds, *and* I caused a potential intercity incident. Oh, and the Set will have all their people released, just for an *extra* kick to the shins."

He winced. "Marasi, we're fighting some of the craftiest and most powerful people in the world. We *are* going to be outmaneuvered now and then. You did well, keeping everyone as safe as possible."

"We'd be dead if you hadn't arrived."

"But I did. You're not a killer, Marasi. Not by trade. Your job is to investigate, plan, and enforce the law."

"And your job?" she asked.

He stood up. "I'm Harmony's sword, Marasi. Recently taken off the weapon rack, the dust blown free. Regardless of what happened today, we need to keep working. Because something big *is* happening in this city. Something extremely dangerous. You lost two good people today—but they died trying to prevent the deaths of *millions.*"

She nodded, rubbing her temples to try to banish her headache. If he and Steris were right . . . if the enemy was trying to sneak a bomb into Elendel . . .

"All right," she said, trying to focus. "We need leads. What do we do now that the Sequence escaped? Where do we look?"

"Working on that," he said. "The man I fought was spiked. So was the Cycle you killed, as was the woman Wayne fought. Each of those spikes requires the death of a Metalborn."

"The kidnappings?" Marasi asked, her stomach turning.

Over the last ten years, the Set's primary activity—the one that had first drawn Wax and Marasi's attention—had been a series of kidnappings of women with strong Allomantic genetic lines. Research over the last few years had proven they weren't alone. Others, both men and women, had been vanishing—mostly from the Roughs, where such disappearances weren't reported. Always Metalborn, or with Metalborn in their family lines.

Wax and Marasi's worries about why had been disturbing. Now, to find members of the Set with access to so many powers . . .

"We tried following the kidnappings, Wax," she said. "Dead ends, every one. Are we *sure* that Harmony didn't see anything about this? Maybe before he was blinded?"

"He can be cryptic, even to us," VenDell said softly from where he sat by the wall. He glanced up at them, his broken face moving strangely. "But I don't think he knows where those people went. When we were hunting for them, we wondered why Harmony didn't feed us more information. Why he didn't look into the secret parts of the world and tell us. I think he's been unable to see details for some time. But he's been . . . concealing his disability from us."

The kandra sighed, suddenly looking tired—his skin going transparent and faintly green. "And . . . there's more, Waxillium. He tries to hide it, but I think . . . something is wrong with Harmony. I see a dark shadow behind him."

"What good is it having God on your side," Marasi said, folding her arms, "if he doesn't do anything to help?"

"He *did* do something to help," Wax replied. "He sent us. A lesson he keeps trying to teach me."

"I will contact him," VenDell said, "and request further aid. But Waxillium is right . . . Constable Colms, we *are* his attempt to do something."

Wax turned to the side, his expression again distant. He hadn't told her everything that had happened to him years ago. She thought maybe Wax had *died* for a moment. Before she'd found him broken in that cold, forgotten shrine. He'd met with Harmony.

Now Wax talked like *this* sometimes. With an authority regarding religious matters that she hadn't heard from priests.

The door opened, and Captain Blantach walked in. She'd changed to a clean uniform, and had obviously run a comb through her short blonde hair, but she still appeared frazzled. Perhaps because of the man who walked in behind her.

Oh hell, Marasi thought. *She brought the mayor.*

27

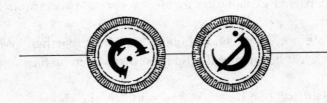

Wax sighed. This had just become a political matter rather than a jurisdictional one. Granted, the entire day had been heading that direction like a galloping stagecoach with no driver. He glanced at Marasi, who nodded. He should take the lead here.

He stepped forward to meet the lord mayor of Bilming, Lord Gave Entrone. A man that Wax had encountered on several occasions now—each more repulsive than the last. And that was saying something, since at their first interaction Entrone had insulted Steris to her face.

Gave had come up in the world, outgrowing his hometown of New Seran. Two years ago he'd landed in Bilming—at the very center of Outer Cities politics—and had somehow proven himself to be the exact sort of person they wanted "standing up" to tyrannical Elendel.

Today he was dressed in formal wear, and even checked his cufflinks as they entered—no doubt to show off the sparkling diamonds set into the wood. Slicked-back black hair, a chin you could use to cut the tops off tin cans. And, of course, his characteristic smug smile.

Lord mayor of Bilming was an important position—probably the most important one outside of Elendel. Which meant Wax had to be careful not to insult him. This would be a delicate conversation.

"Oi!" Wayne said, sitting up. "Hey, Wax! Somebody done sewn a sack of dicks together and made a person! It's even walking!"

The room fell silent. Then VenDell snickered.

"Are you going to apologize for that, Ladrian?" Gave asked.

"Oh!" Wayne said, heaving himself to his feet. "It's Gave Entrone. Sorry, Lord Mayor! I mistook you for something else. Though the resemblance, it's downright uncanny, it is."

"Wayne?" Wax said.

"Yeah, boss?"

"Please stop helping."

"Got it."

Wax's and Entrone's eyes locked. Wax was certain the man had ties to the Set. A partial explanation for his exceptional rise through Outer Cities politics.

"So, here we are," Gave said, rubbing his hands together. "Waxillium Ladrian. The great lawman of the Roughs. Involved in an *illegal* operation in my city!"

"We have jurisdiction here!" Marasi said. "By the code—"

"Code seventeen of the United Justice Act?" Gave said. "We repealed that, you recall? Three months ago."

"You can't repeal it," Wax said. "You don't have the authority."

"We don't have authority?" Entrone said. "To have a say in the policing of our *own city*? Why, that *is* an arrogant thing to assert, wouldn't you say, Captain Blantach?"

"It's technically true, Lord Mayor," she replied.

"Technically," he said, "one of those dirty maskers from the South could pass a law saying they have 'jurisdiction' here. But what right would they have?" He had walked a circuit of the room and halted in front of Wax. "They aren't one of *our* kind."

"I see what you're doing, Entrone," Wax said softly.

"Do you?" he whispered, getting close enough that Wax could smell the mint on his breath. "Do you *truly* appreciate how *delicious* this is? You worked so hard to prevent that stupid bill from passing—and yet here you are, in my hands. By *our* laws you're a criminal, in violation of a *dozen* different codes. Your only fallback is to ignore our authority—the very thing you have spent *months* arguing that we deserve. I have you, Ladrian. You're mine."

"The governor will never stand for this," Marasi said.

Obviously, that was what Entrone wanted. He *wanted* Wax to go crawling back to Elendel for a pardon. And the Supremacy Bill? Well, by insisting Elendel had authority to override local authority, Wax would prove himself a hypocrite. That would give more fuel to the war between Elendel and the Outer Cities. Exactly what this man wanted.

Entrone smiled. Showing no teeth. Just two smug lips that would look *so* much better split and bloodied. Wax restrained himself with effort.

Ruin, I hate this man, he thought.

"Perhaps," VenDell said, standing up, "you might be willing to listen to a . . . higher authority, Lord Mayor." The kandra made his skin turn fully transparent, showing the bones underneath—the skull behind his face, cracked and stuck together with sinew. It was an eerie sight, particularly since VenDell chose to leave the eyeballs normal—and they seemed to float in the jelly that his face had become.

"Ah!" Entrone said. "One of the puppets! Look how it tries to frighten us, Captain Blantach!"

"Er, yes," VenDell said. "I'm an emissary and representative of Harmony."

"I'm not Pathian," Gave said, with a wave of his hand. "Why should I care?"

"About God?" VenDell asked.

"Not my god," Gave replied. "My god is industry, progress, and the indomitability of the human soul. Not some priest who managed to slurp up some juice left by a long-dead entity. Oh! Look, Captain Blantach! It pretends to be shocked by my words!"

"He doesn't pretend," Wax said. "VenDell is a person like any of us. Merely a little more . . . malleable."

"Oh, Ladrian," Entrone said, then had the audacity to pat Wax on the arm. "So easily fooled. Kandra are animals. Puppets. Why, they aren't even really alive. They're mistwraiths *pretending* to be people, and I fail to see how I'm to be *intimidated* by a talking piece of slime that . . ."

He trailed off as he noticed that Wayne, subtly, had edged up close to him.

". . . a piece of slime," Gave continued, "that . . . er . . ."

"Keep goin'," Wayne said, his eyes alarmingly wide. "Keep insultin' my friends. *Do it.*"

Entrone backed away, looking thoroughly unnerved. "You have one hour," he said to Wax, "until I formally announce we're pressing charges. Either break out of here—and perhaps shoot some officers of the law—or call your governor and beg for his help. I'm having a radio box delivered to you."

He retreated in a rush, trying to watch Wayne at the same time. He ended up leaving Blantach behind.

"What a knob," Wayne said, dropping the creepy wide-eyed act.

"I . . . apologize," Blantach said. "I'm afraid I had no choice but to call him."

"It's fine, Blantach," Marasi said. "But you *must* understand. You can't throw us in prison—not without risking the fate of the entire Basin. Please listen."

"I'll see if I can . . . work something out." Blantach glanced over her shoulder and into the constabulary office. "But this is out of my hands now, Colms. Next time, *contact* us before you run an operation in our city."

She withdrew, shutting the door—which had a small viewing window at the top. A moment later a guard delivered a radio box, then lingered outside to keep an eye on them.

Wax sighed, turning to the others. He wasn't about to trust a radio delivered into his hands by an enemy.

VenDell's skin had returned to normal shades. The kandra hesitated, then glanced at Wayne. "Did you mean what you said? Am I actually . . . your friend?"

"Sure," Wayne said. "I mean, you're the stuck-up one that we make fun of, but every crew needs one of those." He pointed at Wax, then Marasi, then VenDell. "Mine has three. Five if you include Steris, since she counts fer two. But you can never have too many."

"I . . . see," VenDell said, scratching the side of his head.

"Point is," Wayne continued, "*we* can make fun of you because we like you. That's how it works. Anybody else does it, and we ram a dueling cane up a part of them that I can't mention, 'cuz I'm working on my language."

"You are?" Marasi said.

"Yup. Ranette keeps sayin' I need to watch what I say, 'cuz there might be children around. Which is real strange, don't you think? Children are the ones who won't understand what I'm sayin' anyway. So why care if *they* hear?"

Wax turned to the door, his mind racing, trying to think of a way out of the current situation—but a part of him realized it was no use. He could walk out of here and ignore Entrone. But that would add another piece of wood to the fire—stoking civil war. Beyond that, could he continue to investigate in the city without being hounded by constables at every step?

How does the bomb factor into this? Wax thought. *The talk of ashfalls. My sister. What is really going on?*

He might have a way to find answers. He felt inside his belt, which he'd recovered and refilled from his ammo stash—the large duffel he'd brought and hidden on top of a building. In his belt pouch, alongside the metal vials, he felt the earring Harmony had given him.

And the other one. Made of trellium.

Damn it. He was going to have to at least try. He pulled the trellium earring out and slipped it into his ear.

He felt a jolt and a disconnect, like the coach he was riding in had hit a bump. Different from when he talked to Harmony. Then he felt *drawn* toward something powerful. A vibration ran through him, forceful, violent. He gasped, the room fuzzing around him.

Immediately, a familiar voice pierced his mind like a spike to the brain.

Faster. I need this to work.

Telsin. He was hearing his sister speak. He thought he could sense some of her surroundings. She was outside . . . no echo of a room.

Our time runs thin, she continued. *The backup delivery device is too obvious. Too easy to stop. I need the primary working. I need—* The voice hesitated. *I sense something,* she said, then stepped to the side.

Her voice grew louder, focused on him. *Out with it. You fought my brother. I know that part already. It . . . Wait.*

Waxillium? Is that you? Ah . . . It is. I can sense you. Found yourself a trellium earring, did you? Clever. Your idea, or was it that god of yours?

"Hello, Telsin," he whispered. No use trying to lie. She could feel him, as clearly as he felt her. He tried to summon some familial emotion. But right now, he felt only haunted by that voice. It was an echo from a long-lost time. A time he'd left behind, but which wouldn't leave him.

So, you're in Bilming. She sounded amused. *Your arrival made a characteristic amount of noise. Good to see that nothing changes. You never could make anything useful of yourself unless you also made a huge mess for me.*

"Telsin," he said softly, "what are you doing?"

What needs to be done, Brother. As always.

"I . . ."

What could he say? All of his objections felt hollow. "You'll get millions killed"? Six years ago, she'd been willing to let her own people die to achieve her goals. She wouldn't care about the people of Elendel. "You'll betray our people"? She'd been willing to betray *him*. "You're playing with forces beyond your control." That was the sort of thing she liked, always dancing closer to the flame.

What did he hope to accomplish? He should have thought this through. He knew better than to walk into the enemy's den without a plan.

Ah, Wax, Telsin said in his mind. *Still pretending, aren't you? Telling yourself that you're the hero? Where was that hero when our family needed him? Off playing in the Roughs. Running from real responsibility.*

I'll tell you what I'm doing. What needs to be done. This world, and everyone on it, is doomed. Unless I intervene. The same way I had to step up and lead after you ran off. You aren't the hero, Waxillium. You never were. You ran away, like a child who can't stand the rules of the—

He pulled the earring out, breathing heavily.

Rusts. All these years later, and she could still get to him. That had been a terrible idea.

At least, he thought, *I know she's actually what Harmony said. Some kind of avatar for the enemy. And she's tense, urgent. She's on a deadline. She's worried. Because I'm here in the city.*

He considered what she'd been saying, about a "primary delivery device" and a "backup."

He looked around the room, but the others didn't seem to have noticed what he'd done. They were lost in their own thoughts or problems. All but VenDell, who watched him keenly.

Wax wiped his brow with his hand. "You . . . mentioned help, from Harmony?" he asked, his voice hoarse.

"It's close." VenDell turned, glancing at the door. "Oh. Rather, I should say it's here. See for yourself."

Frowning, Wax stepped up to the door and peered through the observation window. The guard was staring toward the front doors of the building.

Where Death had arrived.

The Two Seasons would like to retract our dear editor Kyndlip Ternavyl's comments of two weeks ago, prior to her disappearance, when she compared our beloved mayor to "an irascible boar; no smarter, less attractive, and unable to keep from rolling around in every mire he comes across."

stance with which many Outer City dwellers concur: Representation Before Supremacy. Governor Varlance and his

patted his chest where he'd conspicuously hung his military medals.

(Continued on back.)

LETTER TO THE EDITOR

Once again I must object to our continued allowance of ads from Soonie Industries, manufacturers of the "Soonie Pup," who have also ignored my numerous letters regarding their historically egregious depictions of the Ascendant Warrior's companion as a Terris wolfhound, when scholars have repeatedly demonstrated that modern dog breeds were not yet established in the Days of Ash, and that the Ascendant Warrior's Guardian was not a wolfhound, but in actuality a *wolf dog*.

Grudgingly Yours,
Professor Olin Tober
University of Elendel

GUEST EDITORIAL
by Gemmes Millis, Interim Editor
ENFORCE NOSEBALL BAN!

We see them in every unsown field and vacant lot. Vagrants and layabouts, some of them even our own children, congregating in gangs and "playing" the game of Death himself: noseball. These "players" should be going to school or working in factories! Instead, their mal-aimed balls hit unsuspecting motorists and create road debris. The mayor banned this miscreance months ago, yet the conners don't enforce it. R*st and R*in, some of them even join in! Come to a Rally Against Noseball next Steelday afternoon in Tabret's Park, adjacent to the city center, and join a Cause Worth Fighting For!

"BE SURE TO GET MY CHIN RIGHT!"

VISIT THE BANDS OF MOURNING TEMPLE SITE!

Basin Bill Tours now travels to the locale of Dawnshot's famous showdown. Daily re-enactments starring Wevva Cett-Venture and Penelope Portreau. (Additional hot springs day trip packages now available!)

THESE ARE NOT COINS!

They are dangerous Malwish talismans that must be turned in to the authorities for proper disposal. Keep yourself and your loved ones safe from nefarious Malwish witchcraft. Contact N & N at #42 Sixteenth Street for a generous REWARD.

The Man Who Electrifed Time!
The new novel by Bilming-born working man Schrib Welfor. Available now in all fine bookshops!

HELP WANTED ~ Bendalloy Misting cook for new "quick eats" café. Will pay top boxing plus bonuses and bendalloy stipend for off-work recreation. Great hours! One day off a week plus two days off for Survivorday or Harmontide each year. Apply in person at Kevron's on the corner of 2nd & Nellis.

FOOD DELIVERY ~ Order ahead for on-time meal delivery day or night, rain or mist, from any open food establishment. Our trained Steelrunners avoid traffic by knowing all the highways, byways, and throughways. Submit orders to Vema at Steel Kitchen by noon for next-day service.

WEATHER ~ Chance of fog at Lighthouse Point. Break in thunderstorms, but low mist conditions for two weeks or more. High: 26☿ Low: 17☿

ELARIEL
YEARLY
Spring Salon

Come to our flagship store in the City to see our Terris-inspired designs by up-and-comer Idkwyl Elariel.
OPENS BRASSDAY!

CHOC-O-TONIC
Are you skeptical of other sparkle tonics and their alleged "secret formulas"? Searching for a sparkle tonic with flavor you can identify without hiring a chemist? Search no longer! We flavor our sparkle tonic with only the finest imported Malwish beans, roasted and condensed into an invigorating beverage. Ask for it by name!

DRINK! DELICIOUS
CHOC -O- TONIC
PUT A SPARKLE IN YOUR EYE!

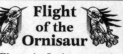

Flight of the Ornisaur

Though I desperately wanted to peek, my regard for my longtime companions compelled me to honor their request, even though the sound of their *merging* was like an octopus kissing a giant slug. For ten minutes.

When I was allowed again to look, the beast before me resembled a featherless version of the paintings of ornisaurs we'd seen at the quarry, with long thin bones and bat-like wings. On either side of the creature's head, where it would normally have had eyes, was KeSun's face on the right and Tabaar's on the left.

"You're absolutely beautiful!" I said, clapping my hands.

"You are an odd one, Miss Sauvage," said the beast from Tabaar's mouth.

They picked me up in a claw and launched from the cliff, the skin of their wings snapping into place like an umbrella canopy.

Below us, the tops of more stone outcroppings materialized against a gradual, soft mist that made it impossible to see where the mists ended and the outcroppings began.

I scanned for signs of Vila. If I were her, I would wait to attack until we entered the mist, so I directed Tabaar-KeSun toward it as I slipped my snake-shaped metal knuckles over my left hand. In my right, I held my umbrella at ready.

We entered the mist, and just as I predicted, Vila's form emerged, arcing toward us until we collided.

"Where's the key!" Vila said.

"Far away from here by now," I replied with a smile.

Vila growled, showing her teeth. What followed was a frenzy of punches and kicks while she tried to hold on to the ornisaur leg. That was to my advantage, though, as Tabaar-KeSun's claw grasped me just tightly enough that I could fight without falling into the abyss.

I beat Vila a few times with the end of my closed parasol, and then, when I had her distracted, I landed a punch with the metal knuckles. As the gold snake met Vila's cheek, I burned chromium

28

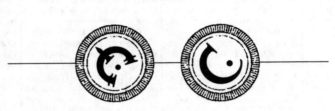

Wax had never seen Death himself, though Marasi had met the creature once. Known as Ironeyes, the ancient Inquisitor had weighty spikes through his eyes, the points jutting out the back of his skull. One of his eye sockets had been crushed during a fight, as recorded in the Words of Founding that Harmony—Sazed—had left. Wax could make out the scars, intermingled with faded tattoos, outlining the eye sockets.

Death wore voluminous black robes and had ghostly skin—looking ill. The hands jutting from his sleeves were so lean they appeared skeletal. Wax had grown accustomed to speaking with beings out of myth; the kandra, even TenSoon, were practically mundane to him these days. But he still felt an unsettling disquiet at seeing Ironeyes. This being was said to escort the souls of the dead to the Beyond.

The entire room outside—filled with desks, constables, and underlings—had grown silent. No one dared turn a page of paperwork; they all stared at that figure silhouetted against the brazen sunlight behind. Something emanated from him. A dread that crushed the soul like a hand around yesterday's broadsheet. A . . .

No, Wax thought. *I do not fear this. I've stared down death already.*

Strangely, the sensation of dread evaporated from him. Had that been . . . emotional Allomancy? It was difficult to recognize in the throes of it, but it appeared obvious in hindsight. Yet this time it didn't affect

Wax as it did everyone else, including Marasi, judging by how pale her face had gone.

Wax took a deep breath, pushed open the door, and strode out past the guard. Wax walked through the center of the room and met up with Ironeyes, who was uncommonly tall. As Wax had always imagined, actually.

"Sword," Death said, focusing spikes upon him. "We need to speak."

Wax gestured into the room with the others, and Death walked past the stunned constables, though one—bearing the shoulder patch of a Seeker—managed to pull out a gun. Not a move Wax would have advised. All Death did was wave absently and Pull the gun across the room to catch it. Then, making it hover between his hands—an incredible feat, the difficulty of which few non-Allomancers would grasp—he flexed. And the gun's barrel *crunched.*

Wax froze. Hell. He'd *never* seen someone do *that* with their powers before. How would you even accomplish it?

Push on the near end, Pull on the far end, he thought. *But damn, the power involved . . .*

The gun dropped to the floor, and as Wax and Death reached the door, they saw that Entrone and Blantach had stepped out of an office, their eyes wide.

"Ah," Ironeyes said, focusing on the lord mayor. "Gave. I never cared much for the members of House Entrone I knew during my mortality."

"I . . ." Entrone said. "This is my prisoner. Who . . ."

"I require privacy," Ironeyes said. "You will return to these mortals their weapons. Once our conference is finished, you will impede their investigation in this city no further."

"I'm not of your religion . . ."

"Death is not a religion," Ironeyes said. "It is a fact."

"But—"

"How would you like to die, mortal?" Ironeyes asked, stepping closer, robes billowing around him. "And when? Quietly? In the night, of a failing heart? Drowning, on one of your new ships as it sinks? Here? Right now? Crushed by the weight of your own stupidity?"

Entrone licked his lips, then whispered, "As you demand, Ironeyes, it shall be done." It appeared that he could indeed be superstitious without being religious.

Wax walked into the room, and Ironeyes swept in after. "Wayne,"

Death said softly, closing the door, "kindly watch the door to make certain we are not observed or listened to."

"Uh, sure," Wayne said, scrambling over to the door and its window. "They're all just standin' out there. 'Cept the few that have fainted. Neat." He glanced at Ironeyes. "That accent of yours . . . real old, *real* interesting . . . I actually kinda got it right."

Death sank down into a chair and seemed to *age* suddenly. Wrinkles sank from the corners of his eyes, crossing his face, and his jowls sagged. He sighed loudly, tipping his metal eyes toward the ceiling. "Lord Ruler," he muttered. "That was a performance, wasn't it? And to think that I was the *reasonable* one in the crew."

Marasi and Wax shared a glance.

"Ironeyes?" Marasi asked. "Are you . . . well?"

"No," he said. "I run low on atium, and so age finally emerges from the shadows. It has always stalked me. Now it senses the kill. I was here in Bilming, seeking answers. They try to re-create the metal, and I thought maybe . . ."

"If you run out . . ." Marasi said, ". . . you die?"

He nodded. "I was going to let it happen. I have lived so much, far longer than my due. But I helped destroy this world—unwillingly, yes, but my weakness led to much sorrow. I swore I would help. And so, I struggle yet to live . . ."

Rusts. Death took a deep breath, and the lines on his face retreated— then regrew when he exhaled. It looked like he was vacillating between decades of age with each breath.

"Trell wants to own this planet," Death whispered. "So your time dwindles, as does mine." He studied Wax with those inscrutable not-eyes. "I've grown too weak to continue hunting those who would destroy this land. My display earlier will get you out of this room, perhaps convince the local constables to leave you alone, but that . . . might be all I can offer."

Wax knelt beside the aging demigod, a thought striking him. "You were in the city, hunting for atium. Why?"

"Because someone here is trying to split harmonium," he explained. "And create the metal again. Though making lerasium would be far more dangerous . . ."

"Do you know what happens?" Marasi asked. "When someone tries to split harmonium?"

Death shook his head.

"An explosion," Wax said. "A *big* explosion. It's what we're trying to stop. Do you have any leads?"

"One, perhaps," Death said, thoughtful. "A man vanished two weeks ago. I only just ran across his name: Tobal Copper. He made some kind of legal disturbance that mentioned splitting harmonium in the months before he disappeared. Finding out what happened to him would have been my next step."

Wax nodded. A lead—a slim one, but still somewhere to start. The way his sister talked . . . it made him feel an increasing urgency.

"Ironeyes?" Marasi asked, stepping over.

"You may call me Marsh," he said softly. "It . . . feels good to hear that name. To remember what I used to be."

"Marsh," she said. "How did you crush that gun?"

"Duralumin," he said absently, "and a lot of practice. Listen, child. Harmony is growing increasingly indecisive. He denies it, but I *see* it. That gives Autonomy—Trell, the god of the outworlders—a chance to move in. She seeks to eliminate us from the stage of galactic politics before we even step onto it, and her followers are already armed with Hemalurgy. You studied the book I gave you?"

"Yes," she said. "And Waxillium practically memorized it." Wax nodded in agreement.

"Your enemy," Death said softly, "has learned how to circumvent one of the most important limitations to Hemalurgy: her agents bear too many spikes. That should open them to Harmony's influence, but it doesn't. Either Harmony is too weak to exploit what they've done, or they've found a way to use Trell's own metal to offset the weakness.

"This is extremely dangerous. So far, I do not believe they've learned the secret to Compounding via Hemalurgy. Identity contamination prevents it; that is our only saving grace. If they could do that . . . or, Lord Ruler . . . if they get atium, or lerasium . . ."

"So . . . what do we do?" Wayne asked from the door.

"What we've always done," Marsh said. "Survive." He looked to Wax again. "The people of Bilming think they are accomplishing so much, building this navy of theirs to threaten Elendel. It is all part of Trell's plan somehow. Be warned. Be careful. She steers them. I've been . . . dull of mind lately, as I try to fight off what is happening to me."

"We'll stop them," Marasi said. "I promise it, Marsh."

Wayne waved to them. A moment later, an attendant arrived with their weapons and equipment. She then withdrew to let them rearm.

"Marsh," Marasi said, slipping a small handgun into her shoulder bag, "have you ever seen a symbol like this?" She quickly sketched three interlocking diamonds in her notepad. They reminded Wax of something. Some architectural designs from around Elendel?

Yes, he thought. *Near the Field of Rebirth.* Actually, it resembled the three-petal shape of a Marewill flower.

"This is my brother's symbol," Marsh said. "He does what he thinks is best. As has always been the case with him. He . . . is not the best at self-reflection, but he *does* want to protect Scadrial. His agents will align with your interests."

"I think I saw through his eyes," Wax said. "Once, years ago. Is he still alive? The Survivor?"

"Alive?" Marsh asked. "It depends, I suppose, on your definition. He's close to alive. How is that?"

"You mean . . . he's a ghost?" Wayne asked.

"After a fashion," Marsh replied. "He's less alive than I am, but perhaps more than other ghosts? It's hard to say. Three of us remain from that original crew. After all this time. Only three. Legs to a tripod, balancing one another. And without one . . . I do not know what would happen."

Wax didn't know what to make of that. Still, it felt good to strap his guns back on, and they had a lead now. A name and, it appeared, permission to leave this office without being chased. He'd take it, even if Death himself was . . .

"I will stay here," VenDell said as they gathered at the door. "I will ensure that Lord Ironeyes is cared for, and look after the constables in the hospital. I . . . do not think I will be of further value to your investigation."

"As you wish," Wax said.

"Just remember what you know, Lord Ladrian," VenDell said. "What you said earlier. Harmony puts people where they need to be, but then they must act. It is his way."

Wax nodded. "Wayne, Marasi—are you ready?"

"I am," Marasi said, slinging her bag over her shoulder.

They looked to Wayne, who put his hands on his hips. "Did either of you know that ghosts was real?"

"Does it matter?" Marasi asked.

"Does it matter if *ghosts* are *real*?" Wayne said. "I think it matters, Marasi. I think it *rusting* does!"

"I'm told it is better to refer to them as Cognitive Shadows," Marsh mumbled.

"Wayne," Wax said, "can we please focus?"

"Fine, fine," he said, sliding his dueling canes into their loops on his belt. "Seems unfair to grouse at a man for getting discombobulated by definitive proof of an afterlife. Dark gods. Death himself dyin'. Rusting ghosts. Guess we gotta keep goin', but after this, I don't wanna see anyone complainin' when I've traded for someone's favorite shoes or whatnot. Hear me?"

Together they marched out through the quiet constabulary office and into the sunlight.

29

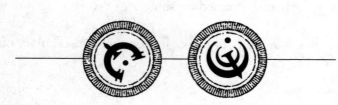

Right, Marasi thought, trying to pull her emotions together. *Conversation with Death. Just another* everyday *conversation with* Death *himself . . .*

She couldn't blame Wayne for feeling out of sorts. But they had to stay focused. Unfortunately, she and the others hadn't even reached the bottom of the constabulary office steps before someone came running down after them. Flushed from exertion—and perhaps stress—Blantach looked a great deal less sure of herself now than she had earlier.

Marasi stepped forward to meet Blantach. "Yes?"

"He's going to send people after you," she said. "As soon as he gets over the shock of what happened in there with . . . you-know-who. I know Lord Entrone. He takes a great deal of pride in how 'modern' and 'forward thinking' he is. He'll decide you tricked him, and will send constables to arrest you."

Wax groaned softly, stepping up behind them. "We don't have time to dodge patrols."

"Look," Blantach said, "I . . . have *no idea* what's going on in this city. I thought I did. Until . . ." She glanced at the office building and shivered. "I had my illusions shattered quite violently. Something dangerous is going on here."

"More than dangerous, Blantach," Marasi said. "Catastrophic."

"Right. Right," Blantach said. "Was that *really* . . . you know . . . ?"

"Yes," Marasi said. "I've met him before."

"Rusts . . ." Blantach took a deep breath and turned to face them again. "I think I can keep Entrone off your back if you let me send an officer with you."

"Out of the question," Wax said.

Blantach stepped closer and met his eyes. "Listen. This is my city. I don't know what—or who—you're afraid of, but I'm not part of it. I want to help, and this is the only thing I can think of. If you have a Bilming officer with you, I can persuade Entrone I've got someone watching you."

She turned, gesturing, and a figure came scrambling down the steps, nearly tripping at the end. The slender woman pushed her overly large spectacles up on her face, but that nearly made her drop the three ledgers she was trying to carry. Shoulder-length black hair fell around her face as she struggled to keep the ledgers in hand. She pushed it back and grinned sheepishly—through lips with bright red lipstick.

It was Moonlight.

"She says she knows you," Blantach said, "and that you might be willing to trust her? Kim is one of our researchers—she's not a field agent, but she knows her way around Bilming and can help you work in the city."

Moonlight . . . "Kim" . . . thrust out her hand to shake—which almost caused her to drop her ledgers again. She scrambled to catch them.

"She looks fun," Wayne said.

"You're just imagining tying her shoelaces together," Wax said, his arms folded. "Marasi, do you know this person?"

"I . . . do," Marasi said.

"From where?" he asked.

Sharing the truth with Blantach didn't seem like a good idea. "We worked on a project together a while ago—she came to Elendel to further some research she was doing."

Wax narrowed his eyes, obviously trying to decide if that made Kim more or less suspicious. Marasi, though, felt maybe she could trust the woman. A little. After all, Marsh *had* said that people with the interlocking diamond tattoos would be on their side.

Moonlight saluted Wax. "I promise to be of use, sir, and not get in your way." She grimaced. "Except maybe by accident."

"I think we should bring her," Marasi said.

Wax nodded. "You're on the team then, Kim. Let's see if you can be of use. A man named Tobal Copper vanished in this city recently. I want to track down where he lived and interrogate anyone who might have known him."

"Oh!" Moonlight said. "I don't have that kind of information *on* me, of course. I just carry around the city maps and details! But I can get you into the records office! We should be able to find answers there."

"Which will let them know what we're doing," Wax said. "The Set is sure to have agents in such an important place."

"I doubt there's another way to get this information," Marasi said. "We'll just have to move quickly, to stay ahead of them."

"Agreed," Wax said after a moment's thought. "Lead on, Kim. Captain Blantach, anything you could do to keep the lord mayor off our backs would be *most* appreciated."

The Bilming City Records and Research Building was a *huge* improvement over the similar offices in Elendel. Marasi had been forced to spend many an hour in closets, searching through thick ledgers of names or broadsheet archives.

This building, however, was a sleek silvery structure, each side more window than wall. Blantach led them inside herself, and a flash of her constable's credentials got them assigned a flock of junior researchers before she bade the group farewell.

In minutes, Marasi and the others were sitting in comfortable chairs in a glass-walled meeting room, sipping tea while waiting for the results. All but Wax, who paced like a caged animal.

Well, Marasi might have preferred some of Allik's hot chocolate, but this *certainly* beat spending bleary-eyed hours sorting through old records on her own. The break gave her a moment to jot down a letter to Allik—saying not to worry if he heard of casualties via the broadsheets.

She paused. Then she added that he should take a short trip to the countryside to visit her father, and stay out of Elendel for the day. Just in case.

She stepped out to send the message—she'd seen a radio station on the way to the archive. As she walked down the too-white hallway, Moonlight emerged from a side passage. Hadn't she gone to the restroom? Marasi glanced over her shoulder and saw that the meeting room where she'd left Wax and Wayne was out of sight.

"Good," Moonlight said softly. "I was hoping you'd take the cue and slip out to meet me."

"I didn't, actually," Marasi said. "We should go explain who you are to the others—there's no reason to keep it a secret."

"I'd prefer not to," Moonlight said lightly. "I'm not here for them. I'm here for you."

"I thought you couldn't interfere?"

"Not without orders," Moonlight said. "I've received some: I can help, but I'm not to reveal myself to the other two. My mentor is worried about their connections to Harmony."

Marasi stopped in the hallway, which was empty save for them. "I'm not going to lie to my companions, Moonlight."

"You already have."

"Only to avoid revealing you to Blantach," Marasi said.

"And do you assume those two tell you everything about their lives?" Moonlight said. "Every little detail?"

"The important ones."

"What did Waxillium and Harmony discuss when he died?"

"That's . . . not important."

"Seems to me that it is." Moonlight stepped around Marasi to stand right in front of her. Not really blocking her way, but making certain Marasi met her eyes. "Do you want answers? We have those. Do you want to protect Scadrial? That's our main purpose. But we *can't* move in the open. That invites our enemies to strike—beings like Trell are too powerful and Harmony is too indecisive. What's he doing to help?"

"He sent us," Marasi said.

"He tossed you into the line of fire and said, 'Good luck!' It's not his fault—my mentor speaks of him quite fondly. But the reality of your planet's situation is dire, and so we *must* move in the shadows. And our secrets *must* be maintained—known only by those who have proven themselves."

"Wax is the single most 'proven' man alive."

"We're not interested in him," Moonlight said. "We're interested in *you*. Doesn't it excite you, to know things that he doesn't—things almost no one else does? The secrets of the cosmere itself?"

"I don't need to keep secrets from others to feel special."

Moonlight smiled. "I believe you. How interesting. Well, for now I'm demanding you keep *my* secret. That's the cost of my aid. I have *met*

Autonomy; I know how she operates. You need me. But if you tell anyone about me, I'll leave."

"That's your play? Extortion?"

"Extortion?" Moonlight said. "It's just a deal. I have agency, Marasi. I don't *have* to help you. I have a lead now—I can probably find my way to this Tobal Copper's place on my own long before you." She shrugged. "Waxillium trusts you. He'll understand when you explain why you couldn't tell him."

She stepped aside and continued down the hallway, her mannerisms changing as she reached the meeting room door. She became jumpy and excited, and—after first pushing on it and blushing when it didn't budge—pulled it open.

Marasi continued on her way, uncertain. There *was* something about how Moonlight talked . . . Chasing petty thugs, or even mobsters with dangerous intentions, had once thrilled Marasi. But the more she learned of the world and the forces moving in it, the less satisfied she was.

Long ago, she'd explained to Wax her philosophy on becoming a constable. She'd envisioned making the entire city safer—not by chasing criminals, but by changing the way people and neighborhoods saw themselves. Lock a man in prison, and you might stop him from committing crimes. Teach a man to respect himself and his community, and you stopped everyone he might have taught, recruited, or bullied.

She didn't want to focus on individuals. She wanted to change the world. At least, that was how she'd thought when she'd first dreamed of becoming a constable. Had she let the day-to-day grind of the job turn her into something else?

By the time she returned from sending Allik the message, the research team had already arrived with answers—and was spreading out relevant broadsheets and city records for Wax. Marasi stepped up beside him—Moonlight sat primly in the corner with a disarming grin on her face. Wayne was pretending to nap, but he had one eye cracked, watching Moonlight.

Don't overdo the act, Moonlight, Marasi thought with satisfaction. *He'll catch you.*

"Tobal Copper," one of the researchers was saying, pointing at a listing. "Age fifty-three. A chemist, specializing in rubber and manufacturing. Worked for Basin Tires, making . . . well, tires."

"He lost his job," another explained, "about five years ago for . . . erratic behavior."

"Which means what, exactly?" Marasi said, surveying the papers set out on the long table.

"Well," the lead researcher said—a Terriswoman with curly hair and a V pattern on her shirt. "We pulled most of this information from a lawsuit he filed against his former employer. Seems that they . . . um . . . 'refused to listen to his vital discoveries about the impending end of the world.'"

Wax and Marasi shared a look.

"Go on," Wax said.

"There's not a lot to tell, unfortunately," the researcher said. "The lawsuit was dismissed before reaching even the first stage of trial. In this, he mentions pamphlets he'd created, but that's not the sort of record we archive. Instead we have his legal case, his apartment lease, and one police blotter record of an arrest."

"For disturbing the peace," the junior researcher said. "He was banging on the doors in his apartment complex, yelling that 'They've almost split harmonium, and when they do, it's going to destroy us all.'"

"We'll leave you with the information," the lead researcher said, patting the papers on the desk. "And we'll keep searching—but I doubt we'll turn up anything else. We keep careful track of the names of anyone arrested, for cross-referencing, and these were the only three hits."

"One more thing, if you don't mind," Marasi said as they prepared to leave. "Can you find any reports of food shipments vanishing? Particularly nonperishable items?"

"Oh, that's been happening steadily for two years now," the lead researcher said. "Captain Blantach has us watching for such reports, as she finds it baffling. Why would the city's criminal underground be so interested in *canned beans*?"

"Why indeed," Marasi said, lifting up a sheet from the lawsuit documents. Where Copper had claimed, *Someone is building shelters against a cataclysm, maintained by inexplicable technology. The city government is in on it, and so were my employers! They fired me because I got too close to the truth. You have to listen. They're splitting harmonium, and once they do, they'll make bombs to turn us into turtles.*

That . . . last part seemed a little far-fetched.

The researchers vanished out the door, leaving Marasi and Wax to read over the three documents in turn. Unfortunately, it *wasn't* a lot to go on. The blotter said that after Tobal Copper had calmed, they'd released him. He had not reoffended.

The last sheet gave an address in an area the researcher said was expensive. Marasi supposed a head chemist would be paid well.

"They probably killed him," Wax said softly, "once the hubbub died down—so it wouldn't look too suspicious."

"Possibly," Marasi said. "But it's equally likely they grabbed him to make him work on their projects."

"Death said he vanished two weeks ago," Wax said. "This trail might be cold already."

"But it's the best one we have," Marasi said.

"Agreed. Kim, do you know where this apartment address is located?"

30

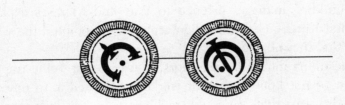

The apartment building didn't look much like a plateau.

Wayne stood with the others, hands on his hips, staring up at the thing. It was too shiny, with too many windows—like a big bottle of something expensive. Buildings shouldn't look like that; they should look like bricks. And have alleys that smelled of what came out of a fellow after he'd had a bottle of something too expensive.

Most of all, he'd expected a plateau.

No, wait, he realized. *There's a canyon next. That's how the story goes. We gotta find that first.*

Comforted, he followed Marasi, Wax, and that Kim woman who tried too hard to be fiddly. The foyer had a doorman and everything. This place *was* fancy. Maybe Wayne should buy a building like that. A doorman sure would be helpful in carrying him up to his flat after *he'd* had too many bottles of something expensive.

Or, well, more often he had bottles of something cheap as piss. Just because he was secretly rich and posh didn't mean he couldn't appreciate terrible booze anymore. He merely had to call it "retro" or "authentic" or something.

The doorman sent for the building manager, who turned out to be a man shaped kind of like a brick—so that was a nice nod to proper building protocol. Marasi and Wax explained they needed to investigate the missing man's apartment, while Wayne took a long walk around the foyer with its enormous paintings of people dancing. They wore suits and dresses, their legs stretched really long, their backs all straight, as if they were made of rulers and not flesh.

Was this the canyon from the story? Ma had said it was beautiful. But no. This didn't work. No self-respecting canyon would have pictures of dancing folks on the walls.

And why did he assume this would be like the story? Well, because he'd thought of it, he supposed. Once you had a thought, you had to keep ahold of it. That was how things was.

The building manager listened to Wax and Marasi's explanations, squinted at Kim's credentials, then grunted. He pointed the way to the elevator, and they all squeezed in.

Wayne didn't much like elevators. It wasn't just being trapped in a little box, or not knowin' how it worked and needin' to rely upon an operator. It wasn't that you could smell everyone a little too much when pressed together, or couldn't see where you were going, which ruined the experience of going up high.

Wait. No, it probably *was* that last one. Elevators were like a carnival ride designed by an overprotective parent who didn't want you getting scared or actually having any fun. He'd had more faith in them when they'd been moved by people, not electricity. Folks were overly trusting of this strange power what leaked from sockets in the walls. After all, Wayne was a primary investor in the technology, and that should have been a big red flag for everyone.

On the twenty-second floor, at the end of a long hallway, the building manager used a set of keys to open a door into a large apartment. He gestured for them to enter, with a grunt.

"Anyone else been in here?" Wax asked.

"No," the manager said.

"He's been gone for two weeks," Wax said. "And nobody came looking? No constables? No family?"

The manager shook his head, grunted, then left them—apparently wanting nothing to do with constables.

"Wonder what his problem is," Marasi said, shutting the door behind them.

"Dunno," Wayne said. "But whatever he has, at least it seems non-communicative."

Wax walked to the center of the room. One wall had narrow floor-to-ceiling windows overlooking the city, with steel girders between. The wall to its right was filled with bookshelves. There was a stylish sitting area to the left, with a smart yellow rug and black furniture. Everything was exceptionally neat, though keeping your place clean was probably easy when you was either dead or vanished.

"So," Marasi said, "they grabbed him or killed him. Then left this apartment alone and visibly pristine. Trap?"

"Trap," Wax said, with a nod. "Give me a minute to use Allomancy to scan about."

Turned out it's really tough to make an explosive trap without *some* metal, even using modern clay explosives. They found three tripwires and one pressure plate, each hooked to a doozy of a grenade. The Set evidently didn't care about a little collateral damage.

"So, whoever you're chasing," Kim said, wringing her hands nervously, "they got here before us. Rusts. I didn't know what I was in for . . ."

"They were undoubtedly behind Copper's disappearance," Wax said. "Be careful, everyone. There might be a trap we missed. Kim, would you encourage anyone in the neighboring apartments to leave for the next hour?"

She left to do so, and the rest of them set to some familiar work: going over a scene for clues. Kim returned a short time later while Wayne was inspecting the writing desk near the bookshelves. She knelt down beside him, looking up at the bottom as he knocked for secret compartments.

"Um . . ." she said, still acting uncertain, "I did as you asked. But . . . why are we bothering to search? Your enemy has been over this place thoroughly."

"Sure," Wayne said. "I can even prove it. See these little drill holes? You make those to be *extra* sure there's no secret compartments, but only if you want to leave the furniture in one piece. Which is less fun . . . but sometimes there are good reasons. Like if you want the room to look normal to a bunch of constables when they visit, so they'll be more likely to get themselves exploded."

"So what is there to learn?"

"Well, you see, this is a kind of fight," Wayne said. "A back-and-forth. A dance. They set those traps in case someone dangerous got wind of the Set. You don't need to blow up ordinary constables. Just the *extra*ordinary kind."

"Like you?"

"Hell no," Wayne said, then pointed to Marasi, searching through books, then to Wax, knocking against the far wall and listening for compartments. "You see those two? They represent the best of two worlds. Wax, now, he's instinct. He's lived a lot, been shot at a lot. He didn't have the schooling to be a constable—he spent his school years learning from Terris scholars about old things people wrote a long time ago.

"But Marasi, she's knowledge. She's spent her life *studying* how to do this sort of nonsense. Sometimes I think she must have read more books on being a constable than have ever actually been written. She talks of crime patterns, preventing chains of poverty, and smart things what make you think maybe being a constable is about *math*.

"Put the two of them together, and you've got both. Instinct and knowledge. Practice and application. The enemy, they looked this place over, sure. They had first crack at it. But they left bombs. That whispers that they're worried they missed something. And so the dance, the fight. Can *we* find what they didn't?"

"Curious," she said. "And what do you add to the team?"

"Comic relief."

She cocked an eyebrow.

"Maybe a little whimsy," he said. "Improvisation. Vision."

"You have a broad imagination, then?"

"There are broads in my imagination almost all the time."

That provoked a smile. Seemed like a nice enough person, when she wasn't pretending. Course, she was probably a traitor of some sort. Shame about that.

"Hey, Wax," Wayne said. "Look at this."

Wax joined him a moment later, inspecting the bottom envelope in a stack from the desk drawer.

"What's that?" Kim asked.

"When you use a fountain pen," Wayne said, "you gotta wait for it to dry. But sometimes you're inna hurry, or you're worried, so you put it away and put something on toppa it. Like this stack of envelopes. Then the ink makes an imprint on the bottom."

"Smudged," Wax said, holding up the envelope. "But maybe legible. This part here, it's underlined. Does that look like a set of numbers to you?"

"A seven?" Wayne asked, pointing at one. The next were too smudged to read. "Then a dash and a thirteen."

"Maybe a combination," Kim said softly, crowding them to see the number. "There are big stacks of lockers at the larger train stations that use numbers like this, where you can pay to store things."

Wax nodded slowly. "Marasi, what have you found?"

"I think these books have all been replaced," she said. "He seems like the type who reads a lot, but these are all brand new. I'd guess the Set took every book in the place, just in case, and refilled the bookshelves with red herrings."

"This looks like the original furniture though," Wax said, and demonstrated moving a chair back so it bumped the wall, right where the paint had been scraped away by repeatedly being hit like that. "It's old. Worn. The carpet too. The room *appears* neat and orderly, because the Set cleaned it up after they did their search—but it was likely a mess before they arrived."

"I think the fellow is dead," Wayne said, tapping the wall and breaking away some putty. "Bullet hole. Probably shot the poor doof in the back while he was sitting here."

"Too specific a conclusion to draw from so little evidence," Marasi said, joining him. She pulled out a little brush and fiddled in the hole, eventually pulling out some flakes of something and putting them in a vial.

"Blood?" Wayne guessed.

"Yes," she admitted. "And what might be a sliver of bone. They must have cleaned the blood off the desk, but removed only the bullet from the hole." She ran her fingers over the wood. "It's worn down. He used this desk a lot. Or bought an old one to begin with. Hard to say."

Wax walked over and handed Wayne a leather cap, like painters wore.

"Found it on the bedpost," Wax said. "What do you think? Have we given you enough to work with?"

"Maybe . . ." Wayne said, slipping on the hat. He walked to the center of the room, then stared out a window, putting it all together. Trying to imagine the man who had lived here, trying to extrapolate from what they knew of him.

"He was respected at first," Wayne said. "A good scientist. But then he found things, heard other things, learned more. He was a chemist, right?"

"For a tire company," Marasi said.

"A front, most likely," Wax said. "He said his employers were making a bomb. I'd bet his chemistry work involved investigating weapon systems and explosives for the Bilming government."

"Yeah . . ." Wayne said, his eyes closed. "He realized they were looking to make a bomb, and heard about splitting harmonium. And he was maybe already a little eccentric. He tried to save the city . . . But he was an odd fellow, and nobody listened . . ."

Eyes closed, he spread his arms out and turned around slowly, smelling the place—and imagining it. Stacked old dishes in the corner. He could still smell them. Frantic nights . . . reading . . . thinking . . .

"They didn't listen," Wayne said. "And when they locked him up, he learned he couldn't use the normal justice system to stop the disaster."

"So what did he do?" Kim asked. "You think the people who killed him were scared that they missed something. That implies he knew something they didn't want leaked. Where did he stash it?"

"He didn't," Wayne whispered. "That's not what this fellow would do. You see, the Set . . . they're going to be wrong about him. Just like Kim is."

"How?" Marasi asked softly from somewhere to his right.

"The Set," Wayne said, "they hold on to knowledge. They *strangle* it, Marasi. But a fellow like this, he might be a little unhinged, but he wants people to know what *he* knows. He ain't going to lock his ideas up in some train station. He'll *share* them. If the government won't listen, then . . ."

He opened his eyes and met Wax's. ". . . he'll do whatever he can to get the information out."

"Kim," Wax said, thoughtful, "which local broadsheet has the worst reputation? The type that publishes whatever nonsense it can get its hands on? Particularly if it's frightening, or a little off-kilter?"

"There are at *least* seven of those," she replied.

"Which one syndicates the writings of that fool Jak?"

"The *Sentinel of Truth*," she said. "I . . . kind of love those . . ." She seemed embarrassed, but she needn't be. Those were good stories. Super dumb, of course, but sometimes you needed cheap storytelling with your cheap booze. Didn't make no sense to read literature while drinking outta a paper sack.

"*Sentinel of Truth* . . ." Wax said. "Do you know the address of their offices?"

"I can look it up," Kim said, digging out one of her volumes of city addresses.

Wayne took off the hat and held it lightly. The poor fellow, Tobal Copper, *was* dead. He hadn't let the Set push him around or force him to work for them. They'd come here to learn what he knew about them and their plans, and they hadn't left him alive. But maybe he'd told someone. Someone the Set hadn't been able to find—because letting go of information, to them, would be inconceivable.

"I've got it," Kim said. "Publishing offices of the *Sentinel* can be found at . . ." She looked up. "Seventh Street. Office 42–13. Nights! The same numbers you found on the bottom of the envelope."

Wax squeezed him on the arm. "Nice work, Wayne."

He shrugged. "It's easy enough when you have a lot to work with."

"That was a lot?" Kim asked, curious.

"Sure," Wayne said, tucking the hat away. "A man's whole life."

31

S teris took a long, deep breath. It was the sort of thing she'd read about
for calming nerves. She'd seen Marasi do it during stressful situations.
Did it work? Steris wasn't certain. But the act was very normal, wasn't it?

She took another deep breath in case she'd done it wrong, letting it
out slowly. Then she stepped into the Senate's main assembly hall to
be assaulted by noise and chaos. The two were so often partners.

Senators shouted across the chamber at each other. Aides fluttered
about, delivering afternoon broadsheets and private reports to their senators. She'd been able to acquire a few of these—not actual broadsheets
from Bilming, but local reprints or summaries received via telegraph.
Emergency editions were common with big stories, each paper rushing
to capitalize.

They wouldn't be the most accurate stories. But they could certainly
start fires. She glanced at a few as she walked past.

CONSTABLES DEAD! BOTCHED ELENDEL OPERATION LEADS TO BILM-
ING TRAGEDY!

SECRET ELENDEL CONSTABLE FORCE UNDERMINES LOCAL POLICING
EFFORTS!

EARLY ACT OF WAR PLACES ELENDEL FORCES IN DIRECT OPPOSITION TO
BILMING LAW ENFORCEMENT! SHOTS FIRED! SEVENTEEN DEAD!

The spins were different, but the flavors were similar. Waxillium had
drawn attention as usual, and she had no doubt that most of the casual-

ti were members of the Set. That wasn't a nuance for headlines. Still, she had sent her children out of the city with Kath. She prayed to the Survivor that they were safe in their grandfather's estate to the south.

For now, Steris pushed through the cacophony, steeling herself against the fluttering of pages, the tumult of words, and made her way to the vice governor's seat. There Steris delivered the proper authorization form for her to take her husband's position in the Senate.

Adawathwyn said nothing about the dire letter Steris had sent earlier, detailing the threat to the city. Why? Did they dismiss her that easily?

People never wanted to listen to Steris. They preferred to nod along and think about other things. She made her way to Wax's seat—her seat. Wax was correct; standing for House Ladrian was her right. Indeed, it was one of the main reasons they'd initially explored a union. Her fortune; his authority. Together they could do great things.

If she could keep her nerve. Yes, she'd taken his spot before, but never for something so vital. So, she stood at the small desk, surrounded by chaos. She'd prepared for this. She'd written down what it would be like. She'd even taken two deep breaths. Yes, her heart thundered in her chest, insisting she was nervous, but what did her heart know? It had spent years insisting she'd never fall in love, and it had been so very wrong. Her heart was no expert in what she couldn't do. It only knew what she had and hadn't done.

As she'd hoped, people noticed her there, standing silently, and some of the arguments dropped off. This allowed Adawathwyn to shout for quiet in the room—and finally be heard. Her forceful tone, unusual for a Terriswoman, brought order at last. Like a teakettle moved from the burner, senators stopped boiling, but remained hot—settling in their seats and muttering softly.

"The governor," Adawathwyn said, "requests an explanation from the acting senator of House Ladrian."

Every eye in the room turned to Steris. Well, she was accustomed to that. People did tend to stare at her. Or glare. Or glower. It depended on how wrong they were, and what level of annoyed they were at hearing her point it out.

"My husband," she said to the room, "has been called back to his duties as a lawman because of a particularly dangerous situation in Bilming. His operation was fully approved by the constables-general, under the authority of the governor himself. Your Grace, everything my husband has done has been strictly legal and documented."

"Sometimes," the governor said, "it doesn't matter if the permissions are in place and the documents prepared. An act can still be improper."

What? *How dare he!* That was the very *definition* of proper! Steris forced down her anger. Some people . . . just thought that way.

She covertly glanced at her note card. She had determined, after deliberating all morning, that she'd need to get the governor into a small-group setting. She didn't want to panic the city, and didn't yet know how urgent the timing was.

She still needed to get a plan in place for evacuating the city. Always plan for the worst. So: get the governor into a more private conversation. In the proper circumstances, he could authorize an evacuation of the city without a Senate vote.

"Your Grace," she said to the governor, "Constable-General Reddi has information of relevance about my husband's mission. I sent him reports with details of my fears this morning. We are facing a far larger issue, even, than the growing intercity aggression. I therefore move that a select council be formed to deal with the emergency in an immediate and timely manner."

A Governor's Select Council would be a small commission—in this case made up of a handful of senators and at least one constable-general— with a limited remit. In the past, they had been used for smaller-scale matters, such as addressing traffic needs in the city hub. But a select council was a potent tool, allowing a concentration of power in a few specific individuals. She was shocked it hadn't been used for an emergency before now; a thorough reading of the law made the application obvious.

"Wait," the governor asked, "is that . . . allowed? I thought those committees were for choosing flowers at grand openings and the like."

The vice governor grabbed him by the arm and pulled him down, where they conversed in quiet, hissing tones—eventually calling over a legal clerk. Several others in the room did likewise.

The governor stood up. "This seems an excellent suggestion," he said, sounding surprised. "Motion to vote on creating a select council on this matter with Bilming?" He pointedly looked toward a few senators in the room—including Lord Darlin Cett, a man with slicked-back, thinning hair.

The Cetts were among the more powerful faction leaders in this incarnation of the government, and the look seemed to say, "You'll be included in this council if you vote for it." It was a shrewd move for the governor, which likely meant he hadn't come up with it himself.

For once, the Senate vote gave Steris the result she'd been hoping for. A select council was to be formed at the governor's discretion, granted authority for twenty-four hours to deal with the crisis at Bilming.

"Lord Cett," the governor said, "Lady Hammondess, and Lady Gardre. Please join me and Adawathwyn in the governor's chambers to strategize until Constable-General Reddi arrives. The rest of the Senate is adjourned."

Steris hesitated. He hadn't called on her. Was . . . that an oversight? Was it implied that she'd join him, or . . .

Or was he leaving her out?

Oh, *rusts*. How could she have missed such a natural possibility? She called for a select council, but then wasn't included in it? She should have seen that coming.

She put her hand to her head, feeling hot and ashamed of herself. The woman who was ready for everything, blindsided by such an obvious move.

As she tried to control her nausea, someone stood up at the back of the chamber—from the observation seats. A figure in a sharp wooden mask painted with red lines. "Your Grace," the Malwish ambassador said, "I should very much like to observe the workings of this council."

"Um, Admiral Daal?" the governor said. "This is a matter of internal Basin affairs."

"Yes, which is exactly why I want to observe," the ambassador said. "I can learn much about a people by how they react to a crisis. I have a pleasure craft, of a personal ownership, docked in the city. Perhaps you would find it useful to borrow, my lord governor? To observe the Basin."

The governor blinked. "Well," he said, "I'm sure the wisdom of a battle-hardened admiral would be of great use to our council. Come on, then."

Oh, rusts. Had he really taken such an obvious bribe? In public? The action cut through Steris's shame, and she glanced toward Adawathwyn. The vice governor had her palm to her face. She'd have to work hard to spin that exchange. But, well, one of the problems with having a pushover like Varlance as governor was that others were fully capable of pushing too.

You can push, Steris thought at herself. *You have to try.*

Ignoring her instincts—which wanted her to sit down and write out how she could have foreseen this situation—Steris hopped out of her seat and ran to the floor, shoving unceremoniously between a pair of senators to reach the governor.

"Your Grace," she said. "I believe I can offer relevant insight to this council."

"Oh!" he said, glancing toward her. "Lady Ladrian?" He then looked to the side, where Adawathwyn shook her head sharply. "Alas," the governor said, turning back to Steris, "I feel the council is already crowded. It was wonderful of you to make the suggestion though."

"Your Grace," she said. "There is a *dire threat* to the city. You need to hear me out."

The governor hesitated.

"She sent a letter about this earlier in the morning, Your Honor," Adawathwyn said. "Some nonsense about a bomb capable of destroying Elendel."

"What is this?" he said, turning toward his vice governor.

"It's true," Steris said. "You didn't even give it to him?"

"Your house has a history of inflating problems," Adawathwyn said. "Remember the time your husband claimed that voting against his workers' rights act would cause an uproar in the city? Or when he insisted the Roughs would form its own country if we continued our tariff plans?"

"This time it's different," Steris said. "He . . . has confirmation from Harmony."

"I see," Adawathwyn said. "And if Harmony *himself* were going to speak to someone, would he not speak to the *governor?*"

"Has your husband seen a bomb?" the governor asked. "Does he have proof to back up your claims?"

"He's gathering evidence now," Steris said.

"Then," the governor said, "why not return to us when you have that proof?"

"Because I need to be in that council with you—"

"Lady Ladrian," he said, softer, "surely you see that this is an important, tense situation. This is not a place for a woman who has been a sitting senator for less than an hour." He smiled. "Indeed, this situation is going to require delicacy and tact, not . . ."

Not whatever it is you are, the unfinished sentence seemed to imply. He nodded to her, then joined the others at the door to the governor's chambers.

Steris was left alone in the center of the floor. Humiliated. She . . . well, she'd have to make another plan. Yes, plan how to deal with this situation. She could take the rest of the day . . .

No. She couldn't afford to spend time planning. She *had* to get into that room.

And in the moment, she thought of one way she might be able to accomplish it.

32

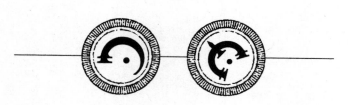

The *Sentinel of Truth* broadsheet offices didn't fit Bilming. Unlike the sleek, modern designs, its building looked like a shack. An older wooden structure, only one story, with a peaked roof, bulging walls, and small windows.

"One of the old buildings," Kim explained, "from when this section of town held a lot of fishing shacks. The push to start knocking everything down and build anew came five years ago, but there are structures like this sprinkled throughout the city."

"Doesn't seem like it's been in operation lately," Wax said, noting the padlock on the door, the dark interior. "Is it still publishing?"

"Releases have been sporadic lately," Kim said. "I had to wait *six weeks* to read the end of the 'Survivor's Last Testament' arc of Jak's explorations."

Rusting idiot man, Wax thought. Ever since the discovery of the "Sovereign" who had ruled and helped the people of the Southern lands, Survivor fervor had been at a high point. Sightings all over the city, particularly on misty nights.

Jak, of course, had capitalized on this and had spent years "discovering" Survivor artifacts in his adventures. It wouldn't be half as bad if the fool didn't mention Wax now and then.

They knocked at a side door, and when they got no reply they tried the door and found it locked. So Wax wrapped a coat tassel around his fist and prepared to smash in the window.

"Wax?" Marasi said. "What are you doing?"

"Beginning an investigation."

"Let's wait a few minutes," she said. "See if the owner returns."

He stopped, his fist a few inches from the glass. "We have a writ of investigation. We can break in."

"If it's an emergency," she said. "And if we've tried other options. This is a private citizen's property, and we have no reason to believe the Set is here. And unlike the apartment earlier, we have no reason to believe a crime has been committed."

"Let me do it," Wayne said, walking up to the window. "You can all say you tried to stop me, but I done pulled a Wayne. They'll let you off."

"It's not about what we can get away with, Wayne," Marasi said, putting her hand to her face. "It's about proper procedure. You can't just smash into any place you want to—the world is changing. People have rights. It makes our job harder, but it makes the world better."

Wax frowned, lowering his hand.

"We can afford to wait a few minutes," Marasi said. "If we're right, we want whoever owns this place to work with us—and breaking in might turn them against us. If we're wrong, then we'll have ransacked some-one's place of business for nothing." She glanced at the sun. "It's lunchtime. The owner might be out—they are still putting out papers, after all, so we have reason to think they'll show up for work eventually."

Wax reluctantly backed down. He expected Wayne to complain, but the shorter man just shrugged and jogged over to a street corner food stand to get something to eat. Marasi and Kim settled down on a bench beside a small nearby park, leaving Wax to put his back to a well-groomed tree set into a little piece of earth with a low fence around it.

Moments like this made him feel old. Not just of body, but of mind. He seemed to represent something that was dying. The lone lawman. And . . . well, it was hard to mourn. Because intellectually, he agreed with Marasi. He'd voted for legal restrictions on constable authority. Society needed robust checks on everyone's power. Even his. *Especially* his.

But at the same time, that made the world seem too big to fix. Out in the Roughs he could beat in a door and talk—or sometimes shoot—sense into anyone who needed it. It had made him feel like he could solve basically any problem.

But that had been a false impression of control, hadn't it? Acknowl-edging that made him uncomfortable. It wasn't that the world was growing more complicated. It was that he was letting himself see it had always been complicated.

A minute later, Wax heard something. He *swore* it came from the building. He narrowed his eyes, burning steel, tracking the blue lines around him to a few moving near the top of the building. An attic? He raised a hand to the others, then slipped out Vindication. Someone was up there. He was certain of it. Had they simply not heard the calls earlier?

He dropped a bullet casing and launched off it, then landed carefully on the roof near where the shingles sloped past a small attic window, shuttered closed. Quiet though he'd tried to be, the metal lines moved sharply right as he landed—then they stilled. Mostly. They were quivering.

He narrowed his eyes at the window. One of the shutter corners was broken, letting whoever was inside peek out. He could see a metal line leading right to the hole. A part of him felt cold, because that metal was almost certainly a gun pointed at him. Shingles rattled under his feet as he engaged his steel bubble—the subtle Push he'd learned to use to deflect bullets. It made the nails in the rooftop vibrate as they tried to escape the field.

Vibrating, he thought, *like that line ahead of me. That's a gun in the hands of someone who is trembling.*

He wasn't facing a Set assassin. Carefully, he raised his gun to the side, pointed away from the window.

"I'm a constable," he said loudly. "I'm here to help."

Silence. Then finally a voice. Feminine, husky. "You're here to kill me. Like you killed Tobal."

"No," Wax said. "I promise it." He stepped forward. "I'm looking for the people who killed him. If I were here for another reason, I'd have shot instead of spoken."

More silence. Long enough to unnerve him, until finally the shutters swung open, revealing a short woman. She had frizzy grey-black hair and a disheveled appearance—a waistcoat buttoned with a few holes skipped, a long skirt that was rumpled as if it spent most of its life in a heap in a corner. She had dark bags under her eyes and a wan appearance, as if she'd been heavier once but had lost weight, like a couch missing some of its stuffing.

"You . . ." she said, lowering a rifle. "Are you . . . Dawnshot?"

"That's me," he said, relaxing.

She brightened. "You're *Jak's* friend!"

Jak's friend? Just because that idiot brought up Wax's name once in a while? He opened his mouth to object, but thought better of it.

"I . . . know of him," Wax said. "Look, something is happening in this city. Something very dangerous. I followed the trail to Tobal's apartment, then here. Please. Did he give you something? Tell you something?"

She leaned out, suspiciously scanning the streets. "Meet me below, at the back." She pulled the shutters closed, and he joined Marasi and Kim at the back doors as they rattled, numerous locks and chains being undone.

Finally, she pulled the door open. "I don't normally talk to conners. Ever."

"'S good advice," Wayne mumbled through a mouthful of something. He walked up beside Wax and took another bite of what appeared to be grease and maybe some bits of meat wrapped in what might have been bread. Or a very large crepe?

"But since you're friends of Jak . . ." she said.

"Sure are," Wayne said, slapping Wax on the shoulder. "Jak and Wax here adventured together out in the Roughs!"

"I guess, then," she said, gesturing for them to enter, "you're not *that* kind of constable. You're the *other* kind."

"Yup," Wayne said. "*We're* the kind what don't like uniforms and shoots people when they try to make us sign paperwork." He took another bite of his wrap.

"What even is that?" Wax asked as Marasi and Kim entered.

"He called it 'chouta.' It's good."

"It looks disgusting."

"Aw, mate. With street food, that's how you *know* it's good."

The building inside was musty and dark, and had numerous trash bins by the door—as if the woman hadn't dared leave to empty them. She watched Wax, rifle in hand—though not raised—as if certain he'd turn on her at any moment.

"Is . . . Jak in the city?" she asked. "Available to help?"

"I . . . um . . ." Wax said. "No. He's on . . . an adventure."

"Don't suppose you can send for him?" she sounded hopeful.

"Afraid not."

She frowned, eyeing him.

"Oh, don't mind Dawnshot," Wayne said, nudging Wax. "He gets coy about Jak sometimes." He leaned toward the woman. "Honestly, he's a little jealous."

"Well, who wouldn't be?" she said, then sighed and began doing up the locks on the door. "Has he ever let you hold the Spear of the Red Sun?"

Wayne looked at Wax, who gritted his teeth. "No," he forced himself to say. "It's too powerful. Jak says I might accidentally awaken some . . . zombies if I'm allowed to touch it."

The woman nodded, locks secured, then waved for them to follow her into the building.

"Good," Wayne whispered to Wax. "But the spear wasn't used for zombies. They was on the Island of Death, with Nicki."

"How do *you* know?" Wax hissed to him.

"I read every one," Wayne said. "Why wouldn't I?"

"You . . ."

"I thought you couldn't read," Marasi said, brushing past them and following the woman.

"Oh, I can read," Wayne said. "But I'm dumb, see, so I can only read things what are dumb too."

The woman led them through a corridor crowded with books—stacks of them, taking up almost every available space. In the next room were a large printing press, some buckets of ink, and boxes of lead type scattered about. Her picture on the wall, hanging askew and showing her in younger years, was captioned MARAGA DULCET, EDITOR-IN-CHIEF.

"So," she said, running a hand through her disheveled hair, "you know who killed Tobal? Was it those people with the golden hair living on the east side? They're some kind of fairy creature; I know it."

"Actually," Marasi said, "we think it was a secretive group plotting to start up the Ashmounts again—and we worry they're working to create bombs of incredible power."

Maraga nodded. "So you do know."

That was a test, Wax realized.

Maraga opened a doorway that revealed a set of old steps. "Well then. Follow me."

She led the way down and Wax followed, waving for Marasi and Kim to stay back a few feet. The air smelled of old potatoes, spiders, and forgotten jars of something that might have once been preserves. Maraga flipped a switch at the bottom, powering a set of electric lights swinging on wires.

Covering the walls of the musty basement room were sheets of metal, scratched in detail—filled with words and diagrams, letters and pictures all cramped up together.

"Figured we'd write it all in metal," Maraga said. "Just in case."

33

Eyes wide with wonder, Marasi walked around the basement. It seemed to have once been used for storage, judging by the piles of old equipment and stacked throw mats. This had all been pushed away from the walls to make room for the metal sheets.

The Words of Founding mentioned metal plates, and Marasi had imagined large, thick sheets with the words chiseled in bold, powerful letters. Instead, Maraga had scratched sheets of tin with a pen, often scribbling out sentences and lines she got wrong. A lot of it was organized as lists. It had a frenzied air to it, but not like—say—the ravings of a madman. More like . . .

Notes, Marasi thought. *A journalist's shorthand notes, connecting ideas and building a story.*

Maraga slumped down on the bottom step, seeming exhausted. "I . . . didn't believe him at first," she whispered. "Tobal. Thought he was another crackpot. But they usually have a good story to tell, something my readers want to hear.

"Then he started to bring me evidence. Information he stole from his employers. I think he was sneaking back in, grabbing ledgers, scraps, whatever he could find . . . Never would let me help. He didn't want me to get too involved." She looked up at the walls. "As if this weren't already enough to get me killed . . ."

Marasi walked closer to offer comfort, but the woman flinched. There was a . . . fatalistic air about her. The air of a woman who had thrown the dice and was waiting to see how the numbers came up.

"How long?" Wax asked, inspecting one of the plates.

"Almost four years," Maraga whispered. "Like I said, I didn't believe him at first. But I've always been interested in the stories that slip through the cracks. The ones other papers ignore because they seem too sensational, or too lowbrow."

"Lies, you mean," Wax said. "You print lies."

"We prefer 'whimsical what-ifs.' Intriguing stories that would be fascinating if they were true."

"So . . ." Wax said, "lies."

"Our patrons understand what they're buying, Lord Ladrian," Maraga said, lifting her chin. "You know. You're friends with Jak himself. It's all about being larger than life, bigger than reality! Our patrons know we stretch to find the more interesting tidbits, the 'might's and the 'could-be's of the world."

He shook his head, obviously unconvinced.

Maraga sniffed. "I did my journeymanship at the *Times,* top paper in the city. Totally respectable. The amount they fudged, slanted, or outright fabricated would scandalize you. At least *I'm* honest about it. Besides, I don't print lies. I print human-interest stories—the tales of people who are ignored by the larger media. Exciting stories, by adventuring celebrities. Cartoons, pictures of funny-shaped vegetables . . ."

"How funny?" Wayne said from across the room.

"Depends on your sense of humor," Maraga replied.

"Crass. With a light seasoning of vulgarity."

"Second box on the left," she said. "Next to your foot."

Wayne located the appropriate box, which was filled with sketches. In seconds he was snickering to himself.

"Anyway," Maraga continued, "the more Tobal brought, and the more I pieced together, the more terrified I became. This . . . was a story. A *real* story. Not a whimsical tale about bug men or the dangers of electricity. This . . . this could get people killed. Could get *me* killed."

She looked up at them, then continued. "Once I believed, we worked for many months, putting all of this together. I started to see things he didn't. Tobal wasn't . . . completely credible. He jumped to conclusions. But he wasn't wrong, not at the heart of the story. And he hadn't made it up.

"He told me that one day he wouldn't show up to our nightly conversation. He said, when that happened, I should run. Take everything to the authorities. But the authorities are involved, so . . . what then? Who to tell? And then, two weeks ago, he didn't show up. One night. Two. Three . . . And I knew. I *knew*. They'd found him."

"I'm sorry," Marasi said.

"Could he still be alive?" Maraga asked. "Might they have just . . . taken him?"

"It's possible," Marasi said. "But . . . we don't think it's likely."

Maraga nodded, looking down at her feet. Then she closed her eyes and seemed to be waiting. For what?

For the dice to land, Marasi realized. *She doesn't trust us. She's waiting to see if we shoot.*

Marasi looked around the room and noticed that Wayne—despite pretending to look at the pictures—was actually watching Moonlight, one hand resting lazily on his dueling cane. Likely with his metals ready, just in case she tried something. Even Wax was watching her from the corner of his eye.

"This is brilliant," Moonlight said instead, staring at one of the walls. "Are these . . . trajectory estimations?"

Marasi joined her beside one set of sketches in tin, which depicted looping arcs. Moonlight was right; it looked like measurements with different estimates of how far a shot could reach.

Maraga stood up, seeming to take strength from the question. "That's right," she said. "Those numbers are the distances the Bilming military *claim* their new guns can fire. They love to send releases to the local broadsheets, extolling their grand navy. It's mostly bravado. They imply they could shell Elendel from twenty miles away, but that's a lie. The guns are much shorter range than that."

"And this?" Marasi asked, pointing at another set of trajectories.

"Poor Tobal's job was to research chemical propellants," Maraga replied. At their confused stares, she continued. "These people, they're trying to develop self-propelled shells. Weapons that could fire *themselves* and fly miles. Or even hundreds of miles. Before hitting and detonating."

Rusts, Marasi thought, her eyes widening. She walked through the room, taking in each of the eight large plates on the walls. She identified one having to do with the "subway" systems of the city, a large interconnected cavern complex that was being "surveyed" to determine where to place train lines. But the truth, according to Maraga's notes, was entirely different—the surveys were seeking caverns that could offer stable underground living conditions.

They're preparing bunkers, Marasi thought. *That's what the supplies are for—they're stocking up for a cataclysm, perhaps?*

Just as people had sought refuge in caverns during the last days before the world ended. Before Harmony's Ascension and the remaking of the land.

"This doesn't make *sense,*" Wax said, joining her. "Harmony says my sister is trying to prove she can rule this planet. If she blows it up, what does that prove? Why build bunkers? Does she honestly think that saving a fragment of us and annihilating the rest would prove her competence?"

"I don't know," Marasi admitted, then pointed at another plate. "This talks about ashfalls. The days of ash and destruction allowed the Lord Ruler to secure near-universal power, at least in the North. So maybe Telsin thinks that would work again?"

"You should read the next plate over," Maraga said.

Together they stepped to the side, reading what appeared to be a list of names. "Dupon Melstrom . . ." Wax read. "Vennis Hasting . . . Mari Hammondess . . . These are some of the most powerful senators in Elendel."

"They're in on it," Maraga said.

"What?" Marasi said, spinning. "All of them?"

Maraga dug in a cabinet and came out with a piece of paper. She handed it to Marasi, who showed it to Wax. A letter from Vennis Hasting, talking about the creation of a bomb of incredible power. It was dated almost a year ago, and implicated many of the names on the wall.

Marasi frowned. That . . . that seemed impossible. This many people in their *own government* knew? Could the Set have its fingers wrapped that tightly around the Basin? She looked at Wax.

"I know some of these people," he said. "Vennis is a rat, of course—but Lady Yomen is a good friend. As close a senator as I trust. This doesn't add up, Marasi. *None* of this adds up."

"Maybe that's why the Senate is so confident," she said, "that they can bully the Outer Cities."

"I know these people," Wax said. "They wouldn't keep a secret like this; they *couldn't.* Everything they've done so far has been about posturing for power. The Supremacy Bill, the tariffs, the 'hard line' they're taking with the South . . . If Vennis knew about a bomb, he'd be advocating for strategic tests to prove how powerful it is."

"They could all be in the Set," Marasi said softly.

His expression darkened. He took the letter, staring at it, and she knew what he was thinking: if the Set's tendrils ran this deep—even into the hearts of his friends among the senators . . .

"No," he said. "There's something very strange here, Marasi. If my sister had all of these people following her dictates, she would *already* rule the Basin. We're missing a big piece of this."

Moonlight walked up to them, nodding toward another of the plates. "You're talking about a bomb? Well, it seems they have one—look at this."

Marasi and Wax walked over, finding another plate with a list of underground disturbances. It was labeled with the words "Underground weapon tests, tracked using seismograph."

"They've developed an underground base beneath the city," Maraga said. "It's where they hide. Lord Mayor Entrone is involved, is probably even one of their leaders. Some of the caverns seem to be weapons testing locations, but others are bunkers they're preparing for some reason and using as a headquarters."

"They stopped the tests recently," Moonlight said. "Wonder why?"

"Well . . ." Maraga said. "They know it works. I mean, they're well past their go date."

"Go date?" Marasi asked, feeling cold.

"Stolen internal memos," Maraga said, pointing to a plate. "Don't know how he got them. Listing target dates for project completion. The weapon was supposed to be detonated two weeks ago." Maraga slumped back down onto the steps. "They killed him the day before that. I thought for sure the end would come soon after . . .

"I . . ." She buried her head in her hands. "I know I should have published this. I'm a coward. In the end, I'm a *coward*. I've been hunkered up here, waiting for the ash to fall, haven't I? Rusts. I was convinced no one would listen . . . Convinced it was too late . . ."

"What is done, or not done, is past," Wax said, firm. "We have the information now. And there's still time to stop this."

"Wax," Marasi hissed, taking his arm. "They have a bomb, and are planning—as far as we can determine—to detonate it in Elendel. They would have done it already, if they could figure out how to get it into the city."

Maraga nodded. "Their self-propelled weapon—the rocket, they call it—is having difficulties. Fuel might be the problem. It's what Tobal was working on for them before he realized what they were planning . . ." She stood up and steeled herself. "I need to show you one more thing." She hurried to some boxes and dug through them as Moonlight unabashedly took rubbings of the plates.

Maraga dug out an evanotype photo. "The crowning jewel," she said softly. "My best piece of evidence. The above-the-fold photo for the story I'll never actually write . . ."

Marasi took it, frowning at Wax, who joined her. It depicted an ashen landscape. In color.

Marasi gasped softly, looking at the stark orange sky, the floating ash, the remnants of a ruined city in the distance. That looked . . . kind of like Elendel, though the ash was heaped so high, obscuring all but the tops of the smoldering, broken buildings and jagged destroyed walls.

"How . . ." Marasi said. "How can you have a *picture* of the end of the world?"

"They didn't have evanotypes in the Survivor's day," Wax said, looking closely. "The colors are remarkable. Did someone take an old photo and paint onto it?"

"I don't know," Maraga said. "But it seems like a picture of . . . of what is *going* to happen. After he found this, Tobal started to get really scared. He barely stayed during our last visits. I think he mostly just huddled in his rooms until they got him. Like . . . like I've been doing."

The basement fell silent, even Wayne sensing the mood and covering up any snickering at his funny pictures. Marasi felt a mounting horror at the sight of that picture. She'd heard Wax talk about a bomb, knew what the enemy was trying to build. Laying it out in stark depiction, however, changed it from abstract to concrete.

This was what they wanted to do. Wipe out everything she loved. Leave rubble and ash in its place. These were bigger stakes by far than any investigation she'd ever done. And the implications of it left her disquieted on a profound level.

She turned around, looking at the plates reflecting the calm electric light. Something ancient. Something new. Just like the picture Wax handed back to her.

A door opened upstairs.

The locks had been fastened, but that didn't stop whoever had arrived.

Wayne scrambled to his feet, hands going to his dueling canes as a single set of footsteps crossed the wooden floor up above.

Wax slid a gun from its holster and positioned himself to watch the steps. A figure descended onto the stairs. A woman with dark hair and a rugged build that seemed in conflict with her small nose and prim lips. She wore a suit: slacks, buttoned white shirt, jacket and cravat.

Telsin. Wax's sister, leader of the Set. She wasn't armed, at least not in a way that Marasi could make out. And she didn't seem to mind that Wax had a gun pointed at her head while Wayne backed away, muttering.

"An address," Telsin said. "The number on the back of the envelope was a rusting *address*? Do you know how many hours we wasted tearing into lockers at train stations?"

34

Marasi immediately reached for an Allomantic grenade, charging one silently in her pocket. Wax edged forward, gun on his sister. Wayne had scrambled back from the steps and was muttering to himself, hopping from one foot to the other. He looked around as if he expected enemies to come bursting in through the walls.

Last time they'd seen Telsin, she had betrayed them to the Set. She'd nearly gotten Wax killed, and in return Wayne had fired a shotgun blast at her chest. The first time he'd fired a gun in . . . well, Marasi didn't know how long.

Telsin had healed, however, vanishing from the bloodied snows where Wayne had left her. She was a Hemalurgist, with at least the power of a Bloodmaker—like Wayne. She had shown hints of two other powers, but it was possible the members of the Set switched out their spikes to gain different Metallic Arts. Regardless, she apparently had enough abilities now that she didn't seem the least bit concerned about facing them alone. Rusts.

"This is marvelous," Telsin said, glancing around the basement. "Remarkable how many of our secrets he managed to sneak out, considering. Who would have thought our greatest danger wasn't armies, constables, or even *you*, Waxillium? It was a miserable, bald old chemist."

"Tobal was a good man!" Maraga said, and ducked behind Wax as Telsin looked toward her.

"Oh, you can lower the gun, Waxillium," Telsin said, settling down on the steps. "The idiot over there will tell you how effective shooting me was."

"Felt good," Wayne said. "Does it need to do more than that? Here, Wax. Hand me a gun. I'll have at it a few more times."

Wax didn't move, and Telsin rolled her eyes. They all stood there, Marasi's grenade vibrating softly in her fingers as it absorbed her power. What now? They were being played, obviously. But how? Would the Set's leader come to see them as a simple distraction?

"Tell us what the Set is planning," Marasi said.

"No," Telsin replied.

"Oh," Wayne said, perking up. "Does this mean I can make her talk? On a scale of one to broken, how much do you fancy your kneecaps, Telsin?"

"I'll heal in seconds, Wayne," Telsin said.

"Not if we yank out the spikes," Wayne snapped.

"Which would kill me," Telsin said. "I'm sure that will give you *so* much information."

"Well," Wayne said, "breaking some pieces off you will still *hurt*, Telsin. I know a thing or two about that part."

"Actually," she said, "it *won't* hurt. Did you know that a Feruchemist can store their pain in a metalmind? Oh, and you won't be able to remove mine from me. We've learned better how to hide those. So torture me if you want, Wayne. I'll find it boring, but nothing more."

She met his gaze with confidence. Wayne glanced toward Marasi, concerned, shying away. Like a puppy whose chew toy had bitten it back.

Marasi was more worried about Wax. He'd frozen in place, gun out and pointed at Telsin, arm straight. Expression . . . grim. Telsin was his last close living relative, and she'd played him for a fool. Six years ago, he'd dedicated a great deal of emotional and physical effort to rescuing her from the evil forces he'd *thought* had taken her. Only to find she'd been working with them all along.

Now, she'd thrown her lot in with a god planning to destroy the world.

"Why are you here, Telsin?" Wax asked.

"To warn you, Waxillium," Telsin said from across the room. "Your next actions will be of the utmost importance. You have two days to solve this problem. Only two precious days."

Wax cursed softly, leaning down beside Marasi and Wayne. "Speed bubble," he hissed.

Wayne threw one up and slowed the world around them. It would also prevent Telsin from hearing, or at least understanding, what they were saying.

"What's she playin' at, Wax?" Wayne said. "She should look more threatened. I shot her. Me. First time in years. And she don't even look like she *cared.*"

"Wayne," Marasi said, "it's not like you gave her your virginity."

"No it's not!" he said. "I give *that* away all the time. This was *special.*" Marasi glanced at Wax. "You all right?"

"I will be," he said softly, staring at his sister—frozen in time. "It's . . . painful. Like an old injury aching again. Because it never healed right."

"Why did she say two days?" Marasi asked. "Wax, she's trying to wrong-foot us."

"I agree," he said. "She's trying to get us to believe we have more time than we do. One of her games." He narrowed his eyes. "Her being here says something she may not realize, though. That she's desperate. She knows she has to stop us."

"But she's not afraid of us," Marasi said.

"Not physically," Wax said. "She's not afraid of being captured or killed by us. Harmony said . . . well, she's—at least in a small way—part god. Autonomy has Invested her with some sort of power and authority, made her the avatar of Trell on this planet. For now. Until she fails."

"Wait," Wayne said. "*Who* is Trell and *who* is Autonomy and *who* is that on the steps?"

"That on the steps," Wax said, "is my sister. A woman representing the god Autonomy. Using the title of Trell—an ancient god from this world."

"Right . . ." Wayne said. "And all three are utter knobs?"

"Utter knobs," Wax agreed.

Marasi followed their gaze back toward Telsin, looking so proud and confident. As she watched, Marasi could *swear* that Telsin's eyes began to glow a soft red. The faintest of light. It was gone a moment later.

"Rusts," she whispered. "This feels like it's way above our pay scale, Wax."

"There's no one else," he said. "But like I said, if she's here, she's worried about us. She wanted to go through with her plan weeks ago, but is having problems getting her technology to work. Now here we are, sniffing about, finding things they couldn't track down. My gut says she's here because she wants an opportunity to mess with my mind. Nudge me the wrong direction. Risky of her, but smart."

They all fell silent, but Marasi had that same sense of cold dread from earlier. Magnified. The Set's plan, the danger Autonomy posed . . . Marasi glanced down; she was still holding the picture Maraga had dug out. Ash falling from the sky, burying cities that had been destroyed.

"What do we do?" Wayne asked.

"Let me think," Wax said. "How much bendalloy do you have? Are we wasting it?"

"Nah," Wayne said. "I've got plenty."

"He's been saving it," Marasi said, "and learning to be responsible with his finances and his use of metals."

Wax glanced at him. "Who'd you take the money from?"

"Someone worthless," Wayne said.

"Remind me to check my bank accounts," Wax said, "if there are any banks left after all of this. For now, the most urgent matter is the bomb. They have it ready, but can't deliver it. So we need to find whatever device they're setting up to launch the thing, then stop it."

"Maraga says the Set is using the bunkers under the city as a kind of base," Marasi said. "If we can sneak in, maybe we can find the mechanism. Or at least learn its location."

"Hard to sneak anywhere," Wayne said, nodding toward Telsin, "with some kind of *demigod* thing watchin' you."

Wax thought for a moment. "I need to confront Telsin, deal with her, maybe try to get information out of her. I want to find that bomb and stop it. I might be able to sort the lies from the truth. But I do agree, trying to get into their base could be valuable. Not sure how we'd manage it though."

Marasi glanced at Moonlight, frozen outside the speed bubble. What did she make of all this? Did she have answers?

Maybe Marasi should tell Wax. Only . . . would that break Moonlight's frail trust in her? The woman could easily vanish again, as she'd done after the fight at the warehouse.

So many secrets. Marasi had become a constable in part to reveal secrets—and here, in working with Moonlight, she had a chance. At something bigger. Something more important. Secrets beyond secrets. She needed more time to pry information out of Moonlight.

"Wax," she said, "we should split up."

He met her eyes. "Two teams," he said. "You find a way into the caverns. I deal with Telsin and follow any leads I get from her."

"Exactly," Marasi said. "I think Kim is trustworthy. She and I had a chance to chat when we were at the archive, and she knows a lot about the city. With her help, I might be able to locate an entrance to the caverns. In there are secrets, maybe the location of the bomb. But an infiltration like that will take time. Maybe too much time."

"So Wayne and I take a direct route," Wax said. "We interrogate Telsin and locate the bomb that way."

"She'll play with your mind, mate," Wayne said.

"I know. But she's my sister. I . . . I need to do this." Wax took a deep breath. "If I'm right, she'll have to give me bits of truth along with her lies. If we can play the game better than she does, it might lead us to the weapon."

"Right," Marasi said. "Whatever you find, send to Steris and Captain Reddi via radio. I'll do the same. That way, we can consolidate our information and leave notes for one another."

Wax nodded, but seemed reluctant.

"You worry local radio operators might be compromised?" Marasi said.

"It's possible," he said. "But I don't know of a better way. I'm going to send something to Steris as soon as we leave here."

"Will you write to Allik too?" she asked. "Remind him I asked him to leave the city? It's selfish of me, but . . ."

"It's all right," Wax said. "It's not selfish to want to save those you love." He paused. "I don't know if we'll have a chance to meet up again before the day is done. So if you don't hear from me, Marasi, know that I trust your judgment. If you have a chance to stop the bomb, do so. Whatever the cost."

"Same for you," she said. "All right. Let's split." Wax nodded to Wayne, who dropped the speed bubble.

And just like that, Marasi had put herself in a position to interrogate Moonlight freely. She *would* share what she found with Wax. And he *would* understand. She felt she should have been embarrassed for keeping this from him, but in truth she was excited.

Wax walked over to Telsin. "You and I need to talk," he said to her.

"Agreed," she said, starting up the steps.

Wax moved to follow, pausing briefly to say something to Maraga. Before Wayne joined him, he took Marasi by the arm. "Hey," he said softly. "Be careful with that Kim character. I think she's fakin' about somethin'."

"I appreciate the warning," Marasi said. "I think she knows more than she's saying, but I don't think she's working for the enemy."

"Right," he said. "Hey, you take care of yourself."

"You too, Wayne."

"Don't I always?"

He said it as if in jest, but there was something to his voice. "You all right?" she asked.

He shrugged. "Just feels off, you know? After six years together, I've gotta let you march away alone. Without my keen observations on life and the world to keep you on your toes."

She smiled, then raised her fist for him to tap with his own. "I'm glad you walked out of the stories and into my life. I'd rather have a friend than a legend."

"Same."

"Wayne, no one is calling me a legend."

"They will," he said with a wink. "You take care. We'll see you later tonight." He slipped an old bowler hat off a rack near the center of the room. He put it on and left a stapler tied with a ribbon hanging in its place. Where had he found that?

Wax and Wayne disappeared up the steps behind Telsin, leaving Marasi alone with Moonlight, Maraga, and the whole cosmere's worth of secrets.

PART THREE

35

Wax nodded to Wayne, and together they dashed out of the news-paper building—Wax pulling Telsin behind him—and into the cover between two nearby apartment buildings.

Telsin sighed as they stopped, then straightened her suit jacket. "Was that necessary?"

Wax gestured, and Wayne scrambled farther along the alleyway to scout the area.

"There are no snipers," Telsin said. "You aren't surrounded. It's just me."

Wax ignored her, absently clicking the chambers on Vindication one at a time. Watching the sky, because each time he looked at her he felt pain. Betrayal. He'd told Marasi he could handle Telsin. But now he questioned that. When had he ever gotten the better of her? She'd always made a fool of him.

This is what you came here to do, he told himself. *This is why you put the coat back on. Because you know she has to be dealt with somehow.*

"What if I towed you to Elendel," he said, "and threw you in prison. Would you just go along with it?"

"Of course not," she said. "I came to talk. To persuade you."

"Of what?"

She met his eyes. "To run, Wax. Return to the Roughs. Take your wife, your children, and *leave.* You have time. Step away and let me do what needs to be done. I'd rather you lived."

"Where was that inclination six years ago?" he asked. "On that mountaintop?"

She sighed, as if at his childishness, then leaned against the wall of the alley. "I didn't want to shoot you, Wax. I didn't expect you to show up and undermine our plans, and I had to do what was required in the moment.

"Wax, I *know* you. I *know* you're overwhelmed by this. It's too big for you; it can't be solved by barreling in, revolver in hand. Go back to a place where you can accomplish something relevant. This next part will be messy, but it's the only way to save our planet."

"You expect me to believe that *you* are interested in the safety of the planet? That *you* are being altruistic?"

"Hardly," she said, her arms folded. "I live here, Wax. If the Basin goes, *I* go. If you can trust in one thing, trust in my sense of self-preservation. Elendel *has* to be destroyed. Or else."

"Or else Autonomy destroys the entire Basin?"

"She has an army," Telsin said, looking away. "Men of gold and red . . . waiting for me to fail. Breathing over my proverbial shoulder. Our best hope is for me to prove I can rule this planet for her—and I need to remove the leadership of Elendel before I can do that." She focused on him. "We'll be better off with her guiding us. Harmony is useless, as you've undoubtedly learned by now. We need someone stronger."

"Someone who by coincidence," he said, "wants *you* to represent her."

"It is a job that needs to be done."

"I'd rather it be done by practically *anyone* but you."

"You don't get to make that decision." Telsin looked up toward the sky. "Once I'm fully Invested—once I'm a Sliver of Autonomy—you'll see. I'll rebuild the Basin. Make it as modern and efficient as Bilming. You realize that Harmony has crippled us? Life is too easy in the Basin, too lush. There's no conflict or strife, so we don't innovate, don't grow. That's what Autonomy has taught me."

Wax, feeling cold, stepped toward her. "So the solution is to annihilate Elendel? Nearly *half* our entire population?"

She continued staring at the sky.

"Telsin," he said, "this *insane* plan won't work. The South will invade the moment we're perceived as weak. The Outer Cities will rebel in *horror* at what you've done. I know the mayors of those cities. They're frustrated, but they're not monsters.

"By destroying Elendel, you'd throw us into chaos. And yes, you'll have strife. But it will end us, as surely as if Autonomy had attacked. This won't give you what you want. Autonomy is *playing* you. Have you considered that? Maybe she wants you to destroy the Basin so she doesn't have to bother."

Again, Telsin didn't look at him. And rusts, he felt like he'd put together another piece. Harmony had talked about Autonomy and the way she pushed people to survive, to prove themselves. A destroyed city might seem like a ruthless enough move to accomplish that, which was why Telsin was pursuing it.

But what about the letter indicating the involvement of Elendel senators? he thought. *This is wrong. I'm making guesses based on incomplete information.*

"Come on," Telsin said, turning to climb up a fire escape. "I hate the smell of alleys."

Wax raised the gun at her and chambered a hazekiller round. An aluminum bullet with a secondary explosive that would blast after it lodged into her—a brutal shell capable of ripping off limbs. Ranette had designed it for him after he'd discovered the Bands of Mourning and had expressed interest in ways to forcibly remove spikes from bodies.

Telsin continued up the fire escape, indifferent. She paused at the first landing and glanced at Wax. "Come on." Then she kept climbing.

Rusts. Wax raised Vindication beside his head, then dropped a bullet with the other hand and used it to launch himself up past Telsin onto the roof. She joined him a short time later, and they both looked out over the city.

"Life really would have been far simpler," she said, "if you'd stayed in the Roughs, Wax."

"Then you and Edwarn shouldn't have vanished."

"We had to go into hiding," she said. "Did Harmony tell you what happened to our parents?"

"It was . . . an accident . . ."

"It was agents of Harmony, trying to get to *me*. Did Harmony ever admit that to you?" She strolled past him. "No, I expect not, based on your expression."

Don't let her play you, Wax. Get information. "I know your bomb's delivery mechanism doesn't work, Telsin. I *am* going to track it down and stop it. Maybe *you* should be the one planning to hide in the Roughs.

Better, maybe you should be asking me for *help*. If Autonomy has an army ready to strike, then we should be figuring out how to fight it together."

Telsin stopped at the edge of the building, elbows on the stone railing, contemplative. "It's pretty, don't you think? A city of the future. All symmetrical, like a perfect face. A beauty without blemish."

"Telsin," Wax said, stepping up to her.

"Oh, stop with the gritty constable growl, Wax," she said. "You see this city? Six years under my direction, and it's doing *far* better than Elendel. You have to admit we've been too sheltered. The Malwish are beyond us, and you haven't even *seen* what other planets are capable of doing. We're so far behind. We're vulnerable."

"I don't see how blowing up the capital is going to change that, Telsin."

"Because you've always lacked vision, Wax," she said. "When something truly expansive lies before you, instead of comprehending it, you *run*."

Wax kept his distance. "Why did you come to see me, Telsin?" he asked. "What is this *really* about?"

"Sibling affection?" she said. Then smiled as he gave her a flat glance in response. "I simply want you gone. Out of the equation. You interfering is bad. Even when you inevitably fail."

Her brother showing up to ruin things is bad, he thought. Telsin glanced away again, but he sensed a tension in her posture. She was legitimately worried that her plans wouldn't come together—that Autonomy would simply send in her armies.

Can't have your own family ruining your masterful plans. It makes you look bad in front of the dark god deciding whether or not to destroy you.

"You can't actually think," he said, "that you can bully me into leaving a case."

"I suppose not," she said softly. "But I wanted to try."

Yeah, she's worried. Telsin knew him, but he knew her equally well. Perhaps Harmony was right in suggesting Wax talk to her. The sharpened sword cut cleanest, and Wax had spent a lifetime sharpening this particular blade.

"Do you remember back in the Village," he said to her, "when you wanted your own room?"

"Father always said it was appropriate for us," she said, "because of our lineage. We shouldn't have to share."

"You planted stolen cash on your own cousin to achieve it. And even *that* wasn't your end goal—you wanted to live alone so that you could sneak out. Everything is a power play for you."

"Because I'm willing to step up," she said. "And take charge. Like I took over our house when our parents died. Like I'm taking over this planet. It *will* happen, Wax. I'm merely sad that I'll have to cut through you to accomplish it."

Wax met her gaze. And he realized something profound.

He couldn't see anything familial in this person.

Familiar, yes. But whatever he had loved was long gone, ripped out and replaced with expansions of the parts of her he'd always hated.

"Last chance, Wax," she said, holding his eyes. "Go back to the Roughs. With Elendel gone, those people out there are going to need someone to help guide and protect them. You can be that person. This is too big for you. You know it is."

Wax opened his mouth to object. To explain that yes, he had run once. He'd been overwhelmed by politics, society, expectations. He'd wanted adventure, dreamed of it in the Roughs—but more, he'd wanted a place where one man could make an easy difference. Where things felt simpler.

He cut himself off, realizing something crucial. She was *wrong* about him.

He'd changed. He'd become someone new, someone who had grown beyond his fears. But she didn't realize it. She didn't know about Lessie. Didn't understand the depth of his friendship with Wayne. Didn't know of his love for Steris, the reason he'd taken Harmony's offer to return from death and try again.

She didn't know him. But she *thought she did*.

Rusts. For the first time in his life, he had an advantage over her. Telsin, by marinating in her own ambitions for years, had become an extreme version of the woman he knew. She'd continued on exactly the path he'd worried about since her youth. But he'd deviated. He'd grown. He'd *changed*.

"I might not be able to fix things in Elendel," he found himself saying. "I might not grasp everything that's happening with you and Autonomy. But stopping a bomb is something I can solve. Something I *will* solve."

She sighed, seeing only the dogged lawman. Her little brother and his fantasies.

"You have no idea . . ." she whispered, looking away. "You can't stop this, Wax. Even if you did find the bomb, there are redundancies upon redundancies to make sure that Autonomy gets what she wants. We need to *prove* ourselves. And I'm going to do that."

Redundancies. What did she mean by that? It didn't sound like the army Autonomy was supposedly sending. Were there other, internal pressures? Rivals? He took a guess.

"Gave Entrone," he said, "is trying to overtake you. Seize your position."

"Entrone is a coward," she said. "He won't move against me. Wax, you're not half as smart as you think you are."

He might not see it all, true—but if Entrone was a coward, then maybe Wax was interrogating the wrong person. He doubted he could break Telsin. But clearly there was someone *else* who knew these plans.

So, I get Entrone to break, he thought.

"You ever stand up someplace high," Telsin said, "and feel the irresistible urge to throw yourself off?"

"No," Wax said, frowning. "If I want to, I jump. If I don't, I don't."

"The curse of Steelpushing," she said, staring out over the city. "You can't feel it. The call to do something dramatic, drastic, *impressive*."

"The urge to kill yourself on a whim?" Wax asked, baffled.

"The opportunity to be afraid," she whispered. "To do something thrilling and new. You know, I resisted getting the spikes for Steelpushing and Ironpulling? I didn't want to lose my nervousness around heights. Then I found new fears, new challenges, new *ambitions*."

Wax nodded slowly. That was his Telsin. The woman who always pushed recklessly for more. More power. But also more experiences. More novelty. More control over others.

"There's an entire cosmere out there," she said to him. "Few ever see or know it. But I have a chance to. A real chance. I'm not going to let you take that from me. I'm telling you, Wax, I'm not going to pull my punches. I'll do *whatever it takes*."

"And I'll stop you. Whatever it takes."

"Ever the moralist," she said, glancing at him. "Standing so tall, pretending you see so high, when in reality you can barely *grasp* the problems you're trying to fix. I've already solved them. Do you want to hear of Trell? Autonomy? What it means to be her avatar?"

A part of him did. But if she wanted to tell him about it . . . if she was offering . . .

Rusts, then she was stalling.

She was desperate, trying to buy as much time as she could. That piece clicked into place. She was talking to him because she had to keep him distracted. The trick wasn't to realize that she was stalling, it was to recognize that as long as he let her tease him with information, she held all the cards.

There was only one way to win this particular game. And that was to leave the table.

"She's going to destroy us?" he said, strolling across the top of the roof behind her.

"Unless I prove to her that we're worth saving," she explained, turning to survey the city. As before, she didn't seem to care that she had her back to him. "Autonomy is . . . odd. She respects those who are bold, strong, able to survive on their own. But she also wants them to obey her. I suppose that is the irony of godhood. Half the time, being 'autonomous' means following her plan. And there's no Whimsy to her—that's a different god.

"Autonomy is rugged individualism filtered through the lens of a god who thinks she knows best. And in that context, individualism is a virtue best applied to finding ways to carry out the plans *she* has outlined. You get to be individual in your chosen path to do what *she* says . . ."

Wax missed the next part, as he had quietly slipped over the side of the roof. With luck, she'd keep right on talking, giving him time to get away.

36

Marasi and Moonlight hurriedly finished up in the basement—Moonlight grabbing a last few rubbings of the wall plates and tucking them away in her case. Together they then climbed to the main floor, where they found the grey-haired editor Maraga standing in the center of a cluttered room, holding an overstuffed travel bag and looking frazzled.

"On his way out," she said to Marasi, "Dawnshot told me to go to family in the countryside. But all of my family is either here or in Elendel. Should I . . . go to them?"

"Probably not wise," Marasi said. Any family in Bilming would be easily tracked down by the Set, and Elendel . . . well, it had a massive bomb pointed at it.

That thought filled Marasi with worry. But she needed to focus on preventing the disaster. She had to leave helping Elendel to her sister.

"Moonlight," Marasi said, "surely there's a place in the city you could send Maraga? A place of safety for someone who did us such great service?"

Moonlight considered for a moment. She wasn't the type to rush into things, it seemed. Careful. Calculating. Finally she slipped a small card from her sleeve, marked with the interlocking diamond symbol. "Do you know the Knightbridge district?"

"Yes," Maraga said, hesitantly taking the card.

"Go to Thirty-Third and Finete, house number one eighty-seven. Knock, show them this, and tell them Moonlight said you could ask for asylum as recompense for services rendered. They'll take you in. Even the Set will have trouble assaulting that place."

"Thank you," the woman said, clutching the card to her chest.

"I'll send someone to collect your research," Moonlight said. "Though I have the plates all copied. You need to go. Quickly."

"I'm going to fetch my sister too," Maraga said. "Please?"

"If you must," Moonlight said. "But be warned, since the Set knows we're here, each moment you waste endangers your life."

Maraga rushed to the door. She paused to look over what she was leaving, then steeled herself and hurried out.

"What about us?" Moonlight asked.

"We need to determine a likely entry point to the underground caverns," Marasi said. "Do you have maps of enemy movements? Lists of places you think might be owned by the Set?"

"Not on me," Moonlight said. "Perhaps we could return to the records office and do some research."

"I think I have a better idea," Marasi said, leading the way out the front door. "Riskier, but hopefully faster."

"I'm intrigued," Moonlight said, joining her as they walked to a busier street where—with some effort—Marasi managed to flag down a cab. She found it amazing how quickly coachmen had made the swap between horse-drawn carriages and motorcabs.

They settled in the rear of the motorcar, and the cabbie—a woman with dark hair in a ponytail—glanced back at them. "Where to?"

"Knightbridge district," Marasi said. "Thirty-Third and Finete."

The cabbie nodded, pulling out into the flow of traffic and taking them westward.

"Clever," Moonlight said to Marasi. "I'm going to have to watch myself around you. But what makes you think our safehouse will have the maps you want?"

"You found me in the caverns beneath Elendel," Marasi said. "Plus, a moment ago you implied such maps existed—you didn't have them 'on you.' Ergo, I assumed this was a good path forward. Your people will have the information we need."

"They might not let you in," Moonlight said. "What then? You'll have wasted time."

"Wasted time," Marasi snapped. "Wasted *time*?" She glanced toward the cabbie, uncertain what she should say.

"Darkwater, dear," Moonlight said to the cabbie, "give us a little privacy."

"Sure thing, Moonlight," the cabbie said, shutting the window separating the front of the car from the back.

Marasi gaped. Then she looked at Moonlight, who shrugged.

"Moonlight," Marasi said, focusing her thoughts, "what kind of game do you think we're playing? Didn't you say your entire purpose was protecting this planet? Now you imply you'd keep me locked out of your safehouse, and the vital information it contains?"

Moonlight settled in her seat, thoughtful. "My organization," she eventually said, "was created to protect and advance the needs of the planet Scadrial. It's not my homeland, but I am committed to seeing it remain stable. There are terrible forces moving in the cosmere; my people are going to need allies."

"So why are you so resistant to helping me?"

"To be honest," Moonlight said, "I'm worried we're being played. Autonomy is adept at misdirection, at false leads and confusing shadows of half-truths. Restarting the ashfalls? That seems . . . outrageous. Impossible even for her. Something is off about all this. A shade too red to be natural."

"So help me find the truth, Moonlight," Marasi said. "Stop toying with me."

"I'm not toying with you," Moonlight said. "This is an audition."

Marasi blinked. *What?*

"Until a little while ago," Moonlight continued, "I assumed we had months to unravel the Set's plan." She tapped her armrest with a fingernail, then looked at her bag, where the rubbings she'd taken were peeking out.

During their short time working together, Marasi had started to see Moonlight as all-knowing—someone mysterious, alien. But that concern in her eyes, the way she was fighting uncertainty . . . that was all too human.

"I'll let you into the safehouse," Moonlight finally said. "And deal with the ramifications later, if this proves to all be another of Autonomy's shadow games. But I'm not sure I can give you everything you want.

"We don't have the caverns in the city mapped, but we do watch their agents." She patted her bag, and the rubbings. "This lists coordinates of the explosions. So if we compare where the blasts have been happening with the places where Set agents appear and vanish . . ."

". . . We might be able to find a way into their testing facility," Marasi said. "I did something similar to locate that cavern under Elendel."

"I remember when all this started to hit me," Moonlight said softly. "When my world expanded, and my personal squabbles—even the ones that influenced the fates of empires—suddenly became so small. You're doing remarkably well."

"My life," Marasi said, "has mostly been expanses of quiet humdrum punctuated by sudden explosions—usually literal ones—of activity. I'm used to working under pressure."

"And dealing with gods?" Moonlight said. "Fighting their influence?"

"Well, we have one on our own side, after all."

"Kind of," Moonlight said. "Harmony isn't terribly reliable these days. At least not in the ways my mentor would prefer. It's less like having a god on your side—and more like having a powerful referee who only sometimes pays attention to your fight."

"Or an observer," Marasi said, "who you're sure could do more to help, but doesn't for some baffling reason."

"Yes, like . . ." Moonlight narrowed her eyes. "Point made. Here, we're approaching the safehouse. Hopefully the Survivor hasn't returned unexpectedly. My mentor isn't always reasonable when it comes to people he sees as Harmony's agents, and might respond . . . poorly."

37

Wayne had read a real interesting book once about a fellow what went back in time. It had happened because he'd turned on too many electric switches at once. That was ridiculous, but the book had been written when electricity had been new—so it was forgivable. People had thought some funny stuff about electricity back then. Wayne himself had tried to fill a bucket with it once.

He found himself thinking of that story as he scoured the nearby alleys for signs of the Set's agents. See, the book had been all about how changing the past was this dangerous thing. The fellow in it had broken some branches off a tree, and when he'd returned to the future, his father had liked eating butter on his sandwiches instead of mayo. Also, sapient lions had ruled the city.

Wayne had thought there was something . . . off about the story. When he'd mentioned it to friends, Nod had told him of another one with the same idea, where a fellow was sent back in time through the intricacies of indoor plumbing and an unfortunately large flush. And *he* had changed things by eating a bagel, then returned to discover that everybody spoke backward and no one wore shirts anymore.

This book had been better than the first one on account of it having more cussing—plus the no-shirts part being universally applied and *very* descriptively relayed—but still, Wayne found the idea uncomfortable.

He traded a beggar—unbeknownst to the fellow—a stack of cash for a dirty handkerchief; Wayne liked it on account of it havin' a little bunny sewn in the corner. He was starting to figure out why those stories bothered him. They had this sense that changing the future was frightening and dangerous.

But didn't people change it every day?

Wayne wondered regarding the choices people made. Rushing through their lives eating bagels, breaking twigs. Each of them changing the future. Shouldn't they all . . . worry about that a little more? Worry how they were changing the future right now, rather than writing books about people doing it in the past? Even if they couldn't know some things, there was a lot they could anticipate. They might not make that future have talking lions or whatnot—but they might make it have angrier, sadder people.

Maybe stories about fellows quietly making the world better were just too dull. Sounded boring, actually. Maybe if the people in them wore no shirts . . .

A hand wrapped around Wayne's mouth from behind. He almost killed the fellow—but it smelled like Wax, so . . .

Yup, it was Wax. The man eased Wayne back into an alleyway, then pulled him down beside some rubbish as someone passed on the street. Telsin, searching around, annoyed.

After she was gone, Wax removed his hand.

"You let her go?" Wayne whispered.

"Call me crazy—"

"You're crazy."

"—but it feels more like I escaped." Wax nodded his head in the other direction and they snuck away.

"I have to say," Wayne muttered, "that there are better methods of gettin' my attention. You're not supposed to take friends captive, Wax, unless it involves a safeword and stretchy ropes."

"Stretchy ropes?"

"More fun if you can move a little," Wayne said. "I got to test them, since I had to be the one getting tied up. You know, on account of the fact that my girlfriend could turn into a puddle of jelly on command. Kind of undermines the point of bondage."

Wax groaned softly as they slipped out onto the street. "I did *not* need to know any of that, Wayne. Could you maybe avoid being crass on the missions Harmony specifically sent us on?"

"Hey now," Wayne said. "That's not crass. MeLaan is a divine being.

Chosen by Harmony. I figure, dating her was basically like going to church, you know?"

"And the stretchy ropes?"

"A, uh, metaphor for us all being bound by God's will?"

They shared a look, then Wax actually grinned as he shook his head. Good. Guy was too uptight these days, what with parenthood, bein' a senator, and having to save the whole damn city now and then.

Hoid pulled up in the car to get them, per Wayne's earlier request—but Telsin was still lurking around. So Wax and Wayne slipped out another way and entered a busy street of bustling people. Full of Bilming idiots what had no idea how difficult they was making life. Though he supposed that was too much of a generalization. There were plenty of people in Bilming that weren't idiots—they came from out of town to gawk at all the idiots.

"Did you get a lead out of Telsin?" Wayne asked as they blended into the crowd.

"Maybe," Wax said.

"Well, I've *definitely* got a lead."

"You do? Thank Harmony."

"Yup. There's a *shining* good pub three streets over. Two different bums swore by it."

Wayne earned a real good glare out of that one. Made him feel all proud of himself. Smiles, then glares, then smiles, then glares. They pulled at a person like taffy, keeping them limber.

"I had to get away from Telsin," Wax said. "I'm sure she was stalling, trying to keep me occupied."

"Seems like she's worried we can stop her."

"Agreed. Which is encouraging. But I won't get anything useful from her. Not in time. We need someone else to interrogate, and she gave me a lead: I think the lord mayor deserves a visit."

"Here now," Wayne said. "Now *that's* an idea."

They stopped on the street, people giving them a wide berth. The folks here seemed to dress with a lot more variety than in Elendel, but nobody wore guns. Wax stood out like a big ol' wart on a fellow's face. The type that you really wanted to pop to see what oozed out.

"We don't exactly blend in, do we?" Wax said.

"Mate, you're wearing a rusting *mistcoat*."

"They're comfy."

"They draw attention."

"You like attention!"

"Depends on who's looking." He eyed Wax. "Never have figured out how to go up stairs in one of those things without tripping over my own feet."

"I've never had any trouble."

Figured. Mistcoats appeared like a regular piece of clothing, but Wayne was sure they was secretly something else. Made of mist or such—and since Harmony *liked* Wax, the coat didn't trip him.

Wasn't fair that God liked Wax better. Wayne didn't *mean* to blaspheme when he got drunk, it just slipped out. And really, if the blasphemy leaked out, didn't that mean he was more pious afterward? That was why he got drunk so often. That, and absolutely no other reason.

The two of them moved to the side of the street, in the mouth of an alleyway, to plan. Wax glared right smartly at anyone who gawked, sending them on their way.

"So," Wax said, "we should choose our next course soon. Because if I somehow actually managed to lose the Set when slipping away from Telsin, they'll surely spot us before too long."

"'Cuz you stand out like pink shoes on a pallbearer."

"'Cuz I stand out like pink shoes on a pallbearer."

"I like the idea of shakin' down Entrone," Wayne said. "On principle, at least. But I worry about how much attention that would draw. So maybe we don't need to interrogate him specifically. After all, we do know where he lives."

Wayne pointed across the city, up the road, to the silvery-white building sitting at the end. It wasn't the highest building in town. The central spire, dominating the very middle of the city, was the highest by a lot. And they were even adding to it at the top, it seemed, with new construction.

Still, there was a certain majesty about the mayor's mansion. The kind that said, "Oi, mate! Don't use words like 'oi, mate' 'round here."

"Entrone," Wayne said, "is obviously involved in all this. He's the type to have secrets written down somewhere, maybe give us a lead on where that bomb is being kept. He's probably got a safe or something full of answers."

"You just said shaking him down would create another incident," Wax said, his hands on his hips, holstered guns jutting out and making basically everybody nearby nervous. "Now you're suggesting we ransack his *mansion?*"

"I'm suggesting," Wayne said, giving it a nice upper-class, Fifth Octant, old-money accent, "that once we have completed our radio communication, we give the esteemed lord mayor an evening turn-down service with mints on his pillow, folded towels in the shape of a monkey, and a light despoiling of his intimate affairs. Done with *only* the most *delicate* attention, mind you. A *courteous* looting. An . . . upper-class plundering."

"Is that so?" Wax said.

Wayne leaned in. "I mean, we'll still break all his stuff and steal his secrets. I just won't fart on his chair before we go. You know. To keep things classy."

Wax took a deep breath. "Well, I suppose that does walk the line between accosting the man himself and doing something that has a good chance of success. Let's do it."

Wayne grinned.

"But *I'll* do the ransacking," Wax said. "*You* handle the distraction."

38

Steris threw open the door to the governor's chamber, where he was holding his private council on what to do about Bilming. Then held that door open for Constable-General Reddi. He'd been invited to the meeting along with his staff. Today that included two other people: Constable Gorglen as record keeper. And Steris.

The governor sat at the head of the meeting table. Adawathwyn immediately glared at Steris through dark brown eyes. The three senators—Lord Cett, Lady Hammondess, and Lady Gardre—were in attendance, as well as Ambassador Daal, his expression unreadable behind his bloodred mask. The shorter man hadn't taken a seat at the table, but instead stood by the wall, his posture prim and sharp.

"Ah, finally," the governor said, looking up from the broadsheets. "Reddi. You . . . Wait. What is *she* doing here?"

"Lady Ladrian?" Reddi said. "Subject matter expert, on my payroll."

As of fifteen minutes ago, at least. Steris had insisted he actually pay her, and she clutched the single coin in her fist as she shut the door behind Reddi. Then she stepped forward and sat down at the table beside him.

"Did she tell you," the governor said, "that I specifically excluded her from this council?"

"Yes, she did," Reddi replied. "And frankly, Your Grace, I thought that an unwise move. She's the wife of the man who alerted us to this crisis.

When Lady Ladrian approached me and explained why I should employ her, I realized she'd undoubtedly have information this council needs."

The vice governor folded her arms on the table, scowling. But the governor . . . he nodded. Steris always hesitated to read too much into people's expressions, but now she wondered. Was there a rift between these two? She'd always assumed Varlance was entirely in Adawathwyn's pocket.

But then, no person ever fit comfortably in a pocket.

"Very well," the governor said. "I'm afraid we started without you. As the information has come in and we've gauged the feelings of Outer Cities governments, we've come to see that our path is inevitable. It looks like war."

"War?" Reddi said.

"It's the necessary course of action," Lady Hammondess said. She had a small gap between her front teeth, of the sort men often described as cute—as if it were the reason for her beauty rather than her flawless skin, delicate features, and long lashes. Curious, how minor flaws became cute when their bearer also happened to be conventionally attractive. "The Outer Cities are building up for war."

"Warships in Bilming," Lord Cett agreed. He was a striking man, if you liked the smooth and well-dressed sort. Steris wondered how much work it took to keep one's rough edges so contained behind powders and soft clothing. "Railroad blockades to the south. Recruitment flyers in the Roughs, offering jobs for 'security forces.'"

"Which is why," Constable Reddi said, "we need to work so hard to soothe the situation and reconcile!"

"Better," Lady Hammondess said, "we should strike first. We've been ignoring the warning signs for too long. If we don't move soon, we will *not* be able to win."

Steris glanced at Lady Gardre, the third of the nobles in the room. The plump woman was much less of a war hawk than the others, far more reasonable. But even she nodded, reluctantly. And it *did* make sense. Every day that Elendel dithered gave the other cities time to build power. Elendel had the advantage of infrastructure, manufacturing, and coordination. But that wouldn't remain an edge for long.

Striking first made sense if you thought war was inevitable. But it wasn't. It didn't *have* to be.

This was the enemy's plan. She was increasingly certain that saber-rattling in the Outer Cities was a cover for whatever weapon was being prepared in Bilming.

Reddi began sputtering. "War with what army? Elendel has barely ten thousand troops, and that's *counting* our navy protecting shipping to the South!"

"We have conscription plans in place," Adawathwyn said smoothly. "And we have a very capably trained constabulary."

Reddi seemed horrified by that statement. Steris had something to add, but she hesitated. Was this the part where she spoke? She could rarely figure that out.

"My people," Reddi said, "are *not* soldiers."

"Pardon, constable," Lord Cett said, leaning across the table. "But no one is a soldier until they're trained to be."

"We're needed," Reddi explained. "Law—"

"We'll be under *martial* law," the governor explained. "Policing crime in the city will get a lot easier with curfews. You can put excess constables into the military force."

Maybe *this* was the part where she should speak. Steris opened her mouth and made a noise to that effect, but they kept talking straight over her.

"I won't stand for this!" Reddi said, throwing himself—paradoxically—to his feet. "This is not the oath my constables swore!"

"You don't get to choose, constable," the governor said. "I hold your commission, and that of every constable in this city. They ultimately answer to me."

"We can quit, Varlance," Reddi said, leaning forward, his hands on the table. "You can't *force* us to fight."

"I—" Steris started.

"Actually," Adawathwyn said lightly, "that's precisely what a draft *is*, Constable Reddi."

"I would—" Steris tried again.

"Yeah?" Reddi snapped. "And who exactly is going to lock us up?"

"Everyone shut up and listen!" Steris snapped. "Or I will barf on the table to get your attention!"

The entire room stared at her.

"I'll do it," she warned. "I keep medication in my handbag to produce the effect. You'd be surprised at how often the option is relevant."

Well, now she had their attention.

"If we are worried about war," she said, "we should immediately begin an evacuation of the city."

"No good," Cett said. "If there is war, we need workers to facilitate industry—and to ramp up production of munitions."

Rusts. That was the correct answer. She'd hoped he wouldn't have thought that far forward. She glanced at the silent Malwish ambassador. What did he think of all of this? Had he anticipated it? She had always kept her focus on members of the Set in the Basin. But who was to say there weren't members among the Malwish as well? Rusts.

"War is not the answer," she said, turning back to the group. "It serves our enemies, not us. Look, I made a list here, to prove the logic of what I say. I'm increasingly convinced that the leaders of the Outer Cities *want* us to be passing legislation that restricts and insults them. They *want* us interfering.

"They have built gunships and militaries, but they *have not* attacked. They caught Waxillium in their midst, shooting up a warehouse, but what haven't they done? They haven't expelled our constables or officials from the city. They've shouted about it, they've drawn up editorials. But they haven't *attacked*. Why not?"

"Because they need *us* to do it," Reddi said. "They need us to give them a reason to go to war."

"The common people of the Basin don't want to fight," Steris said. "Certainly not against Elendel—where they undoubtedly have family."

"Or because they don't think they can win," Lord Cett said.

Steris looked down at her notes. "That's . . . unfortunately a real possibility."

"Why is that unfortunate?" Reddi asked.

"Because," Steris said, "if they know they can't defeat us in open war they might do something desperate. Like unleash a weapon of cataclysmic relevance."

"Returning to your real point," Adawathwyn said. "This bomb you keep harping on."

But Governor Varlance was watching her. He was listening.

"My husband," Steris said, "is in Bilming investigating it as we speak. He produced a terribly dangerous explosion in our laboratory, using rare materials we know the enemy has. We have traced a set of test explosions in caverns underneath Bilming. Something *is* happening."

She met the governor's eyes. "And if our fears about a bomb are true," she said softly, "then the posturing—manipulating us into the position of a bully and tyrant who needs to be resisted—might be intended to give the leaders of the Outer Cities a justification. A way to explain why they had to take such extreme measures. Like destroying us all."

The room quieted, but then Lady Gardre shook her head. "Are we really entertaining these fancies? Doomsday weapons? The real politics of the situation aren't enough?"

She, Steris realized, looking at the quiet woman, *must be the member of the Set.* She'd assumed there would be at least one moving among the political elite of Elendel. For a while she'd worried it was the governor or Adawathwyn, but they were both too obvious. The Set liked to move beneath layers of obscurity.

The governor was far too prominent, and Adawathwyn too actively working for things the Set wanted. She was a decoy; she likely assumed she was the mastermind of her own designs. In actuality, she was just another puppet. Encouraged, but left clean so that her eventual downfall wouldn't lead to real conspirators. Who included, smartly, the woman who was seen as the most reasonable. The most rational.

Steris felt far more comfortable upon identifying her. It was like . . . finding a snake in your intimates drawer. Yes, it was alarming. But at least you could close the drawer and know where it was.

But how to steer the conversation in defiance of that woman? Ah. Perhaps that?

She turned to the constables. "This might be the right time to reveal yourself," she said.

"Huh?" Reddi asked.

"Not you, Constable-General," she said, looking past him toward the lanky Constable Gorglen—the younger man with a long neck and freckles. So unassuming. He met her eyes.

"How did you know?" he asked in a grinding, rough voice that didn't match his frame.

"Process of elimination," she said. "We were promised help, and MeLaan said there were multiple kandra among the constables, but gave only one name. Plus, you walk awkwardly when you have to use a two-legged body."

"Damn," Gorglen—TenSoon—said. "But I suppose you're right about the timing." He stood up before the room of surprised people and made his skin transparent. "Harmony would like me to impress upon you the importance of our current debate—and to confirm what Lady Ladrian is saying. The Set is real. They are planning to annihilate Elendel."

The governor gasped.

Adawathwyn drew back.

Reddi gaped, then spun on Steris. "Why didn't you tell me?"

"I wasn't a hundred percent certain until earlier today," Steris admitted. "I actually wondered if *you* were also kandra, Reddi. I decided against it, as I don't think Harmony likes his kandra impersonating important officials. Except that once. Well, and that other time. But those were exceptions." She flipped open one of her notebooks. "I've been tracking who might have been replaced for weeks now. See? Kandra attendant to the constable-general. Second most likely placement in the city for one of the Immortals."

"And the first?" Adawathwyn asked.

"You," Steris said, flipping back a page. "But I was working with out-dated information. A kandra in your place would take far more care not to be an utterly worthless piece of slime." She made a notation. The room was quiet. "Oh, did I say something awkward again? I *do* make that mistake sometimes, don't I?"

Reddi slumped back into his seat. "I can't believe this . . ."

"It was all but inevitable that they would be among your staff, Constable-General Reddi," Steris said.

"No," he said. "It's not that he's kandra. It's that . . . rusts, Wayne was right . . ."

"I am TenSoon," the kandra said to the room, eliciting another series of gasps. He growled softly. "I hate it when people do that. Harmony is worried. And so *you* should be worried. Especially as Harmony is . . . unable to see certain things lately. We are working blind."

"What can blind a god?" the governor asked.

"Another god," Steris mumbled.

"So what do we do?" Reddi asked. "We can't go to war, not if that's what they want. But—"

He was interrupted by a knock at the door. There were no attendants in the room, just senators and the like, so Reddi answered it himself: revealing a young woman, a radio technician by her uniform, holding a folded piece of paper.

"What is it?" Reddi demanded.

"Communication from Dawnshot," she said, "for Lady Ladrian. I . . .

um . . . thought it was worth interrupting you, even though the people outside said—"

"You did the right thing," Reddi said, taking it.

The poor woman was pale and trembling.

"You read it?" Steris asked.

"I had to transcribe it for you," she said. "That's how it works . . ."

Reddi handed Steris the letter, and she unfolded it. The opening words, bold and dominant, leaped off the page.

Bomb is confirmed real, and already fabricated. City-destroying capacity. Enemy is trying to find a way to deliver it to Elendel. It's time to evacuate the city.

39

Marasi stood before an unassuming townhome, one in a long row of structures along the street, each a different color with a slightly different building shape. Each lawn held a different variety of tree. Bilming ideal: mass-produced individuality.

Marasi hesitated on the threshold. Ruin. Was she ready to meet the Survivor himself? A man she had been taught since childhood to worship, a man who had transcended even the grave. Who had briefly held the mantle of Preservation before releasing it to the Ascendant Warrior. And who had then protected the people of the Southern Continent for years after the world was remade.

Moonlight was confident that her mentor really was him. So how would it feel to meet him?

You've chatted with Death, Marasi thought. *Is this so different?*

Judging by her nerves: Yes. Yes it was.

Moonlight touched her finger to a piece of metal on the door, and the thing unlocked. "Identity lock," she noted, then pushed open the door. The small foyer inside was all hardwood and polish, and there were no paintings or other ornamentations of note. Moonlight headed to the left, into a large room with thick drapes covering the windows.

The walls were lined with maps, illuminated by electric lights. Moonlight slid her bag onto a table by the far wall, where a woman in her twenties—somewhat plump, with a stark blonde bob—was peering at a paper covered in strange writing. She had a small terrier in her lap.

"Moonlight," the woman said after a glance. "You have to read this. Travel to Bjendal has been completely upset. That's *four* primary systems we can't visit without extreme danger, if you count Roshar. I've said it for years: The perpendicularities are no longer viable. They never *were* good for mass transportation or commerce, no matter how hard those fools on Nalthis try. We need a different . . ." The woman trailed off, then turned in her seat, perhaps hearing Marasi stepping into the room. "Hey! You brought a local!"

"Marasi, meet Codenames," Moonlight said. "Codenames, meet Marasi. We're working on a mission together."

"Wow," Codenames said, thrusting the sheet of paper at Moonlight, then hopping to her feet, the small dog under her arm. "You must trust her."

"Hardly."

"You brought her to the safehouse!"

"She forced me."

"No one forces you to do anything," Codenames said, then bounced over and thrust her free hand toward Marasi. "Hi! I'm Codenames Are Stupid. Long story."

The woman had a faint accent, wholly unlike that of Allik or anyone Marasi had met from the Southern Continent. That, plus the way she'd spoken of "locals," indicated . . . another traveler? The presence of an accent indicated she might not be as good at languages as Moonlight was, maybe?

Marasi shook her hand. "Is . . . um . . . the Survivor here?"

"Kell?" Codenames said. "Nah. Haven't seen him in a week or so." She spun toward Moonlight. "What do you think of the report? Worrisome, right?"

Moonlight held the paper pinched between two fingers. "Codenames," she said, "what language is this even in?"

"Thaylen," Codenames said. "Oh! It's a *fascinating* one, Moonlight. You should learn it! Look how the letters interlock in—"

"I'll stick to using Connection tricks for languages, thank you," Moonlight said, spreading out the rubbings she'd taken.

"That's cheating."

"Another word for a clever shortcut," Moonlight said. "Is TwinSoul here? I think we're going to need some mathematics."

"Lily and I will go and grab him," Codenames said, carrying her dog and slipping away into the back rooms.

Marasi had watched the exchange with bafflement, but rather than focus on what she didn't understand, she turned her attention to something she did. One of the maps was of Scadrial—the entire world. A more detailed map than she'd ever seen, far more extensive than the official surveys—it even included the dark parts of the unexplored islands and landmasses to the south.

If that was Scadrial, then what were these other maps? Rusts. How many worlds were out there?

There's always another secret, she thought, remembering her catechism as a child studying the life of the Survivor.

A short time later, Codenames walked back into the room with an elderly man. He looked . . . well, ancient, judging by the long powder-white mustache and the liver-spotted skin, which was a deep tan. He wore a formal suit in the Bilming fashion, so . . . maybe he was from her land? But he also had a short beard with mustaches—a style she'd never seen a man wear in Elendel. Though he stood tall, not the least bit bowed by age, he did seem a little unsteady on his feet—since he gripped the doorframe as he stepped through it.

"Ah," he said, pressing his palms together. "A guest! Welcome to our home, honored guest. Let me get you something to drink."

"TwinSoul," Moonlight said, "we are on a deadline to—"

"Deadlines are no excuse for rudeness," TwinSoul said. "I am Twin-Soul, and you are . . . ?"

"Marasi," she said.

"Lady Marasi!" he said. "Excellent." He immediately turned toward what Marasi assumed was the kitchen. "How do you take your tea?"

"Um . . . mint tea, if you have it. With lemon?"

"Excellent!" he said again. He soon returned with a plate bearing a cup and an array of nuts and fruits. "Please enjoy."

She felt guilty making someone so old wait on her—but at the same time there was a certain forcefulness to how he offered the refreshment. It reminded her of her aunt, who would be far more offended if you didn't accept a drink. So Marasi took the cup and a handful of nuts.

"Now," TwinSoul said. "What have you brought me, Moonlight? Curious, curious." He stepped over to the table and surveyed the rubbings—stretching out his hands and resting them on the table.

Marasi stepped up, curious. There was something odd about his hands that she hadn't noticed earlier: a line of crystal. Embedded in the skin, running along the outsides of his fingers and wrists—almost like a seam on a glove. It was pinkish-red, like rose quartz. The man leaned down, and she saw lines of similar crystal appear from beneath his collar, growing up the sides of his neck and temples. Crossing his skin like little rivers of liquid.

As she watched with amazement, these tendrils expanded from his temples, forming *spectacles*. Completely made of crystal, the lens parts more transparent than the rest. A *second* set of lenses, smaller, formed in front of the others—giving him extra magnification.

"How . . ." Marasi said, glancing at Moonlight. "How does he do that?"

"I fear," TwinSoul said, pulling tight one of the rubbings, "that such information is not lightly shared with an outsider, even an honored guest. I must trust that Moonlight thinks this is acceptable for you to see, but I apologize. I will not explain without leave from our leader."

"It's an emergency," Moonlight said, lounging against a bookshelf with her arms folded. "I had to risk bringing her in." She glanced at Marasi, and seemed to be hiding a smile at Marasi's visible wonder.

She's not as worried about my visit as she implied, Marasi thought. *She sees this as an opportunity to intrigue me.*

It was working. TwinSoul arranged the various rubbings, then raised an index finger. Two lines of crystal grew up the outsides of that finger and formed into a *nib,* like a fountain pen. He absently unscrewed a small jar of ink, then began taking notes.

"What is the emergency, Moonlight?" he asked.

"Autonomy is moving on a much faster timetable than we believed," she explained. "One of these charts lists explosions—once assumed to be due to railway construction. We're hoping you could correlate that with the hotspots of enemy activity we've been monitoring, to find a likely entry point to the caverns."

"Ah yes," TwinSoul said. "Silajana says he would be happy to aid in this. Kaise, would you fetch the appropriate binder?"

"Sure thing," Codenames said, bounding off to do as she was asked. With Marasi's help, Moonlight pulled over a long table and arranged some of the rubbings on it. They left the circular table at the center of the room empty for now, though Marasi couldn't guess why.

As TwinSoul took notes, he absently created a cup from the same rose-colored stone, then filled it from a water jug at the side of the room. When he was finished drinking, he set the cup on a plate—and the stone disintegrated into fine powder, which then eventually vanished. A short time later, he made a thin knife blade on one finger and cut out a specific section of the rubbing.

When Codenames returned a short time later, TwinSoul was settled at the table—on a crystal chair he had created. Marasi fidgeted and checked the wall clock. They'd spent almost half an hour here so far. She didn't know how tight their deadline was, but given what they'd discovered, waiting was unnerving.

"Hmmm . . ." TwinSoul said, scribbling some more notes with his finger pen. As he wrote, a line of crystal grew off his other hand and reached the cut-out section of the rubbing. There it formed a little frame around the flimsy square of paper. A pole grew up behind it, hanging it like a picture for better inspection.

TwinSoul peered at it through his improvised spectacles, playing with his long mustaches.

"I wish my brother were here," Codenames said from a seat nearby. "He'd do this math easily . . ." She looked forlorn as she said it.

"The problem is not merely one of mathematics," TwinSoul said. He stood and walked away from the little workstation, leaving the framed piece of paper behind—and this time the stone didn't disintegrate. He filled himself a much larger cup of water, then stepped up to the circular table and rested one hand on it while drinking.

A crystal city grew up from the table.

It started at his hand, then spread out—like frost forming on steel. His crystal reminded Marasi of a darker version of the pink saltstone Steris had once purchased for decorating the kitchen. Buildings sprouted from it, streets formed as troughs—in minutes a complete replica of the city adorned the table, the circular elevated train tracks of the partially finished high-speed rail growing in last of all.

Marasi's breath caught, then she looked at the old man, who was smiling in a self-satisfied way. He appeared to enjoy the showmanship. Perhaps if she hadn't been here, he'd have pulled out a mundane map. But this was oh so much more impressive.

"It's called an aether," Moonlight said, walking up behind her. "An ancient entity predating the creation of your world. TwinSoul can grow it, manipulate it. Would you like to know more?"

"Yes," Marasi whispered.

Moonlight smiled. "And you shall. Once you join us."

Marasi breathed out softly, then reached out to touch the tip of one of the buildings—which felt solid beneath her fingers, more sturdy than she'd expected. The aether was mostly smooth, with tiny pits here and there.

"I have three likely options for you," TwinSoul said. "I've marked them in deeper-colored roseite."

He pointed toward one building, a little pointer stick—the kind professors used for gesturing at chalkboards—growing between his fingers. The building indicated was indeed a deeper red. It was the central spire of the city, right at the heart of Bilming, rising high above the surrounding structures. Straight along the sides, then tapering sharply toward the unfinished upper floors.

"Independence Tower," TwinSoul said. "This is no surprise—we've known that the agents of Autonomy have been using this as their base for years."

"And there were explosions underneath?" Marasi asked.

"The detonations happened farther to the east," TwinSoul said. "But I doubt that the entrance to those caverns will be right in the center of the detonations, for obvious reasons. Independence Tower is a central hub of activity for our esteemed antagonists, and I'd bet it has an entrance to the caverns."

"But it will be heavily guarded," Marasi said. "What are the other two options?"

"This office building here, my lady," he said, pointing to a smaller structure in the city grid.

She nodded. "Note, though, I'm not a lady. I work for a living."

"It is merely a distinction of respect, Lady Marasi," he said. "From among my people. It . . . translates oddly into your language. Regardless, this office building—the Dulouis Building—is both a hotbed of Set activity *and* at the perimeter of one of the locations with tremors. I consider it the most likely option."

He pointed back at the tall structure. "As you noted, Independence Tower is highly defended—a veritable fortification, a castle in the middle of the city. Breaching it has proven beyond even the arts of the Survivor himself."

"Not for lack of trying," Codenames added. "Their security system can spot ghosts. He hasn't figured out a way to circumvent that."

"And the final location?" Marasi asked.

"It seems of less import," TwinSoul said, pointing at a structure on the perimeter of the city, beneath a section of train track. "An old tire factory."

"Tires?" Moonlight said, stepping up beside Marasi. "Like where Tobal Copper worked?"

"TwinSoul, would I be correct to assume that factory is owned by Basin Tires?" Marasi asked.

"Indeed," TwinSoul said. "You appear to have information beyond mine, my lady."

"That company is involved," Marasi said. "Did your agents notice anything odd about the factory?"

Codenames flipped through one of their files. "Uh . . . let's see . . . Curious. The woman we had watching this location says it's mostly shut down, because very little is ever shipped out of it."

"But things are shipped in?" Marasi said, growing excited. "Maybe an oddly large number of deliveries, given that the factory barely seems to be doing anything?"

"Yes," Codenames said. "Our agent didn't put that together, but yes. From the shipping manifests here . . . Why are they taking in so much, if they're not making anything?"

"Because those aren't supplies for the factory," Moonlight said, meeting Marasi's eyes. "They're stockpiles of food and arms for the cavern underneath. This is our incursion point."

"I agree," Marasi said. "There has to be an entrance to the caverns there, and maybe it will be less guarded than the central spire. We strike here."

"We can get there quickly by rail," Moonlight said. "The section leading from here to there is finished and running."

"Wait," TwinSoul said. "How urgent is this threat?"

"We have reason to believe," Marasi said, "that the Set has developed a bomb capable of wiping out Elendel. Harmony is blinded, and we know the Set have been developing a device capable of delivering their bomb from a great distance."

"They have a dark god breathing down their necks," Moonlight added. "Demanding results. They were supposed to put their plan into motion weeks ago. And with Marasi and her friends getting close . . . well, they have *every incentive* to launch that bomb the moment they can. It could happen at any time."

"By the first aether . . ." he whispered, glancing at Codenames, whose eyes had gone wide. "Moonlight. We should contact the master."

"You're right," Moonlight said. "I hate delaying, but . . . Codenames, is your special friend nearby?"

"Upstairs," she said, scrambling out of the room. "I'll go grab him."

"The master?" Marasi said. "You mean . . ."

"Yes," Moonlight said. "It's time to talk to Kelsier."

40

Codenames's "friend" turned out to be a glowing sphere of light the size of a child's head—though perfectly symmetrical and marked at the center with an arcane symbol.

It floated over to Marasi, then bobbed in the air and spoke with a soft masculine voice. She didn't understand the strange words.

"Was that . . . some kind of spell?" she whispered to Moonlight.

"He said he was pleased to meet you," Codenames said. "And complimented your hair."

"Oh," Marasi said, transfixed by the glowing orb. Nothing held it up; it simply floated, shimmering with a pure white glow, tinged with mother-of-pearl.

Codenames spoke to the sphere in the same language, and it bobbed again, then began to shift and change. It melded into the shape of a person's head—a man with strong, angular features. She was shocked to find that most of the paintings and statues of the Survivor were accurate. Except for the spike through his right eye—a feature that was replicated in the light, same as the rest of his head and hair.

"I'm not surprised to hear from you," he said. "Something's wrong, isn't it?"

"Maybe?" Codenames said. "Honestly, we're not certain, Kell. But TwinSoul said we should contact you."

"Is he there?" Kelsier asked.

"Present, my lord," TwinSoul said, bowing his head to the reproduction of the man's face—though Kelsier didn't seem to be able to see him. "Also present is Moonlight, and . . . a visitor. One Marasi Colms."

The Survivor's image cocked an eyebrow at that. "Marasi Colms. We've been watching you."

Marasi stammered. This man was the center of her religion—she'd prayed to him as a child. And while she wasn't as observant as Steris, it was still . . . daunting to meet him.

He didn't express anger that she was there. Another indication that Moonlight had been playing up that aspect, perhaps to make Marasi feel she was getting away with something.

"Report?" Kelsier asked.

"Dawnshot is in Bilming," Moonlight said, "and thinks the Set is moving soon. Within the day."

"Harmony is blinded, Lord Survivor," Marasi said, piping up. "He admitted it to Wax. He can't see anything, but . . . sir . . . he's frightened."

"Damn," Kelsier said. "I'm twelve hours away, moving quickly via airship."

"That . . . may not be soon enough, Kell," Moonlight said.

"My lord," TwinSoul said, "Moonlight has recovered some disturbing intel. It appears that the Set has discovered the relationship between harmonium and trellium. Beyond that, they've been experimenting with long-range delivery devices. They're prepared to do something stupid."

"Not so much stupid as desperate," Kelsier said. "They know that Autonomy has declared this entire planet anathema. The Set is fighting for survival the only way they know how: by trying to destroy Elendel, to prove to Autonomy they can rule the planet. I thought we had more time though. Why now?"

"No idea," Moonlight said. "But there's talk of a new ashfall. I've never heard *that* before. Plus, we have a *photo* here of a destroyed city. Maybe . . . they tried it out somewhere else, and photographed the results? At any rate, it implies something more than bombing Elendel."

"There have always been two plans," Codenames said. "Autonomy wants to do something catastrophic to the entire planet—the ashfalls could be their plan for that. But the Set is hoping to prove it can dominate the Basin, and that the more extreme measure isn't needed. Like cutting off a finger to prevent the infection from spreading."

The room fell silent, Marasi feeling overwhelmed. They spoke of the end of a planet, *her* planet, as if it were something that they'd known was a possibility for some time. But then again, she was *literally* in a conversation with the Survivor . . . so . . .

"Sir," she said. "Um, Lord Kelsier? I believe they are close to launching this bomb. I intend to stop them, but I'm just one woman. I wouldn't mind help. Anything you can offer."

"I don't have the luxury of holding back," Kelsier said more softly. "I shouldn't have left for the South. I thought Saze would stop it before it got this far . . . We need to do what he cannot. Miss Colms, you have our help. Codenames, how many full Ghostblood agents do we have in Bilming?"

"Um . . ." Codenames said. "Only us three. Everyone else is in Elendel or on assignment elsewhere in the field."

"How quickly can we get the Elendel agents to Bilming?" Kelsier asked.

"Not quickly enough," Moonlight said. "They're all embedded, so we'd have to use dead drops. We could have them roused by early evening, maybe late afternoon, but they would still be several hours away in Elendel."

"Send them to my sister," Marasi said. "She's trying to facilitate an evacuation via the Elendel government."

Kelsier sniffed softly. He didn't seem to have much respect for the Elendel government. "Codenames, you take Dae-oh and see to it. I doubt the field team needs a philologist for this mission. Also alert our members around the Basin. Shri Prasanva, I hate to pull you from your quiet evenings of scholarship, but I fear we're going to need your help."

The elderly TwinSoul stood up straight, then bowed to the floating head. "We are eager to serve, my lord. Silajana sends his regards, and wishes he could send more of his aetherbound to aid in your fight."

"I appreciate the sentiment," Kelsier said. "You and Moonlight are to assist Miss Colms. In fact, I think it is time to do something drastic. Take the stores of purified Dor. The Command is 'Respect.' Authorize the other cells to access theirs as well, and pass the Command to them."

Codenames gasped. Marasi had no idea what purified Dor was, but even Moonlight seemed impressed.

"Do what you can," Kelsier said. "I will try to accelerate my arrival, but the truth is that I don't know how much I can do. I'm traveling over water, and so can't go much faster than I currently am. Dropping things to Steelpush off doesn't do much with an ocean underneath you."

"We will stop this, my lord," TwinSoul said. "Whatever is happening, we will interrupt it. You shall arrive back in Elendel to find a pristine and welcoming city."

"I'll settle for the normal dirty, grouchy city, TwinSoul," Kelsier said. "Go. I'll see if I can shake Harmony out of his stupor. At least he sent Dawnshot; that convinces me the threat is real. Anything that makes Saze take action these days is to be considered significant."

The face melted back into the sphere, and the communication was over. The three immediately burst into motion, going in separate directions. Marasi decided to stick with Moonlight, who rushed to a different room—which required opening another mystical lock. Inside was an armory that would have made Ranette delirious with glee. Guns on the walls, vials of metals in racks, glass knives and dueling canes. A large chain-fed machine gun and some explosives.

Moonlight ignored it all, rushing straight for a safe in the corner. It had no combination or locking mechanism that Marasi could see, though as she peered over Moonlight's shoulder the woman put her hand on the front and said, "Respect me." Some mechanism inside clicked, and the door opened.

"Another . . . what was it . . . Identity lock?" Marasi asked.

"No, this is even more secure," Moonlight said. "It's a lock that is Awake, and can tell from your Intent if you've been given a passcode or if you've stolen it."

A lock . . . that was awake? As in *alive*?

Inside were only three items: a trio of identical glowing jars, big enough that you'd have trouble carrying them in one hand. The glow was similar to the sphere that had followed Codenames, but more intense. Each jar outshone the room's electric lights.

Moonlight took one, the light shining on her face, and turned it over. Awed.

"What is it?" Marasi whispered.

"Concentrated Investiture," Moonlight said. "Unkeyed from any Identity. This is an energy source that can power things like your Metallic Arts."

"Those are powered by the gods."

"Exactly," Moonlight said. "This power comes from a god's corpse. Two of them actually, intermingled. It's *exceptionally* difficult to recover. The things that you could do with this . . . well, that I could do with this. You'd only be able to use it as a hyperefficient replacement for your metals. You

THE LOST METAL • 277

don't know how good you have it here on Scadrial, being able to power your abilities with something so common."

"And your abilities?" Marasi asked. "What are they powered by?"

Moonlight smiled. She hadn't admitted to any abilities, but so far Marasi had seen a man who could create objects from crystal, a woman with a pet . . . sphere . . . and Moonlight, who seemed fairly high in their organization. So what was she capable of doing?

Moonlight packed the three jars in a rucksack, wrapped in some cushioning, then filled it with other supplies, including a few explosives. She threw the sack over her shoulder and took a few guns from the wall. Marasi, with permission, helped herself to a fine-looking rifle—along with an innocent-looking case to carry it in—and some aluminum ammunition. They had it in plenitude here.

"Electrolysis," Moonlight noted. "Aluminum is actually pretty easy to make, once you know the process."

"Wait," Marasi said, hurrying to join her as they left the room, "you can make aluminum with *electrolysis*?"

"Yeah," Moonlight said. "We've been using it to fund our operations for almost two decades now. I'd bet half the aluminum in the Basin came from us originally."

"And you're casually letting me in on the secret?"

"It's a free sample," Moonlight said. "Besides, Dean—he's our chemist back in Elendel—is convinced you'll find the secret soon, and the value will plummet. Dean thinks aluminum will soon be cheaper than tin."

Cheaper than *tin*? Preservation! If every criminal could afford bullets to kill Allomancers, and every citizen could keep a band of aluminum in their hat to prevent emotional Allomancy, it . . .

Well, it would change the world.

"All of this," Moonlight said, "is merely the surface, Marasi."

"Why me?" Marasi asked. "Why not Wax?"

"He's spoken for," Moonlight said. "Besides, Kelsier prefers people like us. The discarded, the ignored. And Wax is a little . . . brazen. People watch him. Track him. Pay attention to him. Not our style, for all that Kell likes to be the center of attention."

"Plus, I suppose," Marasi said with some thought, "having access to a high-ranking constable is useful."

"There's also your uncommon connection to the Malwish," Moonlight said.

"Allik?" Marasi said, amused. "He's wonderful—don't get me wrong—but I think you'd find him to be a little less . . . well-connected than you're assuming."

Rusts. She hoped he'd gotten out of the city. Her gut said that he would go if she asked. There was a certain practicality to Allik that she loved—he was wonderfully, beautifully genuine.

In her line of work, she met so many who made her question the nature of humanity. But then she'd go home and find all the reminders in the world of the best that people could be. And somehow, he was all hers.

Back in the main room, the model of the city had started to crumble. It didn't disintegrate as quickly as the cup had; something made the stone linger sometimes but immediately vanish other times. The chair, for example, still seemed fully sturdy.

Moonlight waved for Marasi to follow her out into the foyer. Here, TwinSoul walked down the steps, gripping the banister tightly for support, wearing a backpack that she thought—from the way it moved, and from the hose draped over his shoulder—might be filled entirely with water.

He'd changed outfits, and now wore some kind of loose-fitting uniform with a bright yellow sash around his waist. He'd strapped on a sword—a slightly curved one in an ornate golden sheath. As he reached the ground floor, he nodded to Moonlight. "Codenames is going to send some messages," he said, "and so can wait for that other woman you sent to reach safety here. I think it is time for the three of us to be about the job. You retrieved the Dor?"

Moonlight tapped her rucksack.

"Excellent," he said, turning to Marasi. "I have been commanded to follow your lead, my lady. With Silajana's blessing and yours, we strike forward. If there is danger, I vow that I shall fight to protect you."

"This . . . could be dangerous," Marasi said, glancing at his ornate sword, noting how unstable on his feet he was. "I'm sure we could use your help, TwinSoul, but . . . I don't know that you should be doing any fighting. Perhaps we two could strike ahead, and call for you when we need your specialized skills?"

"I promise I will not slow you down, my lady," he said. "I have been tasked with aiding you by the Survivor himself."

He said it with calm respect, but his posture and attitude whispered something else. *I'm going with you, young woman. Best not to argue the point any further.*

Right, then. Marasi glanced at Moonlight, who nodded to her. Despite their knowledge and experience, this was Marasi's mission. She was in charge. Good.

"Where's the nearest train station?" she asked. "We need to get to that factory as quickly as possible."

41

It was late afternoon by the time Wax got into position at the lord mayor's mansion, the Silver House. Though nightfall was hours away, he hoped—as he did every day—that the mists would come tonight. It felt like forever since he'd been out in them. Not only did they seem to come less often these days, he also had less occasion to go out at night. The mists felt like a friend from his youth that he still knew but rarely talked to.

He'd been at this all day, having left Elendel a few hours before dawn, but fatigue felt distant regardless. As four fifteen hit, Wax burst into motion. Wayne should have his distraction going in full, which gave Wax the opportunity to bolt across the springy grass to the mayor's mansion. He dropped a bullet and Pushed up to the second floor.

There, he grabbed the outer windowsill and gave a quick Push to the mechanism inside, which should undo the latch . . .

The window rattled, but didn't unlatch. Drat. It had a full lock, one a Push couldn't undo.

All right. He increased his weight manyfold, and a quick *Push* cracked the window and bent the lock, letting him force the window open and pull himself inside.

His boots thumped down on a carpeted floor. The place was messy, but not cluttered. Piles of papers occupied the desk and the nearby tables. A small bar held a collection of spirits, half the tops off, the other half put haphazardly back on the wrong bottle. Books lined a shelf, some put in spine first, others reversed, and a good third of them slumped to the side because the ones at the far end had been removed, leaving the whole thing to slouch like sleepy guards on watch duty.

It was in many ways the opposite of Copper's flat. That had been sterile, pristine. This was lived in. It had the air of a place full of secrets—because a man as important as Gave would employ a fleet of maids and servants to keep things tidy. Except in this room.

Wax didn't have a lot to go on. But the lord mayor *was* involved in whatever the Set was planning—and involvement on that level would leave traces. A bomb somewhere in this city was pointed at Elendel, and this room held the clues that would lead him to it. But where?

Wax sorted quickly through the pages on the desk. Wayne was probably doing Grandma's Been at the Vodka, his favorite ploy for drawing attention but not gunfire. Unfortunately, the Set would be on the lookout for his tricks. They'd created a Metalborn designed specifically to face Wayne. They would know about his propensity for disguises.

The papers didn't give him much. Some shipping manifests to a factory on the outskirts of town. A stack of broadsheets with editorials circled that were critical of Gave. And another, newer stack of them with no such problems. He opened the desk, and there found a curious number of letters from noblemen and noblewomen in Elendel.

Wax recognized several of the names, including Vennis Hasting—one of the more powerful senators. He scanned a letter from him, and it touched on nothing incriminating. Though it mentioned trade negotiations, most of it was pleasantries.

Frowning, Wax fished in his coat pocket and brought out another letter, the extremely incriminating one—also from Vennis Hasting—that Maraga had given him. He was missing pieces here. When had they moved from pleasantries to discussing the destruction of the world?

For now, he stuffed both letters into his pocket. Gave and Vennis were colluding, but he had already known that. He needed a lead on where to find the bomb. Fortunately, after a little more hunting he struck gold. Gave Entrone's calendar.

People usually made certain to hide the most important documents and information. They'd lock up their plans and schemes, but often forgot simple things like calendars. To a trained detective, knowing where you'd been—and where you planned to be—could be incriminating. Back in the Roughs, he'd often had to piece a person's schedule together through interviews and interrogations. But in a modern city, people tended to write it down for him.

The desk calendar was the wide and flat type that displayed an entire month, one day to a box. Previous months had been folded back behind, and were covered in notations in two hands: A sloppier one that, from the letters, Wax assumed was Gave's. And a neater hand that likely belonged to a secretary.

Lots of visits to something called the lab, Wax thought. *With tight scheduling between meetings here at the mansion. So the lab is close, or he has some direct method of getting to it . . .*

Another spot listed *trajectory and distance tests,* and that was surrounded by several empty days. So he'd needed to travel some way for that. Curious. Where could they have launched delivery devices a long distance without drawing attention?

Wax looked up as he heard some muffled shouts. Wayne's distraction was working. He kept searching, scanning for anything suspicious, and something struck him a moment later.

There were no appointments after today.

A coldness spread through Wax as he looked at the last appointment, in Gave's own hand. It simply said, *They arrive.* Rusts. What did that mean?

There wasn't the time for analysis, so he ripped off the sheets—even though that would reveal he'd been here—and moved on. Confident he'd learned what he could from the desk, he tried an old Coinshot's trick: burning steel.

Little blue lines spread from his chest toward viable sources of metal. Most of these were faint, indicating nails in the walls and furniture. Light fixtures, doorknobs, even unseen wires for electricity. More and more, their lives were surrounded by metal—glints of it facilitating everything from the incandescent bulb to the nib in the pen on the desk. He knew some people felt that the day of the Metalborn was over, that modern advances would equalize all people and diminish the advantages of Allomancer and Feruchemist.

Yet he had trained himself—with practice—to put out the lights in a room by distorting the wires in the walls. His versatility improved with each new discovery. And as more metal outlined their lives, he was able to see more and more details of rooms.

He spotted no hidden chambers in the desk, but he did locate the room's safe. Hidden not behind a picture or a bookshelf, but in the floor under a couch—which was a more common spot than the other two, despite popular lore.

Wax set to it quickly. For all his levity, Wayne would be in serious danger during this distraction. Wax didn't want to leave him too long—indeed, Wax heard more cries and shouts as he shoved the couch aside. They were getting louder. The enemy might already be on to him.

The safe had an Allomantic lock. No visible keyhole or combination. It would be opened with Pushes if he was lucky, Pulls if he was unlucky. Wax squinted, judging the metal lines. There was the giant blue one leading to the safe itself, of course. Many Allomancers would stop with that, never realizing that if you peered closer—if you let the lines start to drift and separate . . .

One giant line became many smaller ones, all connecting him to the various mechanisms inside. Pins you could Push in a specific order to unlock the thing. He got to work as the shouts outside grew more urgent. These kinds of locks were secure against most people, and even most Allomancers. But there was a weakness. Wax carefully, subtly Pushed each pin in turn, wiggling them until he found the one that activated a tumbler.

That would be the first. He nudged it and was rewarded when it locked into place. He was in luck—this was a mechanism meant for one who could Push, not Pull. He should be able to open it, though even many Coinshots would have trouble with something this subtle.

First tumbler in place, he wiggled each remaining pin to find the second. Easy. He quickly located the third, Pushed it, and—

And the lock reset.

Wax froze, a bead of sweat trickling down his cheek. What had he done wrong? He forced himself, despite the growing noise outside, to go through it again. Again, the lock reset after he Pushed the third pin.

He pounded the floor in frustration until the answer struck him. This wasn't a lock designed for someone who could Push *or* Pull. It was designed for someone who could do both. The third pin required a Pull.

In short, it was a lock designed for a Mistborn to open. Or in this case, someone using Hemalurgy to cheat.

Which meant he was out of luck. He'd never get this open, not unless he could rip it out and do his Pushes from both sides . . . He didn't have time for that. And there was something more going on outside. Shouts. Alarms, and . . .

And was that *smoke* he smelled?

Rusts. Wax did a quick scan of the room for anything else he could investigate. There wasn't . . .

Wait. That pattern of metal in the floor. Wooden boards in regular straight rows, nailed down in lines. Except for one square of nails underneath the rug.

Trapdoor, he thought, and shoved the rug aside, feeling about until he located the hidden latch. Entrone had the spikes to make him an Allomancer and was quite enamored with his powers, judging by that safe. But he didn't have the *experience* of someone who'd grown up with their powers. A seasoned Coinshot could pick out that pattern of nails in the same way a square of new paint on an old wall would stand out.

The trapdoor led to a very narrow shaft with a wooden ladder. Probably between two walls on the first floor, down into a basement.

As smoke began to stream in around the door and he heard shouts for a fire brigade—along with feet thumping along the hallway outside—Wax decided to abandon the safe. He slipped onto the ladder, then pulled the trapdoor closed behind him. Hoping that wherever this led, it would point him in the right direction.

42

It was odd for Marasi to feel such urgency while sitting and waiting.

The elevated train of Bilming lived up to its reputation. The group of them sat in a private compartment, speeding around the city, bypassing traffic congestion. The train stopped frequently, but each time it did, it bolted back into motion with a jarring acceleration.

It felt almost like she was a Coinshot, each burst of speed from the train a fresh Push launching them ever closer to their destination. She'd read of the Ascendant Warrior's Flight of Destiny in the Words of Founding, when she'd returned to Luthadel at the last minute to save Harmony. In the stories, Vin had traveled a miraculous distance in mere hours.

Now, Marasi likely traveled at that same speed. In cushioned comfort, with a cool breeze piped in from outside. They carried weapons hidden in cases or sacks, and Marasi still wore the simple trousers and shirt she'd donned for her sting. Moonlight was dressed as a Bilming constable, and TwinSoul had shrouded himself in a local fisherman's raincloak. She'd initially worried that his suit and colorful sash would stand out, but he clearly knew how to be inconspicuous.

"For this to work," Marasi said to them, "I need to understand our resources. That means, Moonlight, I *really* need to know what you're capable of."

"Art criticism," she said. "Fighting, if needed. Wisecracks when appropriate."

"I meant any extraordinary abilities," Marasi said.

"Her wisecracks *are* extraordinary," TwinSoul said, his eyes twinkling. "Why, they're so remarkable that I quite often can't see which part of them is supposed to be wise."

Moonlight, in turn, rolled her eyes. "I have three soulstamps on me at the moment: two universal stamps, one Essence Mark. It takes time and preparation to create more—time we don't have—so we'll have to rely on these ones. I can use each stamp multiple times, but no use will last long, since they weren't . . . Right, you have no idea what I'm talking about."

"Moonlight," TwinSoul explained, "has stamps that rewrite the nature of the objects she encounters. One makes a doorway appear where none previously existed. The second repairs a broken or worn object, to make it look new. Is that correct?"

Moonlight nodded. "It's something I'm practicing still—stamps that will work on any object, I mean. Requires Invested ink, on this planet, but we've got the process mostly working."

"So you can make a door appear," Marasi said. "And you can make an object that was broken become new? How many times?"

"As often as I want," Moonlight said. "But only for a limited period in each case."

"Wow," Marasi whispered. "That's . . . magic?"

"Is Allomancy magic?" Moonlight asked.

"Of course not," Marasi said.

"Neither is this," Moonlight said. "To repair something, I merely rewrite the past, making the object think it was well-maintained or never broke. Like I said, universal stamps are a new technology. I don't have them working perfectly yet, but they'll do for now."

It felt magical to Marasi regardless. Allomancy was one thing—it made perfect sense to be able to use metal to Push on other pieces of metal. But rewriting the past of an object? How was that *not* magical?

"You said you have three stamps," Marasi said. "What's the third?"

"It's for emergencies." Moonlight shifted in her seat. "The other two work on nonliving objects only. This one changes a person—me, specifically—in dramatic ways. I avoid using it if possible."

Marasi glanced at TwinSoul, who shook his head in a "leave it alone" sort of way. Well, all right. She hated going into a potential fight without knowing what her options and advantages were, but at least she'd learned something.

The train slowed at a stop, causing them all to lean in their seats at the change in momentum. People piled into the corridor between compartments outside, waiting to flood out into the station.

"And you, TwinSoul?" Marasi asked. "Is there a limit to the things you can make?"

"Alas," he said, nudging his backpack, which was on the floor, "there are indeed serious limits. I can only maintain roseite objects under certain fields of Investiture. Some planets have those naturally, but yours does not, so my roseite creations—outside of our safehouse—must be touching me, or they will disintegrate. It also requires water, drawn from my body, to fuel the creations.

"Beyond that, my ability to form objects is limited by my personal skill and understanding. I cannot make you a gun, for example. The mechanics are beyond this old mind, and the intricacies too fine. Simple tools are the extent of my abilities, though Silajana has bonded some more talented than I in that regard."

"Sil-ah-janah," Marasi said, trying to form the unfamiliar sounds. "That is your . . . god?"

"Both less and more than a god," he explained. "Silajana is one of the primal aethers. They predate Adonalsium, you know, and exist outside of his power."

"They predate the Shattering," Moonlight said. "That *doesn't* mean they predate Adonalsium."

"To my people, this is a sacred tenet," he said to Marasi, ignoring Moonlight. "The primal aethers grant some people a bud of their core." He raised his right hand, revealing a transparent web of stone embedded in his palm, and let light from the window shine through as he held it up before the glass. She could see the bones inside, and it seemed the crystal had somehow entirely replaced his flesh and muscles in that spot.

"This bud connects me to Silajana," he continued, "and through him to all of his other aetherbound. He is the core, and we his web. He is eternal, and we his mortal agents in the cosmere."

That was . . . a lot to take in. But Marasi supposed that all that mattered was that he was willing to help. "Thank you for joining our fight," she said. "I'm glad that Silajana could spare you."

"There is little else for us now," he said, looking out the window. "Until we can return home . . ."

"I'm willing to go with you, Pras," Moonlight said. "If you want to try."

"The forces in my homeland are too strong, too deadly," he said. "Silajana says we must remain in exile. He will decide when and if we are to return. He would not risk another extermination."

The train bolted forward again, causing them all to lean the other direction in their seats. Only three more stops until they arrived.

"Moonlight, can your door stamp help us get into the enemy base?" Marasi asked.

"It will depend on the building materials," she said. "This stamp pretends the people who constructed the place installed a door. It'll be touch and go for it to work on things like natural rock."

"Then we can sneak into the factory from any direction," Marasi said, "and then find the way down into the caverns."

"They've been moving a lot of supplies," Moonlight said. "Large crates of equipment and food. So I doubt we're looking for some hidden stairwell."

"You're right," Marasi agreed. "There will likely be a freight elevator in the main loading bay. Good assumption."

"We could attempt," TwinSoul said, "to pretend to be members of their organization, making a delivery. Perhaps we could hijack a supply truck on the way?"

"Tried that," Marasi said. "It was kind of a mess. I'd rather be more stealthy."

"I agree," Moonlight said. "I suggest we scout the location, find an empty room at the rear, and create a door. They'll have their security focused on entry points, which we can avoid. From there we make our way to the cargo docks and locate the elevator."

A reasonable enough plan. Though Marasi's anxiety increased the closer they came to their destination. Soon the train lurched to a stop, and the three of them piled off. She worried the long case she was carrying—with her borrowed rifle hidden inside—would draw attention, but no one gave her so much as a second glance. Perhaps they thought it was some kind of musical instrument. More likely, they didn't care.

Neither of Marasi's companions were of a Scadrian ethnicity, but Moonlight kept a hat on to shade her eyes. She was shorter than most from Marasi's world, but there was no telling if that was a trait of her people, or an individual body shape. TwinSoul, in contrast, was tall and lanky. His darker skin tone stood out on the street, but most would just assume he had Terris blood—that people's colorations varied far more than those of people with old Central Dominance heritage, like Marasi.

Plus, there was a lot of variety in dress in this city. People seemed to eschew the dark browns and blacks that were more common in Elendel. Vibrant colors, often clashing, were part of the style here. With other oddities too. In the train station alone, they passed a costumed mascot trying to hand out flyers for a furniture store, a couple of masked Malwish tourists, and a koloss-blooded woman in a suit.

Outside the station, atop the platform with steps leading to the streets below, they spotted their target in the near distance: an old brown-brick factory with a mottled sign out front. Even this futuristic city had less-desirable sections of town; many were hidden away beneath the tracks.

Marasi had hoped to find the building quiet, since the Ghostblood spy's records had indicated infrequent supply drops in recent weeks. Today, unfortunately, the building was buzzing with activity—some half a dozen trucks loading up and pulling out through a large bay door at the side of the structure.

"Well," Moonlight said, "little doubt where the loading bay is. We'll probably find the elevator in there."

"Inside the bay," TwinSoul said, "that is currently full of enemy forces?"

"Yeah . . ."

"What if," Marasi said, "we came into the elevator from the back? You can make a door in any wall, right? What if we made one into the elevator from behind?"

"That's possible," Moonlight said. "Though I'm not comfortable with how busy it looks. We were hoping to slip in during a quiet moment."

Marasi agreed—though as she considered it, she realized that had been naive of them. The Set knew that they were in Bilming and actively trying to stop them . . .

Marasi hesitated as she watched several of the trucks roar away from the factory, heading toward the hill with the government offices. Then she found herself smiling.

"They're worried about Wax," she said. "They're marshalling troops, gathering resources . . . I'll bet they're sending it all to deal with him."

"Maybe," Moonlight said.

"Trust me," Marasi said. "Where Wax goes, fireworks follow. The Set is worried about him—and they likely know exactly where he is. Flying through the air does tend to make him conspicuous."

"If you're correct, my lady," TwinSoul said, "then they might not be expecting our incursion here. Their eyes may be diverted toward Dawnshot." More trucks pulled away, and TwinSoul pointed toward the northern side of the city, where a giant plume of dark smoke was rising. "That's the mayor's mansion. Perhaps Dawnshot is being . . . extra difficult?"

"I'll take it," Marasi said, leading the way down the steps. "Let's strike while everyone is distracted."

43

Everyone in the room—including the kandra—gathered around Steris to read the letter Wax had sent. Perhaps they didn't trust her to deliver the information out loud, or perhaps they needed to see it with their own eyes.

Bomb is confirmed real, and already fabricated. City-destroying capacity. Enemy is trying to find a way to deliver it to Elendel. It's time to evacuate the city.

They know I'm after them. I hope that my presence won't cause them to do anything rash. Investigation suggests attempts to deliver by train or road failed and they seek alternative, perhaps some kind of self-propelled artillery shell. Regardless, I suggest you close off all routes into Elendel as a precaution.

There is conflict among the Set. Some want to destroy Elendel, others maybe the entire Basin by restarting the Ashmounts, judging by a strange photograph we've found. I may be able to exploit the schism between them. Either way, my primary objective is neutralizing the bomb's delivery mechanism.

Get as many people out as you can, as quickly as possible, in case I fail.

I love you.
Waxillium

Adawathwyn immediately ordered the young radio operator sequestered—along with anyone who might have heard the communication. Everyone else in the room slumped into chairs at the table, and several looked to TenSoon.

"We should believe Dawnshot," he said. "Harmony has long thought the enemy was working on something like this. The deadline is . . . far more urgent than we realized. Rusts. We need to take this *very* seriously."

"I am forced to agree," Adawathwyn—of all people—said. "I don't much like Ladrian, but . . . this news, with a kandra confirming it . . . My lord governor, it seems we have a gun to our heads."

The governor leaned forward on the table, grim.

Finally, Steris thought, releasing a held breath. *They are giving this the attention it deserves.* Maybe now she could get something done.

"Time is of the essence," the governor said, looking around the table at the three senators and his vice governor. "If there really is a bomb . . . we have to move fast."

"Agreed," Lord Cett said. "How quickly can we get out of the city?"

"That depends," the governor said. "Ambassador Daal? Can I take that airship ride now?"

"So long as the streets aren't packed," Adawathwyn said, "we can theoretically be out of the city via motorcade in under an hour."

"Will that be quickly enough?" Lady Hammondess said. "What is the destructive radius of this weapon, kandra? How far away do we have to get to be safe?"

"I'll send for our families," the governor said. "We have to do this quietly though, to not inspire a mass panic."

Steris closed her eyes, feeling sick. On one hand, she understood their emotions. After all, she had sent her children away immediately.

At the same time . . . Rusts. They were all going to run, weren't they? She met Constable Reddi's eyes. He'd slumped in his chair, looking numb. Sworn to protect the people of the city, and there was nothing he could do. Nothing but sit here and dread what was coming.

She didn't have to do that. She'd dreaded it already. That was the purpose of her lists. She realized, with shock, that her method was actually working. She didn't feel afraid. She didn't feel anxious.

She could function.

She had to evacuate the city.

Steris pulled out one of her thickest notebooks, thumping it down on the table. As everyone else started calling for aides to prepare their escapes, she gathered her thoughts and flipped through her notes. She had seven detailed evacuation plans for the city. Which was best in this situation?

After a few minutes though, the governor ordered the door shut again and all aides temporarily expelled. The room's anxious occupants turned toward him.

"Um," he said, "Adawathwyn has a suggestion."

She had composed herself quickly and now stood up in her immaculate Terris robes, hands out invitingly. "The situation is indeed dire. But I have realized we have a solution . . . upon our arms, so to speak. Lord Waxillium says that there is likely some kind of device that will launch the bomb all the way to our city. But we have Metalborn at our disposal. The greatest wealth of them in all the Basin.

"We should gather Coinshots and station them to Push this weapon away. We can position them atop our highest structures, to watch for the weapon's arrival—or, better, keep people on call in Bilming, watching. They'll be able to tell us when it has launched."

"Pardon me, Adawathwyn," Steris said. "Have you ever been in a situation where modern weapons fire is discharged? Have you *seen* the speed at which it moves? Trust me. If this weapon is launched, when it reaches Elendel, it will impact too quickly for an Allomancer to stop."

The vice governor wilted for a second, then her eyes widened. "What if," she said, "we had an Allomancer with access to all the abilities and powers of the Lord Ruler?"

Several in the room gasped. Daal stood up straight, his masked eyes fixated on Adawathwyn.

"It's an emergency," she said. "A *true* emergency. The entire city is in danger! We need someone who can think the thoughts of a thousand people, someone who can move planets and raise mountains. We need . . . the Bands of Mourning."

Bother.

First off, the Bands didn't work *that* way. They gave a person supercharged metallic abilities—yes—but they didn't contain "all the powers of the Lord Ruler." Unfortunately, the mythology surrounding them and Wax's use of them had only grown over the years.

That said, Steris *had* considered using the Bands—they often factored into her calculations. A powerful relic created by the Survivor—or maybe the Lord Ruler—which granted vast Metalborn powers to the holder wasn't the sort of thing one ignored.

"We can't use the Bands," Steris said. "The people of Elendel made a promise. The foundation of a treaty."

Behind them, Admiral Daal—so quiet through most of the meeting—approached the table. "The Bands of Mourning," he said, "were entrusted to the Faceless Immortals, under the *strict understanding* that the Bands would *never* be employed by your people."

Technically, the Bands weren't to be employed unless the Malwish attacked Elendel. That had been the actual deal, a way of making certain that Malwish aggression didn't go too far.

"Surely, Ambassador," Adawathwyn said, "you can see our need for self-preservation. You wouldn't deny us the means, in this dire emergency, to protect ourselves from this calamity?"

"Surely," Ambassador Daal said, "*you* understand that any action by those in the Basin using this *sacred* relic—however dire the situation—must be seen as an act of aggression against my people. You don't think we've suffered catastrophes that *we* wish we could have used the Bands to stop? We could have been using them to save lives these past six years! But our agreement was that they were too powerful for *anyone* to use."

The room fell silent. *He's playing some kind of game here,* Steris thought. She couldn't fathom what.

"We . . ." the governor said, licking his lips. "We should fetch them. If an Allomancer with enhanced speed of thought could Push away this bomb before it lands, that gives us a chance."

"They don't have as much power as you think," Steris said. "They can't accomplish that."

"Actually," TenSoon said, "there's a possibility."

"What?" Steris asked.

"There are . . . things about the interactions of the powers you don't know," he said. "I have only hints. I think it might be possible . . . to send the bomb away using the Bands. But the deal we made . . ."

"Holy One," the governor said, "what would Harmony say, should it come down to our survival as a city or betraying the Malwish trust. What are his wishes?"

TenSoon stood quietly for a moment, then spoke with a growling voice. "I will fetch the Bands."

SPARKLE TONIC

enough, tell them:
"I KNOW THE DIF
GIVE ME VIF"
(Paid for by the Vif Sparkle Co.)

This was my intention all along," said Jak to a crowd of eager fans, "to train dear Handerwym in the ways of

eyes and sighed.

More details on back: Why the judge let Jak keep the tige

and leeched her steel reserves.

"Give me the compass," I said, "and we'll leave you at the next outcropping."

Vila peered over her shoulder at the approaching stone where the Haunted Man waited.

She glanced at me, her eyes wide, no doubt realizing that without any steel, she couldn't Coinshot away. She was trapped. In her surprise, she forgot to hold onto anything but the compass.

I had not planned on that.

"No!" I screamed, immediately dropping my parasol and reaching for Vila. I serendipitously caught her by the lace of her frilly coat.

"You saved me?" she asked. "Don't you want me to fall?"

"Harmony no," I said.

She clocked me in the face with the compass, which honestly was a bad move on her part. I instinctively let go of her.

As Vila fell, I keeled forward, trying to catch her again, but serendipity is a fickle thing, and my hand missed hers by a hair. Horrified, I watched the mists swallow her. The sudden shifting of my weight, however, threw me from the claw. Suddenly weightless, I feared this might be the end.

Then I felt air pushed by large wings. A claw snatched me and dropped me on the outcropping next to the Haunted Man.

I slid to a stop just shy of the edge, my custom Miele Jedon boots sending pebbles clacking over the side. Bless those shoes and their fashionable yet grippy soles. (You can get a pair at Ardenne's on 9th. They're custom, yes, but drop my name, and the clerks there will be keen to help.)

Heart thumping, my breath coming in gasps, I searched the top of the outcropping. "The compass...we should scour the cliffs!"

Tabaar-KeSun landed and opened their other claw. The compass rolled out, and I snatched it up. Before I could thank them, the Haunted Man took my hand and stared at me with intense, desperate eyes. Given his usual scowl, this new expression was as foreign on him as cheap perfume would be on me.

"My dearest Nicelle," he said, gifting me a rare smile.

"What is it?" I asked, inspecting myself for wounds. Though I'd lost a few buttons from my blouse, at least I hadn't lost the whole shirt, which always happened to Jak at this point in his stories. "I'm fine. I promise."

"You almost fell," he said, cupping my cheek in one of his large, rough hands.

Heat boiled up from my heart, and I couldn't help but smile back. How far we had come from our first meeting!

"You silly man. You'll never get rid of me that easily," I said. "It's you and me exploring the cosmere together forever. Just like we promised."

I let him pull me close, his familiar scent of hellfire and cedar filling me. With the knuckle of his finger, he lifted my chin so that I looked into his stormy eyes.

Was he going to kiss me? Did I want him to? By Harmony, *yes*. In that moment, I realized I'd wanted this for the last six years, every time he'd appeared and (inevitably) upended my life.

"Nicelle..." he said, his voice low and breathy.

"Yes?" I rolled up onto my toes and leaned into him.

"I am so very sorry." He lifted the Compass of Spirits, inserted the aluminum key, and turned it. The little rings

spun until they flowed with ethereal light, which inverted in on itself with a giant pop I felt in my soul more than heard with my ears.

I fell forward onto my knees, the Haunted Man's presence no longer there to hold me up, though the afterimage of him activating the device hung in the air for a moment until it puffed away like smoke from a burnt match.

He had done it. He'd finally entered the ghostly dimension.

And he'd done it without me.

He'd bloody *betrayed* me. Rusting *used* me.

I will spare you the ugly details of my following tantrum, though I did yell some of the delicious curses I'd learned in my time with him. At the end of my fit, my immaculate makeup was smeared, my hat and its raven feathers lay in tatters, and Tabaar and KeSun were suddenly there in their human forms.

"He's gone!" I shouted. "Along with the only way to finish the job, and now we're

stuck a thousand miles from home in the space between continents!"

I thought he'd cared for me. He knew a betrayal like this would hurt me, and he'd done it anyway. Rust and Ruin, I hope he arrived too late to save the world. He and his bloody employer could burn for all I cared.

"He's lucky I can't follow him." I clenched my fist around the metal knuckles until the edges bit into my palm.

The two Faceless Immortals shared a glance before KeSun nodded as if deciding something. Then Tabaar spoke.

"Actually," he said. "There is another way."

———

A note from Handerwym:

It's been two weeks since Nicelle's last letter. (You know how intermittent her correspondence can be.) I can only assume she succeeded in entering the ghostly realm and, Harmony willing, we'll soon know the end of her adventure.

— *Continued next week?* —

'NICKI SAVAGE
is sponsored by

TOBER'S ACCURATE
SOONIE PUP

Patented Pocket!

Trade in a historically erroneous Soonie Pup and get a brand new **Professor Tober's Accurate Soonie Pup** for a mere fivespin!

44

Marasi led the others toward their target. It proved easy to sneak around underneath the train tracks; the buildings down here in this urban twilight were cramped, the streets narrow. Almost like the stories of the old Luthadel slums.

Crowded tenements were crammed up beside factories, refineries, and warehouses. All in the shadow of the tracks—a symbol of progress and unity upon which stormed past every few minutes a tooth-rattling reminder: Wasn't it so nice to live in such a modern city? With a beacon of advancement like the high-speed rail? It cast such a progressive shadow.

She was all for progress in general, but far too often it seemed to stratify society rather than unite it. A high-speed rail was good, but could it be afforded by those who would most benefit? Nice apartments were great, but if they drove those who couldn't live in them to darkness under the tracks, then that made some lives worse while making others better.

She'd been forced to confront this herself as she sought for reform. Good intentions had to be coupled with a realistic look at the effects of your actions. It was entirely too easy to make things worse while trying to make them better.

Is that why I've focused more on the detective side of my job over the years? she wondered. *I was going to change things. But the day-to-day work is so demanding, and the big problems are just so big . . .*

Thoughts for another time. The three of them crept ever closer to the tire factory, using the back alleys. TwinSoul made good on his promise, keeping up—though they didn't have to move quickly, and there was always a wall for him to rest his hand against to keep his balance. Marasi still worried about bringing an octogenarian to what might soon be a battle zone, but bit her tongue on the matter.

As they drew close—only one street away—Moonlight halted the group. Marasi was curious what had prompted the stop, until she noticed a bulbous black motorcar with tinted windows pulling up to the factory.

The lord mayor of Bilming climbed out—accompanied by several tough-looking bodyguards. Entrone hurried through the bay doors, shouting at the few remaining trucks there and waving for them to get moving. Marasi was almost certain she heard the name "Dawnshot" among his shouts.

He soon vanished into the structure.

"Well," Marasi whispered, "*he's* agitated."

"Probably doesn't appreciate his home being burned down," TwinSoul whispered.

Marasi nodded. "Come on. His arrival seems to confirm that we've found the right location."

They took the long way around, briefly dipping out of the shade cast by the railway before diving back in, swimming through shadows until they reached the back wall of the factory. Here they slunk along until they found an old window, boarded up. Marasi had hoped to be able to peek through and find an empty room, but it was boarded up on the other side as well.

"Hmmm," TwinSoul said, resting his aged, bony hand on the bricks. Crystals grew from his palm, creeping along the surface and between boards. "Yes, they really should have sealed this with pitch . . ."

"What do you see?" Moonlight whispered.

"I don't see anything," he said. "But Silajana? Well, he senses a small room cluttered with shelves and small objects. No one is inside, and the wall to the right of the window bears no shelving."

He broke his hand free, leaving a crust of crystals on the wall—which began disintegrating, dropping to dust that in turn burned away into rose-colored mist. Moonlight dug in her rucksack—briefly exposing the glowing jars within—and took out something made of leather. Like a very large billfold, or a toolbelt, it unclipped to reveal three stone stamps.

She selected one, dampened it with some odd glowing red ink, then raised it. "Be ready to move," she said, then pressed it to the wall. The stamp head, remarkably, *sank* half an inch or so into the brick. When Moonlight pulled it back—trailing red mist—it left a glowing red stamp imprinted into the wall, marked by intricate designs and patterns.

The wall then began to *shift*. The bricks groaned softly, then popped and ground as they pulled to the sides—suddenly fluid—and a door emerged in the wall. Like . . . like someone had *unzipped* the stones to reveal it underneath. In seconds the structure had rearranged—many bricks simply vanishing—to create a worn old wooden door with peeling yellow paint.

Moonlight yanked it open and gestured for them to enter. Marasi ducked in first, stepping over some buckets of paint that had been piled against the wall. TwinSoul followed, then finally Moonlight. They crowded into a small chamber, lit by a single red electric bulb. Why were there so many washbasins on the counter, and all of these jugs of liquid? Was this a storage room for cleaning supplies? That didn't explain the red light bulb, which was so dim it barely did anything.

Behind them, the doorway vanished—as if being consumed by the bricks on the sides. "That is the most unnatural thing I've ever seen," Marasi whispered.

"You literally have a friend who can fly," Moonlight said.

"And?" Marasi said, unzipping her rifle from its case. TwinSoul threw off his coat, exposing his suit and yellow sash, then rested a hand on his sword. Marasi listened at the door, and was joined by Moonlight. When they heard nothing from the next room over, Marasi eased the door open and found a pitch-black chamber beyond.

They slipped through it, passing a strangely large number of what appeared to be chairs. Yes, in rows. What in the world? At the far reaches of the room, Marasi fumbled in the darkness, searching for a door. Her hands instead brushed what felt like a series of light switches.

Since the room was clearly empty, she flipped one of the light switches. However, it wasn't the kind of light she'd been anticipating. A streak of illumination burst from one wall and shone onto the other, projecting a brilliant image.

An image of a crumbling city, with ash falling from the sky. Then the image started *moving*.

45

Marasi stared at the moving image, depicting a city in full color—though those colors were mostly muted dark greys and blacks against the brilliant red sky. Ash drifted from above, sprinkling the smoldering ruins. A loud mechanical sound came from the room emitting the light.

"By the first aether," TwinSoul said, stepping up beside her and resting his hand on the back of a nearby chair for support. "What is it? A window into the future?"

"I've never seen anything like it," Moonlight said from the far wall, nearest the image. She hesitantly lifted her hand into the stream of light—and displaced the image, leaving a shadow of her hand on the wall.

Fortunately, Marasi *had* experienced something like this once before. VenDell had shown them a way of projecting evanotype images onto a wall using light. Those had been static, and in black and white. But he'd said something then that had stuck with her: *Harmony implies that if we find this wondrous, it will really burn our metals when the images start moving.*

It appeared the Set had figured out that secret. And they'd found a way to create moving images of another place, using cameras? This room did have the feel of a small playhouse theater, only without the stage.

But . . . was this landscape of piling ash and broken cities the future, or the past? It resembled Elendel, by the architecture, but there was so much rubble she couldn't tell for certain.

"Here, look at this," Moonlight called from the far side of the room, where she'd opened another door.

TwinSoul and Marasi joined Moonlight in a room with a different kind of decor. An enormous table dominated it, with a tiny replica of a city on it. It was like the model that TwinSoul had created, but made out of painted wood and plaster—broken and ruined, the buildings fallen as if in some disaster.

It *was* Elendel; she could see that from the layout. So, not only had someone seen the future, they'd built a model of what was going to happen?

Moonlight peeked into some boxes, then pulled out a handful of fine ash from one, which she let trail through her fingers. Other shelves held tiny props—miniature versions of people lying like corpses. Dead horses made of painted plaster. Broken buildings, ruined motorcars, some large red-painted sheets with depictions of clouds and a blazing sun . . .

And evanotype cameras, set up to look across the table from down low. Seeing that, it all snapped together for her.

"It's a fake," she whispered with relief. "They didn't travel to the future or the past. They created a model of a fallen Elendel . . . then used these machines to craft pictures of a future that hasn't happened. Even that picture we found earlier . . . it's a fake. A photo of this model. They've been *deliberately* constructing a hoax to make people *think* the world is going to end."

"No," Moonlight said. "They've been constructing a hoax to make people think it has *already* ended. But who are they planning to show it to, and why?"

"If there are answers," Marasi said, "we'll find them below." She nodded the other direction, out through the theater room toward the larger doors on the wall near the projecting device.

They peeked out to find a hallway lit with caged industrial lights. The place felt eerily empty, considering the earlier activity. Moonlight went out first. Marasi joined her, and they found a set of doors at the end of the hallway. These doors had windows at the top, so they could observe the loading dock beyond.

A group of armed men and women patrolled here. TwinSoul crouched beside Marasi, then let a tiny—practically invisible—line of crystals sneak under the door.

"Ah," he said. "You see that large wall that juts out to our left, just inside the room? That's our industrial elevator as you had anticipated, my lady."

Marasi could make out the section of wall he indicated—but the front of the elevator would be facing away from them. They'd never sneak through the open cargo bay without being spotted. Fortunately, they didn't need to.

They moved through the hallway to the appropriate location—a blank wall, beyond which should be the elevator.

"All right," Marasi whispered.

Moonlight created another door, then pulled it open, revealing a deep, dark shaft leading down. The elevator must be below, likely having carried the lord mayor and his bodyguards into the depths.

Now what?

"Allow me," TwinSoul said, stepping through the door and steadying himself by grabbing a small box just inside, standing with one foot on a narrow ledge, the other dangling over the void. Marasi reached to steady him, but before she could the door vanished, the wall stretching back into place.

Moonlight hastily stamped again, then pulled open the door. They found TwinSoul hanging from a ladder constructed of roseite stone. He took a long drink from his backpack full of water and smiled. "Shall we?" he asked.

"What if someone calls the elevator back up?" Marasi asked.

"It's an industrial elevator," Moonlight said. "Look how wide this shaft is, how thick the cables are. It will move slowly. Worst case, we can climb on top and ride it up. There's enough space above us here that we won't be crushed."

Marasi nodded, and TwinSoul began climbing down, new rungs forming beneath him as he did so. Marasi stepped onto the ladder, testing its strength. TwinSoul was, it turned out, *exceptionally* handy to have along. She climbed down a little to let Moonlight on too. The doorway vanished again, but Moonlight cracked open her rucksack to let some light leak out, painting the shaft with a pale white glow.

They started descending toward the caverns. And, hopefully, answers.

46

Wax climbed down the hidden passage in the mayor's mansion. Yes, it did seem to be squeezed between two walls; he'd climbed far enough to pass the first floor and reach the basement. Here his ladder emerged into a small room with iron walls and ceiling.

It had supplies on the shelves: dry rations, jugs of water. Looked like some kind of small emergency bunker. Not intended for long-term occupancy, but a safe bolt-hole in case of . . . what? Riots in the streets? Or something more nefarious, like an accidental weapon detonation?

Chilled, Wax inspected the room and found scrapes on the floor indicating a hidden door on one wall. He opened it without much difficulty—though it was made of thick reinforced metal—and found a path into the storm drain. Light peeked in through the grates above, and the scent—though unpleasant—wasn't terrible. Not a true sewer, just a place for washing rainwater out of the streets and toward the ocean.

And a nice emergency exit from the mayor's mansion, he thought, noting numerous footprints in the sludge and dried muddy ones in the concrete tunnel up ahead. A little farther along, he found a small motorized cart, open roofed, perfect to drive in these tight confines. The wheels were covered in sludge, and there were numerous tire tracks in the mud beyond.

There were no keys in the cart, and though supposedly there was a way to start one without them, that was a feat of thievery he'd never studied. Instead Wax pulled the folded-up calendar from his coat pocket and noted again the numerous appointments at the "lab." Back and forth, sometimes a couple of times a day. If Wax had been visiting a secret installation that frequently, he would most certainly have wanted a covert way to travel.

Wax started into the tunnel on foot, but then phantoms from long ago rose around him. For the briefest moment, he wasn't in a drainage sewer in the most modern city of the Basin. He was in a dirty mine adit, haunted by twisted "artwork" made by a terrible mind. Golden light sifting down from above. A meeting with destiny.

Someone else moves us.

A deep breath and a moment of peace banished the phantoms. They'd be with him forever, but they didn't *haunt* him any longer. They were more like echoes than ghosts. Reminders of the man he'd been, the life he'd led, and the people he'd loved. They were remembered, but today he had work to do. He found a service ladder to the street above, and climbed up to go find Wayne. Hopefully he wasn't on fire.

Blessedly, he found Wayne alive and only slightly singed, waiting at the prearranged rally point. A bar, because of course it was. Wayne had picked the spot.

Wax slid into the seat beside his friend, and Wayne passed him a shot of whiskey, which Wax downed with a hiss of satisfaction. They left money on the counter, then slipped out the back.

"You find anythin'?" Wayne asked as they reached the end of the alley behind the bar.

"Some writings that might be relevant," Wax said. "Calendar. Letters. More importantly, a secret tunnel—hopefully leading somewhere useful."

"Nice," Wayne said.

"What happened to you?"

"Eh," Wayne said. "Nothin' that interesting."

Wax looked at him, then at the burn marks on his trousers.

"Couldn't do Grandma's Been at the Vodka," Wayne explained. "Couldn't find a wig in time. So I did Flaming Bunny instead."

"Flaming Bunny," Wax said flatly. "Please tell me you didn't set a rabbit on fire, Wayne."

"Of course not. I couldn't find a damn *wig* in time; where would I find a *rabbit*?"

"Good, I—"

"You use a cat for Flaming Bunny. And those are all over the dang place."

"Wayne. You *set a cat on fire?*"

"Hell, no! What do you think I am? A sadist?"

Wax relaxed a little.

"You throw the cat out a window," Wayne explained.

"Oh, Harmony . . ." Wax said. "*Why?*"

"To *save* it from the flames, of course!" Wayne shook his head as Wax led him toward the storm drain. "That's the plan. You start a big fire, then go around screaming and throw a cat out the window. People believe you and think you're saving pets."

"Then . . ."

"Then you shout that someone has to save the bunny," he said. "You lead everyone in to knock on the doors and get folks outta the place, and everybody gets all crazy and distracted helpin' you."

Wax stopped on the street, gawking at the Silver House with everyone else. It was now almost fully ablaze, a terrible plume of smoke rising from it, like the Deepness itself.

"You did say," Wayne noted, "that following an egregious diplomatic incident, we might as well have some fun."

"That is *not* what I said." Wax sighed.

"What?" Wayne said. "You still on about that cat thing?"

"You really threw it out a window?"

"What would you have done? *Leave it to burn?* I hadda rescue the thing."

"Rescue the cat. From a fire you made. A cat that you kidnapped *expressly for that purpose.*"

Wayne grinned. "Oh, don't worry. I hucked him at a tree real good. Cats always land in trees, so long as you throw them hard enough."

"Why . . . why would you think that?"

"Dunno," Wayne said as Wax started them moving again. "Must have learned it in school."

"Did you . . . go to school?"

"As a kid? Nah. But I burned one down once, before I even developed Flaming Bunny. Maybe the cat thing was on the board or something in there."

"Wait. When did you burn down a *school?*"

"West's Haven?" Wayne said. "Nine years back. It was an evil damn school."

Wax hesitated at the mouth of the alley with the access ladder, thinking. West's Haven . . .

Oh, right. That *had* been an evil damn school.

"Fine," Wax said, pulling open the hatch to the storm drain. "Let's keep moving."

Wayne climbed down. At the bottom, he grunted.

"What?" Wax said, joining him.

"Don't tell Marasi 'bout this," he said. "I told her you ain't never taken me into a sewer. Least this one doesn't stink . . ." He squinted. "Actually, kinda looks like a narrow canyon, with all those lights coming in the top . . ."

"Why would you say that?" Wax said.

"No reason."

They both turned around as the bells of the fire brigade sounded from above.

"So . . ." Wayne said. "Calendar and letters, was it?"

Wax nodded. "Gave has been visiting a place called the lab, though he also left for two weeks for some kind of trajectory test a couple months ago. Disguised as a vacation."

"Huh," Wayne said, pointing ahead. "And the lab is this way, you think?"

"Seems likely," Wax said. He dug in his pocket a moment, then passed the calendar to Wayne.

Who whistled softly. "No appointments after today?"

"I noticed that too."

"'They arrive' . . ." Wayne said, reading.

Wax nodded, giving Wayne a moment with the calendar pages while he pulled out the letters. The light wasn't great down here, but he could make out enough in the sunlight coming through the grates. Reading the two letters again, one extremely incriminating, the other full of pleasantries. What . . .

Oh, rusts. "Wayne," he said, holding up the incriminating letter they'd gotten from the newspaper editor. "This is a forgery."

"What? Really?" Wayne took it. "How do you know?"

"Before all this started," Wax said, "I spent a good amount of time on an operation that implicated Vennis Hasting—who supposedly wrote that letter—in a scandal. I proved that he had been bribing other senators. In order to make our case, Steris and I authenticated letters we'd acquired from him. Rusts. I visited three separate handwriting analysts, and they talked specifically about the distinctive turn of Vennis's strokes. Which aren't right in this one." He felt his eyes widen. "That's what it means . . . *that's* what she's doing . . ."

"Mate," Wayne said. "You've gotta be more clear. 'Cuz I sure ain't following."

"My sister," Wax explained. "She needs a way to seize control of the Basin, and prove to Autonomy she can rule here. I've been wondering how blowing up Elendel achieves that."

"It would remove a whole lot of barriers."

"Yes, but surely the other cities would never follow someone who committed such an atrocity." Wax held up the fake letter. "Unless Telsin could claim she *didn't* blow up Elendel. Unless she had proof—in the form of forged letters—that the *senators inside Elendel* were the ones developing the bomb. With the right evidence, she could make it look like they mistakenly blew themselves up."

"Oooh, that's devious," Wayne said. "She can 'recover' some of the details of that weapon too, so Bilming will 'reluctantly' have access to the technology to protect the Basin from the Malwish. Hell . . . that would work. Remove Elendel. Unite the Basin. Achieve dominance on the planet."

A piece locked into place. Even Gave's letters—the real ones from Vennis Hasting—made sense now. They'd needed handwriting samples, hence the cordial letters between mayor and senator.

"And the lack of appointments after today?" Wayne asked. "Seems like our deadline's even tighter than we feared."

"We need to find this lab," Wax said, starting along the storm drain again. "And hope the bomb is there."

Wayne nodded, joining him. Gave had scheduled fifteen minutes on either side of his appointments for travel to the lab—so it wouldn't be too far.

As they walked, Wax found himself increasingly worried. About what Telsin was doing. About the implications of it all. So he was a little relieved when Wayne broke the silence.

"Sooooo . . ." Wayne said. "When you were in the mayor's office . . . did you notice if he had a nice desk?"

"He had a rather nice one," Wax said. "Why?"

"Did you . . ." He nodded back in the direction of the Silver House. "You know . . ."

"Fart in his chair?"

"Yup."

"Wayne. Of *course* I didn't."

They walked a little farther through the muck, finding a place where kids had obviously snuck down, judging by the graffiti painted on the walls: giant sweeping Terris patterns of V's.

"Okay," Wax finally said, unable to let it go despite trying quite forcefully, "*why* would you even *think* that I would do that to his chair? You explicitly said not to, and beyond that . . . what the hell? Who does that?"

"Nobody, nobody," Wayne said. "It's good you didn't. Gotta stay classy, you know. 'Specially in times like this. Very serious. Bombs threatening cities. Likely detonation today. No time for frivolity."

He paused.

"But . . ." Wayne continued, "if *I'd* been there, and seen that fancy chair . . . Well, I like those chairs, you know? The type that leans all the way back, and is all leather, and firm enough for support, but not so firm that it's uncomfortable. You know?

"And I'd think, 'Damn, that's a fancy chair.' And I'd wonder . . . would the old backyard mistmaker sound different? What if I released a little concentrated essence of Wayne into those perfect leather contours? Would it feel different? Would my cheeks—"

"That's enough. Please."

"Oh, right. Okay."

They continued on a little farther, but something about his words . . . Wax again tried to put it out of his mind, but . . .

"Wayne," he finally said, closing his eyes, feeling angry at himself for continuing the conversation. "I have a chair *just like that* back in my study in the penthouse."

"That you do," Wayne said solemnly. "You do indeed."

Oh hell. "Wayne. Did you—"

"Wax, the whole city is in danger, you know? You need to stop letting your attention drift, mate. First that fixation on me maybe setting government buildings on fire—only twice, mind you, which isn't a pattern, just a coincidence. Now this fascination with what comes outta my backside. Can't we keep focused on important things?"

"Yeah, I suppose."

"Like this art," Wayne said, admiring some graffiti. "Ma was right. This place is beautiful."

"Ma?" Wax said. "Do I *want* to know what you're talking about this time?"

"This just reminds me of an old story with a canyon," Wayne said, joining him as they continued. "A story my ma told me. Last one she gave me. So I remember it well, you know?"

"No," Wax said. "How is this tunnel a canyon?"

"It just is," Wayne said softly, looking up as they passed under another grate, sunlight crossing his face in a checkerboard pattern. "Been thinking about it since earlier today. It's inevitable, you know?"

"I don't," Wax said. "I really don't, Wayne."

"Well it just is," he said. "Even if you don't know it. You're the hero, Wax, and you got a mission. Barm. The nastiest monster what ever lived. You're gonna stop him . . ." He hesitated. "Watch out. Might be some snakes in this canyon."

"It's a storm drain," Wax said, "and I've never seen a snake in the city."

"Yeah, they're damn good at sneaking," Wayne said. "Speaking of snakes: the Set, they'll know that was us with the mansion."

"Undoubtedly," Wax said. "They might push into the mayor's study to recover sensitive documents. I couldn't replace the rug above the trapdoor—so they'll know I found the tunnel."

"Ah, great."

"Great?"

"You're supposed to find a bad guy in the canyon," Wayne explained. "If the story is going to go right, at least."

"Wayne," Wax said. "We're not in a canyon in your mother's story. We're in a storm drain in Bilming, trying to find and stop an explosive device. We—"

He was interrupted by a gunshot just ahead, echoing in the narrow tunnel—and a bullet hit the concrete near Wax's head with a pop, blasting out a chip.

They both immediately ducked to the sides, getting low, and saw shadows moving in the tunnel ahead, just around a bend. Wax picked out two figures crouching beside the curve of the tunnel—the Coinshot he'd fought earlier, and a shorter woman wearing a bowler hat.

"Hey," Wayne said. "Will you look at that. Bad guys *and* snakes. Both at the same time."

47

Marasi's team neared the bottom of the elevator shaft without incident, carefully using TwinSoul's roseite ladder. Red-pink dust crumbled around her as she slowed her climb, the little motes often evaporating in the air below her. Marasi probably had a dusting of them in her hair—smoldering there, like simmering ashes without the heat.

They found the large service elevator settled snug on the bottom of the shaft. TwinSoul expanded his ladder to the sides so all three of them could climb down beside one another. Then Marasi tested the roof of the elevator with her toe. Solid, sturdy metal. She lowered her weight onto it carefully, and it didn't even bow. She nodded to the others, who joined her.

"Now what?" Moonlight whispered.

"Service hatch," Marasi said, locating one set into the other corner. She eased it open. The front doors of the elevator were open, though she couldn't see much more from this angle. She waved TwinSoul over. "Can you see if there is anyone watching below?"

A small line of roseite provided answers.

"Silajana sees two guards," TwinSoul whispered. "A man and a woman, armed with rifles. They are opposite the open elevator door, near a natural stone wall. It appears that we have indeed arrived at a series of tunnels and caverns.

"The guards do not seem observant, and are currently looking at one another rather than the elevator. Should I try to send them to the aethers, their souls left to ruminate on their poor choices in this particular life?"

"She wants to remain quiet, TwinSoul," Moonlight said. "That might be overkill."

"I can handle this," Marasi whispered. "Though it would help if you could lower me through that hole a little, TwinSoul, so I can see."

He obliged, creating a small lattice of crystals to support her as she lowered her head into the elevator, her hair hanging down. The two guards stood amid some large crates, facing each other and leaning back against separate boxes. TwinSoul was right. They weren't paying attention. Actually, they appeared to be flirting. At least, the man was giggling at his own jokes, and the woman was pretending not to be impressed.

From her side pouch, Marasi took out one of her Allomantic grenades and then attached her fishing line. She charged the grenade, then waited—and patience rewarded her when the man said something that finally made the woman laugh. With them distracted Marasi threw her grenade, which activated immediately after touching down. The two guards—focused on one another—hopefully wouldn't notice that time around them had slowed.

"All right," Marasi whispered, holding the fishing line. "Let's go."

Marasi dropped into the elevator with a thump. Moonlight followed more stealthily, prowling forward as she landed. TwinSoul lowered majestically on a pole of roseite with a foothold. He stepped off, then stumbled and put his hand to the wall of the elevator, steadying himself.

The three of them checked the tunnel for any other guards—it was empty—and slipped out, careful not to touch the barely visible edge of the slowness bubble, which was shimmering like the air above hot pavement.

The two guards remained frozen there. The woman's eyes closed as she laughed, the man grinning and fixated on his companion. Hopefully he wouldn't catch blurs from the corner of his eye. Marasi and the others hid in a nearby cross tunnel. She yanked her grenade up and out using the fishing line, and the bubble collapsed.

She snatched the grenade from the air as the female guard's laugh echoed from amid the crates. Marasi waited, tense. Had they been seen? Had either of them heard the grenade hit the stone over the sound of laughter?

Their conversation continued as if nothing had happened. Marasi nodded in relief to the others, and they prowled a little farther down their current tunnel. It was lit by a series of miner's lights on a thick cord on the wall, creating alternating darker sections and brightly lit ones.

"That was well executed," Moonlight whispered as Marasi rewound the fishing line. "Only one way to go for now: down this tunnel?"

Marasi nodded.

"I feel exposed like this," TwinSoul whispered. "We could encounter more guards."

Marasi felt the same, but there was little they could do. They continued along the tunnel, which felt much like the ones she'd entered with Wayne the other day. Smooth, ancient rock—with some rubble here and there showing that chunks had fallen in from the ceiling during the explosive-weapon tests. And perhaps some of the blasts had been used not to test, but to connect tunnels and caverns.

Voices echoed from up ahead. Marasi glanced behind them at the long, exposed tunnel, then pointed forward, toward one of the darker sections where she thought she saw some larger chunks of rubble. TwinSoul lagged behind, despite his promise, as Marasi and Moonlight hurried into the shadows.

None of those speaking were visible yet, as the tunnel turned ahead. Marasi crouched behind some rubble, Moonlight joining her. The stone chunks only just came up past her knees when she crouched, but it was better than nothing. They waved anxiously to TwinSoul, who did his best, stumbling as he arrived and falling to his knees near them.

Then stone began to grow from his hand. It arced up around them, darker colored than his usual roseite. Though it was still pink, the shadows hid the color. He took a long drink from his backpack to restore his water, then—at his urging—they all crouched as low as they could go and let the roseite grow over them, leaving a small section clear at the front so they could see what was happening outside.

A group of patrolling soldiers wandered around the bend. There were only five of them, but Marasi was glad for the cover as they paused and chatted about the lord mayor's visit, then split up in opposite directions. One patrol went back toward the elevator, right past their hiding place. They didn't even look down.

Still, Marasi's heart thundered in her chest until the tunnel fell silent again, and she risked a whisper. "You two certainly are handy."

"Thank you, my lady," TwinSoul said.

"This is only a fraction of the talents members of the Ghostbloods have," Moonlight noted. "You'll be amazed at the things we will show you."

"If I join," Marasi said. "I don't truly know what you are, what you do."

"Well, that is easy to explain," TwinSoul said. "We have three general tenets."

"Protect Scadrial," Moonlight said, standing up as the roseite shell began to disintegrate.

"But neither of you are from here," Marasi whispered.

"True," TwinSoul said, "but my homeland is inhospitable to my kind for now. I joined Lord Kelsier for the opportunity to gain allies and resources for my eventual fight against the dark aether. And having this planet remain safe and uncorrupted is a worthy goal on its own."

"And you?" Marasi asked Moonlight. "You can't go home either?"

"I can't," she said, "but I don't care so much about that. I'm keeping an eye on a particular enemy of the Ghostbloods. Plus I like secrets." She nodded forward.

They continued, and after they checked around the bend and made sure no one else was coming, Marasi whispered to Moonlight, "What are the other two tenets?"

"We share what we know with each other," Moonlight said. "There are no secrets within a team. If you ask Kelsier, even *he'll* tell you what *he's* planning. But you absolutely can't share secrets outside the organization without his permission."

"And the last one?"

"We trust each other," TwinSoul said. "We're a team. A family. You join us, you absolutely swear not to make a move against another Ghostblood. No infighting. No betrayals. No undermining one another. No squabbling over resources or favor."

"We take it very seriously, Marasi," Moonlight said. "And the way you act—your attitude as part of a team—is one of the main reasons we came to you."

And not, she implied, to Wax. They went on, Marasi chewing on those tenets. She swallowed the last one easily. Not moving against one another? Not undermining the mission or goals of another member of the group? That sounded wonderful. More than once, she'd collided with another constable's ambition, preventing her from getting things done.

The other tenet though . . . Not sharing information with those outside? That sat in her gut like a stone. She was a constable for the city of Elendel. Joining the Ghostbloods would be like . . . like swearing allegiance to another country.

But the secrets they knew . . . the things they were doing . . . She doubted that if she joined the Ghostbloods, she'd *ever* have to waste her time dealing with small-time criminals again.

She put it all out of her mind for the time being as they reached an intersection. The rightmost turn was particularly well-lit. There, two long, narrow structures had been built out along the tunnel, one on each side. The path continued between them, as if they were shops on a street.

Peeking around the corner into this tunnel, Marasi could see that one of the two buildings was guarded by thick-armed men. The lord mayor's bodyguards. The two men were distracted though, talking to someone inside. Which gave Marasi an opportunity.

She led the way, crouching low around the corner, and crossed the short distance to the rightmost building. She was joined by the other two as the bodyguards finished their conversation and closed the door, settling into guard postures.

A window on this short end of the building, where Marasi and the others hid, gave her a chance to steal a look. And there he was, right inside. The lord mayor himself, in formal dining wear, hair slicked back with something greasy, sitting at a table. Aside from him, there were two additional guards settling in by the door. Four people in white lab coats huddled near Gave's table, one handing him something to drink.

Marasi frowned, noticing Gave's slumped-over posture. He looked . . . worn. Far less commanding or smug than he was at the police station.

He shook his head. "What odds do you give her," he asked, his voice muffled from inside, but audible, "of getting that bomb to fly. Of actually salvaging this?"

"That's . . . not my department, sir," one of the scientists said. "I'm not an engineer."

"I can't believe it's come to this," Gave said, his voice softening. "I didn't think . . . when I agreed . . . Are they here?"

"Nearly," another scientist said.

"How many?" Gave asked.

"A lot," the woman replied. "An army of soldiers with golden skin and glowing red eyes. Sir, is it true? Are they . . ."

Gave pounded the table. "*I'm* supposed to be in control! She's supposed to fail, and *I'm* supposed to take her place."

"You will, sir," one of the scientists said. "If she doesn't get the bomb working, Autonomy will kill her."

"And invade the whole *rusting* Basin," Gave said, hands to his face. "Maybe the world. Damn. It wasn't supposed to be like this . . ." He downed his shot and hauled himself to his feet.

Marasi shared a glance with the others. They'd known Autonomy was planning some sort of decisive attack if Telsin failed to prove she could control the Basin. It seemed that maybe Gave had been assigned to facilitate that?

It would be convenient for him, she thought, *to have these caverns as a bunker in case a destructive war breaks out above. That would explain the food, too.*

And some kind of invading army? She remembered how awed Miles Hundredlives had been, speaking of the "men of gold and red" as he died. Rusts.

"How many soldiers of our own do we have left in the bunker?" Entrone asked.

"Two contingents," said a scientist who seemed to be in charge—a thick-bodied woman in a white lab coat.

"And Metalblessed?" Entrone asked.

"None," the woman said.

"That woman," Entrone said, "is deliberately trying to leave me short-manned." He started pacing. "While I'm *forced* to support her, lest the worst option play out. I can't believe I let it get this far. We need some kind of military presence to corral those alien soldiers."

"Can we do that?" the scientist asked.

"I don't know," he said, putting his hand to his head. "I don't want to rule ashes. Rusts, Edwarn's plans were always superior. We should have been pushing for those, instead of Telsin's idiotic bomb."

"Yes, my lord mayor," Labcoat said. "Speaking of Edwarn's plans, did you . . . want to proceed with the test?"

He waved for her to do so, and Labcoat sent her two assistants to the far side of the room, the stone wall of the tunnel. Marasi had missed a thick door set into the rock—made of strong wood, with sturdy locks on the outside.

The assistants undid these, opening the door to reveal a group of some twenty people huddled in the darkness. They wore an assortment of different kinds of clothing—some expensive, others just common work clothes. All were grungy and rumpled. With pistols drawn, the assistants picked out a lean woman in a torn evening dress, her face streaked with makeup. She barely resisted, looking too exhausted for anything more than a token protest.

The door was locked again, and the assistants strapped her facedown to a table. Then one took out a silvery spike, long and thin. Marasi felt a chill, then nausea. Was this . . .

Oh, Ruin. Were they making an Allomancer? She'd read about the process in the book Death had given her, but she'd never wanted to see it in person.

Labcoat took out a notebook. "We believe that we've isolated the technique Edwarn was on to," she said. "Indeed, we've refined it. The process involves a very thin spike, my lord mayor, and, oddly, the right mindset."

"Mindset?" he asked.

"You need to know what you're doing and why," the woman explained. "It helps to whisper a Command as you work, though we find it isn't strictly necessary. Trauma on the part of the subject is helpful as well."

At a nod from her, the assistants threaded the long spike through the skin of the woman's upper back. Almost like they were sewing with a six-inch needle. The poor woman made a pained whimper, and the assistant doing the procedure mumbled something to himself, then pushed the needle slowly back through her skin, as if making two holes for some kind of piercing. The woman screamed louder as the process finished.

As soon as the spike left her skin, the holes started bleeding. The woman fell silent, and the assistant washed off the bloodied spike and handed it to Labcoat, who promptly placed it in a solution attached to a device and examined it.

"Roughly five percent Invested," she reported to Entrone. "And as you can see, the subject is still alive. We've essentially excised a piece of the soul and stored it in the metal."

Wait.

They'd made a spike without killing the woman?

That was supposed to be impossible. Granted, Marasi hadn't studied Death's book in as much detail as Wax had, but she was fairly sure Hemalurgy always killed its subject.

"So?" Entrone said. "I don't know if you've noticed, but I don't particularly care if these people live or die. Creating spikes without killing them is pointless. We need Metalborn in huge numbers. *That* will impress Autonomy. *That* will make her realize this planet is a resource, not something to be burned."

"Ah, my lord," the woman said. "This woman *isn't* Metalborn. We've Invested a spike—a tiny bit, granted—using an *ordinary person.* All people are Invested by Ruin and Preservation as part of our very makeup—and we have a little extra Preservation, blessed by the Shards upon our creation. We're pulling some of that out.

"The percentage you get depends on the person. We think it might have to do with how likely they were, genetically, to be Metalborn. But they don't need that extra if the powers didn't manifest in them. It's vestigial. We simply slice it off and use it in a spike. Fully Investing one takes between twenty and thirty people."

"But can you make *Allomancers* from those spikes," Entrone said. "That's the key part."

The scientist glanced at the others. "Sir, this is a fantastic result. A huge step forward in—"

"Can you make me Allomancers?" he demanded. "Now. Today. To show Autonomy."

"No," Labcoat admitted. "We think we need to code this in some way to give a specific Metallic Art blessing. We're working on that. We've had some few gain a power for a short time using one of these spikes, but it gives out soon after."

"Damn," Entrone muttered. "That means Edwarn's Community project here is still valuable." He folded his arms, looking worn down again. "But we have nothing to show Autonomy at the present. I'm going to have to do it. I'm going to have to let her army through. Call all of our remaining loyalists—those not working directly for Telsin—into the caverns."

"But—" Labcoat began.

"We wait," he said, "for Telsin to initiate her plan. We give her every opportunity. And then . . . then if it doesn't work . . ."

"We survive," Labcoat said.

"We survive." He nodded to himself. "I'm going to the Community to see to the perpendicularity." He waved toward the cell at the rear of the room. "They have all heard and seen too much. They are a liability. Execute them."

"Of course, my lord," Labcoat said. Entrone left, leaving the two guards inside, but collecting the two in the tunnel. He slammed the door, making the flimsy structure shake. Fortunately, once outside, he turned and continued farther into the complex instead of walking past Marasi and her team.

"Fetch me some invel gas pellets," Labcoat said to the assistants in the room. "That will be a painless end for the captives. Fion, tell our loyalists to retreat to the caverns. They can bring their families, but nothing else. A priority-one evacuation order. This is the real thing."

One of the assistants left at a dead run, also going farther into the complex. The other began fiddling in cabinets at the side of the room. Marasi and the two Ghostbloods crouched in the shadows, whispering.

"We have to get this information to Kelsier," Moonlight said. "A new way of making spikes could change everything."

"It's still brutal," Marasi whispered back. "Stealing a piece of someone's soul? It's better than murdering them, but I doubt this is something we could use in good conscience."

"You don't understand," Moonlight said. "If they're even *close* to forging Metalborn out of the raw power of souls—if they've had tests that resulted in an Allomancer, no matter how fleeting . . . Marasi, that path could lead to creating spikes using *pure* Investiture instead of souls." She tapped her rucksack, indicating the glowing jars inside.

Ruin. The ability to create spikes in a mechanical way? Even the process of making medallions among the Malwish required Metalborn. If what Moonlight implied was right, then it would change *everything.*

"For now," TwinSoul said, "Silajana reminds us that the planet itself is in danger. Getting information to Lord Kelsier is meaningless if that invasion happens. We must follow Entrone and see if we can interfere with Autonomy's plans."

Marasi peeked around the corner, looking farther down the tunnel. They could sneak past. But the people in that room were about to be executed . . .

"We have to help the prisoners," Marasi said.

"A few lives are meaningless right now," Moonlight said. "We need to keep moving. It's our way."

"It's not mine," Marasi said. "I'm an officer of the law. I can't leave a group of people to be murdered. Besides, he said they'd heard too much. They know something of use to us."

Moonlight and TwinSoul glanced to one another.

"I'm going to help them," Marasi said. "There are only two guards. We should be able to stop those with ease."

"If anything goes wrong," Moonlight said, "it could alert everyone down here. One gunshot . . ."

Marasi hesitated, weighing the risks. It might be foolish, she acknowledged, but she hadn't become a constable to leave people to be murdered. She stood up straight. "It is a risk I will take. Are you with me, or do I do it alone?"

The other two stood. "Let's do it quickly then," Moonlight said.

48

Steris had heard that in a fire, the rats were often the first creatures out. They could smell the smoke before the flames raged out of control—and so, on occasion, you could get an early warning of impending danger by watching the rats flee.

That was what she did now, while organizing her thoughts and listening to the other senators prepare their escape routes. She watched Lady Gardre, the woman Steris was almost certain was a member of the Set. So long as Gardre remained in the city, they had time.

But as the minutes stretched long, waiting for TenSoon to return with the Bands, she began to doubt. Perhaps it wasn't Gardre. Perhaps one of the aides was the real agent, and they'd already fled. Perhaps the Set didn't actually have anyone in the government's inner circle. Perhaps—

An aide bustled into the room—and stepped over to Lady Gardre, whispering in her ear.

"Ah," Gardre said. "I'll need to deal with this." Gardre stood up, straightening her jacket. "I'll be back shortly."

Steris knew she wouldn't be. Her departure meant the city was in imminent danger. She passed TenSoon on her way out, and he drew the attention of the others. They didn't realize.

"Now," Adawathwyn said, striding around the table to TenSoon, "let's see how these work. Give me the Bands. Let me walk Harmony's Path and save the city! I am Metalborn, a Ferring of the mind. Whatever bomb is being delivered here, I can Push it away with the force of a planet! Or I can soar to Bilming and bring justice to those miscreants!"

Ambassador Daal stepped forward, his face hidden behind his mask. "This must be a negotiation. You promised that they wouldn't be used."

"Surely you can see the need, Ambassador," Steris said. "You don't expect us to simply *die* if this could save us?"

"Surely you Northerners understand the meaning of the word 'promise,'" he said, looking at her through the holes in his mask. "I have the authority to negotiate for their return to us." He leaned forward, his hands on the table, and looked straight at the governor—who leaned away, his eyes widening.

"If you use them," Daal continued, "then I demand that they must be turned over to us next, for use during the disaster of *our* choosing. A compromise, yah? If you wish to avoid war, but also use these Bands, that is the *only* solution. You get this chance. We will also get a chance. Deal?"

All eyes in the room went to TenSoon. The kandra had validated the treaty and had become keepers of the relic. It appeared the others thought he could agree to this, and Steris supposed he was as close to an arbiter as they had.

"Harmony is preoccupied," TenSoon said, "but our time is tight. So I will agree to this if the humans do. The Basin may use the Bands right now. But they revert to the Malwish."

"Do it," the governor said. "If it could save the city . . . I agree."

It was not the best situation for a negotiation, and Steris wondered how badly they were being played. Daal must see this as the perfect opportunity to get what he wanted. Regardless, she still didn't understand why TenSoon thought this might work. Yes, the Bands made a person a powerful Metalborn, but Daal acted as if they could win wars on their own—and TenSoon had this distant expression. He met her eyes.

"What?" she asked.

"We believe," he whispered, "there is a way to transport objects large distances using a conflux of Metalborn powers. It is a thing Harmony doesn't yet understand himself. But I wonder . . . if someone feeling the transcendent power of the Bands . . . could solve the puzzle."

Fascinating. She took notes.

TenSoon opened the box to present the Bands—which were in the shape of a large spearhead, made of multiple bands of different kinds of metal. The governor nodded for Adawathwyn to take them. She reached in and touched them, her eyes alight. She picked them up, held them for a moment, and frowned.

"How . . ." she said. "How do I activate them?"

"It was natural for Wax," Steris said, walking over. She hesitantly poked the Bands, and felt nothing.

They passed them around, letting everyone try. Finally TenSoon took them, his face scrunched up in thought. Then horror followed. "They're *drained*," he whispered. "Something has happened . . . How . . . ?"

Without their power, the Bands of Mourning were essentially just a heavy piece of history. Like a statue's broken arm.

The governor gave a groan of despair and leaned back in his chair, squeezing his eyes shut. Salvation had just flitted away on butterfly wings. Steris couldn't help wondering what she was missing. She'd never anticipated this. The Bands could be drained? By whom? And how?

Daal stepped forward and touched them with one finger. "It's true," he muttered. "What have you done? Have you been using these in secret?"

"What?" Adawathwyn said. "No! We haven't seen them in years, not since the treaty!"

Daal picked up the Bands in one hand. "I will return them to my people."

"Wait," Steris said, standing. "That wasn't the deal."

"Wasn't it?" he said. "You had your chance to use them. It happens they are useless to you. Now we must have our chance. I wonder if it is *piety* that makes them work, yah? Or if maybe I am right, and you've been using them all along. Our scholars will know if you are trying to pass off some fake."

Steris looked at him and had the distinct impression that was . . . a prepared speech? Yes. She prepared words to say even in common conversations. His mannerisms felt practiced, rehearsed. But surely she was wrong. He couldn't have been *prepared* for this?

Unless he'd known the Bands would be drained. Unless he'd come to Elendel looking for a crisis that would make them call on the Bands, so he could offer his deal. And then . . .

"I don't know if I can allow this," the governor said.

"I don't know that we can forbid it," TenSoon growled back. "You agreed."

"Ah," Daal said. "Perhaps your Faceless Immortals can actually be impartial? Curious. I had not believed it."

Daal took the Bands' case from TenSoon, who growled low and dangerous—but let it go.

Steris watched with an odd feeling of disconnect. This was . . . this was some kind of Malwish ploy, completely *separate* from the tensions at Bilming. Which made it a problem for another time, when they weren't being threatened with extinction. The Bands were not the solution today. But there was a secret here that eventually she would like to tease out.

The ambassador walked to the door, but paused there, the Bands under his arm. "I did promise you passage, Governor. If this city *is* doomed, as you all think, then . . . if you wish, any of you may join me now. I will drop you at a safer location."

"I'll go," Adawathwyn said immediately. She snatched her things off the table.

"Maybe . . ." the governor said. "Maybe we're wrong. Mistaken somehow about this danger . . ."

"Are you a betting man, my lord governor?" Reddi asked. "Because I am. And I've learned to never bet against one particular man. If Dawnshot says a bomb is pointed at us, it is."

"We need to evacuate the city." Steris thumped her notebooks. "I have the plans here. Full citywide emergency plans for various categories of disaster. I had free time a few summers ago and was bored."

"This is what you do for fun?" Reddi asked.

"Well, the house taxes were already done for the next year," Steris said. "Here. This plan is the best for this situation. It gets the most people out of the city the fastest. The longer we have, the more we save. It's one of my most efficient creations." She looked up to the governor. "Please. We can't leave. We have to protect the city."

"Are you coming or not?" Daal snapped from the doorway. Perhaps he wanted the honor—and political bargaining chip—of having saved the governor.

Governor Varlance glanced from him to Steris. Then toward Adawathwyn—whose robes flashed as she vanished out the door. The other senators hastened to follow.

"You," Steris said softly to the governor, "are the captain of this city. This entire nation. You were chosen by the people to represent them. I need your authority to save as many of them as possible. There will be time for you to escape later. For now, help me save this city."

"You . . . really have a plan?" the governor said. He wiped his brow. "An evacuation plan?"

"Yes. We can do this, Varlance."

He nodded. A quick, hesitant nod, frightened. "I want to try. Where do we start?"

49

There wasn't no cover in this canyon, so Wayne had to do the smart thing: turn into some.

He stepped in front of Wax, who was ducking backward around the corner. Too slow, but fortunately the next shots from the enemy hit Wayne, making him grunt. Bullets *really* hurt. He supposed that was the point, but some other wounds were so big that your body kinda freaked out and decided not to hurt, least at first. Like it was saying, "Whoa. This is gonna suck *hard*. Better take a deep breath."

Bullets though, they didn't send him into shock or anything. So they just hurt. Like Death's own eyes.

Still, it kept Wax from bein' hit. Together he and Wayne ducked back around the curve in the tunnel, out of sight. The two of them waited there, Wax with guns out, ready to fire. They were perhaps thirty yards from where they'd spotted the two doppel-dummies, blocking the way farther through the tunnel.

Wayne rolled his shoulder as the bullet wounds healed, draining his metalminds a little further. He was using up his reserves pretty fast these last few days. Fortunately, most of his work with Marasi hadn't required much healin'. Her missions didn't *usually* involve things like throwing Wayne out windows like he was a rustin' cat.

"Oi!" the not-Wayne called from farther down the tunnel. "We can't shoot you if you keep hidin'! Come out so we can get on with killing you, mates!"

Oh, now that was plain *awful*. She was trying too hard—that wasn't a Roughs accent at all. It was inner-city Roughs enclave accent, with a bit of upper-crust theater thrown in—probably from her dialect coach. The resulting accent was ridiculous, just close enough to his natural accent that it was like rusty old spikes being pulled across a chalkboard.

"What the hell is going *on* with those two?" Wayne whispered.

"I suspect," Wax replied, "that the Set realized they'd need to face us, considering the ruin we made of their plans a few years back. So they spiked a few of their members with powers to match ours and trained them to fight us."

"That one isn't just tryin' to fight me," Wayne said. "She's tryin' to *be* me. You get the same sense from yours?"

"No," Wax said. "Other than the suit, he merely seems to be a competent Coinshot with a few extra spikes. Watch him, Wayne. He can burn up all of his steel in a single terrible burst, supercharging his Push to extreme levels. But he can also drain your abilities if he gets hold of you."

"So long as he has metals," Wayne said.

"The Set has some powerful resources, Wayne," Wax said. "I'll bet his chromium outlasts your bendalloy."

"We'll see about that." Wayne narrowed his eyes, peering around the corner. "That one what thinks she's like me, she's doin' a terrible job. I'm not nearly that annoying."

Wax calmly loaded a few bullets into his pistol.

"Hey," Wayne said. "Don't you say it."

"I didn't say a thing." He snapped the revolver closed. "Unfortunately, any delay is to their advantage. Which means we're going to have to go on the offensive."

"Close confines down here, mate," Wayne said. "Not great for Steelpushing. Real easy to get stuck in slow time while they coordinate to trap us."

"See if you can catch all four of us inside a speed bubble together," Wax said. "It's close confines, yes—but for them too."

"They can make their own bubble, mate," Wayne said. "Even inside ours. But I suppose they can't sculpt one like I can. So we should be good, if we're in close together."

"Exactly," Wax said. "If neither of us can rely on speed bubbles or flying high with Steelpushes, maybe our trained skill will overwhelm their borrowed abilities. We can try to throw that Steelpusher out of the bubble, to freeze him. Just don't let him touch you, or he can Leech your powers."

A good enough plan, Wayne supposed. He dug in his pocket for the aluminum-lined pouch his accountants had given him and pulled out a few beads of bendalloy. Kept it in little marbles, easy to swallow.

He knocked them back. Wax nodded, and Wayne made as big a speed bubble as he could. They ran through it, broke out the other side, and dashed down the tunnel. It was a big concrete pipe thing, a good ten feet or more across, the bottom containing a foot-or-two-wide section of sludge that had partially dried, on account of the lack of rain recently.

The evil twins got a chance to deliberate in a speed bubble while Wayne and Wax moved. But they couldn't do *too* much from inside one. Other than position themselves really well for when the bubble ended. So, the moment Wayne saw motion ahead, he dropped and rolled in the mud. So did Wax.

Bullets went streaking over their heads, where they'd been moments before. Wayne dashed the last few yards to close in on them, then tossed up a large speed bubble—fifteen feet across—to catch all four people. Dueling canes out, he went straight for the evil him, feigning a strike, dodging right, then sweeping with a cane from the left to knock her in the noggin. She barely managed to block him, then slid her weapon along his in a classic maneuver to try and smack his fingers.

He shoved her back and went in again, and the next sequence of attacks hit like a drumbeat—wooden stick against wooden stick. He got a hit on her, but she barely flinched as her metalminds healed her. She returned the blow, and he took it without much more than a faint grunt. Though his ribs cracked, they healed right up.

"Oi!" she said in that exaggerated parody of his accent. "That's cheatin'!"

"You ain't me," Wayne growled. "Don't pretend you are."

She grinned and slid in the mud in an admittedly skillful move, getting past him and dodging his next swing—all while rapping him on the arm hard enough to break the bone. He grimaced and flipped his hand to the side to reset the bone as his muscles pulled it back into place.

He fended off her next attack with one arm while the other healed, letting her force him to retreat. At that moment, Wax flew between them and slammed into the tunnel wall with a grunt. He tossed a handful of bullets in the air, then ducked—tricking not-Wax into Pushing on them instead of him. Wax then slid back across the ground underneath and unloaded his guns toward the Coinshot.

Wayne and the not-him watched it all with shocked hesitation, then Wayne grabbed his second dueling cane out of the mud. The two scrambled back together and exchanged a few more blows.

"Hate doin' this sober," not-him said. "Maybe we should grab a pint, then have at this again in a right proper state of mind."

"Nah," Wayne said, "I drink with bastards, liars, and fools. But I draw the line at someone like me."

"I'm doin' well, then?" she asked as they locked canes, coming in close together. "I'm you?"

"You're something far, far worse," he muttered. "You're someone who *wants* to be me."

"Ha!" she said, breaking the lock and shoving him to the side, making him slide up against the shimmering edge of the speed bubble. It didn't move when Wayne did. They anchored in place, so it wouldn't fall unless he dropped it or was shoved out.

He shook his arms. Damn, she was strong. Looked like natural strength training, which he didn't have time to do. She came at him with a body check, making him grunt as she pressed up against him.

"Hope old Dumad is doing all right," she said, nodding at her companion. "I done stole some of his metal vials without telling him."

"I don't steal," Wayne muttered.

"Sorry! I borrowed it."

"I don't borrow neither! And your accent is sliding from Roughs street into southern Elendel street gang! Gah! You're gettin' it *all wrong!*"

"I love that you're more worried about me imitating you poorly than you are about me tryin' to kill you," she said, shoving her face up next to his. She stabbed him in the chest—he hadn't even seen her drop the dueling cane—with a glass knife. "It's so *you*, Wayne!"

"You don't know me," Wayne growled, managing to kick her leg and make her slip a little. She loosened her grip, which let him rip free and move around her, though her knife sliced him across the chest.

Rusts. He could heal that with the health in his bracer—which these days he wore embedded into the flesh of his thigh. But he was worried about how much she was making him use. That was probably the point.

"Oh, Wayne," she said, turning toward him. "I *do* know you. I've studied you for years! Freewheeling Wayne! Always ready with a joke. Snatchin' what he sees, chasin' the girls. Livin' his life without consequences. Just here for the fun and the booze!"

"Yeah?" he muttered. "And the pain?"

"Eh," she said with a shrug. "You get used to gettin' exploded, now don'tcha."

"Not that pain," he whispered.

They met again, but she was just plain better at the fightin' part than he was. Oh, Wayne was fine with the canes. But he lived his life. And in doin' so, he'd let the trainin' slack off—having a little gum chew out behind the building instead of working into the evening. With Marasi, he hadn't spent quite so much time getting his head knocked in.

But this creature, well, she'd been trainin' something hard. Focused entirely on this day, this meeting, this *fight*. He wasn't brawlin' with some bully off the street, or even some talented Set Metalborn. He was facin' an assassin what had been designed *specifically* to kill him.

She was stronger than he was. Faster than he was. Younger than he was. Better with the canes. He was better with his powers. He was certain of that. But in these close confines, that didn't really matter. And as he traded blows with her, taking hits and forcing himself to heal, he . . . Well, he took more punishment than he gave. Rusts . . . was this what Wax felt like, now he was gettin' on in years?

He rolled to the side, through the muck on the bottom of the giant tube they was in. That put him right to the other edge of the speed bubble, and he slipped halfway out of it—though fortunately, so long as you were touching it at all it included you in its powers.

A motion from where Wax was fightin' made Wayne duck. Wax himself went flying past again, and he soared completely out of the speed bubble. Damn. That was what they'd been planning to do to the other guy.

Wax froze instantly, hanging in the air with a grimace on his face, gun trailing from his fingers and hovering in front of him, mistcoat tassels sweeping around him.

Uh-oh, Wayne thought.

A spray of coins hit Wayne a second later.

"Aw, Dumad," not-Wayne said, turning. "I was havin' fun. *I'm* supposed to be the one who takes him."

"You're inefficient, Getruda," Dumad said. "You play with him. You simply need to hit him repeatedly until his health runs out." He punctuated this by giving Wayne another faceful of coins, knocking him to the ground.

Rusts. This was bad. Wayne healed that, but it was slow—his healing was starting to run dangerously low. And he had to ration it as a result.

"Oi," he muttered, "Death. Betcha fifty clips I survive this." It was a good time for a bet. Because in such a situation, Wayne had to try something truly desperate.

The truth.

He stumbled to his feet, putting his back to the rounded wall of the tunnel. "You think you know me?" Wayne whispered. "You think you know what I've been through?"

Dumad looked at him, then *Pushed*. And rusts, the guy was so strong he could affect the metal *inside* Wayne's body. That was a crazy thing to experience—Wayne was shoved backward from the coins embedded within him. Rust and Ruin . . . that was a power that the Ascendant Warrior was said to have had.

These guys really *were* cheating. No wonder Wax had lost his fight. No wonder Wayne had essentially lost his—the dueling portion at least. But if he could keep their attention . . .

He grunted at the Push. Then he stepped forward anyway, feeling the coins tear and rip inside him. He took another step, leaning forward into the Push.

Not-him hesitated, lowering her canes. He met her eyes.

Then he grinned.

"You can't hurt me," he whispered, changing his accent. "Ain't nothin' that can hurt me more than life already has. You can't kill me. I'm already dead. I been dead for years, sister."

He took another step forward. Most people, they didn't notice accent changes like that. Little tweaks to the tone of your words. But people judged you on them anyway. Their brains associated accents with meaning.

Dumad frowned, seeming disturbed, and raised his hand and Pushed harder. Wayne slid in the mud, the coins ripping farther through him. Then he took another step forward and changed his accent further. Put on his most wide-eyed, excited face. Twisting his voice to be something unnatural. Something terrifying. Something out of a nightmare. Matching this not-Wax's accent, but terrible.

Like the accent he'd hear from his parents and family. Only broken. Wayne didn't need a hat for this one.

"It's easy to do what you do, since you don't care," Wayne growled to the two, making his eyes go even wider. "So long as you can pretend. But real pain, that comes when you realize what you are. What you done. Waking up each morning, knowin' you're worthless. *That's* pain. Anything else? Anything *you* could do to me? Well, that's just a little bit o' fun."

"You're . . ." Dumad trailed off as Wayne's smile widened.

"Thank you," Wayne said, "for tossin' Wax outta here. That way I got a few moments to have you two all to myself."

The coins finally ripped through Wayne's back, letting him lurch forward in a sudden rush. And as he did, he threw himself to the ground. Because amid his display—getting them to focus only on him—he'd dropped the speed bubble. And they hadn't noticed.

From the side, Wax put a hazekiller round straight in not-Wayne's face. Its secondary explosion went off a second later, blowing off half her skull. A second shot from Wax took Dumad in the chest as he was turning, then exploded out his back.

Incredibly, the Coinshot didn't fall. Pewter. Did the fellow have *pewter* to burn and push through wounds? How many spikes did this fellow have, and why hadn't they let Harmony take control of him?

Unfortunately, the man stayed on his feet and ducked the next bullets. He shoved a grate off the ceiling, opening it up to the sunlight, then seized the bloodied not-Wayne and Pushed on a coin.

The two launched up and out. One with a hole in his chest that didn't seem to hurt as much as it should have, the other with half her head gone. She might be dead, though Wayne couldn't be certain. Head shots were tricky. They could end you, but it all depended on the damage done.

Wax maybe should have put another few shots in them as they fled, but the man looked pretty ragged from the fight. Breathing deeply, he slumped back against the wall of the tunnel. They'd come close to losing this fight. Real close.

Wayne stumbled to his feet, aching all over, and used his healing to seal those coin wounds. But they remained sore. He was forced to stop healing to save the last bit of juice in his metalmind. Rusts.

Wayne turned and lurched over to Wax, his clothes a bloody, muddy mess. Wax's, impossibly, were pretty nice—barely marked by the gunk on the floor.

"Hey!" Wayne said. "How the hell aren't you covered in mud? I saw you roll through it."

"I Pushed off a bullet when I did," he said. He put a hand to his shoulder and groaned softly. "Nice job, with the distraction." He met Wayne's eyes. "Did you mean any of that?"

"Nah, of course not," Wayne said, looking away. Ruin, he felt exhausted. And creaky. Like a floor what had been walked on so much, all the boards wobbled.

"Wayne . . ."

"Not the time, mate." He settled down on the floor. "Rusts, I feel old. I'm not supposed to feel old. I'm the spry one!"

Wax settled down next to him on a dry part of the concrete. "You're thirty-nine, Wayne. It catches up to you."

"You infected me, you did," Wayne grumbled. "I never felt old when I was workin' with Marasi!"

"I infected you," Wax said, "with *being old*?"

"Damn right."

"That's ludicrous even for you."

"No it ain't. You done started to think yourself old, and it drilled into my head too." Wayne tapped at his skull. "Ideas is infectious, Wax. More than diseases."

They caught their breath for a few more moments. Unfortunately, they couldn't linger.

"They know for sure we found this tunnel," Wayne said. "If there's some kind of lab at the end of it, they'll be clearing it out as we speak."

Wax nodded and heaved himself back to his feet. He reached out a hand to help Wayne up.

"We need to talk," Wax said. "About you. The way you've been feeling lately."

"Sure. Okay. I like talkin'. But later."

Later was *always* better.

Together, they pressed forward. "I got the woman pretty good," Wax said. "Do you think that killed her?"

"Depends. How's your luck been lately?"

"Awful," Wax admitted. "But at least we know we're on the right trail. Otherwise they wouldn't have tried so hard to stop us."

"Yeah, sure," Wayne said. "I'm glad we're done with the canyon, but the hardest part is yet to come. The mesa, which is gonna gobble you up. Remember to choke it from the inside."

"I'll do my best."

50

M arasi drew up a quick plan—which was the only kind they could afford. Moonlight and TwinSoul stayed near the window, ready to break in. Marasi worked her way up to the front of the building to place a grenade by the door. The slowness bubble would work through the wall, trapping the two guards who stood inside. As she charged her weapon, however, Moonlight ducked around the side of the rectangular structure and scuttled up to Marasi.

"Guards just moved," she hissed. "They're getting gas masks from a bin near the scientists."

Rusts. She couldn't let them release the gas.

"We go in now," Marasi hissed. "Back me up if the grenade fails."

Moonlight nodded, and Marasi kicked in the door and hurled her grenade toward the group of people in the left corner, near the window where she and the others had been spying.

Sorry, TwinSoul, she thought, knowing the grenade would catch him too. Her aim was solid, and the grenade box bounced off one lab table, then fell to the floor near the group of guards and scientists.

The two guards immediately leaped away, one sliding over the table, the other one dashing for the front of the room. One of the scientists was also at the perimeter and—unfortunately—jumped away in surprise.

When the grenade activated, it caught only two of the scientists in gas masks. Luckily, that included the one holding a tin with warning labels on it, presumably the poison tablets.

Marasi's grenade would keep them frozen. But now she had to deal with the others *without* raising an alarm. The free scientist was cringing at the side of the room, so Marasi dashed forward and slammed her rifle's butt into the arm of one guard, who had been pulling out a pistol. Moonlight moved behind her—hopefully dealing with the other guard, because the man Marasi had attacked decided to slam into her, shoving her back against a table full of beakers.

She grunted as he rammed her own rifle up almost to her neck. Glassware shattered on the floor around her, and a part of her panicked. The part of her that still, even after all these years, worried she wasn't good enough and didn't belong.

That part of her was a lot quieter than it had been. Because she *did* belong. This was *her* operation. And though this man was stronger than she was, he was only a common brute. Training beat strength.

She shifted, then let go of the rifle and stepped out with her left leg, shifting the man's weight—and force. As he stumbled, she wrenched out from his grip, rotated around behind him, then slammed his face down into the counter.

She recovered her rifle, sparing a glance for Moonlight, who was struggling. She'd disarmed her guard, but he'd in turn pressed her against the wall. As Marasi took that in, the wall distorted and a door popped into existence behind Moonlight.

Marasi barely caught sight of the stamp in Moonlight's hand as the door opened, and the woman fell backward through it—surprising the guard, who cried out as she pulled him down with her. Moonlight elbowed him in the face to cut off his cry, so Marasi finished off her guard with a rifle butt to the face, then turned to deal with the scientist, who was . . .

Destroying evidence? Marasi cursed and scrambled over to the woman and pulled her away from the trash can where she'd started a fire. Marasi kicked the trash can over, scattering charred notebooks and papers out of it.

"Marasi!" Moonlight cried.

Rusts. The scientist had found a large knife and joined Moonlight's fight. As Moonlight struggled to deal with the guard—who was trying to grapple her—the scientist raised the knife.

Making a quick judgment, Marasi swung up her rifle and snapped off a shot, killing the scientist with a well-placed bullet. The sound echoed in the tunnels like a screamed condemnation. Someone would hear that for certain.

Moonlight finished off her guard with her own knife, then was cut off from view as the door she'd made vanished. Marasi sat on the floor and groaned softly, the shimmering barrier of her slowness bubble just a foot away. She'd taken the risk to save people. She'd known what she was getting into. But now their operation was jeopardized.

So don't let it be wasted, she thought, hauling herself to her feet. As her slowness bubble came down, she pointed her rifle right at the two scientists.

"Make one move to open that tin," she said, "and I will kill you. I'm having a particularly bad day, so I wouldn't test that threat."

The scientist with the tin of poison gas tablets carefully set it down, then both raised their hands and backed away. Moonlight entered a moment later and began binding them. TwinSoul stumbled in behind her, holding to the doorframe for stability.

"I appear to have run afoul of your powers," he said to Marasi.

"Sorry about that," she said.

"I note two disabled guards," he said. "And one dead scientist. So the operation went well?"

"Marasi had to shoot one," Moonlight said, pulling one of the scientists' bonds tight, "to save me. I ruined it."

"No," Marasi said. "It was my fault for not helping fast enough."

"It is done," TwinSoul said. "We should see to the captives and secure an exit. What are those burned pages?"

"They destroyed evidence," Marasi said. "I assume about how they were accomplishing the Hemalurgy. I wasn't able to save it, so . . ."

Moonlight sniffed. "Looks like the cover of a book there. You saved that much."

"But none of the writings," Marasi said.

"I can rewind that later," Moonlight said, "with a stamp." She grabbed the burned remnants and shoved them into her sack. "TwinSoul is right. We should probably begin our extraction—that gunshot will bring people running."

"Extraction?" Marasi said. "Entrone said he was going to help an invading force attack. Moonlight, can enemy troops really reach us from . . . another world?"

"They're probably coming through Shadesmar," Moonlight said. "A dimension overlapping ours. It's how TwinSoul and I got here."

"Autonomy has access to . . . some very specialized troops," TwinSoul said. "Hard to control. Dangerous to unleash. I know their destructive power personally. While I'm more frightened of that bomb, an invasion by Autonomy's forces could also be catastrophic. Fortunately, the local perpendicularity—the portal to reach this world—is far to the south and carefully controlled."

"There's no other way?" Marasi asked.

The two shared a look.

"There are planets," Moonlight said, "where Autonomy has created such portals unexpectedly, and against all understood mechanics. I wouldn't be surprised if she's done that here, or is soon going to. Providing a means for her armies to attack."

So if Wax succeeded in stopping the bomb, there would be an invasion instead. Marasi took a deep breath. Even more reason they couldn't run—not until they knew what was happening with that army. For now though, she unlocked and yanked open the cell door, spilling light across the ragged prisoners. They pulled back from the light like mistwraiths in the night.

"I'm Marasi Colms," she said, fishing her credentials from her pocket. "Elendel Constabulary."

"Oh, thank the Survivor!" a man said, stumbling forward and taking her hand. His suit had once been nice, and he had a few tufts of hair on an otherwise bald head. Did she . . . recognize him?

"You're in Bilming politics," she said. "You served as the local advisor to the Senate."

"Y-yes," he stuttered. "Pielle Fromed. I was head of the opposition party for the Bilming Council. I still am . . . I think . . ."

Most of the others looked like ordinary citizens, but there was a Terriswoman in the rear with kinky hair. That was . . . yes, she was a major newspaper owner, wasn't she? Editor of the *Seasons*? Marasi had been interviewed by her staff the other year . . . It was a newspaper that had been sympathetic to Elendel interests.

Preservation . . . Entrone hadn't merely been experimenting on his citizens, he'd been experimenting on his political opposition. It was shockingly brazen. How had he made these people vanish without anyone getting wind of it?

The editor of the *Seasons* accepted Marasi's help as Moonlight ushered the captives into the main room. "Listen," the woman said. "I think they have an army of some sort! I've . . . I've been taking notes . . ."

She almost fainted as Marasi helped her stand. But she pressed a notebook into Marasi's hands. "There isn't much. But you *must* believe me."

"I do," Marasi said. "We're here to stop them."

"Locate a place they call the Community," she said. "I think it's where their barracks are."

"We'll stop them," Marasi promised, leading her to the others. "We have to get these people out of here," Marasi then said to TwinSoul. "Immediately."

Together, the three of them ushered the poor captives along. They were slow, they were tired, and they were underfed. It took a dangerously long time to get them all into the tunnel. And as Marasi was preparing to lead them back toward the elevators, she heard noises from that direction.

With a sinking feeling, she saw a good two dozen guards—soldiers, really; probably the ones who had been standing watch in the building above—come piling around the turn in the tunnel.

This had just gone from quiet infiltration to full-on war.

51

The Set soldiers, spotting Marasi's group, immediately organized in the tunnel, using the natural curve as cover. Fortunately, this bought Marasi and her team a few precious moments—the enemy didn't know what they were facing, and so took up a defensive posture.

Marasi ushered the former captives back toward the room, though the flimsy drywall would offer very little protection against gunfire.

TwinSoul, however, knelt and put both hands on the ground. "Moonlight," he said, "I'll need extra fuel. Water will not be enough for this."

She swiftly dug out one of the glowing jars and tossed it to him. A line of crystal grew from him and around the jar, opening the top. His crystals began to grow faster—in moments he'd created a chest-high wall of roseite in front of them.

Gunfire rang out from the other end of the tunnel, making the former captives cry out as they crowded back into the room. Rifle in hand, Marasi threw herself against TwinSoul's improvised fortification next to Moonlight. She risked a glance over the roseite mound—he'd made this one opaque, perhaps to give the enemy less information.

She ducked back down as a bullet blasted a few chips off the front of the fortification. TwinSoul clearly had to concentrate to keep this large a barrier up. He had settled down with his legs crossed and his hands in fists, knuckles pressed together in front of him, his head bowed. The crystal-stone had grown up over his arms in an odd way. Marasi turned to Moonlight.

"Can you make a door in the ground?" Marasi said. "There might be tunnels beneath us."

Moonlight shook her head. "Even if there were, the thickness of the stone would be far too great for my stamp."

"I believe, my lady Marasi," TwinSoul said, "that you should allow me to take the people we've freed and hasten them to the exit. It seems these soldiers were guarding the shipping bay above. So if I can push through them, I can get the civilians to safety."

"That would be good," Moonlight said. "Marasi and I can escape farther into the tunnel complex—and the enemy might be so focused on you and your escape that they don't notice us."

"I can't allow that," Marasi said as bullets flew overhead. "TwinSoul, there are at least two dozen soldiers over there. You can't manage them on your own. No offense, but you can barely walk down a corridor without support."

"No offense taken," he said, his voice muffled as the roseite continued to grow up—and for some reason *around* him. "But in return . . . No offense, my lady, but you might perhaps be underestimating Silajana."

The roseite completely encased him, forming a transparent boulder around him. His head bowed, with formal sash in place, he was still fully visible in his cross-legged posture through the rose-colored stone. Marasi frowned as it continued to expand rapidly. The size and speed of this creation seemed to need the help of the glowing substance from the jar, which was being drained as the roseite grew.

Bulges formed at the sides of the boulder, like . . . smaller boulders? Only longer. Then two more formed on the bottom rear of the boulder. Marasi cocked her head, her back to the fortification mound, rifle across her knees. Actually, with the smaller boulder forming on the top, it had almost taken on the shape of . . . of a . . .

Thick stone fingers formed on the ends of the two protrusions at the sides, then massive roseite arms spread out, stone grinding against the stone ground as the lower parts formed knees and feet. TwinSoul at the center, the thing heaved itself up—a twelve-foot-tall stone behemoth. The crystal didn't bend, but had formed joints, like armor.

A man made of rock, like some mythological creature, with a head on the top, broad shoulders, and trunklike legs. TwinSoul sat at its heart, legs crossed, fists pressed together in front of him. But his head rose and his eyes snapped open, glowing softly, as his creation ripped free of the lines of roseite connecting it to the ground.

The fortification started to disintegrate right away, but the soldiers' attention was totally focused on the stone monstrosity that advanced, its head scraping the top of the tunnel. Their gunfire intensified, bullets hitting with a pop and spray of stone. TwinSoul barely seemed to mind. He stepped in front of Marasi and moved his construct's hands in front of him, growing something out of them.

"Behold!" he said, his voice somehow booming through the tunnel. "By the grace of Silajana, Suna, Vishwadhar, and the Twelve Primal Aethers, I am Sanvith Prasanva Maahik va Sila, Grand Aetherbound of the twelve kingdoms, Raj of the Coriander Court. And these people are under *my* protection."

To punctuate his words, a colossal mace finished forming from roseite in his stone fingers—with a huge bulb at one end, like that of a tulip. He let it *thump* to the rock beneath him, shaking the ground.

Some soldiers continued to fire. Others up and ran. Chips blasted off the construct, but the holes filled in immediately. The jar of pure Investiture—still half full—had been overgrown by the roseite and was near the rear of the large stone figure, its glow illuminating TwinSoul from behind.

"Silajana demands that I warn you," he announced, "you have been given this rebirth to bless, encourage, and uplift those around you. By your actions here, you prove this gift wasted. If you are destroyed today by resisting my defense of these innocents, you reject your great blessing—and may not be given rebirth again for many, many centuries. Lay down your weapons and let us pass, or suffer my wrath."

He certainly had a way with words. Moonlight grabbed Marasi by the shoulder, gesturing for them to retreat past the building with the hiding civilians. For the moment however, Marasi remained rooted, amazed by the sight of TwinSoul's construct raising the mace.

"It appears," he announced, "that my offer has been rejected. In turn, your offer of conflict is accepted. Prepare yourselves!" With that, he charged down the corridor, each footstep making the ground tremble.

Marasi finally allowed Moonlight to pull her back. In the flimsy structure—over the cacophony of gunfire, screams, and the impact of stone on stone—they told the captives to arm themselves, then follow TwinSoul to the way out.

Then Marasi and Moonlight exited and hurried down the main corridor, finding a darkened side passage to slip through. Hopefully, this would let them avoid any reinforcements that might come up the main passage.

"Will he be able to get them out, do you think?" Marasi whispered as—using light from one of the two remaining jars—they made their way through the tunnel complex. Marasi spotted a sign pointing toward THE COMMUNITY.

"TwinSoul is the best chance they have," Moonlight replied. "I think he can manage it. He has the pure Investiture—and as long as that holds, he'll be nigh invincible. He can shrink and grow his juggernaut as he needs, to get through smaller corridors. If they try to cut the electricity, he can even push the elevator all the way to the top—or create a new one from roseite."

More gunfire sounded from behind. Marasi hoped it was the civilians arming themselves and firing to protect their retreat. She was certain she heard more footfalls and shouts coming from the main tunnel.

Moonlight looked back and smiled. "Don't worry," she said. "He'll be fine. And this is exactly what we need. Prasanva is an absolute *artist* at drawing attention when he sets his mind to it."

"You willing to keep going forward?" Marasi asked.

"If there really is a perpendicularity here," she said, "then . . . yes. As much as I want to get out with this information, protecting the planet must come first." She hesitated. "I'm new to this large-scale sort of thinking. Spent a long time looking out for myself and my own goals. Sorry if I come off as terse or too quick to want to retreat."

Marasi nodded, noting some light up ahead. She slipped forward quietly, and Moonlight covered up the jars in her rucksack. Together they approached another tunnel, lit with mining lights. The natural tunnel vanished to the right, but to the left the stone had a different cast to it. Marasi pointed at the jagged sections of rock on the ceiling and walls.

"They blasted here," she whispered. "This is a section they opened up and expanded."

Moonlight pointed to another sign. The Community, whatever it was, could be found this way. Marasi held out hope that Gave and the Set weren't *quite* so zealous as to let Autonomy's armies in. He'd sounded hesitant, at least. Smarmy as the man was, even he realized this was extreme. But he also had seemed worn down. As if he felt he couldn't fight or resist.

As they snuck farther along the blasted-out tunnel, Marasi was pulled out of her thoughts. Were those sounds coming from the tunnel behind them? Something following them?

Moonlight seemed to hear the sounds too, because she turned and glanced that direction. They shared a look, then hurried forward, hoping to stay ahead of whatever it was.

52

As Wax and Wayne neared the end of the tunnel, Wax noticed his friend sniffling and trailing behind. In the light streaming through the holes in a passing manhole cover, Wax saw that Wayne had sudden bags under his eyes.

"This might not be the best time to store up health," Wax whispered softly.

"I'm runnin' low," Wayne mumbled. "I feel like I'm gonna need every bit I can store. That, or I'll die one of these times somebody shoots me. That's right terrifying, it is. Don't know how you all deal with it." He paused. "If we get inna fight, I'll stop. Just need to squeeze a little extra in during breathers, you know."

Wax didn't say anything. This was more a matter of comfort to Wayne than anything practical. Wayne wouldn't be able to store up much in the time they had. It took a Feruchemist months storing health to get a full metalmind.

The tire tracks stopped at the end of the tunnel, where the giant concrete tube dumped out over the ocean. Wax was used to the relatively sheltered and calm waters of the Elendel docks—where the waves were so placid, you could be on a large lake. Here on the promontory that Bilming occupied, the waters chopped and churned, crashing against the docks. No wonder the Bilming navy was made up of such hulking metal monstrosities. He could see them in a row in the near distance, six terrible petrol-powered warships, each larger than the one before.

It was strange to think that, even combined, they posed an insignificant threat compared to the bomb Wax was hunting. All that work to create weapons of war, invalidated by a single discovery.

He gestured to a final hatch and ladder, which must lead to the lab. As soon as he and Wayne emerged onto a street by the docks, a door slammed nearby. Wax spun, scanning the warehouses.

"There," Wayne said, pointing. "Third one down. Someone was watchin' out the window too."

The two glanced at each other, then took cover as gunfire exploded from the window. Conventional bullets and guns, his steelsight told him.

No aluminum weapons, Wax thought. *They sent those Allomancers to try to deal with us, but didn't have time to otherwise prepare. We might finally be ahead of them.*

He increased his weight with his metalmind, then Pushed the next round of gunfire away—flinging the bullets back through the wooden walls and glass windows. Curses followed, giving him and Wayne a chance to scramble closer. Wayne nodded, so Wax increased his weight and hit the entire building with a Steelpush, anchoring himself from behind.

The wall shook, and a section was ripped free by its nails and a window housing. Wayne leaped in through the hole and dropped a few gunmen inside. Wax followed with Vindication raised, three precise shots bringing down the gunmen Wayne couldn't reach. As they fought, a truck revved its engine and barreled out on the other side of the warehouse, tires screeching. Wax caught sight of two others ahead of it. A small convoy escaping into the evening.

A quick survey of the large room told him an entire story. Laboratory desks and machinery, stripped bare in a frenzy. Debris on the floor. Torn corners of paper still stapled to the wall where charts or schematics had been hastily ripped down. Dangling chains indicated that something had been constructed here, built in the center of those desks.

They hadn't expected Wax to dare raid the Silver House or find the tunnel. He was only one step behind now.

Wax launched himself after the truck, decreasing his weight and flying through the large garage doors to track the truck as it screeched around another corner, nearly toppling in its haste.

Wayne would take care of the stragglers. Wax *needed* to know what was in those trucks.

He roared into the air in a rush, gaining height, and spotted the last of the three trucks heading back into the heart of the city. He'd spent the whole day running to catch up, to tease together plots that had been in motion for years. He was tired of half answers, of feeling like he was a hundred steps behind his sister.

Now he had solutions in sight. Those trucks held real answers, perhaps even the bomb itself. He'd be damned to an eternal pit of ash before he let them get away.

He Pushed off a manhole cover, gaining more height. From there, streetlamps—which were just starting to come on as the sun neared the horizon—became his anchors, like stepping stones across a lake. He Pushed on a pair at a time for lift and momentum, then began using buildings as enormous anchors. Then a moving car, to gain even more speed, borrowing its momentum.

Air became a whistle, then a roar around him—his mistcoat tassels whipping and snapping. His furious pace let him gain on the three trucks, even as they moved at speed on the highway. He had almost reached the last one in line when a slot opened in the back door and the barrels of several automatic rifles—aluminum—peeked out.

They'd saved the good weapons for themselves as they fled. A hail of aluminum bullets followed. Wax moved by instinct. His pursuit so far had been too direct, making him an easy target.

He dodged to the side as the bullets cracked in the air. He lurched away from the highway over cars full of startled civilians, then between two buildings to give him cover. There he ground to a stop, boots on asphalt, tassels falling still around him.

This isn't right, he thought. His path following the trucks had been obvious, but their path along the highway was more so. Could they be playing him yet again? He launched himself off a bullet, then gained speed by Pushing against the buildings to the sides, rattling windows—cracking a few as he warped their metal housings.

In Elendel, he had to hold himself back. Moderate his actions to minimize property damage. But Harmony had set Wax on this path, and you didn't bring Dawnshot out of retirement to play nice. The lives of millions were at stake.

He'd break a few windows to stop it. Hell, he'd break a few necks. He barreled up over cars, ignoring the cries of startled pedestrians as he moved parallel to the highway—trying to gain enough speed to catch up to the enemy truck, but keeping buildings between him and it. At the right moment he ducked back out, shattering windows, and darted across the highway—finding the third truck exactly where he'd hoped it would be.

It was in a pack of civilian vehicles, so Wax dodged behind cover again and followed, parallel, for another minute. He soared down that side street, feeling . . . alive. Propelled by steel, a bullet in flight. Perhaps he'd been without this for too long, and so had forgotten the rush, but he felt more in control than he ever had before.

Have to stop that truck slowly, he thought. *In case the bomb is inside.* He assumed the device couldn't be detonated simply by being jostled—his experiment the other day had shown that the real explosion required specific mechanical intervention. But he had to be careful regardless.

At the next intersection, he glanced right and saw what he'd hoped to see: the truck, in its haste to stay ahead of him, had pulled away from the pack of civilian vehicles into a more open stretch of the highway.

Wax darted in, over the edge of the highway, and increased his weight tenfold. He slowed in the air as a result, and hit the side of the passing truck with a Steelpush, *grinding* it into the highway's sidewall. It jostled more than he would have liked, but it did slow.

Wax changed trajectory, staying alongside the truck, forcing it into the sidewall until its tires burst and it stopped. He hit the ground near the broken rear door, sighting three unsteady gunmen within. He took them out, then drilled a bullet right through the front wall of the truck, hitting the driver in the back of the head. But other than those people, the truck was empty.

It *was* a decoy.

Damn it!

He launched back into the air, Pushing off the truck, bending and warping the crumpled roof as he sought height. Such a Push could only take him up so far—the farther you went from your anchor, the less force you could Push upon it.

He reached the zenith of what his anchor could provide and spun, scanning the city below, searching for . . .

There. The second truck was racing along the highway ahead. He almost darted straight for it. But . . .

Three trucks. At least one decoy. He spotted another far ahead, on the straightaway. This *was* too easy. They were so visible on a highway like this; they could keep his attention, draw him away from . . .

He hovered there, still Pushing, holding himself upright—though wind began to blow him to the side, upsetting his anchor. As he began to lose altitude . . .

. . . he spotted it. A fourth truck with the same markings, winding its way through the side streets perpendicular to the highway. It was heading inward, toward the center of the city. He barely glimpsed it as it moved behind some buildings.

That was the one he needed to catch. He left the others, hoping his instincts were right, and dropped into the city. He slowed with a Push on the top of a parked automobile, cracking the windshield with his weight, then warped the hood as he landed. He launched forward through the center of a park, scattering a flock of ravens, then bounded up the side of a building—barely reaching the top as his Push gave out.

There was an invigorating thrill to the motion. The city was so full of metal, so packed with obstacles. In a chase, each could be an advantage. Wax could soar over buildings, get height, track the vehicle—and gain on it, as the truck had to keep to the roads and deal with traffic.

Wax dropped over the side of a building, then propelled himself between two others with the force of a swimmer pushing off the wall at the start of a lap. He swept around corners and almost seemed to be able to ride the cries of the people below, like a bird riding thermals in the desert.

Chases in the Roughs had their own charm. But nothing there could truly compete with the thrill of landing *inside* a building via the balcony, charging through, and emerging on the other side to find his quarry right below. A balcony railing was a springboard, and nearby structures let him fine-tune his descent.

Here, he could fly in a way he'd never been able to in that land of dust and stone. He could acknowledge that—no, *embrace* it—now that he had let go of his past.

The people in the truck ahead pulled open another slot on the back door. Wax sighted with Vindication, but not toward the window. Toward the door itself.

He plugged it with a hazekiller round, one with a secondary explosion designed to rip apart Hemalurgist bodies. It blasted the door to shrapnel and split open the rear of the truck. As the gunmen stumbled away, Wax got a view inside. No bomb, but a ton of boxes, ledgers, and documents.

That would have to do. He let the truck pull ahead as the gunmen started laying down fire. Wax increased his weight and shoved on a grate below him in the street—bending and twisting it out of the way as he dropped through and entered the storm drain tunnels again.

He twisted in the air, delivered two bullets into the tunnel wall behind him, then Pushed off those—and the remnants of the grate that had plunged into the mud—to send himself screaming through the tunnel right under the street.

Wax came out a second later, blasting a manhole cover off into the air. He landed, one foot on either side of the open manhole, and increased his weight many hundreds of times—completely draining his metalmind. Then he Pushed.

His feet skidded a few inches on the concrete.

The truck crumpled as if it had hit a solid wall, the front mashing like tinfoil, doing unfortunate things to the driver. The back end of the truck lurched up into the air, then slammed down, trailing loose-leaf pages. One of the wheels rolled completely free, straight through the front window of a nearby building. A liquor store, Wax noticed with a wince. Wayne would *not* appreciate that.

The street fell quiet as other cars stopped, their drivers cowering in their seats or—more commonly—staring slack-jawed. Wax took a few deep breaths, his pulse racing, his body electric. His mind . . .

Focused on the job. He released another breath, and was surprised by how calm he felt. A part of him . . . a part of him had worried about returning to the field again. Worried that by experiencing these kinds of thrills, he'd view his normal life as mundane, lacking.

It didn't happen. He could go on a chase like that through the city anytime he wanted in Elendel, as long as he wasn't *quite* so flagrant about the property damage. He could even bring Max along, and have someone to share in the joy. He didn't need this, not as he once had.

What a wondrous thing that was to confirm. He took a deep breath, then rounded the truck.

53

Marasi and Moonlight were being hunted.

Something was back there, something that seemed not quite human. It made a sound like nails or claws on stone, accompanied by unnatural growls. Marasi hurried through the blasted-out tunnel, Moonlight at her side, trying to balance their speed. If they moved too quickly, they might run straight into a patrol. But if they slowed too much, then whatever was back there would catch up to them.

So they moved in fits, hurrying a distance they could see by the light of mining lamps, then pausing to scout out their next rush forward. This part of the tunnel complex was far more built up than the one they'd come from, with many more turns. But they were able to follow the signs, heading ever closer to the Community. They passed more drywall rooms, some clearly occupied, and they had to find improvised cover several times as groups of people hurried past.

These weren't soldiers though. Mostly workers or scientists. Judging by their whispered conversations, Entrone had ordered everyone to their quarters. There was a sense of frantic worry to the people—but also a single-minded anxiety. That helped, as they weren't paying much attention to their surroundings.

As Marasi and Moonlight hid from one of these groups beside some boxes, Marasi worried the thing chasing them would catch up. Yet it was creeping along, not rushing. Perhaps . . . perhaps it was hiding too?

Moonlight eventually whispered for Marasi to wait, then ducked into a room that—through the cracked door—seemed unoccupied. She emerged moments later with two lab coats, and they started moving through the corridor as though they belonged there. The disguises were flimsy, but no one gave them a second glance, despite Marasi's rifle.

Soon, a voice echoed through the tunnel. "Stay calm. Don't worry. I am in the Community making preparations for our new arrivals. I want all of you to settle in and wait. This is what we've planned for; we are ready."

It was Gave Entrone. His voice came from some speakers that lined the hallway—a technology that was becoming more common since its invention a few years back.

Hearing his voice finally undermined Marasi's hope that Gave would resist the invasion. This complex, the supplies . . . everything about it indicated the truth. This was a bunker, the launching point of an invasion—and a place for Entrone's favorites to be protected from the coming annihilation.

A haunting worry whispered this was only part of it. Marasi had to stop Entrone, but that wouldn't protect Elendel from the bomb Telsin had trained on it. For that, she had to trust that Wax and Wayne were fulfilling their half of the mission. Her duty was to deal with this oncoming army. The men of gold and red.

The tunnel eventually expanded to a large cavern. But curiously, the far wall was straight wood, from floor to ceiling. And it felt like that wall bisected the chamber—which, judging by the slope of the blasted-out ceiling, was extremely large. The wooden wall had several darkened rooms built up against it. Indeed, the entire chamber was silent and mostly dark, lit only by a few emergency lights.

Marasi and Moonlight stopped at the mouth of the cavern. Was this the Community? Why split the cavern like that? Whatever the reason, the order to quarters had been obeyed, and apparently any soldiers in the area had gone to deal with TwinSoul. That let Marasi and Moonlight enter the cavern alone.

Soon after, those sounds came from behind again. Taking Moonlight by the shoulder, Marasi pulled them between two buildings beside the large wall. From this scant shelter, she watched as something entered the mouth of the cavern. It stood on four elongated legs and had an unnervingly long neck, with a head that wasn't entirely canine. It had features that, even shadowed as they were, evoked an image that was . . . too human. A dog's nose, or something approximating it, but human eyes set forward on its skull.

It had no clothing, but also no fur. Two spikeheads jutted from its shoulders. She'd heard of something like this before—Wax had encountered something similar in the tunnels beneath Elendel. Now, after studying the book Death had given her, she recognized what it was. A Hemalurgic monstrosity.

One use of the art was to create Metalborn. But the Lord Ruler had also used Hemalurgy to create twisted versions of human beings. The kandra had arisen from that work, as had the koloss. Creating those had required precision use of spikes—the knowledge of a god. If you tried to approximate such designs, you were likely to kill your subject. Or stumble into some kind of half-creation. A twisted mutation, leaving a being's soul mangled by the spikes.

The Set, it seemed, had found a permutation that was viable but grotesque. The thing sniffed the air, then prowled carefully into the cavern. It knew they were there. It paused where Marasi and Moonlight had stopped to inspect their surroundings—a spot that was barely thirty yards from their current hiding place. The abomination made a hooting sound that echoed in the cavern, and other voices—dozens of them—replied.

Moonlight gripped Marasi's shoulder, then pointed. She'd made a door in the side of the structure they'd been hiding by, and they slipped into a dim room built up against the wooden wall bisecting the chamber. Two windows looked through it.

Marasi didn't have a good view through them, not from her corner next to Moonlight. The door vanished, and a few moments later scratches sounded at the wall they'd passed through. Silence followed, then a thumping at the main door. It held, for now.

Marasi unslung her rifle, glanced at Moonlight, then nodded toward the windows. Perhaps they could escape through those? She stepped over to look through, and found . . . a town?

Neat rows of houses lined streets within a vast chamber, bigger on that side than this one. It was lit from above with floodlights. Someone had painted imitation flowers and grass on the floor in wide swaths, and others had erected sculptures meant to imitate foliage. People in everyday clothing—skirts, trousers, day dresses—walked the "streets," though there were no horses or automobiles she could see.

"What in Preservation's name?" Marasi whispered. "I suppose . . . this is the Community they built for themselves to escape the destruction above?"

She frowned. A short time ago, she might have theorized it was designed to withstand the second ashfall, but she was now mostly certain that was a hoax. The bomb and the invading army were the true threats.

Behind them, the thing stopped scratching at the door. She wasn't certain that was a good sign; it might have gone to get help.

"There's something off about this entire place," Moonlight said. She rapped on the window. "I think this is one-way glass. See the tinting? And those people in the next chamber? They don't appear to have heard the order to quarters or the fighting. They're too calm."

"We could still escape in there."

"Those twisted things will follow us," Moonlight said. "The strain the Set has developed can track like a hound, but think almost like a person."

"Can we fight them?" Marasi said, checking her ammo.

"I'm not . . . natively a soldier," Moonlight said. "I can defend myself if I have to, but . . ." She seemed concerned as she glanced toward the door.

Shouts came from outside. Troops arriving.

"You have another stamp," Marasi said. "One you said can transform you."

"Into someone else," she said. "Someone with a different past, different training, different . . . talents."

"Can *that* person fight?"

Moonlight took a deep breath. "Yes. Better than fighting though, she should be able to vanish. Hide. But the person I would become . . . she wouldn't be *me*. I've always wanted to try this specific transformation, Marasi, which is why I have the stamp. But it's dangerous.

"This one won't wear off as easily as the others—it will be permanent until I decide not to maintain it. And when I'm someone else, stamped like this, I don't think the same. One of these times, I'll change and never come back. Yet, with the jar of pure Investiture as a power source . . . I can try this. I can really try it."

Moonlight dug out the stamp, then stared at it with the same air Marasi had seen in Wax when cleaning one of his guns.

"You're telling me," Marasi said, "that transforming yourself into another person *isn't* magic?"

Moonlight grimaced. "All right. I'll admit those ones feel more mystical. It all makes sense if you understand the Dor . . ."

Marasi glanced through the window, then back at the front door. Shouts were converging outside. Rusts . . . it sounded like a lot of soldiers. Marasi raised her gun, then hesitated.

"Those monsters track through scent. What if you made me a door in this wall, and I jumped through? Next, you could distract them—make a big fight of it—then vanish, like you say. They might not know what happened to me; they might assume we both ran."

"That's a solid plan," Moonlight said. She took a deep breath. "All right. I *have* wanted to try this. I intended to convince Kell to give me some of that Investiture so I could. Never thought I'd be using this in the field though. I can fight them in this form, but that would leave you alone."

"I can't just run, Moonlight," Marasi said. "It's my fault we drew those troops. Beyond that, the Basin is my home. I can't leave it to Entrone and his plans."

Moonlight nodded sharply. "Let's do it. I should have an advantage, as they might come after me with batons and bayonets. Too much gunfire could disturb whatever they're doing in that Community. You'll notice the Set hasn't done the smart thing here, which would be shooting up this entire room with prejudice."

"Forward then," Marasi said.

Moonlight dug something from her sack, a little device that she read some numbers from. "If I ask, give me the distance twenty-seven sixty-three, inclination twelve degrees. And show me this map." She held out a notebook. "I don't have time to explain why." She popped the top off the jar of Investiture, then dipped her stamp into that light and used it on the wall—making the door for Marasi. "That should make it hold longer than usual." Then she held the other stamp to her wrist. "I hoped to have Kelsier here to pull me out if things went wrong. You might have to reexplain to me why I need to fight those soldiers."

"What do you mean?"

"I might not have all my memories," Moonlight said. "This will *completely* rewrite my past. My soul will think my parents moved to a different kingdom on my homeworld, and that I was born and raised there. I will change personalities entirely. I wrote it all out, but . . . well, I'm never *quite* sure how an Essence Mark will function until I try."

"Wait," Marasi said. "You didn't mention *that* part of—"

Moonlight pressed the stamp down on her wrist.

Then began to transform.

54

Unlike TwinSoul—who had tapped the pure Investiture like a keg, drawing it forth slowly as he needed it—Moonlight took the entire jug in one metaphoric slurp, sticking her hand into it and drawing it in. Her hair shrank to a bob and became *luminous*. Incredibly, her skin managed to outshine it—glowing from within like her core was ablaze. But with a white fire somehow far more pure than any worldly flame.

Power swirled around Moonlight, and she even appeared to rise off the ground, though she was simply up on her tiptoes. She let out a long, satisfied sigh, then turned to Marasi. Glowing like some divinity of lore. A being of radiant energy. She smiled through too-perfect lips, blessed from within by her natural brilliance.

The glow started to fade almost immediately, but she knelt on the ground and began drawing with her finger. She consulted the map, and the notations on it that Marasi showed her. She nodded, and light flooded from her, leaving a traced image on the ground. It looked a little like the map—a quick sketch of the Basin, but with a strange rune at the center.

Once she finished, her light stabilized, then brightened. She sighed in satisfaction again and stood in the center of the circular drawing of light. Only then did she address Marasi.

"Ah!" she said, her voice slightly higher pitched than before. "A mortal! How are you, child?" She searched around the room without waiting for an answer. "I seem to be in an unexpected location."

"You're in Bilming," Marasi said. "Underground."

"Don't recognize it."

"The Elendel Basin?" Marasi said, and was rewarded with a blank stare. "You just drew a map of it on the ground."

"Oh," Moonlight said, looking at her feet. "So I did. How curious." She clasped her hands behind her back, humming softly to herself. When she noticed Marasi gaping at her, she looked to one side, then the other. "Ah. Did you have a boon to request of me, child? Something I can do for you?"

"There are soldiers outside," Marasi said, pointing as the door began to thump and crack. "Who want us dead."

"Bother," Moonlight said, then began moving her hands in the air, drawing a complex network of lines that hung and glowed there. She finished with a flourish, and the lines faded into the wall, which stopped cracking, despite the people pounding on it.

"Who are they?" Moonlight said. "Nasties from the Rose Empire? Or another group of Wyrn's faithful, come to waste their time trying to fight their betters?"

"Uh," Marasi said, "they're just bad people. We had a plan to—"

"We?" Moonlight asked.

"You and I, before you changed."

"I have always been Shay-I," she said, gesturing. "Blessed of the Shay-ode."

Riiiight. Okay.

"O blessed one," Marasi said, trying something else, "your power is incredible, and your being divine. Please, will you grant me a boon?"

"Why, of course!" she said, perking up. "So polite! A rare quality in mortals."

"I need to escape through that door," Marasi said, pointing to the one in the rear wall, "which will soon vanish. I need the people outside to think I have left another way. With you. I understand you can vanish . . . ?"

"Vanish? I'll use Aon Tye-A," Moonlight said. "But that is quite the blessing you ask. I'd need distance and inclination . . ."

"Oh," Marasi said. "Twenty-seven sixty-three, inclination twelve degrees? But can you really vanish—"

"Fine, fine. But if you flee through that door, they'll find only me in here. An imperfect solution, devised by someone with poor planning skills. Here."

She tapped Marasi on the forehead, then drew some symbols in the air with one hand. A second later a *duplicate* of Marasi appeared, made with some of Moonlight's power. It started moving, though when Marasi tried to touch it, her fingers passed right through. That made it even more unnerving.

"Are you still here?" Moonlight said. "Scoot along, scoot along. Shay-I has it all in hand, child. I'll deal with these, then make a great show of vanishing. Be certain to deliver the proper offerings for the blessing I've magnanimously gifted you, and be pious in your treatment of your gods."

"Yup," Marasi said. "Pious. I'll be pious." She stepped toward the door, then paused, noticing the last jar of light in the rucksack. She took the bag—which seemed to have some other useful equipment in it too—but handed Moonlight the burned notebook and leather folio of stamps.

"You'll want these later, great one," Marasi said. "They're very important. Please take them and keep them safe."

"Fine, fine," she said, then shooed Marasi away with one hand, waving toward the breaking lines on the wall—which was being pounded in force now—with the other. "Hurry. They are almost through."

Marasi threw the rucksack over her shoulder and—with regret—left her rifle. She needed to be inconspicuous, so the pistol she stashed in the rucksack would have to do. She also left the lab coat, counting on her clothing—still that of a common delivery driver, intended to blend in with the workers for the Set—to conceal her.

She then pushed through the door. As she closed it, she glimpsed Moonlight standing beside the Marasi doppelganger, drawing lines of light in the air with both hands as the far wall buckled and began to break.

Marasi ducked away from the windows—which were indeed one-way glass, disguised on this side as part of a large checkerboard pattern. She threw the rucksack over her shoulder and slipped into the peaceful neighborhood, hoping that this strange version of Moonlight would stick to the plan.

55

In the back of the truck, Wax found a mess of papers and equipment. And three corpses.

Feeling a grim sense of purpose, Wax climbed in and checked each of the corpses—just in case they were feigning. He stopped before the final one. She was bloodied but breathing, and when her eyes slipped open there was a faint red glow to them.

"Ah," she said in a rasping voice. "You *are* good at this. We thought we had taken enough precautions. Yet here you are. Breathing down our neck. Such drive. Such *individualism*. A shame that Harmony got you first."

Wax backed away, leveling the gun at her.

"This body soon expires," the creature said. "You need not concern yourself."

"What are you?"

"You know what I am," she whispered.

"Trell."

"Your sister becomes Trell," the thing whispered. "The name and mythology I prepared for her to adopt. But she has not achieved it yet. And I am not Trell. Rare is it that I speak to one directly as I do you."

"Autonomy," he whispered.

"Yes. Pierced by my metal. Soul open to my touch . . ."

Wax drew back farther, uncertain what to think.

The woman smiled, blood on her lips. "You have nothing to fear from me. I will not intervene against you and your efforts. Your sister does not understand this, Sword of Harmony. She pleads with me to act, but cannot see: It is only in the struggle to survive that a person—a people—achieves their potential."

"This city," he said. "Everything in it. This is your fault."

"It is the fault of those who strive for more," Autonomy said. "And to their credit in the accomplishment. Though, I do not think your sister understands the nature of true Autonomy yet. Her attempts have a . . . fabricated, forced uniqueness to them. Not the raw wounds of true individualism.

"She will learn. The longer she holds the power, the longer she becomes an avatar of my nature, the more she will see and understand. If she survives. You should be proud of her. Though she flirts with her own destruction, her efforts have kept this world alive. I would have attacked it years ago otherwise."

Wax frowned, stepping closer. "Where is the bomb?"

"Aaah. It is not the bomb you should worry about. It is the destruction I have sent if that bomb fails."

"I think you're bluffing," Wax said.

"Think what you wish. But you yourself know the strength—the capacity—one has in those moments before death. It is when the soul is pushed to the limit that true exceptionalism manifests. And so, there must be a consequence—as final and terrible as death—for failure."

"And what must we do," Wax said, "to get you to leave us the hell alone?"

Autonomy's bloody lips smiled. "Prove you deserve it." She closed her eyes. And the body stopped breathing.

Rusts. Could he believe a word of what Autonomy had said? Could he risk ignoring it? Either way, it left him more rattled than the chase had.

He quickly began digging through the papers in the back of the truck anyway. He found much of it chopped to shreds, then soaked in buckets of water. They'd been trying to prevent him from getting the information.

Fortunately, he found a notebook that was only halfway soaked and began flipping through, reading records of test launches. Rusts . . . these "self-propelled rockets" could travel thirty or forty miles. How had they launched them without anyone knowing?

The ships, Wax realized. *That's why they built the navy—so they could test weapons out on the ocean.* The notes confirmed it. He checked the dates of the latest test.

They matched the dates of Gave's "vacation." They'd sailed out into the ocean to run tests. But the rockets had failed, or at least they hadn't performed to desired levels. They couldn't quite reach Elendel—though the notebook was full of ideas to get them to go the little farther they needed.

He put together everything of use he could find, then shoved it in a duffel bag he found near the corner. He had so little time to make sense of this, but surely somewhere in all this mess was a hint of where to find the bomb.

He slung the duffel over his shoulder and stepped out of the truck. People had begun gathering, including the poor shop owner who ran the liquor store. The man stood outside, mourning his shattered window.

Though Wax should have been on his way, he hesitated, then walked over and pressed some cash into the man's hand. "Sorry," he said. "Trying to prevent a catastrophe."

The man gaped at the money, but before he could reply, Wax spotted something just inside the broken window.

"Hey," he said. "Is that a case of *Logshine?*"

A short time later, Wax touched down at the laboratory where he'd left Wayne. As he'd hoped, the younger man had dealt with the enemies, even tying a few up. Now Wayne had settled down with a handkerchief that had someone else's initials on it and was wiping his nose. He looked miserable.

Wax had never been forced to store health, so he could only imagine how it felt—particularly in the middle of a job. And now that the thrill of the chase was over, Wax was tired. Rusts, he shouldn't join investigations without any sleep. He wasn't twenty anymore.

He walked over to Wayne, who blinked up at him. Then Wax raised two bottles of Logshine, a beer brewed in the Roughs—best there was.

"Rusts, Wax," Wayne said. "Where did you find *those?*"

"Amazing what comes up in the line of duty," he said, handing one to Wayne.

"I ain't had a bottle of Logshine in years." The man actually teared up. "You . . . Rusts, mate. You really do care about me, don't you?"

"I think it's time," he said to Wayne, "that we take a bit of a breather."

"Can we afford to?"

"I need to dig through what I found," Wax said. "And if we keep running into fights exhausted, we'll get ourselves killed. I think we can spare a half hour or so. Sound good?"

"Good?" Wayne said. "It sounds *rusting amazing.*"

56

Sneaking through this strange cavern unseen proved impossible for Marasi. The floodlights on the ceiling left little in the way of shadows, and the homes were built around a central park—including fake grass made of some wood chips painted green. Nothing would be more conspicuous than someone being furtive.

So, feeling utterly exposed and half expecting to hear gunshots, she walked down one of the picturesque rows of townhouses. Trying to pretend she belonged. After the urgency of rushing from one fight to another, it felt surreal.

No one in this cavern appeared to have any idea of the battles beyond it. She passed couples walking hand in hand. A man worked on a play structure in the yard of a home, his children eager for the swings to get connected. A man in a white uniform strode past, delivering jars of food to each home, humming to himself.

It was bizarre. It was all too peaceful, too normal . . . and there was no metal. The windows had wooden frames. The buildings were made of brick or clay, no need for nails. The street had no lights or lanterns.

It was glaring once she noticed it. In fact, the only metal she was able to spot was in those floodlights high in the ceiling above. That made her even more aware of the rucksack she carried. Aside from the glowing jar, Marasi had some ammunition in it, and a few small explosive charges, along with bandages, cash, and some lockpicks and other tools. Moonlight was the type of woman who liked to be prepared.

Marasi pulled the sack tighter against her shoulder. Unfortunately, she was drawing attention. People turned to watch her as she passed. Conversations between promenading couples died. Eyes lingered on her, as if she were the one person on inspection day who'd neglected to wear a uniform.

Perhaps best to hurry through this strange neighborhood and see if there was some way out the other side. Yet would that actually help? Her intel said there was a way to the portal through the Community. She needed to find it.

The lord mayor mentioned going to the Community, Marasi thought. *He could be in here somewhere. Maybe he would lead me to it?*

As two women on the road passed by quickly, wearing day dresses and moving at a brisk pace, they shot several furtive glances at Marasi. That posture . . . Marasi's instincts said they were going to tell someone about her.

Those same instincts told her to go the other direction. But . . . she needed to find the people in charge. She almost asked Wayne what he thought, then felt like a fool. Over the years, she'd grown to rely on him. Not having him at her back . . . well, it felt wrong.

After a split second of consideration, she broke into a trot to follow those two women. They hurried into a two-story townhome with wooden trestles along the wall outside, being climbed by painted ropes to imitate vines.

Marasi peered in through the door and found the women clustered around not soldiers or officers, but a stately, middle-aged blonde woman. She wore a fine grey-blue dress: short overcoat, long skirts with a slight bustle. It was a style that had been popular a decade ago. The stately woman met Marasi's eyes, then hurried over and took her by the arm.

Marasi's instinct was to dodge away, but it wasn't a threatening move.

"Hurry, hurry," the woman said to Marasi. "Inside. You've already been seen by too many, dear. Drenya, close the drapes!"

Befuddled, Marasi let the woman pull her into the well-furnished room as Drenya closed the drapes. The third woman lit an oil lamp on the table. It felt . . . quaint to see it after years of electricity inexorably creeping into every home and light sconce.

"Fialia," the stately woman said, "fetch the others. Kessi will want to meet her, obviously. And Abrem. He has been keeping notes. Hurry, hurry!" She then patted Marasi on the arm absently. "How are you, dear? Hungry? Thirsty? You must have had such a difficult time of it. You're a survivor. Good for you."

Drenya peeked out through the now-closed drapes, watching. She was a mousy younger woman in a dress that could have used some more color. "I don't think Gord saw her, bless the Survivor."

"Word will get to him eventually," Fialia said, pausing by the door. "He'll go straight to the mayor."

"I'll deal with Lord Entrone," said the blonde woman, who settled Marasi in a seat. "Go!"

Fialia left and Marasi let herself be seated, trying to understand. They didn't want the mayor to find out about her, so were these dissenters within the Set? But their clothing, these homes, this place . . .

And this woman. The stately blonde patted Marasi's hand, then vanished into another room. Perhaps a kitchen? Marasi almost bolted. Perhaps they were trying to distract her from stopping Mayor Entrone? But then the blonde woman returned with some biscuits and tea.

Marasi gaped, flummoxed by the idea of a tea break in the middle of a dangerous incursion into enemy territory.

"Look at the poor thing," said Drenya from the drapes. "It's probably been *years* since she saw real food."

"It's all right," the blonde woman said, offering the biscuits. "Don't be afraid. We have plenty here—like in the old days. You remember?"

"The . . . old days?" Marasi said.

"Yes, before the disaster," the blonde woman said. "Before the ashfalls. We are safe down here."

"It was built to keep us protected," the other woman said, stepping up. "You must be so strong to have survived up there, to have found your way here."

Up there.

Oh, rusts. It finally came together for Marasi. All this time she'd assumed the pictures of ash falling, the strange moving image made with the models above, was a part of a plot to threaten the outside world. But no. The hoax hadn't been planned to be used in the future; it had already been perpetrated. On these people.

Rusts. They thought the world had been destroyed. And that they had been protected from it.

"How long," Marasi whispered, "have you been down here?"

"Seven years now," the blonde woman said, patting her hand. "Though we lived in much smaller caverns originally. This town—'Wayfarer,' as we call it—is about five years old."

"It was terribly difficult to build," the other woman added. "But it's *so* much nicer. Makes you think of the old days, doesn't it? With a sky and sunlight? Trees and plants?"

Marasi numbly took a biscuit and bit into it, partly to keep the blonde woman from forcing them on her. It was good, Marasi noticed absently as her mind raced. These people . . . they'd been tricked into believing the world was ending. Forced to live in a bunker underground. But why? Surely the Set had plenty of willing participants in their schemes; why keep some of them so ignorant? And how did this relate to the impending army or the bomb?

A few other people soon piled in, along with Fialia. Three women and one man, a stocky fellow with a belt full of stone tools.

"No metal," Marasi mumbled.

"Well, naturally," the blonde woman said. "The metal mutants can sense it. The only metal we dare use is a little aluminum to make lights and the speakers for the public address system."

The four others huddled, gaping at Marasi. Did she really look *that* much like she'd survived an apocalypse? She supposed her outfit was a little worse for wear, after multiple gunfights and struggles for her life. Plus the rucksack, and having no chance to wash up . . .

Well, maybe she did.

"You poor people," Marasi whispered.

"She's in shock," said mousy Drenya.

"Can you tell us what it's like up there?" the man with the toolbelt said, stepping forward, a cloth cap in his fingers. "Are the ashfalls still strong? It's been a year since we saw an outsider."

"There have been others?" Marasi asked, confused.

"Once in a while someone from above finds their way through the tunnels, and our protections, to the town," the blonde woman said, patting her hands. "I keep telling the mayor that we don't *need* those protections—that we can take in far more people than we have now. But Gave Entrone is a stubborn man. He insists that outsiders are too dangerous."

"Gave," Marasi said. "Your . . . mayor?"

"Yes, he's from the other caverns originally," the blonde woman said. "Ones underneath Elendel. There are several complexes, and occasionally people from that one move here."

"Entrone is a tyrant," the man with the tools said. "He won't let us help the world above. Won't let us search for survivors. Won't even let us explore the caverns. And when people like you come—"

The blonde woman shot him a glare.

"It's all right," Marasi said. "I need to know. Please, there are secrets here you don't understand."

"Well," the blonde woman said, "when outsiders like you arrive . . . they get shipped off to one of the other caverns. We never get to talk for long."

"And they . . . tell you about the world above?" Marasi guessed, connecting the clues.

"A world of ashes," one of the other women said. "A destroyed land full of terrible metal mutants."

"I saw one once," the man said. "A terrible, twisted thing. Poor soul. It broke in here, and the lord mayor's security force killed it."

A Hemalurgic abomination, Marasi guessed, *let loose in here on purpose to keep these people frightened.*

"Newcomers," the woman said, "can't help sharing how terrible things are—then get taken away. We think the lord mayor doesn't want them frightening us."

"Quite the contrary . . ." Marasi said. "They're actors. Brought in to prove his lies."

Marasi looked around the room, meeting their concerned eyes. They were worried for her. They had no idea.

The blonde woman patted Marasi's hand yet again. "We keep hoping that we'll get word that people we knew . . . had survived . . ."

"I had three daughters," said the man with the tools. "In Bilming? It's been corroding me ever since I was saved, not knowing what happened to them. Please, miss. Do you have news of any pockets of survivors up above? The last refugee who came down here, he said the entire city was a wasteland, completely destroyed. But . . . *some* people must have lived . . ."

Marasi frowned. "Wait. You were *saved?* How did you end up here?"

The blonde woman forced another biscuit on her, and shared a glance with the others. "It was a random lottery," she finally said. "The scientists who discovered the impending eruptions realized they could save only a few. So they made an impossible decision, randomly selecting people."

"It wasn't *completely* random," one of the women said. "It was weighted toward women of childbearing age, for obvious reasons. And an emphasis on Allomancers or those from the lines of Allomancers. Again for obvious reasons."

"We couldn't bring our families," the man said, looking down. "We argued for it, once we woke here. Oh, how we tried to get the managers to see reason. But . . . eventually . . . we felt the earth shake, and we knew . . ."

"Then the lord mayor arrived," the blonde woman said, "and instituted stricter protocols."

"Tyrant," the man muttered.

"We still feel it shaking now and then," one of the women said, looking up. "From the explosions of the Ashmounts. It must be deafening out there. We are occasionally allowed up to glimpse your world, but not often. Too dangerous. Still, I've seen how it is out there. The distant rubbled city, the red sun, the suffocating ash. Like a funeral shroud . . ."

"How do you see these things?" Marasi asked.

"An observation room," the woman explained. "There's a ladder to it at the edge of the cavern."

That wouldn't lead to the room Marasi had seen with the projector—they were too far from there. She suspected that entire room was a test chamber, and that these people were somehow shown something more authentic-seeming, without such an obvious light and projector.

Regardless, she was now certain that was what the ruse was for. Along with actors sent to reinforce the illusion—who were then taken away "to another cavern," so that they couldn't slip up and reveal the truth. As long as none of the actual subjects of the experiment were allowed to leave, no one would ever know.

But why? So much work, for what?

Except . . . Allomancers.

"Some of you are Allomancers?" Marasi said.

"Yes," the blonde woman said. "I'm a Rioter, though not even my family knew about my powers. Fialia is a Lurcher. Kessi a Soother."

"I had two Allomancer parents," the man said, "but I never got any powers myself. The others are similar."

That was the final piece. Marasi knew what was happening. And as she put it together, another revelation struck her. She *did* know the blonde woman. There was a reason she was familiar.

She was Marasi's distant cousin Armal Harms: a woman who had been kidnapped by Miles Hundredlives and the Vanishers seven years ago, during Wax's first case in the city after his return.

57

Marasi should have left right then. There was little she could learn from the people caught in the Set's experiment. Yet the implications weighed her down. So she sat in that plush seat with a biscuit, feeling overwhelmed, surrounded by people who'd been lied to for years.

Wax had been the first to notice that the kidnapped people had a history of Allomancy in their families. They'd thought them all women at first, though a few other mysterious kidnappings during the same time period had proven to be men.

Marasi and Wax had searched for these people for years, on and off. They'd worried that the Set had done terrible things to them, but had never imagined anything like this. Locking them all up in a bunker? Convincing them that the world had ended?

One of the Set's primary long-term goals was to gain access to Allomantic powers, and the fact that the Set had so much access to spikes indicated that some of those who had been kidnapped had met with gruesome ends. But this group, and the fact that only the most important Set members had spikes so far, whispered of a much longer-term plan. Down here, they'd have a literal breeding ground for children likely to be Metalborn—excellent for recruitment, or for creating spikes. It turned her stomach in knots, particularly when she thought to look at the women in the room and noticed that two might be pregnant.

That playground the man had been building earlier suddenly took on a darker cast. Yet . . . these people didn't seem terrified their children would be taken. There was a hope, and a good one, that Marasi had found them in time. Not to prevent all the trauma, unfortunately—these people had been stolen from their families and lives and locked down here—but at least the Set hadn't started turning them into spikes yet.

The lord mayor called the Community "Edwarn's project," she thought. This whole thing had been the scheme of Wax's uncle, a long-term solution to providing Allomantic powers to the Set. She suspected that upon his death, much of this infrastructure had been co-opted, with Telsin taking command and Autonomy breathing down their necks. A cavern that had been designed as an Allomantic eugenics experiment had now expanded to become a bunker housing the lord mayor's loyalists. Further experiments with spikes were leading to different innovations.

But this old experiment remained, and the people trapped in it. Marasi had stumbled upon the solution to one of her most troubling unsolved mysteries. She could rescue these people. Assuming she could save the world itself first.

"I know you," Marasi said to the blonde woman. "You're Armal Harms, aren't you?"

"Well, I *was* a Harms," the woman said. "Before marrying down here. Did I . . . know you?"

"I've only seen pictures," Marasi said. "I'm Marasi Colms. Steris's . . . cousin." It was the lie they'd always used, before her father had been willing to publicly admit to his infidelity.

"Steris?" Armal asked, perking up. "Is she . . . I mean . . . ?"

"She's alive," Marasi said. "Armal . . . they all are. You've been lied to in a terrible way. I don't know how to be more delicate about this. There was no ashfall. The Basin didn't fall. It's a hoax." She grimaced. "You were all kidnapped by some horrible people."

Those in the room looked at one another.

"Ash sickness," one of the other women said.

The mousy woman nodded, then patted Marasi on the shoulder. "You're disoriented, seeing delusions, dear."

Marasi sighed. Of course the Set would have come up with an excuse like that—they'd want a fallback explanation in case someone snuck through the defenses.

"I can't prove it to you now," Marasi said. "Though I will find a way. Please, consider my words. They will soften the blow when you have to confront the truth. I'm a senior officer in the Elendel Constabulary." She pulled out her credentials. "For years I've been trying to trace you: people kidnapped by a mysterious organization called the Set. They have other plans in motion—even more dangerous ones—which is why I can't stay. But the truth is, Armal, that you were taken because they wanted Allomancers. And they are willing to play the long game to get them."

Armal glanced upward—as small feet thumped on the upper floor, and the laughter of children drifted down.

"You *have* to agree it is odd," Marasi said, "that you were kidnapped by a group of armed men during a robbery."

"They had to act that way," Armal said. "To hide what they were doing. To avoid a mass panic."

"Posing as a group of thieves?" Marasi asked.

"It worked in the Words of Founding," she replied. "The Survivor himself pretended to be a thief."

Marasi didn't have time to continue this argument. "I need to locate Gave Entrone," she said. "Do you know where I could find him?"

At that very moment, as if decreed by Harmony, a voice blasted from a set of speakers outside. Echoing in the vast cavern through the public address system.

It was Gave Entrone, the lord mayor.

"Be warned, people of Wayfarer," he said in a tinny broadcast voice. "A dangerous outsider has been spotted slipping through the outer tunnels, possibly coming in this direction. She is likely armed, and known to be very, *very* ash-sick.

"Treat her as extremely dangerous and report sightings of her to your neighborhood tranquility officer immediately. Do not approach her. Do not engage with her. She has killed already, and will kill again if given the chance."

The group of people all looked upward, and Marasi tensed. How far would their congeniality extend now?

"Hell," Armal said. "We have to hide her."

"Others saw her entering," the man with the tools said.

"We'll rough up the room," Armal said, "and claim she threatened us and ran out." She looked to Marasi. "You're confused and ash-sick. But . . . do you remember how to get out of here? The path through the caverns?"

"Forget that," said the mousy woman, suddenly fierce. "Do you have weapons? Anything we could use to overthrow Entrone?"

"We're *not* going to overthrow him!" Armal said. "All we need to do is follow our plan: sneak up to the surface, find survivors, and bring them here. Prove to everyone that we can do something to help. That will shift the lord mayor to our line of thinking."

That was a noble philosophy. And also completely hopeless. Marasi did *not* have time to try to persuade them further. "Where is Entrone?" she said, standing.

"He has a new mansion at the edge of town," Armal said. "Large, with the broadcast station in it. It's dangerous there because he needs metals to work the devices—if mutants ever invade, they'll go for him first."

"How very brave of him," Marasi said, hurrying to the window—the others moved aside for her. "No doubt he has a nice tunnel to the surface too. You know the flat outer walls? Those have one-way glass. They watch you through it."

"Ash sickness," one of the women hissed.

"Is there . . ." Marasi said, trying to figure out how to phrase it, "some kind of portal around here? Rusts. I don't even know what it would look like. A large construction of some sort, maybe? Or an area that is specifically off-limits?"

They just stared at her, confused. *Should have expected that,* Marasi thought. Of course they wouldn't know. They were captives, not confidants.

But something about that puzzled her. If Entrone was creating a portal for Autonomy's army, why would he do it *here,* near these people? Why not do it in a more isolated portion of the cavern complex, away from his test subjects? Yet he'd specifically said he was coming *here* to open the portal.

She glanced to Armal—who was holding Marasi's credentials, a frown on her face. "Why would you go to the trouble," she said, "of carrying fake credentials? Going all the way to create a fake stamp, for this year's date . . . ?"

"She must be far gone," one of the others said.

Armal met Marasi's gaze, her frown deepening.

"It's because I'm telling you the truth," Marasi said. "Now I need to get to Entrone and stop him."

Armal shook her head. "Marasi, we can help each other. Don't do anything rash. We don't like the lord mayor, but we don't want violence. There has been too much death already. If we hide you, we can talk, plan."

"No time for planning," Marasi said, hurrying back across the room and seizing her rucksack. "Go ahead and rough up this room. Tell them I'm extremely dangerous—tell them at length. Maybe it will delay them a little." She fished a pistol out of her rucksack—making them gawk at her. All but Armal, who took it in with a disappointed expression.

"Look," Marasi said to them, "things are about to get *very* dangerous and *very* confusing in here. My friends have dealt with a large number of their soldiers, so there's a chance I can handle Entrone alone. But if I don't come back, you *need* to overthrow him. Millions of lives might depend on it."

"We can't do that," Armal said. "Even if we wanted to, we don't have weapons."

"You *are* weapons," Marasi said. "If we can just get you . . ."

Metals. That was why there weren't any down here. The Set had imprisoned a large group of people who either had extraordinary abilities, or were likely to give birth to people with them. Telsin and the others knew that unless they were careful, they'd be overpowered by their own captives. Hence the lack of metals and the story of "mutants" who could sense it.

How did you keep a bunch of dangerous people captive? You convinced them that they weren't actually captives.

Marasi turned and met Armal's eyes. "Which way to the lord mayor's home?"

"I . . ."

Marasi held her gaze until Armal glanced back down—at Marasi's credentials—and then looked to the side.

"You know, don't you," Marasi said. "That what I'm saying is true? Or at least you suspect. You've always known something was wrong."

"I have a family," Armal said. "Children and a husband I love."

"And if Entrone wins," Marasi said, "they are doomed to a life in darkness. Armal, he is planning to take your children from you. You need to find yourselves some metals and fight back with everything you have."

"Find metals," one of the women said, with a sniff. "What do you want us to do? Lick rocks, hoping there's some iron in them?"

"I don't know if I believe you or not," Armal said. "And I'm . . . I'm not going to fight, even if I had the weapons. Maybe I can take you to where Entrone lives. But that's all."

Idiot people, Marasi thought, grinding her teeth. Then she felt foolish.

They weren't idiots because they were scared. They had been abused, lied to, locked away without the sun.

She shouldn't be berating them. Indeed, in her shame at having done so, she felt an odd moment of clarity. These people, and those like them, were the reason she did what she did. Her reason for being a constable. It was her job to rescue them.

"Just take me to Entrone," Marasi said. "I'll find a way to handle him." She lifted the rucksack to her shoulder.

Then froze as she heard it clink.

58

Wayne watched as Wax held the bottles over his head, then Pushed the caps off with a quick flip of Allomancy. Handy, that. When God had been designin' Allomancy, had he considered that Coinshots would make good bottle openers?

Wax held one out to Wayne, who wiped his runny nose on his handkerchief, then took the bottle. He sighed, his head pounding, his body aching. Damn, he hated storing health. Made you feel like the stuff a fellow found between his toes after wearin' his shoes too long.

He lounged back against the support running alongside the front of the billboard. They'd flown up here, naturally, because Coinshots liked being in the sky. Plus, Wax liked bein' blatant. And what was more blatant than havin' a beer in front of the city's stupid propaganda poster?

The thing had a ledge in the front, so sitting was comfortable enough. This was presumably for the workers to erect the image: a nauseating picture of a fellow looking toward the sky, with lines of light spreading out behind him. INDEPENDENCE THROUGH SHARED STRUGGLE, it said. Wayne could have eaten the beer bottle wrapper and dumped a load the next day that made more sense than that.

The offending billboard was up high, pointed inward across the main highway. Toward the city's central spire, Independence Tower, nicknamed the Shaw. After old Kredik Shaw.

Wax held his bottle out, and Wayne reached forward to clink the necks together. Then Wayne tipped his head back and drank, welcoming the strong taste. Hoppy, bitter. Like a good beer should be. Out in the Roughs they knew that. Why clean it all up, make it taste like somethin' other than it was? City beers . . . they were for people that didn't actually like beer.

The suds felt good on his throat, which turned all scratchy when he stored health. Like he was perpetually sick all the time, every day—but normally didn't notice it because his body was good at covering it up. Only the moment he started storing health, the sickness got the upper hand.

Wax took a long pull on his own beer and relaxed into the taste, his eyes distant. Content.

"Remember that time," Wayne said, "when you went to take the tops offa the bottles, but I'd smacked the beers on the table first, so they squirted out all over your head?"

"Which time?" Wax said.

"Heh," Wayne said. "That joke never gets old."

"Because it was ancient the first time you tried it."

Wayne grinned. "I was thinkin' of the first time, after you caught Icy Ben Oldson. You know, when Blinker was your deputy?"

"I remember."

"Can't believe you worked with that guy," Wayne said, taking another drink. "He couldn't shoot worth a bean."

"He had other skills," Wax said. "You can't shoot worth a bean either, it should be noted."

That was true. But honestly, Wax had terrible taste in deputies.

"I do remember that first time you got me by shaking the bottles," Wax said, sipping his beer. "I remember it well. It was the first time you really seemed to smile."

"Yeah, well," Wayne said, "I'm good at pretendin' to be things I ain't, you know? I eventually put together how to feign bein' a person who was worth somethin'. It's a good lie. Still manage to believe it." He took a drink. "Mosta the time."

"Wayne . . ."

"I don't need a speech, Wax." Wayne rested his head back against the metal support, closing his eyes. "I'll be fine. Just gotta put on the hat . . ."

"You've been feeling worse lately, haven't you?" Wax asked. Annoying, perceptive fellow. "This isn't only about MeLaan."

Wayne shrugged, his eyes still closed.

"Out with it," Wax said. "I gave you a beer. You owe me an answer—those are the rules."

Ruin that man. He knew the rules.

"I've just been thinkin'," Wayne said softly. "Rememberin' my family, and how ashamed my ma would be of me for turnin' out to be a murderer. I've been workin' all these years to pay it off, but I don't feel no better. So I guess I'm beginnin' to wonder: Maybe I can't *ever* do enough good to balance the bad I done. Maybe I'll always be worthless."

"You can't pay it off, Wayne," Wax whispered. "That much is true."

Wayne opened his eyes.

"Durkel, that man you killed," Wax said, "he's always going to be dead. Nothing you can do will change that. No number of good deeds will bring him back or earn you forgiveness."

Wayne looked away, feeling sick—and not just because he was storin' up health. "I know I said I didn't need a speech, Wax. But I don't know that you need to rub it in, neither."

"Fortunately," Wax said, "you don't need forgiveness, Wayne."

"Now that's nonsense."

"No it's not." Wax leaned forward, pointing with his bottle. "Wayne, would you do it again, if you had the chance? Rob a man for his pocket change? Shoot him when things get heated?"

"What? Of course not!"

"So," Wax said, leaning back, "you don't need forgiveness. Because *you* aren't the man who killed Durkel. Not anymore. The man who did that, well, he's dead. Buried beneath six feet of the clay and rock that passes for soil in the Roughs. You haven't been him for years."

"I don't think it works that way," Wayne said.

"Why not?" Wax replied, taking another pull on his beer. "What's any of this for, if people can't change? If there's no chance for you, Wayne, there's no chance for anyone. We might as well shoot a man the first time he does anything wrong, because hey . . . he'll never change, so who cares?"

"That's not fair."

"You're not fair," Wax said, "to yourself. I've watched you, Wayne. You didn't become my deputy because you wanted redemption. You don't keep fighting alongside me because you need to be forgiven. You do it because of the man you've become. You do it because you want to make the world better."

"Maybe you're wrong," Wayne said. "You don't know what's in my brain, Wax. Maybe I *am* corrupt, through and through. You know how I am when I get in a brawl. Maybe I'm doin' all this to get a chance to fight and kill folks. Because I *like* it."

"Nope," Wax said. He finished off his beer, then held the bottle out, dangling between two fingers. "I don't buy it, Wayne. I know you. And I *respect* you. Admire you. There are times I wish I could be as good a man as you are."

Wayne sat up, squinting at him. "Wait. You're serious?"

"Damn right."

"Mate, I burned down a building today. And not one what you're supposed to burn down, like a school. A big important building."

"Yeah, and what did you do with that fire?" Wax asked. "Did you light it and run?"

Wayne shrugged.

"No, you got everyone out," Wax said. "You specifically led a group of people knocking on doors to make sure everyone escaped. You lit the fire because you needed to, but then you made sure that . . ." He hesitated, double-checked his bottle was empty, then looked at Wayne with a frown. "Wayne. Schools aren't *meant* to be burned down. Just because we did it once doesn't mean it's all right."

"No, see," Wayne said, finishing off his own beer, "I figured it out. Schools *is* meant to be burned down. Imagine you was a kid, and you woke up and found the school was plumb gone? Well damn, that'd be the best rusting day ever!"

Wax sighed.

"I figure," Wayne continued, "that's why the city keeps building more schools. Have you seen how many there are these days? The government is saving them up, in case they need to make some kids happy. Then they'll burn 'em down."

Wax eyed him. So Wayne smiled and winked, letting him know that this might have been an exaggerated-story-type thing.

Wax leaned back. "I can't tell with you sometimes . . ."

"That's the problem though, ain't it?" Wayne said. "Because I do terrible stuff! Ranette told me that Durkel girl—apparently, visiting her is the *worst* thing I coulda been doin'. I've been making her life awful all these years even without knowing it!"

"And you care?" Wax asked.

"Course I do!"

Wax inclined his head toward him. "Proof. You're a good person."

"Fat lot of good it does when I still mess everything up, mate. I still grab stuff sometimes, even when it's not my friend's and I ain't joking. I don't think about it until later. And I realize, maybe that fellow *liked* his cigar box."

"You mess up a lot less than you fix, Wayne. You can't deny it. You are a *good man*."

Wayne fell quiet. Because . . . because he liked Wax. More, he trusted Wax. Wax was right about things.

Could he . . . be right about this?

Wax leaned forward. "You can't keep digging up the corpse of who you used to be, Wayne. You can't keep toting it around. Let him stay buried. Consider who you *are*, not who you left behind. That's what I've learned these last few years. It's made all the difference."

Huh. It was platitudes. Easy words to say. But Wax didn't just say things. He never had. Wax meant things.

Maybe . . . maybe it *was* time to bury that corpse. Because rusts, it was feelin' heavy lately. What would life be like if he weren't carryin' that thing? Maybe a part of him was ready, and had been for years. He'd stopped shakin' when he held a gun. His body was ready to move on. Could his mind allow it?

He scanned out over the city, his head pounding from storing health. Cars bustled below, representatives of a new world, with fancy new buildings throwing long shadows as the sun started to set. The whole Basin was changing.

Why not him with it?

He let himself stop storing up health. Truth was, it wouldn't do much. His head cleared, and his aches faded.

"Right, then," he said, sitting up. "We needta solve this thing, Wax. I've got this bad feeling—had it all day—that we're on a trail that is far, *far* too cold for comfort."

"Agreed," Wax said, pulling over two duffels. "Look through that. See what Steris packed us." He pushed over the first of them—his ammo pack, retrieved from a rooftop.

Wayne took it and undid the ties and zipper, while Wax dug in the other and took out some pages, holding them up. The billboard had some electric lights on it, to make the thing visible at night—which was good for readin'. Huh. Maybe Wax had a good reason for pickin' this spot after all.

Wayne began counting ammo for Wax's guns, setting it aside in little pouches. "So," he said, "they was testin' some flyin' bomb out in the ocean?"

"They were only testing the delivery device," Wax said, shuffling papers. "No bomb on it yet. That would be too dangerous. Plus, it wasn't ready yet. I've got schematics for the bomb here, and until recently they were having trouble creating a big enough battery to make it portable."

"But they figured that out?"

"Unfortunately," he said, handing a schematic over—as if Wayne would have any use for it. "Look there. Finally have it working, portable but *large*. That's what's giving them such a headache. They have these rockets that can fly a good thirty or forty miles, but not with such a huge payload." He shuffled more pages, then handed another over. "This schematic is a dead man's switch. An extremely pernicious one. They don't want anyone disarming the thing. And here, a design for a much larger rocket. Maybe a last chance at making this work, but they're worried it won't fly far enough . . . and might catch Bilming or other towns and not just Elendel."

Wayne grunted, tucking the pages in his pocket. Then, digging further into his own duffel, he found a sandwich.

"Hot damn," he said, unwrapping it. Pastrami? Hot *double* damn. "Good thing you ignored me and stayed with that woman. She's quite a catch."

Wax gave him a flat look.

"I was wrong about her, all right?" Wayne said, digging out a second sandwich and tossing it to Wax. "I'm wrong about people a lot. Maybe even myself."

Wax smiled, then dug into the sandwich. Wayne did the same, and he hadn't realized how hungry he was. Some canteens followed—alas, just water. He wished for another beer. But no, they had work to do. One would keep them limber. Any more would be dangerous.

Wayne dug out a replacement metalmind for Wax, filled with extra weight, and tossed it to him. Next were some vials filled with metal flakes, all in a little sheath. Eight of them had been removed already; eight remained. "These ain't your normal sort."

"Harmony sent them," Wax said. "Said they were special."

"Did he now . . ." Wayne said, eyeing the last one in line, with a red cork. He set those aside, then took out a small pouch of metals with his name on it. Rusting woman had even sent him some bendalloy. "So, where do we go, Wax? You said they were buildin' one final rocket, biggest of them all. Where do we find it?"

Wax scanned the notes. "They're worried, Wayne. Up against the wall. There's notations at the end here, from today. They are *terrified* that Autonomy will cancel their whole project—violently. So they're scrambling to fend us off, and for any last chance at victory. But where . . . how . . ."

Wayne continued fishing in his duffel, then pulled out a strange wicker ball with a weight at the center. "Is this something Ranette made?"

Wax grinned, waving for Wayne to toss it over. Then Wax launched it into the air with a Steelpush. "Max must have helped Steris pack. Sent me a little gift." He launched it higher next time. Then higher.

Then he caught it and froze.

"What?" Wayne said.

"I know where the bomb is," Wax said. "You need height. Height first, then you can launch something far. Plus, they needed to build a big rocket someplace where people wouldn't be able to poke around. Get as much height as they can, in a secure location . . ."

Wayne breathed out, and the two of them turned toward the center of the city. And the Shaw, the enormous tower there—which had new construction on top, supposedly adding a few new floors. Or was it a different construction project entirely?

"Damn," Wayne said, noting the number of lights on in the upper floors of the tower, and the floodlights on the top. "They're busy tonight. Backs against the wall indeed . . ." He looked to Wax. "It's a mesa. That spire. *That's* the mesa."

"What mesa?"

"In my ma's story," Wayne said, "it all ended at the mesa. The lone peak in the center of a flat landscape."

Wayne eyed his friend to see if he complained they weren't in that story. Because in this, Wax would be wrong. They *were* in it—or at least living alongside it. Because Wayne had decided it was so, and that was the way of things.

"A mesa, eh?" Wax said, letting one leg slip out over the edge to dangle. "Yeah, I can see that."

"I could never figure out the part that happened next," Wayne said. "In the story, the lawman went to the mesa to find the bad guy—Blatant Barm, worst villain there ever was. But Barm *was* the mesa."

"He . . . was the *mesa*?"

"Yeah, like he'd transformed into it," Wayne said.

"That . . . doesn't make much sense."

"Sure doesn't," Wayne said. "I never could figure out why Ma told it that way."

"Maybe it doesn't mean anything," Wax said. "Maybe she came up with it because something needs to happen in stories."

"Nah," Wayne said. "You didn't know my ma, Wax. She was *good* at stories. Real good. It meant somethin' . . ." Wayne took a deep breath. "If we've gotta get to the top, that's gonna be a *rough* ascent. There aren't any other buildings around it nearly as tall. You won't be able to Push us up there."

"We'd be exposed to snipers trying that anyway," Wax said, squinting at the floodlights high atop the Shaw. "We'll have to go up the inside . . . Ruin, Wayne. You're right. It's going to be rough."

Wayne's foot thumped against something from the ammo duffel. He frowned, then knelt and pulled out a wooden box that had been tucked at the bottom. It had Ranette's symbol on the top.

Wax breathed out softly, almost reverently. "Steris packed it."

"What?" Wayne said, opening the top.

He revealed a gun. Stocky, with a barrel a good *four inches* across. Unlike anything he'd ever seen.

"Something special." Wax took it out, then removed other pieces from the box to assemble something that looked a bit like a single-barrel shotgun, only with a much wider bore. It had a big central ammo wheel—almost like for an oversized revolver—which held slugs bigger than shot glasses.

Wayne whistled.

"We just call it the Big Gun," Wax said. "I'd hoped I wouldn't need it. It wasn't built for a lawman. It was built . . . for a sword."

In the distance, the sun finally sank beneath the ocean horizon, like a great big piece a' dough bein' dropped in to be fried up nice and toasty. Wayne held his breath. Then mists began to curl in the air. Growing like vines from invisible holes, pouring out into the city.

"Well," Wax whispered, "that's a welcome sight." He glanced at the gun in his hands. "This next part is going to be bloody, Wayne. How much healing do you have left?"

"Not much," Wayne admitted. "I can handle a bullet or two. That's it."

Wax took a deep breath. "I'll want you to stay back. To let me do what Harmony has decided I need to do." He cocked the strange gun, chambering an enormous bullet. "We're going to get to the top of that building and stop the launch." He paused. "Funny. I don't know if I could have done this a few years ago. But I know who I am, what I'm fighting for, and why. There's a certain peace in that, no matter how bad this is likely to get."

"Rusts," Wayne said, his stomach in a knot. "Wish I felt the same. Wax, after all this time, it's still hard for me to sort out. I kill a man, and it ruins my life. Then I join you, and I've gotta keep killin' them. Poor sods. You know?"

Wax shouldered the strange gun, then put his hand on Wayne's arm. "Yeah. I know. But maybe your ma was right about the bad guy being a mesa. Being the *land itself.* Maybe that's what she was saying, Wayne: It's the world that we have to worry about. Individual men, yes, they can be evil. But we should worry *more* about the world itself making them so."

"What do you mean?"

"Well," Wax said, "do you think you'd have fallen in with the Plank Boys if your mother hadn't died in that accident?"

"Absolutely not," Wayne said.

"Nearly every man I've had to shoot? He had a story like yours. It's the sort of thing Marasi is always talking about. You have to stop the Blatant Barms of the world, yes. But if you can create a world where fewer boys grow up alone . . . well, maybe you'll have far fewer Blatant Barms to face in the future. Maybe that was what your mother was saying."

Huh. "Yeah," Wayne said. "Yeah, that sounds right." He stood at the edge of the billboard ledge, the two of them facing the spire. Wax slid the last of those metal vials Harmony had given him into the aluminum-lined sheath at his belt. Wayne downed some himself.

"Wayne," Wax said, "do you remember how this started? This new life, after the Roughs? I'd given up after Lessie's death. You came to me in Elendel, and *you* pulled me out, Wayne. I was content to sit around, stewing in my own self-reflection. Then you showed up and grabbed me. Told me there were train cars being robbed mysteriously. Set me on the path chasing Trell . . ."

"I suppose," Wayne said. "Doesn't mean I'm the hero."

"Nonsense." Wax glanced at him. "This is who you are. No amount of complaining, no phantom guilt, no whispering lying voice that says otherwise is going to change that. 'You're meant to be helping people,' Wayne. 'It's what you do.'"

Wayne cocked his head. "Was that . . . a quote or somethin'?"

"It's what you said to me seven years ago. When people needed me, but I was too afraid to pick up a gun."

"You *remember* that?" Wayne said. "The exact things I said?"

"Of course I do. Those words changed my life."

Wayne let out a howl of laughter. "Damn, Wax. I just *say things*! You're not supposed to actually pay *attention* to them!"

"It was meaningful!"

"Ha. Listening to *me*. Might as well write the stuff I say on a plaque or something. 'You're meant to be helping people. Also, remember—ain't no fellow who regretted giving it one extra shake, but you can bet every guy has regretted giving one too few.'"

They shared a look as the mists began to curl around them, headlights illuminating the roadway beneath like a river of light running toward the Shaw. Then they both nodded.

"You ready for this?" Wax asked.

"Let's do it," Wayne replied.

59

Armal and her nervous little collection of townspeople insisted on taking Marasi together. They hurried along a "back road" of Wayfarer—a path lined with fake trees, simulating a park.

It worked. The Set's "tranquility officers" started a door-to-door search behind them—along the main road—but had to maintain the illusion of being a friendly neighborhood watch. This promenade gave Marasi cover, letting her slip past.

Entrone's home—constructed over the last year—was so large that she sensed resentment from the others. He should have been smart enough to keep it modest; he likely didn't spend much time in it. But the man's ego apparently demanded something ostentatious—including a third floor with large picture windows on all sides. As they approached, Marasi decided it was probably just another observation center. Maybe with a few false rooms at the front to keep up appearances.

"All right," Marasi said to Armal and the others, "think about what I've said. Please."

They huddled among the fake trees and bushes. Rusts. Marasi wasn't certain they'd be of much help. All the same, she hurried to the building—which was on a small stone hill.

She was spotted by people gathering outside their townhomes, in deliberate defiance of Entrone's orders. Some pointed. Well, the time for sneaking was gone anyway. Feeling alone, Marasi used Moonlight's picks to undo the lock on the mansion's back door, then slipped in. She passed through a kitchen that seemed a little too clean and quickly found another door, held shut with several deadbolts. Right, then. She wasn't getting through that with picks.

She took a deep breath. There was so much that could go wrong with her plan. But she was out of resources and out of time; once in a while you just had to do things Wayne's way.

She attached one of Moonlight's explosives to the door, took cover behind a cabinet, then blasted the thing off. A second later she burst through the smoking doorway, pistol ready. The two people in here had ducked to the floor at the explosion, though the small charge—intended for this kind of use—hadn't done much damage to the room. They had been monitoring some radio equipment. A closed door on the other side of the room led farther into the building, and a strange glowing light came from beneath it.

"Down," Marasi said, her gun trained on the radio operators. The two didn't look armed, and they hastened to comply.

Radio equipment. Marasi crossed the room, hauled the woman to her feet, then gestured to the equipment. "This broadcasts to the town? Through these microphones?"

"Y-yes," the woman said.

"Turn them on," Marasi ordered.

The woman hurriedly flicked some switches. Then Marasi sent the two technicians outside and trapped them in a slowness bubble from a charged grenade. She didn't have time to do more.

When she returned to the radio room, the door on the far end had opened and people were entering to see what the ruckus was about. And rusts, one of them was Entrone himself, appearing weary, bags under his eyes, wan complexion making him look like a corpse dressed for a funeral in his fine suit and formal hat.

The room behind him glowed with a white light. Marasi glimpsed a large chamber with a white floor—the source of the light—but she didn't have time to study it now. Instead she leveled her gun at Entrone, but his bodyguards immediately stepped in front of him.

"I told you, gentlemen," Entrone said from behind them. "The rat we've been hunting doesn't hide in the dark. Wait long enough, and it will come to you."

"By the authority of the Elendel Constabulary," Marasi said, "I order you to lay down arms and metals, then submit to arrest."

Entrone sighed in a long-suffering way, like a man who had just been given a bedtime ultimatum by his three-year-old. So Marasi fired. She dropped one of the bodyguards, but the other returned fire.

Marasi ducked back into the kitchen, narrowly avoiding the shots. "Think about this, Entrone!" Marasi called into the room. "Are you really prepared to kill so many? Can anything be *worth* such a terrible act?"

He didn't respond. Rusts. She'd hoped to get him talking. She exchanged a few more shots with the remaining bodyguard, then reloaded.

As she did, she heard footsteps. Dodging back by reflex, she narrowly escaped getting caught in a slowness bubble. Not made by her, but one that had extended through the wall. She could pick it out by the faint shimmering of the air.

She peeked through and saw the bodyguard frozen in a slowness bubble just inside the doorway. Entrone was safely beyond it. But how . . . ?

That bodyguard shares my Allomantic power, she realized. *He was trying to catch me in the bubble, but put it up a hair too slowly.* If she hadn't dodged, she'd be trapped in that bubble with him while time sped up around them. Giving Entrone plenty of time to get reinforcements.

It was a tactic she had employed herself on several occasions. It chilled her to realize she'd nearly been caught in it. The slowness bubble took up a chunk of the kitchen and most of the doorway into the radio room.

Entrone paced, separated from her by that slowed time. Gunfire would be useless; they could only glare at one another. She didn't have a good angle to see into the room beyond him, but that glow . . . it reminded her of something.

Entrone settled down in a nearby chair.

"Why, Entrone?" Marasi asked. "Why lock all these people away like this? Why pretend the world has ended?" With that corner of the doorway not caught in the bubble, her voice should be able to reach him. Unfortunately, he refused to take the bait, instead simply leaning back in his chair.

Maybe I'm approaching this wrong, Marasi thought. *He's not going to volunteer anything. But what if he thought he was the one getting information out of me?*

"Wax and Wayne have stopped the launch," Marasi lied, taking a risk.

"Elendel is safe. You're trapped, and soon this place will be flooded with constables."

Entrone didn't laugh at her immediately, which was a good sign. She hoped he'd try to pry for more information.

"That's nonsense of course," he said. "It—"

Then he stopped. Because his voice echoed outside the building, projected into the city. He glanced at the radio and saw it was on. He gave her a dry look.

"I think," he continued, "you are seriously ash-sick, young woman. Please, let us help you."

Then he reached over and flipped off the radio.

Damn.

"Clever," he said to her. "But what do you think would happen if those in the Community knew the truth? They're a bunch of cowed civilians. They've been imprisoned here for seven years, never knowing the truth. Never caring to know it. You really think they'd help you?"

Marasi winced. So much for that plan.

The guard remained frozen in place between them. Eventually he'd realize he hadn't caught her, and would drop his bubble. But that could take time, inside one of those. She knew how that felt.

"Entrone," she said, "you don't have to go through with this."

"With what, exactly?" he said.

"You're going to open a portal to let Autonomy's army begin an invasion of our world. I know the plan."

He grunted, then slumped forward further. He was still slime—the way he'd casually ordered the execution of those captives had proved it—but he was also obviously burdened by events. Perhaps she could shake his conviction.

"Why?" she asked, genuinely curious. "You know they're here not to rule, but destroy. Lay waste."

"Because if I don't," he said, "she'll send them anyway—and then I'll be one of the ones who gets killed. We can't fight them. They'll annihilate our forces."

"Will they?" Marasi said. "From what I hear, Autonomy is frightened of us. Worried we'll outpace her people technologically. If she could destroy us easily, she'd have done it already, right?"

"It takes special circumstances to create one of these portals," he said.

"Even for her. Can't just be anywhere, or anytime." He turned, looking over his shoulder. "The timing gave us a deadline."

Rusts. That room behind him . . . that was where the portal would open, wasn't it? She'd assumed there would be some kind of gateway, but it was the ground that was glowing. Rusts . . . maybe he hadn't wanted a big mansion out of pride. Maybe they'd built it here to hide the fact that the portal, whatever it was, would appear here.

"The location . . ." he said, turning back. "I think it's because of those people, oddly. Such a large collection of Metalborn. And we were required to bring in a strange power, a glowing light. That's part of the key."

"But—"

"Are you a Survivorist, constable?" he asked.

"Yes," she said.

"Then you know our prime tenet," he said, looking up and meeting her eyes. "The one we're taught from childhood?"

"Survive," she whispered.

He nodded.

"Not like this," she said. "Not at the expense of others. Kelsier didn't give up without a fight. He didn't simply go with what the Lord Ruler demanded. He taught us to survive *despite* obstacles. Not to let ourselves be slowly crushed so we could gain a minute or two of extra breath."

"Interpret it how you wish, constable," Entrone said, rubbing his brow. "I think these troops will come even if Telsin is successful . . . to *help* oversee us, in this new world. One where we serve Autonomy."

"That's an excuse," Marasi said. "Worse, it's cowardice. You're the mayor of this city. Your duty is to the people, Entrone."

He laughed, standing up. "You can't possibly be that idealistic."

She blushed.

Was she?

Yes, she was. And proud of it.

I have to find a way to close that portal, she thought, looking through the bubble of slowed time toward the room with the light. Again she thought it seemed familiar. White, with a mother-of-pearl sheen. Yes. It was like the pure Investiture from Moonlight's jars. The floor had been dug out, then filled up with the stuff, making a kind of pool in a recessed portion of the ground.

"A great deal of power in one place . . ." she said. Allik always said that you weren't supposed to store too much harmonium in one place, or "strange things happen, yah?" He didn't know what those things were. But Marasi swore she could make out a warping of the air in that room. That liquid was somehow powering the portal.

Entrone had stepped up to the faintly visible barrier of the slowness bubble. It was smaller than the ones Marasi made, closer to the size of Wayne's bubbles. Entrone shook his head at the trapped guard.

"You're like him, if I recall," Entrone said, walking to the side. "A Pulser—capable of making bubbles of slowed time."

Marasi didn't respond. Entrone strolled sideways, near the wall separating the radio room from the kitchen, where she couldn't see him through the doorway anymore. The bubble filled most of the radio room, but there were some portions at the edges that weren't touched by it. His voice continued a moment later.

"Do you ever feel," he said, "embarrassed by your useless power, constable? I know your sister is an embarrassment to your father. But at least he *acknowledged* her."

He had done his research; a few years back, that barb might have bothered her. Now Marasi recognized it for what it was—an attempt to put her off balance. She focused on the glowing pool. The surface was beginning to ripple. Was there another way into the—

At that moment, Entrone ripped through the wall itself, circumventing the slowness bubble. Rusts! He'd sounded so worn out that Marasi had nearly discounted him. Now he crashed through the wood, shattering beams like they were twigs.

Marasi shot him in the chest, but the wounds *healed* immediately. Faster than Wayne's did. He gave her a grim smile.

Marasi unloaded the entire magazine into him, and did little more than poke a few holes in his suit. He grabbed her by the front of her shirt and lifted her. Dust from the drywall streamed from his clothing as he pulled her right up to his face. Still in his grip, Marasi hit him on the side of the head with the butt of her pistol. He just grinned. She did manage to knock his hat off though.

"I'm a god now, little bastard," he said to her. "What strength do you have to stand against me? Your Allomancy? Pathetic. Your weapons? Laughable. You have no power to threaten me."

He turned and threw her out the window with a crash, back into the main cavern.

It *hurt*. A sharp blinding pain all across her body. Cuts and slices, followed by a dizzying hit to her head and shoulder as she slowed and stopped in a heap. Through teary eyes, through the pain, she saw his shape—shadowy to her vision—climbing out the window after her.

"The army is coming," he said, his voice growing softer as he stalked forward, his nice coat disheveled. "I imagined I'd be some grand lord, ruling in a new world. But I guess . . . I guess . . . we all have to do what we must to survive."

He reached for her. She tried to pull back, noting another group of shapes stepping out from the shadows outside the building. Had Armal and the others followed her up to the mansion?

She had hoped they would overhear Entrone admitting the truth via the radio. But perhaps . . . perhaps they'd been close enough, in their curiosity, to hear him speak now . . .

Please, please *have heard him.*

Gave Entrone loomed over her.

"You're right about my powers," Marasi said with a cough. "I've found uses for them. But they aren't where my strength comes from. Not really."

He grabbed her.

"My strength," she whispered, "never came from Allomancy. Rusts . . . I learned that lesson as a child. It doesn't come from weapons, or even the credentials I carry."

Please . . .

Entrone raised her into the air as a distinct *clink* sounded. He froze, then turned to see Armal. The source of the sound was a jar she'd dropped to the ground. Once full of light. Now empty.

A replacement for metal, Moonlight had said. But supercharged.

"I'm a constable, Entrone," Marasi whispered. "My strength isn't in myself. It comes from the people."

A Rioting, with the power of a thousand Allomancers, hit their emotions like a physical wave of force.

60

S hame hit Marasi like a wave.

The Rioter's art. Pick an emotion, then blast it into a person on full automatic. It was easier for emotional Allomancers to target their powers in a direction instead of at a specific individual.

It caught Entrone, judging by his stumble, but it also *pounded* Marasi with a sense of worthlessness. A sure knowledge of her own irrelevance and insignificance. Memories bubbled out from her soul: times she'd failed, times she'd fallen short. Had she ever *not* failed? Had she ever *not* been worthless?

She'd spent her childhood hidden away by a father who was embarrassed by her. She'd spent her youth dreaming of far-off legends, only to make an utter fool of herself when one of those legends walked into her life. Though Marasi's romantic feelings for Wax were long since abandoned, the shame of how she'd thrown herself at him—to be rebuffed—was oppressive.

She gasped, rolling to her knees, head bowed, with drips of blood from a slice on her scalp trickling down her cheek.

She was *nothing*. She'd *always* been nothing.

Wax let her join him because he felt bad for her. She'd lived in his shadow for years. Unable to find her own constable partner, so she'd needed to borrow his. Unable to solve important cases without his help.

The weight of it smothered her, reminding her of everything she was not. And everything she would never be. And . . .

And it was nothing new.

She'd felt it all before. Less powerfully, yes, but none of this was novel. She'd lived with some of these fears for her entire life. Others she'd pushed through during her professional years. They were illogical.

Logic didn't matter. Just emotion. But she could handle that emotion. She took a deep breath, whispered that it would soon pass, and shouldered it.

She could weather this.

Entrone wasn't so capable. He curled up on the green-painted stone patio and whimpered softly. All the regeneration powers in the world wouldn't help if he couldn't move—and without his aluminum-lined hat he was completely subject to Armal's control.

Some soldiers came running up, but one of the other townspeople dealt with them using what appeared to be a Soothing. It seemed that Armal had spread the Investiture around as Marasi had suggested.

Ultimately, the plan had worked. Marasi had succeeded in her primary job: empowering the people. She could rest now, and ride out the Rioting.

Except . . .

Except that portal was still opening. The invasion force was still coming.

This worry—narrow, focused, cutting through her shame like a knife—drove Marasi to focus. Because Marasi . . .

Marasi *could* function.

She began moving, feeling as if she were crawling away from it: her pain, her sorrow, her shame. With each grueling inch, she felt herself growing stronger. Shrugging off those lies. Embracing the person she'd become. A woman who didn't care whose shadow she stood in—as long as the job got done. A woman who didn't care if her father, or society, was ashamed of her—as long as she was confident in herself.

A woman who could, painfully but determinedly, pass Entrone huddled on the floor. And—with a breath of relief—get outside the directional force of Armal's Rioting. The emotions vanished like smoke on a windy day. Marasi breathed out a long sigh, but there was no time to relax.

"Be careful," she said to one of the others as they came up to her. "Entrone is Metalborn. He can heal and has incredible strength."

Marasi wasn't certain how long Armal's power would last, but it seemed that she'd been granted exceptional abilities—like when Vin had drawn in the mists, as recorded in scripture.

Rusts. Could that glowing light be the body of a god, just like the mists had been? Marasi limped back into the mansion. She ignored the frozen guard. For him, this would all have passed in seconds. Perhaps he was still responding to her dodging out of the way of his bubble— or maybe Entrone had just ordered him to block the doorway.

Fortunately, the lord mayor had ripped her a new path. She pushed through the broken remnants of the wall, limped past the radio station, and stumbled up to the portal doorway. Most of the mansion, it turned out, was a sham. The vast majority of the space was taken up by this one room with the glowing floor. Radiant light had been poured into a pool twenty feet wide, and it was beginning to churn. Glowing brightly. Lighting the walls a ghostly white.

She didn't have to think hard to grasp the mythological implications of this place. Rusts. That was raw, concentrated power. A single jar had given TwinSoul the power to create a stone body twelve feet tall, a second had transformed Moonlight into another person, and a third had given Armal the power to Riot emotions like the Lord Ruler himself.

This pool had to hold thousands of jars' worth of the power. She stepped forward, then felt the most awful premonition: she was close enough that she *saw* them, in a place with a dark sky and misty ground. Thousands of inhuman soldiers with golden skin and glowing red eyes. Living statues. They carried rifles of an advanced design, and their stares seemed to bore holes in her mind. The men of gold and red had arrived. Bearers of the final metal, Miles had called them. Destroyers.

Marasi stumbled back from the pool, daunted, as the pains of the fight started to flare up; the bruises and cuts from being thrown by Entrone.

But before the call of that power, her pain seemed distant. Inconsequential. Once upon a time, she'd given up the Bands of Mourning. She didn't need to hold power like that.

Today, she realized something else. She didn't need power like that, but duty wasn't about what you needed. It was about what was needed from you.

Centuries ago, the Last Emperor Elend Venture had been faced with a similar problem: how to dispose of a great deal of power. She knew what she needed to do.

A second later, she burst out of the building to find the clustered men and women of the Community speaking with the guards—calming them. Armal had finished tying up Entrone. He struggled, but strangely was unable to break free.

"Macil is a Leecher," Armal said, gesturing to one of the nearby women. "He might be able to heal, but we've sucked the strength out of him."

Marasi nodded, teeth gritted against the pain and the echoes of the Rioting she'd survived. "I need every Allomancer in this cavern gathered here, *right now*."

"Why?" Armal said, walking up to her.

"There's a well of power in the room nearby, and it's opening a portal to something terrible," Marasi said. "We're going to stop it the old-fashioned way. By burning up all of the power with our abilities."

61

With Wayne clinging to his back, Wax bounded across the city to the Shaw. He made one last jump from the top of a nearby skyscraper—one that was half as high as the Shaw—and launched them toward destiny, mists curling in their passing.

There were some balconies over halfway up the tower, just inside a strong Coinshot's reach. If the enemy had any measure of foresight, they'd be ready for incursions at those locations. They were still his best choice. The higher he got, the less ground he'd need to cover inside, where he'd likely have to fight for every inch.

Wax angled them toward a wide balcony with two broad, dark windows looking into the structure. Wax's Push—the anchor too far away—was barely enough to get them to it, and they landed lightly amid some small planters.

"Aw . . ." Wayne said, dropping off his back. "We was supposed to go smashing through that glass! All dramatic-like!"

"That's an excellent way to get cut to shreds," Wax said, ducking to the side—out of sight of those windows. "I can't heal. You can barely heal. And there's a door *right there.*"

"The Ascendant Warrior did it," Wayne grumbled.

"When?"

"Right before killin' the Lord Ruler."

"Since when have you known that sort of thing?"

"It's in a little kids' book that Max and I read sometimes," he said. "Right about my level."

Wax tried the door in the wall to the left of the large windows, but it was locked. "Assassinating the Lord Ruler?" Wax asked. "Isn't that a little violent for a children's book?"

"Mate," Wayne said, "it ain't *violence* if it's *religion*. Don't you know anythin'?"

"Apparently not," Wax said. "I—"

He cut off as floodlights turned on in the room beyond, shining through the windows with blazing intensity. Wax pulled up against the wall, Wayne next to him. He dared a glance inside, and saw figures behind and between the lights, their silhouettes raising weapons.

Gunfire cracked like thunder, shattering the window.

"Damn," Wayne said as the gunfire tapered off. "Those are *soldiers,* mate. I came down here to the Basin all those years ago 'cuz of a cute little case involvin' train cars what got robbed in a funny way. How in Ruin's own name did I end up getting mixed up with dark gods, armies, bombs destroyin' cities, and . . . and *ghosts,* Wax. We still ain't talked about the *ghosts.*"

Wax unhooked the Big Gun from inside his coat, where he carried larger weapons while flying. "Can you keep their attention while I try to flank them?"

Wayne smiled. "Scary Tree? We could do Scary Tree!"

"Do you have enough health stored for Scary Tree?"

"Mate, I don't need health for Scary Tree," Wayne said. "Just you watch."

Wax nodded, whipping off his mistcoat and handing it to Wayne along with a spare gun—which Wayne took with a shocking level of calm. Usually they needed to throw some bullets in the fire or something to do Scary Tree.

Wayne proceeded to shoot the weapon from beside the window into the room beyond—mistcoat tassels waving—persuading everyone he was Wax. Wayne even did some eerily impressive vocal imitation.

People fixated upon Wax. They had tunnel vision about fighting the infamous lawman Coinshot. It was even worse these days—where news of his exploits had been exaggerated by the broadsheets. He supposed that finding and using the Bands of Mourning themselves hadn't hurt his reputation.

While everyone was distracted by Wayne, Wax unlocked the door with a quick Push from the side on the deadbolt. When he'd glanced in through the window earlier, he'd noticed that a wall separated the room with the soldiers from wherever this door led. On cracking it open, he found a small hallway.

If he guessed right, their enemies would soon use this hallway to try reaching the balcony. So he slipped inside and Pushed himself up to the ceiling directly above the door on the other side. He held there, using nails in the floor. As anticipated, a small group of armed men snuck into the darkened hallway, light from the floodlights in the room beyond spilling in around them. Blinding them.

In the old days, Allomancers—Mistborn in particular—had been regarded like shadows. Or the mists themselves. Silent, hidden, practically formless. Wax could well understand the origins of those myths as the three soldiers passed underneath him in a tight cluster. He dropped and disposed of them the old-fashioned way: a few coins flung in the air, delivered noiselessly into their brains from behind. No crack of gunfire. No shouts of pain. Just the thump of bodies on the floor.

They'd left the door open, and he peeked into the main room. Those floodlights had been prepared for this and could move on wheels. Likely they'd had scouts watching for Wax bounding over the buildings below, and positioned their ambush where they thought he'd enter.

Wayne's distraction was working well. The soldiers had pushed the floodlights into a line across the middle of the room and were arrayed in the gaps between them, shooting aluminum bullets.

As Wayne had noted, these people weren't like the common street criminals Wax and Wayne had fought earlier in the day, with their rough clothing, mismatched and rugged gear. These wore red uniforms and carried sleek weapons—modern rifles. They knelt with precise postures, firing carefully. Several were slipping forward along the left side of the room to get an angle on Wayne.

Unfortunately for them, they weren't watching their own flanks. And while aluminum guns might not be affected by Steelpushes, the enormous floodlights were. Tapping weight to make himself sturdier, Wax Pushed into the room, smashing the lights into one another—and crushing the soldiers who had set up between them.

He crashed all of this into a mess against the far wall, then decreased his weight and slid across the ground, using nails in the wall behind as an anchor. On the other side of the room, he positioned himself and Pushed again, sending some of the wreckage sweeping outward to catch the remaining soldiers—and sending them and the broken lights out the window into the mists.

A moment later, Wayne sauntered into the now-darker room and tossed Wax his mistcoat. "Sorry for the bullet holes."

"A few holes won't . . ." Wax said, then noticed—in the weak light of the room's flickering ceiling light—that there had to be at *least* sixteen holes in it, even in some of the tassels. "How did you not get shot?"

"By not bein' where the bullets was," Wayne said.

Wax threw on the mistcoat duster. He had three guns on him. The Big Gun in his left hand. The Steel Survivor, aluminum but loaded with normal lead slugs. And Vindication, with aluminum bullets in the ordinary chambers and two hazekiller rounds ready for dealing with Metalborn.

"We're really going up the inside?" Wayne said.

Wax nodded. They would need proper climbing equipment to scale the outside, even if there weren't Set sharpshooters around.

Wayne pulled out a dueling cane. Wax met his eyes and shook his head.

"But—" Wayne said.

"Harmony knew," Wax said softly. "He knew what I'd need to become."

It seemed he had a moment to pause, though more enemies would undoubtedly be on the way. So he reached into his pocket and took out a small sliver of metal. He slipped it into his ear, then carefully—ritualistically—checked Vindication's chambers to be certain there was a round in each.

As before, he felt a faint disconnect from the trellium earring. But he didn't see visions. He felt Telsin's attention come on him, and heard—faintly—what she was doing. Giving orders. Sounding frantic.

She was above. At the top. He could *feel* it.

Waxillium, she said in his mind. *You should have left the city as I suggested.*

He clicked to the next chamber of his gun. "I have come," he said, "to clean up our family's mess."

Very dramatic, she said. *You—*

"Don't make me do this. Don't force it, Telsin."

She didn't reply at first. The only sound was that of him clicking, chamber to chamber.

You are still just a frightened child, Waxillium, she said. *All these years later, and you still can't take a risk. Can't see beyond your own limited mindset. I'm going to become something incredible.*

"I'll see you dead first," Wax said softly.

Wax, she said, *you're thirty floors away from me—and there are hundreds of soldiers from the Hidden Guard between us. My best. Reserved to stop you here.*

He snapped Vindication closed.

Oh, Wax, she said. *You have never understood. You can't beat me. You've never had the vision for that. Whatever you try, I'll always be ahead of you.*

He slipped Vindication into a holster, then downed an extra vial of steel—one of the ones Harmony had sent him. Finally, he hefted the Big Gun in one hand. Ranette had warned him what it was capable of doing. So he put up his steel bubble, even though the enemy was armed with aluminum.

"Funny, Telsin," he said, "that you claim to be the one with vision—when you've always underestimated me. If you'd *actually* had foresight, you'd have killed me when I first came back to the city seven years ago."

Before you could learn what I was doing?

"Before I came to love the things you're seeking to destroy."

He ripped the earring out and tossed it aside, then walked into the hallway and looked inward, toward where it ended at a cross hall. Footsteps and calls sounded from beyond a doorway there marked STAIRS. They went silent a moment later.

"Mate," Wayne said, stepping up. "You're sure about this?"

Wax raised his gun in two hands and strode forward. "Stay behind. Follow once I'm done. But don't engage. It's time for Harmony's Sword to do his job."

62

Wax strode toward the stairwell and slipped out the Steel Survivor, loaded with ordinary lead bullets. He shot—then Pushed—twice, drilling a bullet through the wood on either side of the door. He was rewarded with shouts of pain from soldiers hiding within.

Telsin assumed that if she stuffed enough soldiers between them, it would slow him. But Wax was a Coinshot. The more you put between him and his goal, the more debris you gave him to turn into weapons.

He ripped a fire extinguisher off the wall next to him, then tossed it and Pushed it forward—his weight increased—and ripped the door to the stairwell off the hinges, slamming it against the men hiding inside. Predictably, several others ducked through the opening to try shooting him. He downed them each with a bullet to the head.

Then he shot the fire extinguisher, blasting white smoke and chemicals into the chamber. Finally, he lowered the Big Gun in his left hand and launched a shot. The massive explosive shell detonated amid the white smoke, spraying shrapnel through the hallway and out around Wax—where his steel bubble Pushed it away. He strode through the storm of steel untouched.

It was a gun built just for him: a grenade launcher designed for maximum shrapnel. And those it didn't kill, it would outline. Wax stormed through the doorway, tracing the lines of steelsight across the chaotic space, and downed shadows that tried to aim at him through the smoke.

Looking up through the smoke, he found a modern skyscraper stair-well. A straight shot to the top, assuming he could get past all the troops. Men and women fell on the steps as his gun flashed. Like those he'd faced before, these were dressed in sleek uniforms and didn't carry a trace of metal on them. But Wax had plenty to work with regardless. The stairwell had a metal banister and wrapped around itself, leaving a hole up the center. He almost flew straight up it, but he couldn't afford to leave enemies at his back. Plus he needed to carve a path for Wayne.

So, Wax launched a grenade up through the center of the stair-well, which detonated in another hail of shrapnel and screams. He launched upward, then Pushed outward, forcing the metal banister out and away from him in a circle, pinning it to the wall—and taking any people still standing with it. Indiscriminate firing started from above, so he dropped back down, narrowly avoiding aluminum bullet hail. Another grenade—fired up through the gap and detonated in exactly the right position by a careful Push—made them curse and stop.

He dashed upward, keeping his momentum, and Pushed off a fuse box, then a metal sign indicating the floor number. Sweeping up the steps, firing—yes—but just as often using chunks of metal debris as weapons. Grim, he advanced, never touching down, building a wall of metal—bullet casings, shrapnel, debris—ahead of him as he continued to Push, constantly repositioning, soaring up the stairs and bounding over corpses.

Once, Wax had run from his calling. He'd seen a duty that required him to not just find answers, not just solve problems, but to become some-thing terrible. Something that Harmony—manacled by the powers of Preservation—couldn't do himself.

Tonight Waxillium embraced that duty. He became destruction incar-nate. For to worship Harmony was not only to worship Preservation—it was also to worship Ruin, with all that implied. There were times for careful caution and empathy. And there were times when people pointed a weapon capable of killing millions straight at his home, his family, his constituents.

Wax ascended the stairwell as a tempest, constantly seeking upward. Toward the false heaven of a monstrous god. And as he did, he noticed mist trickling down the steps—there was a small vent to the outside on each floor. Enough for Harmony's blood to spill in. It rarely came indoors, but it coated the steps tonight like a ghostly liquid.

Metal plinged. Metal he couldn't see. He ducked back by instinct—and a second later another explosion shook the stairwell. He found himself bleeding from shrapnel along one arm; they'd found grenades of their own. But as the resistance pressed forward to stop him, they found him still quite hale.

Vindication aimed true, dispatching aluminum death. The enemy bunched up with wooden shields and furniture to block his way, but Wax lobbed a grenade into it, then used the wood—now embedded with steel fragments—and a Push to force them back. When they went down, Wax landed behind the barricade and heard calls from above, giving him time to reload the Big Gun with another six grenades. He locked the weapon closed, then gritted his teeth.

These soldiers might have thought themselves prepared. They might even have fought Coinshots before.

But they'd never fought Waxillium Ladrian.

He had to take another hit of steel as he advanced. He was using it faster than he expected. He dropped the vial as shouts above accompanied soldiers throwing lines and nets across the central column to prevent him from flying up.

Wax pressed on, relentless. Heavy as a truck at some times, light as a bullet at others, he drove himself upward. Allomancy made the stairwell tremble—the concrete was reinforced with steel he could sense and use. It bent beneath his will, the concrete cracking, stairs rupturing and throwing off the aim of those trying to fire at him.

Time seemed to slow as he hit the next batch of soldiers, and he avoided their gunfire, then increased his weight and lodged a bullet in one's skull, then slammed that person back into the others. He crumbled the steps completely beneath the feet of the next group.

This wasn't about a case. This wasn't about a mystery. This wasn't about questions. He *couldn't* stop. He couldn't *afford* to stop. If he did, life ended. He fought with grenade, bullet, and steel. He fought as the sword, put where it needed to be. For all he hated that it was necessary.

Finally—trailed by the mist, trailing death—he reached the top. The end of the stairwell. There didn't appear to be a way up to the roof from here, but he'd reached the top floor. Breathing heavily, he glanced down through the center of the stairwell—flickering electric lights illuminating broken, crumbling concrete, ripped apart as if by cannonballs. Railings twisted and covered in wreckage.

Groans, like the hollow moans of the damned, echoed up from below. Wayne's head popped out to look up at him from one floor down; he was covered in dust and chips from the broken steps.

"Did you know this was coming?" Wax whispered to Harmony. "Is this ultimately why you brought me back to Elendel? Was this why you had Lessie watch me? Did you always know?"

There was no answer, of course. Wax wasn't pierced by the right metal currently, and couldn't commune with God. Still, he felt as if he could feel Harmony trying to push through, trying to see. Fighting Trell's influence.

"Don't ask me to do this again," Wax whispered, turning away from the carnage below. "This wasn't an adventure. It was a massacre. I'll finish the job, but don't ask me again. Find yourself another sword. You don't know how this feels."

In reply, he was given a distinct impression. Almost like a memory implanted directly into his mind: an exhausted, overwhelmed man lying broken on an ashen street, in front of a shattered city gate. Surrounded by death.

Wayne arrived a moment later, scrambling up the last cracked steps. "Mate," he said softly, looking back down the stairs. "I ain't . . . I mean . . . *Wow.*"

"It isn't over yet," Wax said, easing open the door to the top floor. The two of them slipped into a large marble hallway, with fine pillars and lush red carpet. Another force was gathering at the far side, before a broad set of double doors. Wax and Wayne took cover behind a large pillar, but they'd be flanked as soon as the troops moved forward.

Fortunately, this final group seemed to be the dregs of the enemy forces. Steelsight showed him few, if any, aluminum guns. Indeed it revealed metal weapons, zippers on clothing, keys in pockets. These people wore uniforms, but not like the others—more security officer, less soldier.

Wax downed another metal vial and quickly reloaded, then . . . Rusts. Those cuts along his arm were throbbing. He pulled a self-clinging bandage from his pocket and wrapped it around his arm, best he could. Hopefully the damage wasn't too bad. His hand still worked fine.

"They aren't well armed," he whispered to Wayne, "but there are a *lot* of them. Building security, I'd guess. I'll go—"

"Stop," Wayne said, holding his arm.

"What?" Wax whispered.

"These ones ain't into it," he said. Then as Wax frowned, he continued, "Those other ones, the ones who came down first? They wanted us dead. They wanted to prove themselves. They wanted the fight. These poor sods? These are the last defense. And they *ain't into it*."

"You might be right," Wax said. "But we have to keep moving. Telsin could initiate the launch at any moment."

Wayne nodded.

Then he started shouting.

63

Hey," Wayne called loudly, his voice echoing in the marble room. "You all, out there? I know you!"

Wax gave him a glare, but Wayne ignored him. Wax knew a lotta things. But tonight the fellow had become Ruin incarnate. Wax wasn't wrong. But he didn't have to be right neither.

"I know you!" Wayne shouted, louder.

The hall fell quiet save for the clinking of weapons and the shuffling of feet. Wax glanced out from the side of the stone pillar, perhaps thinking he might use Wayne's voice as a distraction. Wayne grabbed his friend's arm, then shook his head.

"I know you," Wayne continued loudly, looking up toward the ceiling. "Yeah. I know how you feel. You're guards. Watchmen. Fellows what was hired to protect the building. You don't know about this nonsense—about cities being destroyed, about dark gods. Sure, you seen creepy stuff, but you ain't here for that. You're here to put coin in your pocket the honest way.

"You were supposed to go home tonight. Hug your kids. Have a meal—maybe cold, but filling. You were supposed to go drinkin' with buddies, or get a good night's sleep for once.

"But now, here you are. Gun in hand. Wonderin' how you got where you are. Sure, you're only facin' down two blokes. But you heard what happened below. Maybe just rumbles, but you heard. And you *know* there used to be a hundred or two *actual soldiers* between those two blokes and you. Now there aren't any of them left."

Wayne let that thought linger. The room had gone so quiet you could have heard a man cock a pistol from a hundred paces. Wayne squeezed his eyes shut, remembering. Feeling. Then he continued, softer.

"Yeah, here you are," he said. "Your hand is slick on the grip of your gun. Your heart, it feels like it's tryin' to rip outta your chest and run away. But you think, 'I ain't got no choice. I signed up for this. I gotta shoot.'

"You're *wrong*. You *don't* hafta do this, mate. To hell with what you said you'd do. To hell with it all. You're in the wrong spot, and you *know* it.

"There's a door to your right. I don't know where it goes, but at least it ain't in here. In a moment, Dawnshot and I, we're gonna come out killin'. If you stay and fight, maybe you'll get lucky. Maybe we'll kill you, and you won't hafta spend the rest of your days feeling crushed on account of what you've done this night. Shootin' lawmen, then hearin' about an entire city bein' destroyed—full of kids, and families, and men what just wanna live like you do.

"But maybe you won't get lucky. Maybe you'll actually pull that trigger and hit one of us. And if you do, it's gonna be bad. Worse than bad. It will follow you your whole damn life." He paused. "Anyway, I just wanted to say my piece. I hope there's one that listened. When we come out, if you got your gun holstered and you're makin' for that escape route in the chaos . . . well, we ain't gonna aim for you first."

He looked at Wax, who pulled his bandage tight, then nodded back. He'd dropped the Big Gun; it was out of ammo. But he raised his regular revolver, armed and ready.

Sometimes you needed what he'd done. You needed a sword. But Wayne figured sometimes you needed something else. A shield? Or maybe that was too poetic. He didn't know much about poetry.

Sometimes what you needed was a guy who had been there before.

The two ducked out from behind the pillar, weapons out, and saw a whole host of people pushing and scrambling to get through that exit. Wax lowered his gun, dumbfounded, and Wayne grinned as *every damn person* left. Sure, a few at the tail end glanced back—with concern, like maybe they were the guys in charge of this bunch and didn't want to leave their posts. But when the army left you alone facing two trained Twin-born with notches in their stocks running to three digits . . .

In seconds, the marble entry room was empty. Wax shared a look with Wayne, then they walked to the large wooden doors at the far end and threw them open, to reveal a grand staircase leading up to some kind of ballroom with a skylight. Standing at the top were a man in a suit and a woman with a bowler hat, her head completely healed, flipping a dueling cane in one hand and trying her best—but failin' somethin' awful—to imitate a Wayne grin.

"These idiots again?" Wayne said with a sigh. "All right. I'll tackle the one with the hat. You—"

"No," Wax said softly.

"No?"

"No," Wax repeated. "They were built and trained to defeat us. That man knows exactly how to hunt me."

"So . . ." Wayne grinned. "I take the fellow, you take the woman?"

"Damn right," Wax said, smiling. "Remember he's a Leecher. Don't get too close, or he'll wipe out your Allomantic abilities."

"Mate," Wayne said, "I'm depending on it. Let's do this."

64

The Allomantic grenades in Marasi's hands vibrated so powerfully, she thought they'd shake her flesh free of her bones. The Allomancers from the Community gathered around the edges of the glowing pool, which was rapidly vanishing—their hands thrust in to touch it, draw it in. Their skin glowed as they filled with power.

Marasi had waded straight into the middle. And she could feel those troops on the other side, in a place that was somehow distant and impossibly close at the same time. Waiting.

She needed this power gone. Now. Marasi continued to draw in strength, charging her grenades. She had no idea how much they could hold. She'd never had access to this kind of strength before.

"It's too much!" a man cried. "What do I do with it!"

"Burn it!" Marasi shouted. "Use it!"

"For what?"

"It doesn't matter!" Marasi yelled. "We only need to get *rid* of it!"

Bursts of emotional Allomancy washed over her as Armal used her powers to Riot. Metal in the radio room vibrated and ripped apart. The Allomancers in the room channeled every bit of energy they could.

The pool shrank further. Marasi thought—through the blasts of confidence Armal sent—that she could sense the troops on the other side getting *agitated*. Then she felt something different. Something *emerging*. They were coming through. She understood it in a flash—you had to *want* to come through the portal. To command it to let you through. They were beginning the process.

No you don't, she thought. Then she dropped both her grenades, and used the same mental command to open the portal to them.

The movement on the other side stopped. Frozen in time as the Allomancers around her continued—wide eyed—drawing from the pool. Siphoning away the awesome power until, at last, the glow faded. The room was suddenly a normal ballroom again, with a hewn-out rock pit in the floor some three feet deep.

She was left with one final impression from the other side. Shock. Judging by how much energy she'd put into those grenades, it would be a while before the army discovered what had happened.

The other Allomancers slumped against one another, exhausted. She had never thought that using their powers would be so much work, but she felt wrung out as well. Not simply from what they'd done here—but from all of it, taking place in such a short time.

She limped to the edge of the pit and let them help her out.

". . . Now what?" Armal finally asked.

"Now," Marasi said, lying back on the rock, "we hope that my friends have had an easier time of it than I have."

65

*F*igures, Wayne thought, dashing up the steps. *Wax would want me to face the evil version of him. While he gets the easy job. My evil twin probably spent the afternoon drinkin'. She'll be a snap.* Especially since she'd gotten her face half blown off earlier in the day.

The steps led to a large ballroom, with red-carpeted floor and no furniture. A skylight kept out the mist above, but for the most part this was a wide-open room with high ceilings and no obstacles. No cover either. The two backed away a little as Wayne and Wax charged up the steps—Wax doing a steel-assisted flying leap at the end, because of course he did.

Wayne kept his eyes on the woman, pretending he was going to engage her. As soon as he drew close though, he broke to the left and tackled the Coinshot. The man cried out in shock as Wayne knocked them both to the carpeted floor.

Rusts. His cologne smells terrible.

The man scrambled to get free, but Wayne took hold of his suit coat and clung on. Wayne knew how to fight beside Wax, which translated into knowing how to fight against him. *Gotta stay close to Wax, otherwise he'd do something smart, like fly up high and shoot you till you died of it.*

The man grunted, trying to pry Wayne off, seeming baffled by the whole experience as they wrestled on the ground. Eventually he put his hand on Wayne's face and Leeched him—the bendalloy in Wayne's stomach vanishing.

Wayne grappled anyway, trying for a headlock, but the man was *strong*. Too strong.

"You know," Wayne said, "you're too handsome to be a copy of Wax. You oughta get a scar or something."

The man tried to seize Wayne's hand and pry it free, but Wayne let go with that hand—then grabbed the man with the other, grinning, staying close.

"You miscreant!" the man growled. "Go and fight Getruda, as is your task. I must prove myself against Ladrian!"

"Why?" Wayne said as he tried to get his arm around the man's neck—but also palmed a bit of bendalloy and popped it into his mouth. "Why do you two have this *freakish obsession* with copying us?"

"Survival," the man said with a grunt, "of those most worthy. Trell demands that her servants *prove* themselves. Against adversity. Against society. Against the roles we take. And when there are several who fit the same slot in life . . . well, only the strongest can survive and be rewarded."

"Rusts," Wayne said. "That is one of the most messed-up things I've ever heard, mate."

Not-Wax pried Wayne's fingers free with pewter-enhanced strength. "It is the way of Autonomy. To find our place in the coming pantheon of rulers, we *must* be the best versions of ourselves. It is not we who are copying you, but you who seek to take the places which are rightfully ours."

Wayne shifted positions, but then felt something tremble on the front of the man's coat. Wayne rolled out of the way as one of the man's buttons— metal, evidently—burst free and shot off like a bullet.

"Damn," Wayne said, rolling over. "Did you steal that button trick from Wax?"

The man stood, glaring at Wayne while pulling a gun from his holster.

"Of course you stole it from him . . ." Wayne said. "You really *are* tryin' to become him. I thought you weren't as freaky as the not-me over there, but you're just more classy about it, eh?"

The man started firing, but Wayne tossed up a speed bubble. Anticipating the look of shock on the man's face when he found out that Wayne still had his Allomancy, he repositioned.

The essential trick to defeating the not-Wayne, Wax knew, would be staying close enough to her that she couldn't leverage her speed bubbles. So when Wayne broke left, Wax broke right, surprising the short, squat woman in the bowler hat.

"Oi!" she said. "That's not fair! Fight someone your own size! Or at least your own stench!"

She tossed up a speed bubble moments before Wax drew close enough to be within its perimeter. From his perspective, she became a blur of motion. Fortunately, he'd worked with Wayne long enough to know what to do. He changed his trajectory and shot the floor with an ordinary bullet. As she came out of the blur, leaping for him, he Pushed himself out of the way to avoid getting hit by a dueling cane.

"Oi!" she said. "Stand in one place so I can clobber ya in a fair-type manner, ya rustin' sod."

"Is that the best you can do?" Wax said, backing away—dodging her strikes but staying close enough to be inside a speed bubble if she made one. "Really, I thought you'd be harder than this."

"Stop quotin' lines from your wife last night," she snapped, "and fight me!"

She tossed up another speed bubble, catching Wax—but making it appear that Wayne and the Coinshot were frozen mid-conflict. Wayne was wrestling the fellow for some reason.

Whatever. Wax shot the woman as she drew close, but she barely flinched. She seemed to have a lot of health stored up—and that made sense if she'd begun preparing to fight him and Wayne years ago.

He jumped back, floating on a slight Steelpush to the perimeter of the speed bubble, where the air shimmered. He had to separate her from her metalminds. Wax clicked Vindication to a chamber with a hazekiller round, though she'd healed from the last one of those he'd hit her with.

Where to shoot her? He'd memorized the Hemalurgy book Death had sent them, but it would be hard to blast her spikes off her, as she would be wearing them deep in her core. Her healing power came from her metalminds though, and many surgeries embedded those in arms or legs. A pin through the arm bones was easier to recover from than one in the chest, and easier to swap out if required.

She growled and dropped the speed bubble, then attacked—clearly trying to get him to dodge too far out. But his years beside Wayne had given him a gut instinct for the precise distance to stay from her—which unfortunately meant he had to stay dangerously close to her attacks. During his next jump to get past her, he had to stay low enough that she was able to get a solid hit on his leg. It didn't break anything thankfully, but *rusts* did it hurt.

She saw that and grinned wickedly. "Oh, that pain. That pain is *delicious*. Get in here. That was just an appetizer."

Wayne stayed wary, putting up a speed bubble and watching the Coinshot try to take aim at him. That trick with the button worried Wayne. His remaining stored-up health would probably let him survive a hit or two, but not much more. He felt so exposed.

I have to watch out for that super-metal he has too, Wayne thought. *Or . . . actually . . . that's probably my best way of beating him . . .*

After gauging the direction the man was swinging his arm as he aimed, Wayne repositioned and dropped the bubble. A series of *bangs* sounded as the man's shots missed. Then Wayne dodged in from the other direction and tackled him again. This time the man managed to keep his feet.

Wayne grunted. "You know, Stinky—can I call you Stinky?—I can respect what you're doin'. Gettin' into a man's head to figure out how to beat him? That's good strategy. But . . ."

The man Leeched away Wayne's bendalloy, then shoved Wayne off and started punching, his face turning red with anger. Wayne dodged the blows, then leaped forward and grabbed him yet again.

"But weren't you worried?" Wayne continued. "About contamination? Wax, you see, *isn't* a complete waste of a person. While you obviously are. So by pretendin' to be him, you might have *accidentally* ended up doin' something useful."

The man growled, shoving Wayne aside, then fired a few shots. Wayne took one of those—ouch—but managed another hit of bendalloy. That was the key. People expected a man like him to run out of such an expensive metal.

But the fellow didn't know. He wasn't merely fighting Wayne the amiable miscreant. He was fighting Wayne Terrisborn, filthy rich snob with way, *way* too much money to burn.

"You know I can heal, right?" Wayne said after dodging back out of a speed bubble. "Shootin' me is kinda stupid."

"Not if it *hurts*," the man snapped, though he stopped firing. Mistake that, lettin' Wayne talk him out of it. He couldn't know that Wayne was running low on health—but then in general, you beat a Bloodmaker by makin' them use up their metalminds.

Instead, the man fished in his pocket and brought out a pair of what seemed to be aluminum handcuffs. Wayne swallowed a wisecrack. That . . . was actually a good idea. If he could grapple with Wayne for long enough to lock him to something, then get away, he could shoot Wayne full of bullets at his leisure. The only way out would be for Wayne to cut his own hand off.

As he was considering, the man gestured at Wayne with the cuffs— which he didn't need to do, but Wayne could admire the nice pose—and released a *terrible* wave of Allomantic strength, one that ripped the carpet up by its staples and sent Wayne tumbling backward.

Rusts. Even his metalminds—embedded beneath the skin of his thighs—felt those blasts. Still, Wayne had been ready for it. So he *pretended* to be dazed, but instead watched keenly as the man covertly pulled an aluminum flask from his inner coat pocket and took a hit. Wax had said every time the fellow used that super-Push, he'd have to replenish his steel.

Now I know where you keep that flask, friend.

With another speed bubble, Wayne rushed in close. The man groaned as—once again—Wayne grabbed on to him.

"You annoying little *prick*," the man snapped.

"Oh, mate," Wayne said. "You sweet mama's baby." He pulled in closer. "You ain't even *begun* to learn how annoying I can be."

"I'm supposed to like the pain," the woman said, circling Wax as they continued their dance—him trying to stay just far enough from her to avoid being hit, but not so far as to give her a chance to back up and make a speed bubble. "That's something I didn't know about him. Learned it recently, ya know? In the tunnel? He likes pain. I have to like pain. Enjoy fear. Savor misery."

Wax didn't reply, focused on keeping the right distance.

"Do ya know why?" the woman asked, feinting in, making Wax hop backward. "I didn't at first. Freaked me out! I hadn't *seen* that innim. More I thought though, the more it made sense. He *must* like the pain. Otherwise he'd have ended things long ago. It's the only answer that makes any sense."

She lunged, and he dodged a little too far, because she broke and threw herself the other direction, rolling to the ground and becoming a blur. Wax cursed, dancing away—noticing something from the corner of his eye that made him feel comfortable backing up. A moment later, his back pressed up against Wayne's.

"So, how're things?" Wayne said.

"Could be better," Wax replied.

"I hear you," Wayne grumbled, giving them a speed bubble. "Wanna try something new? Shake it up?" He waggled one of his dueling canes in his hand.

"Sure."

Wayne tossed a dueling cane into the air, and Wax tossed *him* Vindication, loaded with aluminum bullets. "Ignore the hazekiller chambers," Wax said, snatching the cane from the air. "Lever on the top activates those."

The bubble dropped, and Wax met Getruda with dueling cane against dueling cane—a crack of wood nearly as loud as Vindication, as Wayne took a few shots at Dumad.

Wax smiled at the sound. It was in some ways silly to enjoy hearing his friend fire the gun. But it wasn't the action that mattered. It was the wound that had finally healed.

Wax parried the next set of dueling cane blows. She was better than he was—but this change-up obviously had her confused. She started at him in a more defensive posture, and he was able to briefly fend her off, then deliver a strike on her thigh. Looking for where her metalminds were embedded deep under the skin, where Allomancers couldn't interfere with them.

Not either thigh, he thought, hitting again. She, like Wayne, seemed not to mind the hits. Indeed, her eyes flashed with pain at each one, and her smile widened. At the same time, she didn't have the wild sense of pleasure he'd seen from some who truly enjoyed pain. She was trying to brute-force train herself to think like she believed Wayne did.

In some ways, that was even more disturbing.

She eventually came in more aggressively, and after he took a hit on his side—one that might have bruised a rib—he forced himself to retreat. His arm was still aching from the shrapnel earlier, and rusts . . . he was beginning to wear out.

So when Wayne came past him, Wax tossed him the cane back and caught Vindication as Wayne threw it. He'd fired all but the hazekiller rounds.

"More dodgin' and hittin'?" the woman asked Wax with a yawn. "I don't really mind, as it's fun watchin' you squirm. But I would rather not waste all night."

Wax needed to try something different. So with steelsight, he located a suitable piece of metal: a doorstop by a nearby door. He leaped over and grabbed it, then turned back as the woman came at him in a blur.

Time to try something old-fashioned.

Wayne landed another grapple on the Coinshot. The man had given up burning away Wayne's metals, and tried something smart. He took to the air—forcing Wayne to hold on tightly as he dangled. The Coinshot fired into the skylight, then they smashed through into the dark misty air. As they did, a shard of glass sliced the fellow along the arm something fierce.

Huh, Wayne thought. *Look at that.*

The wound didn't heal. He wasn't a Bloodmaker. So there *was* some limit on the number of spikes the Set could stick inna person. Or maybe Trell/Telsin just didn't want them to be so powerful they could challenge her.

Being in the air let Wayne control the fight far less; he really had to hold on, since if he dropped from up here—well, healing that would take basically all Wayne had. The need to hold on with both hands let the guy snap the handcuffs around one of Wayne's wrists. Rusts.

Wayne *did* get a glimpse of the apparatus set up on the rooftop though, among the construction. It included a long, sleek weapon that looked an awful lot like . . . well, a sausage. And sausages looked like a fellow's knob.

That had to be the rocket, and it hadn't been launched yet, which was a very good sign. Wax's sister stood there among some engineers, wearing jacket and cravat, the mists staying far away from her—like she had an invisible glass bubble. Her waiting with hands clasped behind her back, and staring off into the darkness . . . that seemed a bad sign.

The Coinshot let them go down lower, then used a Push off some apparatus to jerk them forward, then another Push sent them backward. The jarring motion dislodged Wayne, who dropped with a grunt of annoyance to the rooftop. Not far enough to need much healing, but still.

Damn, damn, *damn.*

Well, if the fellow was going to fight dirty, Wayne could do the same. Granted, Wayne would fight dirty *anyway,* but he felt better about it in moments like this. He ran toward the broken skylight, where hopefully he could drop down to help Wax fight Getruda.

Wax used the metal doorstop like a bludgeon, Pushing it at the woman. She dodged by instinct, as something that large would hurt more than a bullet.

Wax leaped over her as she rolled, then he Pushed the doorstop toward her again, hitting her in the arm and snapping bones.

She growled, agony breaking through her facade. It made her stumble and slow momentarily as she waited to heal—which let Wax reposition and shove the doorstop straight into her foot, shattering bones there too.

It bounced to the side, and he used a Push to soar in that direction, grab it, and shoot it again. By then she'd healed and managed to get out of the way—but this weapon made her keep dodging. Whenever she was distracted, or the bludgeon fell far enough away to be awkward retrieving immediately, he hit her with a bullet Pushed from his fingers. He didn't pause to reload. He just kept beating her down.

Her quips trailed off. He grabbed a chunk of metal from the broken skylight and used that too. He kept throwing things at her, relentless, a flurry of steel she had to dodge, or be slowed by pain and healing. Soon she seemed more *angry* than anything else, and she kept trying to find a way to engage him directly.

Wax didn't let her. He cut the woman on one side. Then the other. Then he delivered a bullet directly into her arm—and caught sight of a glimmer of metal. The wound healed over in a moment, but he knew what he'd seen. Her metalmind.

A second later, Wayne came thumping down from above, breathing heavily and muttering under his breath. Wax reached out and had his fingers in the right place to be inside the bubble when it appeared. Since any part of your body touching the perimeter would work to hold you in it, with that brush of the fingertips he was able to step in and join Wayne.

"Mate," Wayne said, "fightin' you is rustin' hard."

"Likewise," Wax said.

"It's *fun* though," Wayne noted. "He's *real* annoyed."

"Well," Wax said, "I'll admit I've often wanted an excuse to shoot someone short, with an exaggerated accent, wearing a bowler hat."

Wayne eyed him.

"It's the oddest thing," Wax said. "Can't rightly say what causes it. Instinct, I guess."

"I wear a coachman's hat," Wayne grumbled, shaking his hand—which had a handcuff on it. "It's *different*." He took a deep breath, then pointed toward the sky, where Dumad was hiding in the mists. "I need to draw him back down. Shall we?"

Wax nodded, and as the speed bubble dropped they both made for the woman. This drew the Coinshot's attention, as he couldn't afford to let his ally be double-teamed. He landed back on the carpet, then released a barrage of Pushed bullets. As he did, Wax tossed Wayne a chunk of metal, then used a careful Push to separate the two of them. The bullets soared through the space between them.

Wax turned back to the woman, as his Push had put him closest to her. She had healed from the hits she'd received, but she appeared to be slowing, gasping for breath, covered in sweat. He knew that feeling. He ached in a dozen places, and even the adrenaline from the fight was fading before the exhaustion of an entire day spent racing a deadline.

He raised Vindication, hazekiller round chambered.

"Can you at least tell me why?" he said. "Why are you so fixated on imitating him? This goes further than trying to know your enemy."

She drew in a ragged breath. "You ever been nothin', Dawnshot?" Before he could reply, she shook her head. "No. You've always been somebody. Had two names. Even when you ran, you still had the money . . . the knowledge . . . a life spent knowin' that you were in charge of yourself. Running away was a luxury for someone like you." She paused, flipping one of her dueling canes and catching it. "Well, we don't all have that. Some of us, we take the chances we're given. And becoming someone we're not? Well, that's temptin'."

Wax kept the gun on her. "Walk away. I don't know you, but I can promise you this: They've lied to you. Trell, the Set. They've *lied*. You are somebody. And someone out there misses you."

She grinned. "They said you'd get into our heads. They said it! But see, I'm smarter than you think. I got into your heads first."

She came running at him. Wax turned Vindication a fraction of a degree and pulled the trigger—delivering the hazekiller round into her right shoulder. The secondary blast came a moment later.

Ripping her arm clean off.

She lurched to a stop, gaping at the wound. It didn't heal, as that arm had held the metalmind that stored her healing. She might have another metalmind elsewhere—having several was smart—but if so, he'd forced her to use enough healing to drain it. Because the arm didn't heal.

The wound was gruesome, but not as bad as one might imagine. Head wounds bled a ton, but if you separated a limb . . . well, it was awful. Yet there was always less blood than he expected.

She looked to him, almost pleading, but kept running at him. So, with a sigh, he tossed a bullet in the air and delivered it into her head with a surgical Push.

Her body dropped. Wax sighed, feeling wrung out. Now . . . where had Wayne run off to?

The Coinshot raised his hand toward Wayne, preparing to do his trick with the super-Push again.

Wayne braced himself, then got pushed back into a heap, barely raising a speed bubble in time. He glanced up and saw a bullet inching through the air about a finger's width from the edge of the bubble. He rolled aside as it broke through the barrier, deflecting in the process, and went zipping past him.

Right. Okay. He gritted his teeth and launched forward, dropping the speed bubble and charging the fellow. Not-Wax was expecting this, of course. Wayne had pulled this trick multiple times. The guy flung out some bullets, which Wayne dodged.

Resigned, not-Wax raised a hand to begin grappling Wayne.

Who hit him square in the face with a dueling cane instead, smashing his nose. The man cursed and backed up, bloodied.

"Yeah," Wayne said, "that's better. Not so pretty anymore."

The man howled, raising his gun.

Wayne slapped the free side of the handcuffs down on the man's wrist. The Coinshot, bleeding from both face and arm, gaped at this. Then, after letting out a howl of rage and frustration, he *Pushed* them into the air with a powerful force. Exactly as Wayne had hoped, though the force of the launch nearly ripped his arm out of its socket.

He dangled off the fellow, then grabbed on and climbed his body, holding his coat as they shot high, high, high into the air. Up through the mists in an incredible Steelpush, going many times the height Wax could have managed with the same metal. That super-metal—duralumin, it had been called?—was really something.

"You know," Wayne said over the howling wind, "your problem is that you specialized too much!"

The man grabbed Wayne by the throat, no longer bothering with the guns. They continued to rise, then exploded from the top of the mists into a land bathed in starlight.

"You did everything you could to learn to fight Wax," Wayne said, "but you didn't train to defeat me. That says you've been too single-minded. You should pick up a hobby or somethin'!"

They finally crested the height of the Push and began to drop. As they hit the mists again, the man shoved Wayne free, leaving him to dangle by the handcuff. With his other hand, not-Wax reached into the inside pocket of his jacket.

He came out with a yellow handkerchief, a bunny sewn in the corner.

"I suggest," Wayne called up to him, "taking up pickpocketing. It's rusting useful!"

And with that, Wayne tossed the man's aluminum flask full of metals away into the darkness.

The man watched it go, his eyes widening in horror. The wind picked up again as they fell. The man scrambled, searching his body frantically.

"No others?" Wayne shouted. "Too bad!"

Not-Wax reached for Wayne as the two of them plummeted, his eyes bloodshot and enraged. But fallin', it happened fast. Faster and faster, the more you did it. Wayne had always wondered why that was.

"Hey!" Wayne shouted. "When you meet Death—"

They crashed through the skylight, then slammed to the floor with a crunch.

All went black.

A few minutes later, Wayne blinked open his eyes and groaned. The healing he'd stored had been enough. Barely. He rolled over and looked at the Coinshot's crumpled, broken body.

"Aw, man," he muttered. "We dropped too fast. I didn't get to say my awesome line."

He found the keys to the handcuffs in the man's pocket, and unlocked himself. Ruin, his body hurt. He'd have bruises something fierce in the morning. The metalmind had repaired the worst parts first, and saved him from dyin'. But it hadn't been enough for anything more than an economy-class-type healing, and now he was all tapped out.

"When you see Death," Wayne said, kicking the corpse in the side, "tell him he owes me fifty clips."

He wandered over to Wax, who had removed the metalminds from the disembodied arm of the woman who absolutely was *not* a clone of Wayne. Takin' those out was smart. There were stories of Compounding Bloodmakers regrowing a whole damn body from a limb that got ripped off.

"We should remove their spikes too," Wayne said. "Just in case."

"Let's stop the bomb first."

"Your sister is up there," Wayne warned. "With the rocket thing, ready to shoot off."

"Right, then," Wax said. They crossed the room to the skylight.

"Why'd you keep so close to fight?" Wayne asked. "You shoulda stayed up high. Best way to fight someone *maybe* a little like me, in purely superficial ways."

"I couldn't. She would have run out the time. I needed to stay in close, force her to engage me."

Huh. Well, maybe both of them had wanted things personal this time. They positioned themselves in the center of the room, ready for Wax to grab ahold and launch them both up into the open skylight—toward the mist, which cascaded down like a ghostly waterfall.

But Wax paused.

"Mate?" Wayne asked.

Still staring up, Wax fished in his pocket, then brought out a small earring. Shaped like a bent nail. A religious icon for a Pathian, but to him, so much more.

He rarely put it in, except when he had to. Tonight he hooked it into his ear, and then he whispered something.

66

I did my part," Wax whispered. "I became your sword. I want you to do your part now."

My part, Harmony said in his head, *is to put you where you can—*

"No," Wax said, reloading quickly while staring up at the mists. "Not good enough. Not *damn near* good enough, Sazed. I can kill men. I'm far too good at that. But I can't kill a god. If Autonomy intervenes, I will need you."

Autonomy won't intervene, he said. *It's not our way, as it exposes us. She has Invested your sister, but mostly to let Telsin communicate with her followers and visualize plans in greater complexity than an ordinary human. She will not fight you. You won't win this next part with bullets.*

"Can I kill Telsin?"

I'm counting on you trying to. But . . . I'm not certain. She might be so highly Invested that you can't. If so, Telsin will die only if Autonomy withdraws her power.

"I'm still going to want your help."

I—

"What can you *do*?"

I . . . I do not know. I can perhaps stun her. Briefly interrupt her Connection to Autonomy. Maybe.

"Be ready," Wax said, raising his reloaded gun in one hand, then seized Wayne by the arm. Wayne nodded and held on. Wax Pushed off the nails in the carpet, sending them soaring up into the mists and onto the rooftop.

Wax felt better immediately, entering the mists. His fatigue washed away, his pains fading. The mist was something ancient, older than Harmony. It had seen the Ascendant Warrior and the Last Emperor stop the end of the world. It had seen the Lord Ruler rise before that, and protected—perhaps threatened—the world when it had been new.

You've done something to me, Wax thought at Harmony, nudging them to the side and landing on the roof. *Odd things have been happening to me all day. Is it an aftereffect of holding the Bands?*

No, Harmony said. *It is something else. But it didn't work as I'd hoped.*

Mists wrapped around Wax as he walked across a cold rooftop to confront Telsin. Her eyes glowed bright red, painting the nearby mist bloody. It stayed away from her. The way a dog lurked outside the range of a man who had kicked it in the past.

"You're right," she said. "I *have* underestimated you."

Wax stopped a distance away, Wayne at his side. Behind Telsin was a hulking contraption with the rocket on top. Hidden from sightlines below by the "construction" at the perimeter of the rooftop, it was bathed in floodlights. Engineers worked on it furiously, sparing him nervous glances.

"Wayne," Wax hissed, gun trained on Telsin, "go help those engineers take a lunch break."

"Gladly," Wayne said, hurrying over. It didn't take much work to get them corralled into a corner.

Wax stood there, gun on Telsin, feeling . . . unnerved. He'd made it this far. He'd found the rocket. This should be it, shouldn't it? But what did he do now?

Don't get blindsided again, he thought. *Six years ago, she got the better of you. She must have something planned today too. Don't fall for it.*

"So," Telsin said, her eyes glowing brighter, "here we are. Now you're going to let me destroy Elendel."

"Like hell I will," Wax growled.

"What would you give up, Waxillium," she said, "to save a *planet*? How many people are you willing to sacrifice to do what needs to be done?"

She stepped closer. He cocked Vindication, thrusting it forward. Rusts.

"Autonomy likes you," Telsin said. "She called you a masterpiece. I disagreed, but here you are, and I find myself persuaded. Harmony knows he's growing impotent, that Discord is near, and so he created you. A sword. Who can act when he cannot."

She stepped closer, ignoring Vindication. And why shouldn't she? Harmony had said the gun wouldn't do anything. Her smile as she advanced reminded him of when she'd turned on him. Of how it had felt to be betrayed by his last living kin.

That moment. That *terrible* moment when he'd realized that by saving her, he'd not only gotten himself shot, but potentially gotten Steris, Marasi, and Wayne killed as well.

That horrible moment lived on. Like crystallized agony deep within him. One last tie to his old life. He needed to defeat that as much as he did her.

"Do you think Harmony could do it?" Telsin asked, gesturing to the rocket. "If this were the only way to protect the people of this world? Could he sacrifice one city to save the rest? Or would indecision freeze him? Like a constable on their first day on the job."

Rusts. She didn't seem the least bit concerned by their arrival. Something was wrong. Something was *profoundly* wrong.

"Well," Telsin said, "*I'm* strong enough. *I'll* see it done."

Rusts, rusts, *rusts*. This was all wrong. A quiet conversation on a rooftop? A doomsday device apparently stopped? And yet Telsin was so rusting *confident*.

You're not merely a sword, Wax, he thought. *You're a detective. That's the life you chose. Be the person you decided to be. Not the one you've been assigned to be.*

Wax focused his thoughts, pushing away the pain of betrayal. *Think. You found those charts of launches. None of them could travel far enough. So . . .*

He lowered his gun. "It doesn't work."

Telsin froze.

"The delivery device," he said. "All this time, and it still can't lift a bomb this big, can it? You'd have fired it by now if it could."

Telsin shrugged.

The detective in him grasped for connections. If she legitimately thought that the world would end if she didn't destroy Elendel, she'd have launched it anyway. On the hope that it worked. Because if she failed, everything ended anyway—so why not try?

Feeling cold, Wax raised his hand and increased his weight. Then he Pushed against the rocket. The whole construction collapsed, and the enormous weapon—the bomb—hit the rooftop with a resounding, *hollow* clang.

It was a decoy.

Telsin's eyes went wide.

He turned and looked across the city, softly blanketed in mist, made indistinct—like a dream. Here in the mists he could think; he could make the connections that had eluded him all day. Where was the bomb?

They'd been planning this for years . . . waiting until the delivery device was ready. Building the launchpad high to give themselves the best chance. Those were the right threads. He'd followed the correct clues.

Problem was, in the end, they hadn't been able to get it working. So when Wax had arrived earlier in the day, they'd panicked. They'd moved their bomb somewhere else. But where? Surely they weren't going to deliver it by train or by road. Too obvious. Plus, he'd told Steris to close both routes into the city. So what? They had to move and install their bomb on a new delivery device. So . . .

The docks, Wax realized, pieces clicking into place. *They were genuinely surprised when I located the tunnel from the mansion. Why put their lab out there near the docks, instead of secure in this tower or one of the caverns?*

Because they had another delivery method, a backup. In case the rocket never worked. And when I arrived in town they acted, taking the bomb from here to . . .

He spun, searching the darkness, and somehow he was able to see *through* the mist. As if it thinned just for him. Distant, beyond the city, he picked out the trailing lights of something out on the open sea. An enormous warship, a Pewternaut-class vessel that had been docked all day. A show of force, he'd thought.

But also the fastest way to carry something large toward Elendel. A method that couldn't be stopped by a railway or road blockade.

The bomb was on that ship.

"She thought you'd find it," Telsin whispered. "I think she prefers you to me. I'm . . . not sure how I feel about that."

Wax's mind raced. How to stop it? He rushed up to the edge of the roof, looking between the steel rods of the construction facade.

"Wax?" Wayne asked, hurrying up. "Nearly gave me a heart attack when you toppled that bomb there. What's going on?"

"The rockets never worked," he muttered. "Not well enough."

"Autonomy wanted to figure them out," Telsin said. "Turns out advanced ballistics and self-propelled rocketry proved a little beyond our grasp. Curiously, with this power I can . . . see hints of what is to come. But the mechanisms? Well, that takes experimentation, learning, iteration . . ."

Rust and *Ruin*. He couldn't reach that ship. It was already too far out in the ocean, far beyond what a Steelpush could manage. His anchor would give out, and he'd drop into the depths.

". . . Mate?" Wayne said, worried. "Wax? What's wrong?"

Could he get to Elendel fast enough? He doubted he could outpace that ship. And even if he could, what would he do when he arrived? The ship would almost certainly detonate the bomb as soon as it drew enough of the city into the blast radius.

"Oh, give it up, Wax," Telsin said, stepping closer. "Admit that I'm right. Did you know, that's the most infuriating thing? When we were young I'd invite you to join me, but you'd *judge* me instead. You always thought you were too good for me."

He turned, surprised at the vitriol in her voice.

"I've hated you for decades," she hissed at him, her eyes pulsing an even deeper red. "Because you could never just admit it. Well, today, *I'm* doing what has to be done. You're going to watch. You're going to weep. And I'm going to Ascend."

How?

There *had* to be a way!

"A new world begins tonight," Telsin said. "Emerging from Elendel's smoldering ruin. The Basin will be devoted to a new god, one who isn't weak. Isn't divided.

"All day you've hounded me. But now you're the one who is caught, and the ship is free. The bomb is on its way. You can't stop it. Go ahead. Throw yourself into the night, Wax! You'll end up swimming in the bay.

"Or maybe you'll hurry to Elendel, to join everyone who will die in the blast. The bomb is rigged to blow if the ship is stopped or struck by weapons fire. It's too late. I've *won*. I—"

Hit her, Harmony, Wax thought. *Cut her off. Now.*

Telsin gasped. She stumbled, the red glow to her eyes fading, her lips parting, and fell motionless to the rooftop.

Her body is pushed past its limits, Harmony told him. *Waxillium . . .*

she's being sustained only by the power. Get Autonomy to withdraw. Stop that ship!

Wax met Wayne's eyes, which were pleading with him, worried. The answer. What was the answer?

Wax looked down through the broken skylight, where mist was pouring in like water into a drain.

He could barely make out a corpse below.

67

S teris stood at the central station, where people piled onto a train—a cargo train, as those could carry more people. She checked items off her list. Another district evacuated.

Broadsheets were getting wind of Steris's efforts. Entire octants being evacuated? Mysterious gas leaks used as an explanation? People were fleeing by car in larger and larger numbers, but she'd planned for that. It was part of the evacuation projections.

She nodded to TenSoon, who came prowling up, still wearing the constable's body. "Daal and the senators have fled the city. News that they are gone is spreading."

"That's troubling," Steris said. "But inconsequential before our current need."

His expression became distant. "Yes, but they took the Bands. I shouldn't have brought them out, shouldn't have let them go. I've been away from human politics for too long." He looked at her. "I didn't know, Steris. I didn't know they had been drained. I feel we were played somehow. I don't do . . . human very well anymore."

"We will deal with the problem of the Bands," she said, "if we have the luxury of surviving what is coming."

He growled softly, but it seemed more like a sigh than a sign of disagreement. They both turned as Governor Varlance walked up, wiping his brow with his handkerchief. He'd begun the meetings today wearing white face makeup, but little of that remained, just some patches on his cheeks.

His presence lent a great deal of authority to Steris's orders. People were comforted to see him, the governor, directing efforts. Simply by standing near her, he had probably saved thousands of lives.

It had proved difficult to keep him from talking and spoiling the effect by being . . . well, himself. "How are you doing?" she asked him, making a notation as another train chugged away. "Perhaps some more coffee?"

"No," he said. "Thank you." He paused and spoke more softly. "How many do you think we can save?"

"It depends entirely on how much time we have."

"Assume there's not much," he said, his voice growing even more hushed. "Lady Ladrian, we just received a report from intelligence operatives in Bilming. Something has happened."

She felt a coldness deep inside. "Artillery launch?"

"No," he said. "Bilming has launched one of its *warships* toward Elendel. Full speed."

A warship. She turned and waved toward Reddi, who was instructing his constables to keep lines organized as people were loaded onto the next trains.

He jogged over. "Bilming has launched a warship," Steris said.

"A single warship?" Reddi said. "We can handle that, even without a navy of our own."

"Indeed," the governor said.

Only one ship? Going at full speed?

Oh no.

The answer was obvious to her.

"The ship *is* the bomb," she said, her eyes wide. "Wax said he was going to try to interrupt the artillery launch. So they sent a ship instead, at full speed, laden with explosives."

"Blessed Preservation," Reddi whispered, then looked at the vast station still full of people. They, including the ones already evacuated, represented only a fraction of the city's population. "Can we shell it?"

"And detonate the bomb?" Steris asked. "They wouldn't have chosen this delivery mechanism if destroying the ship would stop the bomb."

"So Dawnshot has failed," the governor said, slumping to the side against a pillar. "Elendel is lost."

"How long do we have?" Steris asked.

"At full speed from Bilming?" Reddi said. "Not long. Hours at most. Most likely less than that."

"We can get away," the governor said, "if we leave *now*. We have to get on this train!"

Steris stood there, numb. The other senators had already evacuated. They would rant all day that she was wrong, but when there was a whiff of actual smoke, they broke down the doors to flee.

But she knew. She *knew*.

She slammed her hand against her notebook, surprised at her forcefulness, causing the panicking governor to hesitate.

"That ship," she said, "will not reach this city."

"How do you know?" the governor said.

"Because my husband, Waxillium Ladrian, will prevent it."

"And if he doesn't?" the governor said.

Steris flipped through her notebook to the disaster scenarios she'd anticipated, landing on a specific page full of projections about the dangers of offshore earthquakes.

"He will," Steris promised. "But we need to evacuate the region nearest the bay just in case. And prepare for the possibility of a tsunami." She flipped to a map of the city, pointing. "We need these areas evacuated next in case the best my husband can do is detonate the weapon early."

"But . . . if Dawnshot fails . . ."

"He will not fail," Steris said. She took the governor by the arm. "I need your help. Don't go. Stay. Be a hero, Varlance."

"But . . ."

"My husband will stop the ship."

"How do you *know*?" he asked. Nearby, one of the trains let out a jet of steam, and last call was shouted. Governor Varlance took one step that way, but then looked to her.

"Some things," she said softly, "cannot be planned for in life. I struggled to learn that, Varlance. But there is one thing I've learned that is true: No matter what else happens, Waxillium Ladrian *will* get wherever he needs to be. Somehow."

68

Marasi undid the final latch and heaved open the heavy metal hatch. Her arm and leg still ached, but she'd overcome her immediate exhaustion.

No army had appeared. The soldiers in Wayfarer, with Entrone captured, had backed down. Most everyone else—by the lord mayor's orders—was confined to quarters.

Everyone was waiting to see what happened next.

"We should have known," Armal whispered from lower on the ladder. "This much metal, by their own admission, would have drawn their 'mutants.' This hatch was never to lock them out, but to lock us in, so we could never visit the observation room unsupervised."

Marasi climbed up into the observation chamber, which was indeed different from the projection room she'd visited earlier in the day. This one was a simple round room with one flat wall—the "window" that displayed a destroyed city and falling ash. Apparently opening the hatch triggered the system.

Knowing what she did, Marasi could see the flicker of the image as proof of its fake nature—but to someone who had never encountered anything like it, it would be astonishingly convincing. Somehow appearing on the back wall without the projector streaming light through the room in a way that could be interrupted.

Marasi helped Armal and the others up through the hatch. The four were immediately transfixed by the image. In the next room they found the projector—set up to shine onto the back of a sheet and create the image in the main room.

As the four former captives inspected the equipment and put their hands between it and the sheet, Marasi found and opened another small door—one to the outside. It let the mists pour in, revealing that they were in a small, nondescript building in a warehouse district. The door looked out onto a street—and a good portion of the city was visible beyond, twinkling with electric lights.

Armal and the others gathered around her, staring. Marasi could only imagine their emotions. They'd believed her enough to fight Entrone and the Set, but seeing this . . . knowing what had been stolen from them . . .

"I'm sorry," Marasi said. "I—"

"Have you appreciated it?" Armal whispered.

Marasi frowned as the woman regarded the city.

"These seven years," Armal said. "Have you *used* them? Have you *appreciated* them? I spent them wishing I could have even one more day of my old life. That I could show my children a world of lights and life, instead of stone and shadow. Please. Tell me you *lived* those years of freedom."

"I . . ." Marasi said.

Had she? She had spent much of that time with Allik, and that had been wonderful. And she'd accomplished much in her career. But was it what she wanted, ultimately?

Or, was it *all* she wanted?

She'd seen and learned so much. And yet . . . these poor people, kept in the shadows. How much sooner could they have been saved if Moonlight and her people had been more *forthright* with what they knew? Marasi and the Ghostbloods had been working toward the same goal for years, and she had never known it.

People suffered when the truth became a commodity to be speculated upon.

For now she looked up—peering through the mists, toward some spotlights shining high above. Was that . . . the top of the Shaw in the distance? Lit up so it blazed in the mists like some kind of mythical beacon?

As she watched, something flashed there, and the lights—in an explosion—went out.

69

It had taken Wellid far too long to decide he hated the ocean.

He had volunteered for this duty—sailing the Pewternaut A16 from Bilming to Elendel—because he'd figured it would be the safest. On a giant ship made of steel? The biggest the world had ever seen? Protected by the thick hull from enemy bullets?

He figured that at least—once the war started—he'd be aboard the most indestructible ship ever built. Yes, they were going to engage Elendel, but he'd prefer that to being in Bilming where that crazy lawman swooped around.

But now here he was, the familiar glow of Bilming retreating in the distance. Ordered to keep watch on the deck as they steamed across the choppy waters. Keep watch for what? There was nothing out here but churning froth and mist. They were even cutting lights on the ship, now that they were out of the bay and beyond any other vessels they might hit.

He'd thought that sailing out on the ocean would be serene, but not tonight. The crash of waves, the thrum of engines. And other . . . phantom noises from out there somewhere. Splashes that didn't match the flow of the water. Distant screeches that might have been gulls. Only what gull screeched at night?

Spooked by the sounds, he slid open the hood on his lantern. Unfortunately, that just lit up the mists—making a blazing halo around Wellid. He couldn't make out much of the waters; the ship's deck was pretty high up in the air. When he'd signed on, he hadn't realized how intimidating it would be to look down. It was like he was atop a three-story building, the water all the way below.

"What are you doing?" a harsh voice said from behind. Gabria? The more senior sailor took him by the arm and quickly closed the lantern's hood. "Didn't you hear the order? Once we're out of the bay, we're running dark. Do you want Elendel to be able to target us?"

"I thought I heard something," Wellid said, prying his arm free. "I'm on watch. Aren't I supposed to watch for things?"

"If you hear something suspicious," she said, "report it. Don't open your lantern unless *absolutely* necessary. Didn't you listen to the briefing?"

"Sure I did," he said. Though his mind *did* tend to wander.

"Why are you wearing a life jacket?" she asked. "That wasn't ordered."

"I want to be safe," he said. "Hey, Gab? What are you going to do with your reward?"

With the lantern shielded, he couldn't see her in the darkness. But she seemed to stare at him for an uncomfortably long time. Was he missing something?

"Reward?" she said.

"Sure," he replied. "The great reward we were promised. For this mission?"

"Wellid, what do you think we're doing?"

"Delivering a payload," he said. "To Elendel. It's a weapon, right? We drop it off, then we get out of there?"

Another uncomfortable pause. "Yes," she said. "Get out of there. That's right. But I'm not doing it for the reward."

He should have expected that. The others, well, they were all a little bit more . . . diligent about all of this. Trell. The impending war with Elendel. They'd have probably volunteered for this mission even if it hadn't been aboard a giant indestructible warship.

"Keep that lantern shielded," Gabria said, "and fetch me if you hear or see something suspicious. *Credibly* suspicious."

She stalked off across the deck, leaving him alone with the cold mists and indifferent waters. He was supposed to patrol, but they hadn't given him a specific route. So after listening to those waves, and feeling like he could hear the darkness watching him, he walked in the direction Gabria had gone. Logically he'd need to stick close to—

What was that?

That thump against the hull *surely* hadn't just been his imagination. He was near the back of the ship—um, the aft of the ship, sir—and the sound had come from farther along. He inched forward, wielding his lantern in a shaking hand. Even shielded, it let out a *tiny bit* of light. Letting him better make out the ship's back railing.

That noise was nothing, he told himself forcibly. You heard things in the mists. Everyone knew that. He shouldn't say anything, because Gabria had—

A hand reached up from the darkness below and seized the top bar of the railing. A shape followed, pitch black, vaguely human, heaving itself onto the deck. It had *tentacles* waving behind it, a hundred of them curling like the mists. In that shadow, Wellid saw a misbegotten shape. A thing that wasn't human, a thing that *couldn't* be human. The mists seemed to know this, for while they played with the waving tentacles, they stayed away from the figure. It *repelled* the mist.

It was a mistwraith, Wellid knew. A terror from the deep, a relic of ancient times. A thing of stories and legend come to claim his soul.

He found his voice and screamed. With fumbling fingers, he threw open the shield on the lantern, bathing the deck in light. Revealing . . .

A man. Tall, with prominent sideburns, his vest and cravat peeking from underneath a thick duster—mistcoat tassels spraying out behind him in the wind.

Dawnshot was here. On the *ship.*

Gabria spun from farther down the walkway. "Wellid, why—" She cut off immediately, seeing Dawnshot there. She gaped long enough for a second man to climb up over the railing, land with a thump, then pull on a damp bowler hat.

"No!" Gabria finally said. *"How?"*

Dawnshot flung wide his mistcoat, revealing what had been obscured before: a large metal spike protruding from his lower chest, where it had been pounded right through his clothing to pierce him directly between two ribs.

Slowly, awareness returned to Telsin.

She found herself on the rooftop, near her failed decoy. Even before Wax's arrival, she'd been worried. Autonomy's deadline was today. Maybe she could have gotten more time—made the rocket work—except . . . except for *him.*

She growled softly and rolled over to find one of the engineers shaking her arm. What had happened? Her Investment from Autonomy should have prevented a blackout like that. She felt . . . wrung out. Her core cold, her arms sore from scraping the rooftop, her skin clammy. Rusts. She felt practically *mortal* again.

What is happening? she asked Autonomy.

You, the distant—too distant—voice said, *are failing me.*

No. The bomb is being delivered! I'm . . . I'm . . .

For the first time, she took in the wreckage around her. A broken rooftop. Bent steel girders. A smashed remnant of her missile-launching construction.

"What . . . what happened?" she hissed.

"They took spikes from the bodies," the woman said, pointing. "Ordinary ones, not made of your metal. But one granted . . . duralumin."

No.

Telsin heaved herself to her feet and stumbled to the edge of the building to stare out over the bay. The force of Wax's Push had bent and crushed the very underlying girders of the skyscraper here, leaving the rooftop cracked and sloped.

Your failure begins, Autonomy said, voice increasingly distant. *You are not worthy.*

The fire inside Telsin died. The power that had for so many months warmed her was leeching away. Her skin began to turn grey.

No! she thought. *No! The bomb cannot be stopped. If they interfere, they will destroy themselves and the city.* Potentially both cities. Rusts.

We . . . shall see . . .

Telsin gasped and fell to her knees, trying to reassure herself. It was just Wax. He'd been an annoyance since childhood, but he'd never *actually* interrupted anything she'd set in motion. Honestly, he probably hadn't even reached the ship. A jump like that was nearly impossible, and his aim wasn't *that* good.

Was it?

Wax downed a vial of metals from his belt, replenishing his steel. That jump had been incredible, with Wayne on his back, a flash of rushing wind and power reminiscent of holding the Bands of Mourning. He had barely made it to the ship after slowing their final approach with

Allomancy—eventually landing them near some portholes a few feet below the open deck. He expected to get an earful for making Wayne climb the rest of the way.

A sailor reached for her gun, and Wax for his own. But before either of them could draw, Wayne flung a handful of bullets into the air and Pushed them to streak through the air, dropping the woman.

"Ruuusts," Wayne said. "Is that what it's always been like for you? That was so easy!" Wayne eyed him. "Gotta be honest, almost ruins your reputation, mate. If people knew how easy bein' a Coinshot was, they'd all stop talkin' about how great you are."

Wax shook his head, pointing Vindication at the second sailor—the trembling one holding up the lantern. Wayne had of course insisted on a spike for himself. Ruin. Wax hoped what they'd done hadn't been *too* blasphemous.

No, Harmony's voice said in his head, *not blasphemous, Waxillium. More . . . a sense of industrious recycling.*

"Good to know," Wax muttered.

I cannot see where the bomb is, Harmony told him. *I can see only what you do. I didn't know the ship was the delivery mechanism—but I am afraid the device will have redundancies and dead man's switches. Take care. We cannot afford to detonate it by accident. I fear that even at this range, it would be deadly to many innocent people.*

Strange. He'd come all the way around to finding God's voice in his head comforting again.

Wayne seized the fellow with the lantern by the arm, holding tight and staring him in the eyes—though the man didn't seem to need any further intimidation.

"The bomb," Wax said. "Where is it?"

"The . . . the payload?" the man stuttered, then pointed to a nearby door. "In the munitions hold. A-all the way down. Follow the red lines painted on . . . on the walls."

Wax shared a glance with Wayne, then nodded.

"You can't go inside!" the man said. "The weapon is fragile and might explode, so only the experts are allowed to touch it! You'll blow up the entire ship!"

"Then mate," Wayne said with a drawl, "I suggest you find a way to not be on the ship anymore. Real fast."

Wayne let go. The nervous fellow glanced from Wax to Wayne, then—with a sense of panic—threw himself off the ship into the churning waters below, taking his lantern with him and leaving the two of them in darkness.

"Damn," Wayne said. "I meant for him to find a lifeboat or somethin'."

"The people on this ship are going to be zealots," Wax said. "Considering they're on a suicide mission." Shouts from farther along the deck, including other lanterns being unshuttered, indicated that someone had noticed what was happening.

With increasing urgency, Wax led the way to the metal door the man had indicated. A Push slammed it open, revealing a stairwell to the decks below. He surprised several sailors coming up, armed with rifles. They didn't get a chance to fire before Wax dropped them. He then soared to the landing. This entire ship was metal—steps included. It made for some easy—

Wayne crashed down beside him, thanks to a maladroit Steelpush. He scrambled back to his feet.

"That part's harder than it looks," Wayne admitted. "You sure you got my spike in the right spot, mate?"

"I studied the Lord Mistborn's book thoroughly over the years, Wayne," he said. "If I'd placed the spike wrong, you'd be in an extreme amount of pain."

Wayne grunted, then grabbed one of the rifles from the fallen sailors. He nodded to Wax, and—despite calling for the sailors to surrender—they had to shoot a few on their way down. Following the red lines, they reached a small hold labeled MUNITIONS DUMP.

Someone really ought to explain, Wax thought, unlocking the door and slipping the key into his pocket, *that leaving a guard outside with the key is a terrible practice.* He stepped over the body of the guard and joined Wayne inside the room.

It was square, perhaps thirty feet across, and had three very large barrel contraptions—covered in wires, maybe five feet tall—near the center, spaced about five feet from one another. There was another device on the far wall, also rigged with wires—these leading to the three barrels. There were no obvious timers, control panels, or anything of the sort. It was, frankly, baffling.

"Careful, mate," Wayne said as he inspected the contraption. "Be *real* careful."

"It's some kind of dead man's rig," Wax said. "These three barrels are the explosive devices, each with its own power source. Disarm one, and it will send a signal to detonate the other two via that contraption on the wall. Wayne, tell me you still have those schematics."

"Course I do," Wayne said, digging in his pocket. "Got lots of interesting stuff in here." He pulled out the schematics Wax had given him, then spread them out on the floor.

You are right, Harmony said in Wax's head, processing the information far faster than he could. *Actually, it's worse than you think. The control device is sending a pulse every twenty seconds to the three barrels, telling them not to detonate. If that stops, they'll go off.*

That is combined with a dead man's rig. If something happens to one of the bombs, the other two will detonate. Even if we had three people, one disarming each barrel at the same time, it wouldn't work. The timing is too precise for humans. You'd end up detonating two of the bombs.

"How much destructive power are we talking about?" Wax asked, folding out the bomb schematics. "What if we set a charge, get out of here, and let it blow in the middle of the ocean?"

Waxillium, Wayne . . . Harmony said, and Wayne perked up, apparently hearing the conversation too. *This is a new kind of explosive—the direct transformation of matter into energy. I don't think Autonomy or her agents understand how destructive this is. Looking at this, and how much metal they've used, I suspect they severely underestimated this bomb's power.*

If we were simply talking about harmonium blowing up when combined with water, then yes: you could detonate it safely out here in the ocean. But a blast caused by splitting harmonium with trellium . . . My friends, I have no *idea how much power that would release. I can't exactly be sure what will happen if something this powerful is ignited. It could set the very atmosphere ablaze.*

If not, it would potentially vaporize not just Elendel and Bilming, but many cities nearby as well. Your sister is desperate, and Autonomy is callous. I doubt they tested anything on this size or scale in those caverns. We can't let this explode. But . . . I also can't see a way to disarm it.

Wayne whistled softly. Wax carefully backed away, not touching any of the wires. The only safe thing to do would be to get this ship—and everything it contained—as far from civilization as possible.

"So," Wayne said, "guess we get to steal a ship, eh? That's new."

70

Steris didn't have nearly enough time.

But she had learned, from both accounting and contracts, never to be overwhelmed by scale. Dealing with sums of money in the millions didn't make a thousand boxings less valuable. In a similar way, being unable to completely evacuate the city—or even a region of it—didn't lessen the value of a single life.

So she left Constable-General Reddi to handle the main evacuation and hurried with the governor to the city docks. Her master plan included these people leaving via boat, which meant tons of people now crowded the docks. If that bomb exploded nearby, all of these would be in serious danger. In addition, she worried about flooding. She knew only a little regarding this possibility from the studies she'd read—but that was enough to make her alarmed.

She had to rectify this miscalculation. Get as many people away from this region as she could. The governor took command of the dockworkers via their foremen. Following her instructions, he sent them to begin wrangling people for a retreat farther into the city.

Steris set her notebooks out by a lantern on a workman's desk, sitting beneath the dark night sky, on the road above the bay, worried about her low resources in this region.

"Steris Ladrian?" a voice said from behind her.

She turned to find a group of eight men and women in nondescript clothing. "We were told," said the man at their lead, "you could use our help."

"Did the governor recruit you?" she asked.

"Actually—"

He was interrupted as Governor Varlance came jogging up, followed by several workers.

"You," Steris said, ripping out a page and thrusting it toward one of the men. "Train conductor? I need all of these people gathering here inside those cargo trains. You," she said, pointing to another. "Crane operator, right? I need those cargo bins moved into positions blocking the streets here, arranged to stem and slow a flood of water, in case of a tsunami.

"Construction workers, congratulations. You're now constables. Wear your brightest hats and vests and get the people from these three sections moving inland away from the docks. I've outlined a route for you. You won't get far, but putting buildings between you and the ocean is essential.

"Dockworkers, I need ropes. As many as you can find. We're going to make stable anchor points where we can start human chains to grab anyone who might be swept away if there's a flood. Hurry! Our primary concern is a blast out in the bay. Our secondary concern is flooding."

The majority of the foremen ran off through the mists, calling for their crews. It was rather fulfilling how alacritously they obeyed. She wasn't accustomed to people simply doing what she said; in the past they'd always needed a great deal of persuasion.

"I've noted the structures I believe are strong enough to withstand a blast or flood," Steris said to the governor. "We should evacuate people in this region to the middle floors, congregated away from windows."

"This . . ." the governor said, looking over the plans. "This is incredible! Why haven't you shared any of this?"

"It's mostly done for my own amusement," Steris admitted. "Or my own anxiety."

"What a waste," he said, picking up one of the sheets. "I thought your evacuation plan was exhaustive, but this is even more so. It's *brilliant*. You have detailed plans like this for other disasters?"

"Only fires, earthquakes, hurricanes, sudden invasions, dust storms, droughts, food shortages, and mass pipe breakings. There are seven more I want to get to."

He stared at her, his eyes wide, several of the remaining officials gathering around and nodding as they looked over her maps, instructions, and plans. "Your talents," the governor whispered, "have previously been *wasted,* Lady Ladrian."

What . . . What was this emotion?

Feeling *appreciated?* She'd felt appreciated before by Wax, yes, and occasionally Marasi. But to see it in the eyes of virtual strangers, to have her overplanning seen as a *talent,* not a bizarre character flaw . . .

By the Survivor. This warmth inside. She'd always said she didn't care what people thought of her. And she'd worked hard to build that bubble around herself, a protection against the way she was normally treated.

But this . . . this was a remarkable feeling. Was this what it felt like to be *proud* of who you were? Instead of worried you were embarrassing those around you?

Miraculous.

"What is next?" the governor asked. "What else can we do?"

"I want to sink those ships," Steris said, pointing to the large cargo vessels out in the bay that were waiting to be called in to receive passengers. "After bringing their sailors in safely first, of course."

"Excuse me," one of the remaining foremen said. "*Sink* them?"

"I think it might slow the water," Steris said, "in case of a tsunami. You read what happened to the island of Alicago three years ago? No? Well, anyway, think of speed bumps. Large cargo ships on the surface will glide over the water, or worse be carried with it and slammed into people on the docks. Scuttled on the bay's floor though, they'll create drag and slow the force of the wave if one comes."

Again, instead of objecting or complaining, the foremen simply accepted her explanation—and her orders. Only one seemed concerned. He hesitated as the others began to move off.

"What is it?" Steris asked.

"His Honor the governor," the man said, "told us there wasn't much time left. To get those ships sunk might take hours, ladyship. We'll have to take tugs out to them—not many of the cargo ships have radio yet—and then explain to the captains, probably fight them on it. Then the scuttling process . . . it's not as easy as it sounds. I'd guess four, five hours to get this lot sunk. At least."

Rusts. Well, that wouldn't work.

Someone cleared their throat behind her. One of the eight people who had approached her first. Oh, right—she still didn't know who had sent them, or even who they were.

"Perhaps we can help," the man in the lead said. "You are certain this is legal? The mass sinking of private ships?"

"Yes," the governor said. "On my authority. If we are so fortunate as to have overreacted, the city will pay for the losses incurred by the ship captains."

"Ohhh . . ." Steris said, leaning toward him. "Varlance, that sounded positively *heroic*."

"Really?" he asked, eager. "Heroic?"

"Decisive," she said. "Very leaderlike."

Nearby, the leader of the eight people nodded to her, then launched into the air.

Oh! Allomancers. She had all the official ones working on the main evacuation. But having these to sink ships would certainly help. And then she could use them to help carry the injured or infirm away with Steel-pushes.

The others followed one at a time, until only one remained. He nodded to Steris, and on the back of his hand—mostly obscured—she saw a red tattoo.

"Your sister," the man said, "sends her regards." Then he launched after the others.

That was the last of the meaningful actions Steris could take. From here, she could only make certain her plans were being executed. Everything else rested on Waxillium. None of this would matter if that bomb reached the city.

You'd better be on that ship, Wax, she thought.

71

Clearing the ship proved to be an ordeal. Even worse than that time Wax had decided to teach Wayne "the value of hard work" by making him muck out a stable all on his own. Yeah, he'd learned the value of hard work—it turned out to be three clips. Least, that was what Jeffy had charged to do the job for Wayne.

This time, there was nobody else to do the job. After locking the door to the room with the bomb, they set out to take control of the ship. Wayne kept the key in his pocket, in case Wax had to face another Coinshot.

They didn't meet any. The ship had only a skeleton crew; seemed they'd saved most of their troops to protect the Shaw. It took some time to fight their way to the bridge regardless, given the need to check every corner and flush out people trying to ambush them. Wayne thought every crew member on board had been mustered to try to stop them.

When, half an hour or more later, Wax finally Pushed down the reinforced door to the bridge, they found a disturbing sight. Four people—three women and a fellow—dead on the floor from self-inflicted gunshots. All wore officers' uniforms. They'd killed themselves rather than fall into custody.

"You know," Wayne said, shouldering his rifle, "I thought the weird ones would all be in the Roughs, you know? City folk, they were supposed to be educated. And . . . and refined. And not bleedin' *zealots*."

Wax checked the bodies to be sure, then stepped up to the ship's front controls. They were a confusing mess of levers, along with a giant ship's wheel that appeared to have been locked in place. The ship was still moving at full speed through the mists, and *rusts*. Wayne thought he could see the glow of Elendel on the horizon. They were getting close.

Wax stopped at the controls, then cursed softly.

"What?" Wayne said.

"It's wired to the same system," Wax said. "Harmony? Can you confirm?"

Yes, unfortunately, the god said. *With you to give me sight, I can see that it's wired into the bomb.*

"If we undo the locks on the controls, it blows," Wax said. "I should have foreseen this. We wasted time coming up here."

"But—" Wayne said.

"It makes a brutal sense," Wax said. "They guided the ship here, then locked the course down before killing themselves. The thing will explode the moment it stops—as soon as it hits land. We're not on a traditional ship. This is a *rocket,* like the one they built to fly to Elendel. Self-propelled. Needing no controls. Set to detonate the second it hits."

"Mate," Wayne said, pointing out the front windows. "I see lights."

You have approximately twenty minutes, Harmony said softly, *at current speed.*

"We have to risk trying to defuse the bomb," Wax said, rushing out onto the deck.

Wayne scrambled to follow, tripping on bodies. "Wait! You said that if we tried, we'd almost *certainly* blow the thing!"

"Do you have a better idea?"

"Maybe," Wayne said, halting beside the railing—mists coursing past like a river in the sky.

Wax froze, turning back to him.

Did Wayne have a better idea?

Actually . . . actually he *did.* He looked out at the ocean and realized something. This ship here . . . well, this was a lot like a lone mesa. It fit way better than the Shaw had. Yes, a solitary mesa in the middle of flat lands . . .

And it needed to gobble up the hero.

"You said that this bomb," Wayne said, "it blows up big if detonated proper. But one part of it is ettmetal, right?"

"Harmonium," Wax said. "Yes. And?"

"And that stuff is so unstable, it blows up if *water* touches it. Except in a *smaller* explosion? One that won't level cities and such?"

"It's still bad," Wax said. "But not catastrophic. But if we fiddle with one of the devices by pouring water into it to detonate the ettmetal, the others will simply go off."

"Unless," Wayne said, "we were using a speed bubble. See, there's that device on the wall, right? And if we fiddle with one of the bombs, it's going to detonate the other ones?"

"Right," Wax said.

"So, what if we put up a speed bubble that leaves *out* the device on the wall? We could work on one of the barrels, detonating the harmonium in it so the *real* explosion can't happen. We set that explosion off, then kick *that* barrel out of the speed bubble. It'll send a warning to the other two barrels, but that signal will have to pass along the wires outside the speed bubble, to reach the box on the wall. So the signal will be frozen in time and can't come back! We could work on the other barrels during that time."

"Wayne," he said, "do you have any idea how quickly electricity moves? Even assuming you could do something incredible—like speed up time by a factor of a thousand—that wouldn't be nearly fast enough to outrun an electrical signal."

Oh.

Wait, Harmony said to them. *This could work. I have a way. Wax, I gave you a vial with a red cork.*

"I have it," Wax said, fishing in his sheath of metal vials. He frowned, and came out with . . . a handkerchief.

"Barely used," Wayne said.

"Wayne . . ."

Wayne grinned and handed Wax his rifle, then fished in his pocket. "I thought it needed to be somewhere safe. So I made a nice little trade."

"Harmony," Wax said, "if you can make this work, it will still detonate the ship, right?"

Yes.

"Wayne," Wax said, ". . . setting off the smaller explosions would kill everyone in that room. An ettmetal blast like that isn't something you survive, even if you had full metalminds."

"Ah," Wayne said as the ship hit a wave, water spraying up along the side. "I'd figured out that part. I just needed to know if the idea worked. And I needed to confirm one other thing."

"Which is?" Wax said.

"That the plan doesn't need you, mate," Wayne said, and he Pushed. Shoving Wax—via the barrel of the rifle he was holding—outward off the ship and through the mists. Wayne felt real proud of that Push. He did it like Wax did, crouching down first to give it a little lift.

His friend gave him a look of outrage . . . and maybe regret . . . as he vanished into the misty darkness over the waters.

"Land safely, mate," Wayne whispered. "And survive."

He tipped his hat, then pulled out the red-corked vial. "What the hell is this, anyway?"

Earlier in the week, you all conducted a test, Harmony said. *Splitting harmonium.*

"Same test our enemies have done a hunnerd or more times."

Yes, but this one was different. I have no idea what happened, but Wax did something different from everyone else trying this. Because he didn't merely blow up the room. He created something. Something amazing.

Wayne held up the vial, staring at the metal dust settled at the bottom.

That, Harmony said, *is the faintest bit of lerasium, Wayne. A metal from legend. A metal found by Vin at the Well of Ascension, and used to make Elend Venture a Mistborn. A metal that hasn't existed for centuries, and as far as I know, hasn't been made in millennia. Drink that vial and you'll be a Mistborn, able to use all of the metals. There's a little of each one in there.*

"Why didn't you have Wax drink it earlier?"

I don't want to reveal this happened, as I don't know why or how. I don't know what he did. Besides . . . he might have already had a dose, inhaled during the explosion.

Huh. That explained a few things.

Wayne knocked back the vial. Then he waited. Nothing happened.

"That's anticlimactic," he muttered.

You have to burn the lerasium, Wayne.

Oh, right. He searched, and found a new metal reserve. Neat. He reached out and burned it.

A flash of light.

A fire in his veins.

A feeling like a kick to the face.

Damn.

"How does this help?" he asked.

You can now burn duralumin.

"That fancy metal that not-Wax was using to make those big Steel-pushing explosions?"

Exactly.

"I don't need to Push though."

Wayne, using duralumin burns all the metals in you at once. Every single bit. The more you have, the more powerful it is. It doesn't just work on steel. It works on any Allomantic metal.

Wayne paused, the ship rocking, then whistled softly, understanding. "You mean . . ."

How much bendalloy do you have left?

He fished a pouch out of his pocket.

Hmm. Maybe enough to—

Wayne fished another pouch out of his other pocket.

Okay, and—

And the pouch in his sock. Uncomfortable, but handy.

Wayne, how many pouches do you have?

"Seventeen," he said. "I'm a fancy rich guy now. Will that be enough?"

Oh, Wayne. Yes. I think it will.

Wayne turned and took the steps down at extra-fast speed—grabbing a canteen off one of the corpses. He swallowed mouthfuls of metal beads on his way, stuffing himself with bendalloy. Echoing noises warned him about sailors trying to break into the room to detonate the bomb, but they didn't have a key. He dealt with both men, then burst back into the room. Electric lights flickered on the walls, and he could hear the chugging of the engines somewhere farther inside the ship.

. . . And suddenly he wasn't alone. A figure—mostly transparent—stood beside him, a tall bald man. Terris. And another *darker* fellow stood behind him. Not in the skin tone sense or anything. Like . . . this other one was a shadow. It mimicked Harmony as he held out his hands to Wayne.

"I knew," Harmony said softly, "that I had to bring Wax to Elendel. It is possible to see future needs. I understood it would be *good* to make this choice, though one doesn't always know why. Even if one is a god." He hesitated. "I thought I only needed Wax. It seems that I was wrong."

Wayne tossed up a speed bubble, so that time didn't move so quickly. He needed a moment to compose himself.

"It *should* be Wax," Wayne said. "He's the one that fixes messes like this."

"No," Harmony said. "You have practiced all your life with speed bubbles, Wayne. Wax would be brand new at them. You might be the only person in the world who could do this."

"That's kind of depressing," Wayne said, turning to Harmony. "Really, *I'm* the best you could do? Ain't you God?"

Harmony's eyes softened. "Wayne. You aren't the best I could do. *You're the best there is*. And no being, neither god nor mortal, could have wished for more than one such as you."

Wayne wanted to reject that. But damn, if God was sayin' it . . . maybe . . . maybe Wax was right? About Wayne?

Damn. Had Wax been right *all along*?

"You don't have to do this," Harmony whispered. "I will never again force such a choice upon someone. Unfortunately, it is the only sure solution that I can think of, and my thoughts move with exceptional speed. This preserves, but it . . . destroys."

"The only solution that is sure," Wayne said. "There's another?"

"It is possible—very slightly possible—that you could use your new powers to Push hard enough against upcoming sources of metal to hold the ship back, treading water, while we gain more time and figure something else out. It would be exceptionally difficult, but it's plausible."

"You can see the future," Wayne said. "Would it work?"

"I can see *probabilities*," Harmony said. "I can see what *might* happen. It is, at times, frustrating."

"And . . . what are the chances that other option works?"

"One in a hundred, maybe."

One in a hundred? A one percent chance at survival.

. . . And a ninety-nine percent chance it failed. Meaning a whole ton of people got vaporized.

Damn. What a day to leave his lucky hat behind.

"There's this family what doesn't have a daddy because of me," Wayne said, stepping forward. "You'll take care of them?"

"Of course."

"Will Wax survive this?"

"Normally, no person could," Harmony said. "Considering explosions in water are exceptionally dangerous. Fortunately, this one will be channeled mostly upward—and Wax has pewter now. So long as he burns the metals in those other vials I gave him, he should survive the blast. I will . . . do what I can to help Preserve him. But Wayne, there is nothing I can do for you. This blast will be too big."

Wayne nodded, then hesitated, looking toward Harmony. "Will this . . . earn me forgiveness?"

"Oh, Wayne," Harmony said. "You've heard this from Wax. You have to hear it from me too, I think. You can't do this for forgiveness. You need *no* forgiveness, not anymore."

And . . . he was right.

Wayne wasn't doing this for forgiveness, or out of shame, or out of a need to prove himself. He *wasn't* the man he'd been when Wax pulled him out of his hiding place. He was someone different.

"Wayne," Harmony asked, "do you know who you are?"

"Yeah, I know who I am," Wayne said. "I'm the *God. Damn. HERO.*" He paused. "Sorry."

"Under the circumstances," Harmony said, smiling, "I understand. Each of those barrels has a hole in the top, to draw in air once the explosion starts. The harmonium has been removed from its oil bath and is currently being heated. That means if you pour water in, it will detonate the harmonium. That will destroy the mechanism that heats up the bomb, and will prevent the much greater explosion. Once you pour, use your Allomancy to Push the barrel out of the speed bubble."

"Right, then," Wayne said. "I'm gonna need your hat."

"My . . . hat?"

"Gotta sculpt a speed bubble just right," Wayne said, "and put everything I have into the Push. Burn so much bendalloy in one moment, it practically melts me from the inside—slow time so much, even *electric signals* get dull."

"I don't wear a hat."

"You're God. Improvise somethin'."

Harmony paused, then touched Wayne on the head. He felt it start to glow, as if something had been settled there. Earrings too. He felt earrings like a proper Terrisman wore. Something he'd maybe always been, just in secret.

It wasn't nothin' magical. But when he wore someone's hat, he thought he could understand them. And who was better to understand than God himself?

"Good," Wayne said, adopting the proper accent. Old-fashioned, but Terris. Like Harmony. He dropped his speed bubble and gathered his power. "Hold on to your robes, my dear friend. This is going to be unlike anything you have seen before, I think."

Marasi strode toward Blantach's constabulary offices, Armal and a few of her friends in her wake, through a dark city content with its own business. Ignorant of the crisis.

Yet she felt something in the mists. Wax always talked about them in this supernatural way, a way she rarely felt.

Tonight though, they seemed to be holding their breath.

Steris froze on the docks. Her workers and constables were still busy doing as she asked, but something felt . . . odd? About the moment? She turned toward the waters and looked out across the misty sea.

Gripping the little silver spear she wore at her neck, she said a prayer.

"Now!" Harmony said.

Wayne made the perfect speed bubble. Most Allomancers with his powers couldn't change the shape of a bubble. But bendalloy was so expensive, people couldn't really afford to practice.

He could. He'd probably done this more than any person alive. In that moment, he made a bubble that contained the three barrel devices—but had a hole to exclude the device on the wall that coordinated the explosions.

Then he burned duralumin and *Pushed*.

People didn't often refer to speed bubbles and slowness bubbles as Pushing and Pulling, like they talked about Steelpushes and Ironpulls. But it was the same. What Wayne did, it was Pushing on reality itself. Distorting it, shoving it inward, warping it.

Today he Pushed harder than any person in history. He Pushed like a god, on account of wearing Sazed's own hat. On account of that strange metal, and on account of Wayne bein' the hero. Time squeezed in around him, compressed like coal bein' made into rustin' diamond. Further, further, as a whole damn stomach full of bendalloy was burned in an instant.

God himself froze. Standing motionless. The bubble crystallized into a visible sphere. Lights that had been blinking halted, half-on. Something funny even happened to his eyesight, everything going all strange until he took another vial of Harmony's metals and burned steel to see that way instead.

Go.

Canteen in hand, Wayne flooded the first bomb. He ducked back as the water dripped, then Pushed that barrel right out of the speed bubble as the explosion started. It transfixed him momentarily, fire and light erupting from the barrel, all outlined in these strange blue lines. As if that barrel was releasing its soul to the afterlife.

Cracks started to appear in his crystallized speed bubble. Damn. Wayne leaped to the second barrel and poured, then Pushed it out too. It sent electric warnings up the wires—but the box that controlled the detonation was stuck in slow time, the signals moving like molasses.

Damn, how fast was he moving? And he'd thought he was getting slow because of old age. Heh.

He slammed into the third barrel and dumped the rest of the canteen's water out into it. He Pushed it, then turned, gazing out at all three barrels hanging motionless in time. He was going so fast, only the first one was exploding, and that because he'd taken the longest to Push it out. The blast was completely halted now.

He let out a breath and dropped the canteen. He'd been gobbled up, it was true. But when that happened, you strangled the monster from the inside.

His crystalline speed bubble shattered.

And all became red light and blossoms of fire.

72

Wax struggled in the dark waters.

Then something erupted to his right. A flash of light, blinding and dazzling. Followed by a shock wave in the air, and another in the water. For both, he thought he glimpsed—briefly, through the omnipresent light—the sight of a figure dulling the wave directly in front of him. A calm Terrisman standing tall on the surface of the water, with one hand stretched forward.

Then, darkness again. Wax blinked, his eyes blinded by the blast. Debris rained around him. Splashing into the choppy waves.

In moments, Wax was struggling to stay afloat. He'd hit the water hard, and thought he'd broken at least one leg. Wayne, trying to save his life? That frustrating, infuriating . . .

. . . that wonderful man.

"Farewell, my friend," Wax whispered, choking on his emotion. "You incredible *rusting* man. Thank you."

As the waters grew more choppy, Wax had to struggle harder. He forced through pain, grief, and fatigue to keep himself—barely—afloat. He burned his steel, then . . . something else. Something deep within, which kept him warm.

Despite that, he was lost in darkness, and even the mists kept their distance. With his leg not working, with his coat dragging him down, with the exhaustion of a nation's hopes weighing on him, he felt himself begin to slip. Begin to lose his fight with the waters. Begin to . . .

What was *that*?

A tiny light, drifting closer. Small, yet unyielding in the mists. It resolved into . . . a lantern? On a small boat? How . . .

The boat motored right up to him, and then a man in a coachman's outfit with white gloves stood up on the deck and reached out to Wax.

"Carriage," Hoid said, "for you. Sir."

73

The shock wave hit Steris like a thunderclap. She gasped in surprise, her ears ringing from the sound of the detonation. Rusts.

She and the governor had been carried via Allomancer far into the center of the city—close to their original evacuation command post—following their efforts at the docks. But that obviously hadn't been far enough to escape completely. Around her, windows rattled. Any closer to the docks and they would have shattered. And the buildings nearest the explosion . . .

Fortunately, the only ill effects she felt—standing atop a building this far from the blast—was that shock wave. And so, after her initial panic, she watched that brilliant light in the distance slowly fade.

A moment ago, that explosion had been like a momentary sun on the horizon, magnificent and ominous all at once, blazing through the mists. Now, in seconds, all that remained were the afterimage and the faint ringing in her ears.

The governor peeked up over the rooftop's stone railing, where he'd ducked at the initial explosion. Then he stood up straight. "He's done it, hasn't he? Preservation! He's done it! He detonated the bomb early! The city is saved!"

Steris nodded, exhaling a long breath. Wax had been exactly where she'd hoped he would be. Now that she'd seen that light—then survived the detonation—a new worry struck her.

You'd better not have been on that ship when the explosion happened, Waxillium Ladrian, she thought. *You . . . just . . . just have gotten off, all right?*

"Will the tsunami come?" the governor said.

"Yes," Steris said. "Imminently."

"We . . . uh . . ." The governor straightened his cravat. "We *actually* helped, didn't we?"

"Yes," she said. "The dockside buildings are going to be a disaster zone in the weeks to come—we'll need to rebuild. But I think we evacuated most people from the dangerous section."

Water was pulling back rapidly from the docks as she watched. Receding in advance of a tsunami. Hopefully it would not be a big one. The studies she'd read were inconclusive about how water would react to explosions.

"Thank the Survivor," the governor said. "I'm . . . glad you let us retreat. I worried you'd insist on staying by the docks."

"There is no need to go down with the city," Steris said, "if the city isn't going down."

He nodded eagerly. He was actually quite an agreeable man. Which made sense. He'd been chosen by people who wanted to steer him. People who'd never expected him to put his hands on the helm and take control.

She blinked, her eyes bearing the afterimage of that explosion.

Just . . . be safe . . . Steris thought toward that distant, now faded, point of light. *Please.*

74

Wayne floated.

Floated someplace high. Damn. Was that the planet *itself* beneath him? It *was* a sphere, as everyone said. He'd always hoped maybe it would be, like, doughnut shaped or something. To throw the smart folks for a loop.

Felt kinda strange to be all the way up here, in the darkness. He leaned forward and felt a disorientation, like he should be falling. He was woozy, unsteady.

Huh. Who'd have thought being dead would be so much like being drunk? He could write a whole damn book of scripture about that, he could.

A figure hovered next to him. Vast. His robes like the infinite colors of creation, his essence seeming to expand into the darkness of space itself. But at his core, he had the appearance of a bald, kindly Terrisman.

"Hey, God," Wayne said. "How's . . . um . . . creation? Time and space? Reality? You know, things?"

"Good," Harmony replied. "Because of you."

"Now wait," Wayne said. "I ain't gonna be a *ghost,* am I?"

"No. You were Invested when you died, so you will persist a short time, but will soon join the Beyond."

"Good, good."

"You don't find that idea concerning?"

"Hell no," Wayne said. "I *already* done gone and died. That was the part that I worried would hurt." He gaped down at the planet below. "It's so *big*."

"Yes, Wayne," Harmony said. "I realize that a person might become intimidated, seeing all this. Recognizing the vastness of what they've lived upon. It is a lot to take in, I think. It can make a person feel small, insignificant, and—"

Wayne grinned. "And I saved the whole damn thing!"

Harmony paused. "Well, I suppose you did. With some help from Marasi and Waxillium." Harmony gestured toward a red haze, swirling away from the planet as if in a funnel, vanishing into the distance.

Wayne felt something from it. An angry sort of respect. Begrudging. Her avatar had been defeated, and so Autonomy withdrew her touch from the planet.

"Is that it, then?" Wayne asked.

"For now," Harmony said. "She was overextending to try to bring us down quickly, I think. Telsin and the Set's failure is an enormous setback, and Marasi was quick to collapse the portal to this planet. My vision returns, and I will try to take care I am not blindsided again."

"You sound afraid?" Wayne said, cocking his head.

"Nervous," Harmony said, his expression distant. "I can see pieces moving in the cosmere. Aligning. Pointed at us. We are not free of their influence. But we have . . . time, now. Time to prepare. Thanks to you, Wayne."

"Me," Wayne said. "I saved the *whole damn world*. I . . . I'm probably the best constable who ever rusting lived!"

"I . . . suppose . . ." Harmony said, "that Vin, Elend, and the others weren't constables . . ."

"Wax ain't never saved the whole world. And most of the others in the octant constabulary? They couldn't save a coupon for free beer, even when I gave it to them. Stupid kandra giraffe man. Wayne, the best conner in the whole damn world . . . Ha! Eat that, Reddi. Eat it with hot sauce and *cry*!"

Wayne felt something happening as he said it, though. A kind of . . . stretching feeling. Like he was being pulled somewhere. Somewhere . . . warm?

"Before you go," Harmony said, "is there anything you would like to know? I'm not truly omniscient, but my knowledge far surpasses that of mortals. Some have a final question for me before they go. Have you such a request, Wayne?"

Huh. Any question? That was a hard one. He pondered a moment. "So," he said, "before she left, MeLaan told me that I was the best lay she ever had, and I was wondering—"

"Wayne," God interrupted, "what is it Ranette always says to you?"

"Try dodging this?"

"The other thing."

"Don't ruin the moment by bein' all skeevy?"

"Yes, that one."

"Right, right," Wayne said, nodding. "Good point. Good point. You're smart, maybe even as smart as Ranette. Suppose that makes sense and all." He continued to think, though that stretching sensation . . . it was getting stronger. What could he ask? What . . .

Then he grinned. That was *perfect*.

"I'm gonna assume Wax and them will be fine," Wayne said. "You already promised that. So I ain't going to waste a question on them. And you can't trick me into doing so. You'll take care of them. I know you will."

"To the best of my ability," Harmony said.

"Good. Then tell me this, God," Wayne said, pointing at him. "Was that the *biggest damn explosion* a person ever made?"

Harmony raised an eyebrow. "*That's* your last question? Your final request of God before you pass into eternity?"

"Hell yes! Figure now that I'm dead, I'll get the other answers right soon. You ain't going to trick me into asking a useless question. So tell me. Was it?"

Harmony smiled. "Ah, Wayne. I suppose that most other things that could rival it—like the detonations of the Ashmounts—would be categorized as acts of God. Therefore, I declare that it is. Yes, Wayne. You exploded yourself in the biggest *damn* explosion a person has ever made in the history of our planet."

"Make sure Steris knows," Wayne said, grinning. "She's always complainin' about my exploding things. This time I saved her hide by doin' it. Plus, I made the explosion *smaller*. That's gonna break her brain. I made it smaller, and it was still the biggest one what ever was."

He felt himself really going now. So, he held out a hand to God. Who, smiling, shook it.

"I knew you'd glow," Wayne said, with a wink.

With that, Wayne stretched into another place, into another time. He stretched into the wind. And into the stars.

And all endless things.

EPILOGUES

MARASI

TEN HOURS AFTER DETONATION

Somehow, the sun was already rising again when Marasi stumbled off the train in Elendel. She might have expected the train to be empty, considering the disasters—both prevented and diminished—that had marked the night.

Yet the train was packed. Some traveling to aid those in the water-logged and broken northwestern quarter of Elendel. Others coming to check on family. Others returning home from the evacuation to seek a place of comfort in this strange time.

She let them swarm around her as she stood on the train platform, feeling disjointed. Out of place. Part of that was fatigue. She'd had perhaps two hours' sleep back in Bilming, after coordinating with Constable Blantach, who had finally accepted the evidence of Entrone's malfeasance. The testimonies of the people who Marasi and the others had saved—especially the journalists and politicians who TwinSoul had escorted out—would prove vital.

It felt wrong to leave the lord mayor and his remaining accomplices in the hands of a constabulary department that had up until recently answered to him. But honestly, Marasi wasn't certain what else she could do. An Elendel invasion of Bilming wasn't feasible, considering the disasters and the political situation. She simply had to hope that the testimonies, the explosion, and the overwhelming physical evidence would be enough to force the Bilming constables to do their jobs.

At the least, it seemed that Wax and Wayne had left the Set's organizational structure—and military forces—in shambles. They'd found Telsin dead on the top of the Shaw. Written, by her own fingernail, on the strangely grey skin of her arm had been the words:

You have proven yourselves. For now.

The way her god had left her was eerily reminiscent of how the Ascendant Warrior and the Last Emperor had been discovered at the end of the Catacendre. Strangely peaceful, and . . .

And rusts, Marasi was zoning out. Standing there as confused as a Roughs bumpkin her first time in the city. She forced herself to start walking, moving with the last straggling passengers to leave the train. She needed a bath. She needed something to eat. And she needed . . .

A frantic masked figure burst from the crowd ahead, having fought his way against the flow of traffic. She wasn't certain how he'd talked his way through the ticket gate, but Marasi finally let herself feel a measure of comfort as Allik crashed into her with a powerful embrace.

This, she thought as he held her tight, *was what it was for.* This and a million other people. But to her . . . it had been for this most of all.

Allik pulled back and raised his mask. He'd been crying.

"It's all right," Marasi said, wiping his tears away. "Allik, I'm fine. I promise. I thought you were outside the city?"

"I returned early," he said. "And these tears aren't for you, love. We tried to get word to you, but . . . it was chaotic, and the lines were busy . . ."

Her world started to crack. "Who?" she whispered.

"Wayne," he said.

No. It was impossible.

Wayne was practically immortal. He was like . . . like a rock. The kind you got in your shoe and couldn't get rid of.

No . . . no, he was the kind you leaned against. When you needed something stable. He . . .

He was her partner.

She knew their job was dangerous. She knew they risked their lives each day. Still, she'd always assumed she would be the one who . . . who . . .

"Wax?" she choked out.

"Fine," Allik said. "Well, all but one leg, yah? But he will heal up."

He winced. "He says . . . Wayne stayed behind. Detonated the bomb. To save the city . . ."

She grabbed him then, because that break in his voice matched the one she felt inside her, and she needed to hold to something. As they embraced, she felt grief welling up to destroy her.

She . . . she wouldn't accept it. She wouldn't believe he was gone. He'd . . . he'd survived worse than this. She would come home one day and he'd be sitting in her kitchen helping himself to the chocolate.

And if that never happened?

I can't deal with that right now, she thought. *Not on two hours of sleep.*

She let the delusion linger. So it could erode, like a stone in the waves, over time.

Allik took her by the shoulders. "You," he declared, "look like you are in need of copious amounts of baked goods. Delivered with an urgency rivaling that of a warleader in battle. Yah?"

"Yah," she said, embracing him again. "A thousand times yah, Allik."

An hour later—full of exotic cakes and biscuits—Marasi snuggled in the overstuffed chair of her small flat. She'd finally changed, but not into pajamas. Instead she wore her uniform. Long skirt, blouse, constable's overcoat.

Allik had given that an odd glance before he'd slipped out—with characteristic apologies—to buy a bottle of wine. The thing was, as tired as Marasi had felt, another emotion dominated. A sense of displacement. An awareness that something was *wrong.*

She was struggling to deal with the idea that Wayne was dead. Most of her refused to believe, for her own sanity. That was part of it. There was another part though. A sense that something was unfinished, that a question hung in the balance. One she had to answer before she could truly rest.

So it was no great surprise that soon after Allik left, a knock sounded at the door. It was a young messenger girl, of the variety you could easily hire in town for a few clips. They knew the ins and outs of the many tenements, apartments, and winding streets of the octants better than most postmen.

The girl delivered a small envelope before scampering off. Inside was a card with the symbol of the interlocking triangles. The Ghostbloods. There was an address on the back.

Marasi checked her things. Credentials in her pocket. Handgun in the holster at her side. Insignia on her jacket. She didn't bring a rifle. Today, she didn't need to be armed so much as equipped.

She left a quick note for Allik, promising to return soon, then made her way out into the city. Her city.

She loved Elendel. The sheer variety of people. The way that the broadsheets were already selling the story of the detonation. Some called it a warning shot from the Outer Cities, others a deliberate attempt to cause a flood—as if blowing the city up wouldn't have been a more effective choice. A surprising number actually had the right facts.

DAWNSHOT AND DEPUTY SAVE DAY.

DARING LAST-MINUTE RACE TO SAVE ELENDEL!

BILMING BOMB PREMATURELY DETONATED BY CONSTABLE COURAGE!

She wondered what they'd say when they got hold of her story. A hidden cavern full of kidnapped people being used to try to create Mistborn? Moving photos and Hemalurgic monsters? It was the sort of thing that would fuel broadsheet stories for decades.

She strolled toward her destination. Savoring the scents—good and bad, but always potent—the sounds, the *feel* of a city so alive that even a disaster couldn't stop it.

The Ghostblood base in Elendel was more ostentatious than the one in Bilming. A grand old-school estate, with stained glass and manicured grounds. Marasi was ushered in without needing to knock, then led to a dimly lit room. She assumed she was to sit here and wait, until she noticed someone at the far side. Seated in a comfortable—but enveloping—chair, fine shoes catching the light, his face lost in shadows. But one feature was plain: a single spike pushed through his right eye.

The Survivor himself.

She'd met Death, chatted with kandra, heard Wax speak of Harmony. She was no newcomer to figures from lore stepping out of shadow and into her life. This was different somehow. This was the man who had started it all. The man who had survived his own murder. This was the man she'd been taught to worship and revere.

Here he was. And it was the most intimidating experience of her life. She tried to speak, and found her mouth dry.

The door opened and TwinSoul entered, stabilizing himself against the door handle. Though she'd known him only a short time, it still felt right to give him a hug, which he returned.

"It is good to see you well, my lady," he said to her. "And to hear of your accomplishments."

"Oh!" Marasi said. "TwinSoul. Moonlight, she—"

"We've heard reports," TwinSoul said. "She was . . . forced to use her stamp?"

"Yes," Marasi said.

"She will be difficult to recover," Kelsier said from the shadows. "I may have permanently lost my best agent to this fiasco."

Marasi's first instinct was to rush to apologize. She stopped herself. "You'd rather we let the invasion happen?"

Kelsier leaned forward, and she thought she caught a hint of a *smile* on his lips. Perhaps the stories were true. That he might be a brutal man, but he wasn't a *stern* one. But who knew? Could you really trust stories from hundreds of years ago? And if you could, surely a man changed after living—or, well, not staying dead—for four centuries.

"Go ahead, TwinSoul," Kelsier said.

"Marasi Colms," TwinSoul said, "I am proud to offer you membership in the Ghostbloods. If you accept, I would be honored to become your mentor, as is our tradition. You may join me on my next mission, to track Moonlight down and attempt to restore her natural personality."

"This offer comes with access to everything the Ghostbloods know," Kelsier said. "We don't keep secrets from one another."

"Even you, Survivor?" Marasi asked, curious. "Do *you* keep secrets?"

He didn't respond to that. But he did smile again.

"There is lore and arcana we have access to," TwinSoul said, "that will delight and awe you, my lady. Our duties lead us to fascinating places— all in the service of the very thing you want: protecting Scadrial."

"It is not an invitation," Kelsier added, "that we extend lightly."

So here it was. The question. Did she accept? Lately, she'd wanted so badly to do something more. Every glimpse she got of the larger conflicts—the larger cosmere—made her want to see it in full. Like a woman peeking at a sunset through a slit in the wall.

And yet.

"How long," she said, "did you know about the Set? How long did you know what they were trying to do? Who Trell was?"

Silence.

"We provide answers," TwinSoul said, "*after* oaths, my lady. It is our way."

"Did you share with Harmony?" Marasi asked.

"Saze," Kelsier said, "is . . . erratic lately. There's a problem brewing with him. One I fear is going to make even today's events seem trivial by comparison. We must, unfortunately, work in secret. We are too small, too weak, as of yet. In the open, forces in the cosmere would crush us."

She didn't disagree, not entirely. Every lawwoman understood the need to work covertly at times.

And yet.

Marasi turned their card over in her fingers, then held it up and looked at the interlocking bloodred diamonds.

Was this really what she wanted? She'd been dissatisfied in her service on occasion. But was there any job you *didn't* dislike now and then? As she turned the card over again, she remembered why she'd first become a constable. Not just to solve crimes. To solve problems. To make the world a better place, not merely protect it.

She couldn't do that from the shadows, could she? Others might be able to, but Marasi? She'd have to lie to so many people. That violated the fundamental oaths she'd taken.

Have you appreciated it? Armal had asked. That question haunted Marasi.

"Once," she said, "about seven years ago, I thought everything I'd ever wanted had fallen into my lap. I *thought* I'd figured out what I wanted. Then he walked away. That rejection was among the best things that ever happened to me."

"My lady?" TwinSoul said.

"I guess," Marasi continued, "it's hard to know what you want. We never have all the information. We merely have to do what we can with what we have." She met Kelsier's shadowed gaze. "If I join, will you let me share what I discover with the constabulary?"

"What do you think?" Kelsier asked.

"I think," she said, "that I am a servant of the people." She moved to set the card on the table beside the door. "That any power or authority I have comes from them. They are not served by darkness and lies, no matter how well intentioned."

"Be careful," Kelsier said before she could put the card down. "Are you *certain* this is what you want?"

"No," she said. "My job isn't to be certain. My job is to do the best I can. Even with limited information." She dropped the card.

She still needed to find something. An answer for herself. But this *wasn't* it.

"I'm a servant of the government," Marasi said, "and of the law. Things that you, I believe, have historically had a problem with, Survivor. I appreciate your help on this mission. I'd accept it again in the future." She shook her head. "But I'm not a good match for your organization. I won't keep secrets when the truth could save lives."

She needed to know what was hidden here—but she was a detective. She'd find answers without selling her soul. Even if it was to the Survivor himself.

Kelsier did not seem like the type of man who appreciated being rejected. But he did eventually nod in acceptance. She shook hands with TwinSoul, offered to help him with Moonlight anyway, then let herself out.

Back into the city.

Back to the people of Elendel.

And as she walked among them—hearing their concerns, their fears, their uncertainty—she remembered things she'd lost to the doldrums of daily work. Plans for her life she'd followed for years, but had eventually grown beyond.

Had she grown back into them, then? Wiser, more understanding, more nuanced?

It was then, wrung out and exhausted, yet victorious, that she realized what she wanted.

All she needed was a plan.

Prasanva—TwinSoul—watched her go, then shook his head. Unfortunate. And also remarkable. He liked seeing people uphold their personal codes. The aethers, after all, had created all people to think differently from one another.

As the main hallway door shut outside—and Marasi Colms left—Dlavil eased from the shadows behind Kelsier's seat. The short man bore an intricate and fearsome mask, wooden and painted—but when he spoke, his accent was not that of the Southern Scadrians. It was of Silverlight.

"We will need to deal with her," Dlavil said softly.

"She is a woman of integrity," TwinSoul said. "I will not permit harm to come to her."

"She knows our secrets," Dlavil said. "She knows this base. She saw what you and Moonlight can do. She glimpsed the maps, the powers, the knowledge. She is dangerous to us now."

"We offered these things freely," TwinSoul said, "and although she rejected us, she did *not* take from us. Master Kelsier, rein him in."

"Enough, Dlavil," Kelsier said, flicking on the light and leaning back in his seat. "TwinSoul is right. She knows nothing that couldn't be learned from a cursory exploration of the cosmere. We might have to move bases, but that's our own fault. Moonlight was so certain she'd join."

Dlavil held his tongue, his eyes inscrutable behind that cursed mask. TwinSoul hated being unable to get a full read on the man's expressions, but Dlavil—like his sister who ran amok on Roshar—wore a mask that he never removed; it was grown in to the point that it was practically part of his skin.

"I mean it, Dlavil," Kelsier said. "You will *not* move against her, or anyone in this city, without my permission. You understand?"

"Yes, Lord Kelsier," Dlavil said, and withdrew through the back door.

Kelsier sighed audibly, rising from his seat. He joined TwinSoul beside the window, where they looked out at the city.

"Good work yesterday," Kelsier told him. "Very good work, old friend. We almost lost everything."

TwinSoul bowed his head in acceptance of the praise. It felt good.

You are blessed, Silajana said in his mind. *And worthy of commendation.*

That felt even better.

"It should never have gotten this far," Kelsier said. "Something *is* wrong with Sazed. It's getting worse."

"What do we do, my lord?" TwinSoul asked.

Kelsier narrowed his eye. "I," he whispered softly, "am going to have to have a difficult conversation with 'God.'"

STERIS

TWO DAYS AFTER DETONATION

On the second day of the city's recovery, Steris finally got to bring Waxillium home from the hospital. They limped out of Hoid's car, Wax on crutches, then looked up at the enormous skyscraper that held their suite. Wax stared at it, his eyes faintly haunted.

"Thinking of the Shaw?" Steris asked softly.

He nodded. "On that rooftop, Wayne made me get him a spike. If I hadn't listened, he wouldn't have been able to Push me away."

"So you could have done what?" she said gently. "Stayed with him to die? He knew what he needed to do."

Wax looked to her, and she saw the same pain in his eyes that she'd seen after Lessie's second death. Tempered this time, but haunting nonetheless. She hated seeing him in pain. It happened far too often.

"I should have at least said goodbye," Wax whispered. "He left the Roughs because of me . . ."

"And he lived because you gave him a second chance," Steris said. As he was staring up at the roof, she covertly consulted her notes from the books on trauma she'd been reading. "This wasn't your fault, Waxillium. You need to allow Wayne his agency, allow him to have made his own choice. You would have sacrificed yourself for the city; we both know it. So let *him* have the same decision."

He was silent for a moment, and she tried—anxiously—to figure out what he was feeling. Was that scrunched-up face annoyance? Or was it pain? Ruin, had she made it worse?

"You're right," he said softly, then blinked tears from his eyes. "You're right, Steris. I need to let him be the hero, don't I? Harmony . . . he really *is* gone."

She slipped her notebook into her pocket and held him close, ignoring the world around them. She dimmed everything else, like an old gas lantern with a dial. Turned it down until only the two of them remained. Only the two of them mattered.

He held to her, then took a long, deep breath. "Marasi still doesn't believe he's gone. She thinks he's going to come sauntering back in a few months, wearing a straw hat and telling us how great the fruity drinks are in the Malwish Consortium. But she's wrong. This time it's over."

"Yes," Steris whispered. "He's gone. But *nothing* is *over,* Wax. You said the same thing when Lessie died. It wasn't true then. It's not true now. It will take time for you to believe, but you can trust that it will happen."

He squeezed her hand. "Again, you're right. How *did* you get so good at this, Steris?"

"I learned from Wayne."

"About . . . helping people deal with pain?"

"No," she said, then slipped out her notebook. "About cheating."

Waxillium smiled. The first genuine one she'd seen from him since the incident. Then he handed her his crutches and dropped a spent bullet casing to the ground.

"Oh!" she said. "Are you sure this is wise?"

"I might be getting old, but I'm not frail," he said, then grabbed hold of her. "You ready?"

"Always," she said, feeling an exquisite thrill from anticipating the flight. She leaned into him.

He propelled them upward, using the metal installations he'd had erected here to give him a series of appropriate anchors. A rushing, exhilarating ascent with wind in her hair, and the insignificant world became more tiny. Until it was only the two of them and the sky.

Wax landed them carefully on the platform outside their suite. As he took back his crutches, Steris fished for her notebook.

"I think . . ." Wax said. "I think I'm going to be all right."

"Good," she said, flipping a few pages. "I have a Wayne quote for the moment."

"A what?"

"I figured," she said, "it would be a way of remembering him. To keep a few appropriate lines handy. Is that . . . morbid? That's morbid, isn't it? I'm sorry."

"No," he said. "I mean, it might be, but he'd approve."

She grinned. "'Oi,'" she said. "'Here you carried a girl all that way, mate, and you didn't grab 'er butt, even a little?'"

"You just made that one up."

She proffered the notebook, showing the line written there.

"Well, I mean," Wax said, "we've got to do as he says."

"It's the only proper way to honor the dead."

He seized her then, pulled her into a kiss, her figure sculpting to his and pushing against him in all the right places. It felt amazing—like they were liquid, aligned, alive, alight.

And yes, a proper butt-grab was involved. It almost toppled them to the side, unbalancing Wax on his good leg. They broke the kiss before an accident could befall them, but stayed close.

"Thank you," Wax whispered. "For being you."

"It's the only thing I am good at," she said. "Other than throwing cows at people."

Wax frowned.

"That is something Wayne said on occasion," she said.

In response to that, he looked to the sky. "Thank you, Wayne. Wherever you are. For letting me have this. For *making* me live."

She forced him inside then, so he could sit. He wasn't supposed to put weight on that leg, cast or no cast. Even if he could cheat by making himself lighter.

Unfortunately, Kath had been a little quicker than she'd expected, and the kids were already back from the Harms estate down-Basin. So Wax, in flagrant disregard for medical instructions, knelt and scooped Max up in an embrace.

"Daddy!" Max said. "You did it! Kath says you did it!"

"Did it?" he asked.

"Stopped the bad guys! Saved the world!"

"I suppose," Wax said, "I did a little of both. Wayne helped a lot though."

"Jennid at school," Max continued, "says that you're *also* supposed to get the girl when you save the world. But that part is stupid. I don't like girls."

"What?" Wax said. "Not even Mommy?"

"Dad," Max said, with an exaggerated sense of long-suffering—as if this were the most obvious thing a boy had ever had to describe. "Mommy's not a *girl*, she's a *mom*."

Steris smiled, moving over by Kath as Wax took little Tindwyl and held her tight, letting her grab at his sideburns.

"This came for you," Kath said softly, taking a letter from her handbag. "A short time ago. It looked important."

"Thank you," Steris said, taking the letter—which was addressed to her—and noting the governor's seal on the front.

Her panic was immediate. She'd worried about this. She'd written down the possibility, but surely it wouldn't . . . it couldn't . . .

She ripped it open, her hands shaking with terror. He'd need a new vice governor, now that he'd formally fired Adawathwyn. *Surely* he wouldn't . . .

Dear Steris Harms Ladrian,
    I would like to meet with you and discuss a possible appointment in my government. Considering your invaluable service during the recent crisis—

Oh no. Oh *no*. Not that.

—I have decided to ask you to accept a position as the city's Disaster Preparations Officer. I would assign you a seat on my council and provide a task force for your use, ensuring the city is prepared and outfitted for any and all potential disasters or relevant dangers.
    Please reply with times that will work for you, so we can sit down and talk. On a more personal level, I'd like to give you my most sincere thanks. I am being hailed as a hero and a decisive leader. I would not deserve either of those accolades without your intervention.

Disaster . . . Preparations Officer?
She blinked.
Why . . . that wasn't terrifying at all.

That might actually be *fun*.

Wax gave Tindwyl to Kath, then hobbled over to Steris—nodding passively as Max explained at length about the new marbles game he'd been playing. Looking over her shoulder, Wax read the letter, then took her by the elbow.

"Steris," he said, "that's *wonderful*."

"I don't deserve it," she said. "The tsunami wasn't nearly as bad as I'd feared it would be."

"Love," Wax said, "you *do* deserve it."

She turned to look him in the eyes.

"What if instead of quoting Wayne," he said softly, "we honored him in a different way. What if we decided to make an effort to let ourselves be happy? What do you think of that, Lady Ladrian?"

"I think, Lord Ladrian, I should like that very, *very* much."

And she could already imagine an entire list of plans to make certain it happened.

ALLRIANDRE

FIVE DAYS AFTER DETONATION

Allriandre climbed the steps one at a time. Feet like lead. Legs like slag. Back bowed, as if weighed by bars of steel. Her ashen clothing bore a few new marks from the forges, which threw sparks when she passed. Her job didn't involve working those—she sorted bits of metal for melting down.

When she arrived at her small flat—on the seventh floor, in a building with no elevator—she could already hear Miss Coussaint yelling. Despite her exhaustion, Allriandre picked up her pace. She hurried to the door and threw it open, to where her daughter, Ruri—three years old and still small for her age—huddled in her blankets. Terrified again.

"Why would you think *toothpaste* was for *drawing*?" Miss Coussaint shouted. She was a woman with a hierarchy of chins, the last—most swollen—one lording over the others like a terrible regent. She glanced up as Allriandre entered, then held up the toothpaste jar. "Did you *see* what she did *this time*?"

"I'm sorry," Allriandre said, exhausted, but she scooped up Ruri as she came running into her arms to escape. "Thank you for watching her."

Coussaint looked her up and down, noting the dirty face, scraggly hair, burned clothing. "Rent?" she demanded. "It's been three days."

"He's never been late with a payment before." Wayne, the man who'd murdered her father. "I'm sure he'll show up soon."

"I need to do some renovations," Coussaint said. "Maybe when he comes, you can—"

"Thank you, Miss Coussaint," Allriandre said, stepping aside so the woman could leave. "For watching her. It is an enormous help."

The woman huffed, but squeezed out of the room and went clomping down the steps. Allriandre pulled her daughter close, and thought for a moment about her choices. About how the best schooling in the city didn't mean much when you were in debt to the wrong people. About how something you loved so much—like the girl she held to now—could also be a reminder of one of the greatest mistakes you'd ever made.

She was exhausted, but she plopped Ruri down, and together the two of them painted with toothpaste on the wall until the girl was laughing again. Until Ruri understood that mistakes could sometimes turn into amazing, wonderful, cherished things. With the right perspective.

A knock came at the door.

Allriandre froze, then quickly wiped her hands on a rag. She hadn't been expecting anyone. Rusts, she barely *knew* anyone. All of her university friends had gone on to marriages, office jobs, and nights spent socializing. Her family still lived out in the Roughs, and she'd made sure they didn't know what had happened to her. Because they had their own problems.

She opened the door hesitantly and saw two men in suits outside— one tall, one short. Her stomach immediately dropped. Were these Bleaker's new collection men? They usually showed up a week *after* she received her monthly payment.

"Miss Allriandre?" the shorter of the men asked. "I am Mister Call, and this is Mister Daring, of Call and Son and Daughters Accounting and Estate. Might we come in? We have a matter of some importance to discuss with you."

"I don't have the money yet," she said quickly. "I can't pay you until I do. There's nothing in here for you to take."

The two shared a glance, then the shorter man gestured again. She reluctantly let them in.

"If you," she whispered, "hurt my daughter . . ."

"We are not who you appear to think we are," the taller man said with a cheerful air, looking at the toothpaste-covered wall, then the ragged furnishings. "We represent the estate of Master Wayne Terris-born of 662 Inkling Lane."

"Oh," she said, feeling relieved. "Him. Wait. Did he finally get smart and decide to stop insisting that I meet him in person?"

"Indeed he did," the taller man said, setting his bowler hat on the counter. She winced, noticing the mushed-up apple Ruri had dropped there. The little girl came and climbed into her arms. Strangers made her nervous.

"Why are you late?" Allriandre asked. "His payments always come on the first of the month."

The taller one coughed. "You haven't heard? You . . . don't read the broadsheets?"

"Do I *look* like I have time for broadsheets?" she asked. "If you have my payment, that's great. I could use it. But I *really* need some sleep. So . . ."

"Miss Allriandre," the shorter man said, "Master Wayne passed last week. It was quite spectacular—he was the one who detonated the bomb. Did you hear about that?"

She'd heard rumblings of it at the forges. Not his part in it. But the whole flood and, and the evacuations . . . and . . . Wait.

"He's dead?" she asked.

They nodded.

Rusts. How did she feel about that? Happy? The man who had killed her father was finally dead. She should be overjoyed, shouldn't she?

Instead she felt confused. A little angry still, yes. That would never leave her. A hint of relief. But mostly . . . sorry. Sorry for how it had all turned out. Sorry that wounds long dulled sent a pang through her now and then. Sorry for mistakes. Mistakes didn't always turn into something better, not by a long mile. But she could understand now how they happened. Even the big ones.

The taller man set a large folder onto the room's only table. "Shall we?" he asked.

"Shall we what?" she replied.

"Miss Allriandre," the shorter man said, "you are the primary beneficiary of Master Wayne's estate."

"What's that amount to?" she asked. "Three balls of gum and an unpaid bar tab?"

"Currently," the tall one said, "it's twenty million boxings—liquid—

along with majority stake ownerships in several important holdings, equating to at least another hundred."

The room fell silent save for Ruri's sniffling, which the girl solved by wiping her nose on Allriandre's jumpsuit. Allriandre barely noticed.

"Did you say . . . *a hundred and twenty million?*" she whispered.

"Give or take, depending on the market," the taller man said. "He invested wisely—in a brilliant way, actually, against most conventional wisdom—using a considerable amount of aluminum as collateral. Turns out electricity, fabrication, and power were the place to be six years ago."

The shorter man pulled over a chair for her. "Please," he said softly. "Sit down. We have some things to go over."

"A *hundred and twenty million,*" she repeated, her eyes wide, barely able to think. Her debts—from her failed art studio—equated to barely ten thousand.

"Yes," the taller man said, setting out some papers. "By my estimation, you have become the fourth-richest person in the city." He looked up. "There are a few holdbacks, mind you. Accounts that Master Wayne set aside for other things. But that equates to less than five hundred thousand in total. Everything else . . . well, it's yours."

She sank down into the chair.

The short man pushed over a note. Handwritten, stained with something. "He wanted you to have this."

It simply said, *Sorry.*

As if that could explain all of this. Overwhelmed, she took the note, then held it close to her chest. With money, she could bring her family to Elendel. Resolve their problems. Build the life for them all that she'd promised when they'd put everything into sending her to the city.

Ruri grabbed at the card, getting toothpaste on it.

"What are the holdbacks for?" Allriandre asked. "Not that I'm complaining. I'm merely curious."

The two shared a look.

"Various things," the shorter man said. "Each one of an . . . individual nature."

KELSIER

THREE WEEKS AFTER DETONATION

Kelsier, the Survivor, liked high places. Fortunately, the city as it had become contained plenty of them.

He was one of the few who could remember a time when the grand keeps of Luthadel had been considered lofty, stretching up sixteens of feet into the air. Today they would be quaint compared to the city's dominating skyscrapers. The monoliths of modernity.

Kelsier didn't see quite as he once had. One eye saw as a mortal, the other as an immortal. His spiked eye not only pinned his soul to his bones, but gave him a constant overlay of blue, letting him see the world as a being like Sazed did. Outlining not only sources of metal, but all things. The very axi that made up matter had their own polarity, influenceable with Steelpushing under the right circumstances.

One eye of the gods. One eye of the common men. As he had always tried to see the world.

He had a spectacular view from the top of the skyscraper today. He could remember the joy, the *freedom* he'd felt all those years ago when he'd first crested the top of the mists and seen the stars. Now, those stars were naked and bare most nights. Even if the mists were out, it wasn't too hard to find a building that reached up beyond them, presenting them to full view. Stars. Suns. Planets.

Each one a potential threat.

A figure walked along the edge of the skyscraper's top toward Kelsier. Harmony wasn't accompanied by his dark double, the shadowy version that sometimes appeared these days. A representation of his other self.

"Marsh is going to live," Sazed said, settling down beside Kelsier. If you didn't look directly at him, you could *almost* ignore the fact that his essence extended into eternity.

Sazed spoke like he always had, though he was literally a god now. Kelsier wasn't certain if that was because Harmony presented a personality that was familiar to Kelsier, to put him at ease. Or if the man who had once been Kelsier's friend was actually the same person somehow.

"Marsh will live," Kelsier said, musing. "Does that mean we have atium again? Or did you find another way?"

"The kandra found atium dust in Waxillium's destroyed laboratory," Sazed said. "It appears that if you detonate harmonium against trellium—or, I suppose bavadinium would be its true name—it creates some small amount of atium as a by-product."

"Lerasium?" Kelsier asked.

"I'm sorry. That is all annihilated in the explosion. We've tested it several times now."

Damn. Another dead end.

"It wouldn't work on you anyway," Sazed said. "Not in your current state."

"Doesn't matter, Saze," Kelsier said. "We need Allomancers—*real* Allomancers, like in the old days—to face what is coming. This problem with Trell never would have happened if we'd had proper Metalborn."

"So you agree with the Set?" Sazed said. "And their monstrous undertakings in the name of creating Metalborn?"

Did he? It was difficult to say. Sometimes to make an omelet, you had to break a few skulls. He didn't like what the Set had done to innocent people, and would never condone such actions. But if Hemalurgy was demanded, there was always someone around who was the strict *opposite* of innocent.

"You don't know where the Set's experiments could have led," Sazed said. "Even the simple act of trying to breed Allomancers . . . it leads to darkness, Kell. Trying to create perfect people through forced breeding? You don't have to be Terris to find that idea nauseating."

"Perhaps Ruin and Preservation should have thought about that before giving genetically derived powers to only part of the population. My goal is to democratize this. Take the power away from the few, give it to the many."

Lerasium would have been the easiest way, but it seemed he would have to keep hunting. That gave him hope for himself though. Lerasium wouldn't have worked on him, and Hemalurgy had proven ineffective on what he'd become. It held his soul and body together, but no more.

There had to be another way. He had hope. Ever, he had hope. Hope he could control the metals again. Hope he would be able to soar again. Hope he'd be able to touch the metals he could see in the world all around him.

The two sat in silence for a time. They did that more and more, during their infrequent meetings. Perhaps because both knew it was better than arguing.

"I'm fond of heights," Kelsier eventually said. "More so than when I was fully mortal. Perhaps a part of me holds a grudge against the ground, and what she did to me in those caves. Maybe I just try to get as far from her as possible." He paused. "Explosions to make atium. I wonder if there will ever be a way to get it that *isn't* traumatic."

Sazed didn't reply.

"How could you let it get this far, Saze?" Kelsier eventually asked. "This was almost the end."

"I had it in hand."

"Like hell you did. You're lucky that lawman could function after what you put him through six years ago. Lucky that the other one was a Slider. I still can't figure out how he managed that partial detonation in the ship's hold."

"Luck is a different thing for a god who can see futures, I think," Sazed replied softly.

"Immaterial. This ran to the last minute. You should have stopped Trell *years* ago. But you didn't. Why?"

Sazed stared out over the city. Beyond the city. To things Kelsier couldn't see, even with the eye of a god.

"You can't protect this world, Saze," Kelsier said. "We have to face it. Something's happening to you."

"I have it in hand."

"Do you? Do you *really*?"

Sazed remained there, seated, with his eyes closed. And damn, looking at him was disorienting. On the surface was his friend, the calm Terrisman. But he *extended*. Somehow he was the very stone they were sitting on. The city. The planet. And *beyond*.

And there was a darkness within him. A different face from the one he showed. The powers were in imbalance. Ruin had always been stronger.

"What would you have me do?" Sazed asked.

"There are potential allies out there," Kelsier said. "Moonlight's world, perhaps. Or the land of the aethers. Hell, maybe even Mythos. We need a way to reach them."

"Shadesmar—"

"Is unreliable," Kelsier said. "I know you're barely able to get the kandra out into the wider cosmere; it's untenable for large-scale travel. Besides, crossing it anymore is like walking into the hands of various gods who absolutely want us dead. There's got to be a better way."

"What are you proposing?" Sazed asked.

"Lead us into a new technological age," Kelsier said. "Help us find ways to defend ourselves, and perhaps accomplish even more. Autonomy consistently shares with her people the things they can accomplish with electricity and industry. You don't."

"People should discover it on their own," Sazed said. "If they do not, there are subtle consequences. We should let the decades play out, becoming centuries, and let humankind find their own path to the cosmere—"

"No," Kelsier said. "We can't wait centuries; we can barely wait decades. If you don't do something, we *will* discover technology on our own—when enemy armies bearing it arrive to destroy us. Lead us to a revolution, Saze. Bring us into a new world."

"The one we've arrived at isn't progressing quickly enough?"

"What do *you* think?" Kelsier asked. "Another few weeks, and they'd have had that rocket working, wouldn't they? They'd have delivered it straight into the heart of Elendel, and millions would have been vaporized—and we'd have never known it was possible. Well, none of us but you."

Sazed looked down. "I will . . . consider."

"Consider?" Kelsier said. "This is all going to get worse, unless we can stand against the outsiders. Yes, their army withdrew from Shadesmar—you're welcome for my people's help with that, by the way—but only because Autonomy is regrouping.

"They're going to come back, and we need to be ready. With technology. More, with our most powerful resource. We *need* Allomancers and Feruchemists. Is there a way to expand our access to Metalborn? They have the seed inside them, don't they? The heart of Preservation?"

"I don't know," Sazed whispered.

"Are you lying?"

"Have I ever lied to you, old friend?" Sazed opened his eyes and met his gaze, showing infinity within those depths.

"I," Kelsier said, "am going to protect our people. Whatever it costs. Please tell me I won't ever have to protect them from you."

"That depends," Sazed said, "entirely upon you, old friend."

RANETTE

SIX MONTHS AFTER DETONATION

Ranette's honeymoon had been dreadful. Full of *relaxing* and *reading books* and *seeing sights* in Malwish. Not a single gun. She'd barely been allowed to draw schematics and designs.

"You'd better appreciate this," she grumbled to Jaxy as the car pulled up to their place in Elendel.

"You liked it," Jaxy said, poking her in the side. "Don't pretend you didn't like it."

"Having fun gets boring too quickly," Ranette muttered.

"Just think how refreshed you are," Jaxy replied. "How many ideas flowed when you didn't have to worry about deadlines or delivery dates!"

"I like deadlines," Ranette said.

Jaxy eyed her.

"Fine," Ranette said. "It wasn't *awful*. It was *almost* enjoyable. Even if that place is weird. I wish Wax hadn't discovered it. Then maybe we'd have gone to the Roughs."

"The Roughs," Jaxy said. "For our *honeymoon*."

Ranette shrugged. "You're the one who likes that dumb restaurant."

Jaxy rolled her eyes as the car—strangely—didn't stop at their place. It kept driving.

"Wait," Ranette said, turning and looking back.

"There's something you need to see," Jaxy said.

"This isn't more 'fun,' is it? I'm so full of it by this point, I feel like barfing it all right back out."

"You are *so* romantic," Jaxy said, taking her arm.

Ranette huffed. Well, she'd been careful not to spoil the actual honeymoon with this kind of behavior. She'd been *nice* and *enjoyable* and *perky*.

Okay. Not perky. But *not grouchy*. Most of the time. And admittedly, the Southern Continent *had* been something special. Even if tensions were . . . well, growing tenser. There was constant talk of closing the borders to Northerners. It seemed that tourism was at an end.

Regardless, they were home now. This was *supposed* to be her time to gripe. That was how a relationship worked. Push and Pull. She'd given. Now she could take a little. Now she could . . .

"What the *hell*?" she asked as the car came to a stop outside her shop. A little place on a small plot of land—which had been expanded somehow to a *very large* place on a small plot of land.

"A wedding gift," Jaxy said.

"How in the world did you afford this?" Ranette said, throwing the door open and stumbling out.

"I didn't. It's not from me."

Ranette looked back.

"Some nice men showed up," Jaxy explained, "with a sum from Wayne. After . . . you know. They said I was supposed to do something nice for you, but—the instructions said clearly—'Not in a skeevy way.' He suggested a renovation to the shop."

Ranette couldn't help smiling at that. She had been surprised by how much she'd missed Wayne. Once he had learned—shockingly, people *could* learn—how to not be slime, they'd actually become friends.

Of course, he'd gone out in the most incredible explosion ever. So she hadn't felt *that* bad. If you had to die, then hell, that was the way.

She was still trying to figure out how to get her hands on some of those explosives. The things she could build with something that packed that much of a punch . . .

"He left a note," Jaxy said, handing it to her.

Hey, it said. In crayon. *These two fellows in suits told me I gotta write this and make decisions about this stuff, just in case. Apparently they think* my job is "high risk." I told them that if they wanted their jobs to become high risk, they should try pushin' me harder to do stupid stuff.

But . . . I guess, if you're readin' this, I'm done and gone. Buried. Maybe burned. Maybe I got eaten. I dunno. Whatever happened, I hope it's Marasi's fault, because she's always tellin' me I'm gonna get her into trouble and it would be nice if that hat were on her head instead.

Anyway . . . I want to say thanks. For not throwin' the Wayne out with the Wayne, ya know? Enjoy the gift. Build something real awesome.

"Damn," she said, putting her hands on her hips. "I really do miss that little miscreant."

Jaxy smiled, leaning into her, holding to her arm. "Ranette. That was almost *kind*."

"I mean it. I miss him." She smiled. "Wasn't ever a person I've known who was more fun to shoot."

MELAAN

NINETEEN MONTHS AFTER DETONATION

The messenger flitted off across the dark ocean of Shadesmar, glowing faintly.

MeLaan sat in a boat kept afloat by some kind of glowing substance on the hull. The blackness beneath was like a liquid, more viscous than water. It was supposed to be perfectly transparent—if a person slipped into it and sank, you were said to be able to watch them fall, and fall, and fall.

"Do you know," MeLaan said, "what those messengers even *are?*"

"An Invested entity," her guide said, "which can read Connection to find anyone, anywhere."

"That's . . . kind of unnerving."

Her guide—Jan Ven—shrugged. She was a creature with four arms, chalk-white skin, and large almost reptilian eyes. Her white hair was wide, like blades of grass. Sho Del were apparently rare out here, but made excellent guides. Something about having a direct line to their gods.

The envelope was stamped with the words SILVERLIGHT MERCANTILE. Inside she found a note from Harmony. Short, to the point, empathetic. Wayne had stopped the attack on the city. And had died in the process.

Her breath caught. She found herself trembling.

Rusts. She was supposed to be better than this. Immortal. Stoic. Why couldn't she be like the others?

She'd known she wouldn't see him again. But this? She'd wanted him to find someone else. For his own good. And if she was being honest, for her own good. Because he made her forget what she was. Because with him the world was too interesting, and that made her forget what was smart.

Dead? He . . .

It was supposed to have been a mere fling. She was just too damn awful at being immortal. She folded the letter, then placed it carefully into her jacket.

"Bad news?" Jan Ven asked, paddling them softly across the infinite black expanse.

"Yes," MeLaan whispered.

"Do you want to put off the landing?"

MeLaan turned. There was *land* ahead. And lights that seemed too alive for the cold fire of this strange place. People crowded around, hundreds of them, with strange outfits, many with odd red hair. Lost.

This was her task. To save those people.

"No," MeLaan said, standing. "I have a duty here."

After all, she could remake, rebuild, and regenerate her heart. That was what her kind did.

WAXILLIUM

TWO YEARS AFTER DETONATION

The most difficult thing about commissioning Wayne's statue had been deciding which hat it should be wearing. In the end, the answer had been obvious. They had to make it changeable.

So it was that Wax and Steris stood before a remarkably accurate bronze depiction of Wayne wearing a removable bronze version of his lucky hat. He was larger than life-size, smiling slyly, with an outstretched hand. Likely so that he could pick your pocket with the other, but most people would think he was offering help.

They figured they'd replace the hat once a year. Keep things fresh, interesting. It wasn't the official unveiling yet, but the artist had let Wax and Steris come to see it. Fences kept others away as they promenaded along the Field of Rebirth at the very hub of Elendel. The knoll where people had first emerged after the remaking of the world.

The statues of the Ascendant Warrior and the Last Emperor were just far enough away that if Wayne's had been alive, he could have hit them on the backs of their heads with an occasional thrown pebble. That seemed appropriate.

Steris knelt down to read the inscription.

"'You're meant to be helping people,'" she read, then noticed a second, smaller inscription plaque at the bottom, near the base. Wax winced as she read this one too.

"'Ain't no fellow who regretted giving it one extra shake,'" she read, "'but you can bet every guy has regretted giving one too few.' I can't believe you used that quote."

"The lower plaque can be removed," Wax said quickly. "We'll change it up now and then too. But . . . well, that quote *was* something he explicitly asked for."

She stood up and shook her head, but he could tell she was already thinking this would be a good place to put some of the more choice quotes she'd recorded.

Wax remained standing, looking up at the visage of his friend. The dull ache remained. Always would. But Wax had been living his life. He, Steris, and the kids were preparing for another tour of the Roughs. A political tour, to drum up support for their bid to become a province in the changing face of the Basin.

Two years of hard work had staved off civil war. Real progress had finally led to a national assembly for the cities of the Basin. The Roughs were next. Some there wanted to be their own country; he hoped to persuade them they'd be better united.

The gate to the fence slammed, and shortly Marasi stepped up to the statue, wearing Wayne's actual lucky hat. Wayne had left it to her. A last-minute addition to the will, they'd been told. At first, Wax had thought *he* hadn't been left anything specific. Then certain items had started . . . showing up.

He held up the latest one for Marasi to see.

"A desiccated frog?" Marasi asked.

"Taxidermied," Wax said. "Was in my coat pocket this morning. Along with a note apologizing. Apparently the instructions had been for a *live* frog, but they hadn't quite been able to bring themselves to do it."

"You ever find out who he paid to do this?" Marasi asked, taking the frog by one leg.

"I assume it's the men who handle his estate," Wax said, "from how polite and apologetic the notes are. I haven't had the heart to confront them about it."

"You should just let it keep happening," Steris said.

He frowned as she stepped up to him. "You don't think it's gross? Last time was half a sandwich."

"It is obviously gross," she said. "But . . . well, it shows remarkable planning on Wayne's part. It's the sort of thing we should encourage."

"He's dead," Marasi pointed out.

"It's the sort of thing we should respect, then," Steris said.

Marasi eyed the frog. "They say that in gift-giving, it's the thought that counts. So . . . um . . . how do we interpret this?"

Wax sighed. "I'm sure they'll run out of items on his list soon enough."

Both women stared at him.

"Did you *know* Wayne?" Marasi asked. "When in his life did he *ever* let a joke die?"

It was . . . a fair point. And from what they'd learned about Wayne's remarkable finances, he'd had the money to keep this joke going for a long, long time. And, well, things like the frog were aggravating. And endearing. Both at once.

Just like Wayne had been.

"Are you ready for your trip, Marasi?" Steris asked.

Marasi grimaced. "Physically? Yes. We're packed. But mentally? Emotionally?"

"You'll do wonderfully," Steris said. "You're going to be the best rusting ambassador the damn Basin ever had!"

Marasi cocked her head.

"Using respectful language," Steris explained, looking up at the statue of Wayne, "considering the location."

"She's right," Wax said to Marasi. "You're exactly what we need. A Basin woman with a Malwish partner. A distinguished public servant with a record for being fair but tough. The leaders of the Southern nations will listen to you."

Marasi nodded, her expression firm.

"Have to be honest," Wax said, broaching the topic, "I'm a little surprised to see you leaving the constabulary behind. A part of me thought you'd never walk away. It was your dream."

"No," she said. "My dream was to do more. Always has been."

"I suppose you can do that as ambassador," Wax said.

Marasi smiled, arms folded. He was happy to see how confident she'd been lately.

"You're planning something," Wax said, finding himself amused. "What is it, Marasi?"

"I realized a while ago that there was something I wanted to do, something I wanted to accomplish," Marasi said. "But I needed experience I didn't have yet. I think becoming ambassador will help."

Wax frowned at that, trying to pick out what she meant. But before he could press further, Steris spoke.

"Hopefully you can calm the tensions," she said. "If anyone can get them to start opening up trade with us again, it will be you."

He agreed with the sentiment. Wax hadn't been in the meeting where the Bands had been brought out and found drained, but it smelled of a setup to him. Unfortunately, since the events of the detonation, relations had grown increasingly tense. The Basin felt the Bands had been taken unjustly, and the Malwish claimed that the Basin had shown aggression by even considering using them.

But the Bands were merely a symbol. Part of a larger power play. A new faction in Malwish—the one in control of their unification—kept talking about how Northern disasters had caused them so much hardship over the centuries, and warned that the discovery of these bombs was only the next step. They saw the North as chaotic, unpredictable.

Listening to this group, the Malwish Consortium had forbidden things like tourism and even most forms of trade between continents. Most importantly, they'd forbidden any transfer of harmonium to Northern interests.

No harmonium meant no airships. And no Investiture bombs, though trellium was the rarer component of that particular device. Unfortunately, the Basin had enough of both metals squirreled away to be dangerous. And despite his arguments against it, the Basin had been looking into developing weapons using those remnants.

They'd entered a new age. War was one of the main disasters Steris had to spend her time preparing for. It wouldn't come to that. Hopefully. If only he could figure out who had drained the Bands . . .

Don't go down that path, he thought.

Yet if he didn't ask those kinds of questions, who was he? Lawman? Father? Senator?

Questions were part of who he was. He just wished he knew for certain that the choice was his. Though, as he considered—his old instincts working on his behalf—he thought maybe he could piece to-gether what Marasi was planning. Judging by the way she was glancing back at the line of political picket signs in the grass nearby. By the way she'd strategically chosen such a high-profile appointment.

She said she needed experience. Negotiating, perhaps. Soothing egos. Trying to get people to get along . . .

"Rusts," he said, pointing at her. "You're planning to run for governor."

She jumped at the exclamation. Then blushed. *Then* she raised her chin and nodded.

Wax looked to Steris, who was smiling. "You knew?"

"She needed help planning," Steris said. "But the secret wasn't mine to share."

"I had to really decide," Marasi said. "Had to know for myself, Wax. I need experience. I need to see if I'm any *good* at this sort of work. But . . . yes."

Huh.

"I found I couldn't content myself with a constable's job," she said, "after what I'd seen and learned. I needed to be able to change things. *Actually* change things." She glanced at him. "Do you think I'm foolish? For years, in my youth, I thought maybe I was being trained to enter politics. I ran away from that, but now . . ."

They locked eyes. And she seemed to realize, for the first time, what she was saying. Who she was saying it to. Yes, he understood that feeling. He nodded to her, then glanced again at the quote on Wayne's plaque. Those words he'd said, years ago now. *You're meant to be helping people.*

Another figure approached, this one wearing a long black coat and hat. He stepped up beside them, inspecting the statue through spiked eyes.

"It looks good," Death said.

"How is it," Steris said, "you walk around without drawing attention?"

"Emotional Allomancy," he said absently.

"You seem better," Marasi said. "The treatment is working."

"Thank you," he replied. "I prefer not to taste of my own offerings. It seems I won't have to for some time." He turned to Wax. "Greetings, Brother."

Wax felt at his abdomen, where he bore his spike. Though he'd been assured being called "brother" by the likes of the kandra and Death didn't mean he was immortal, it did make him uncomfortable. He'd joined the ranks of an extremely disturbing group. The spiked.

"I've considered removing it," Wax said.

"I will help if you wish," Death said. "But not all of them can be removed. I nearly lost one once that would have ended me. Still find it amazing that I survived."

"Perhaps it's in the blood," Steris said.

"Perhaps it is at that." He hesitated. "Harmony wants me to express his regards."

God could have spoken into Wax's head because of the spike. But he had—by Wax's request—vowed never to do so, unless asked. He said he wouldn't even watch.

The spike, though, continued to perpetuate a problem. Who was Wax? Father, lawman, senator? Or was he none of the three? A part of him still worried, after all these years, that he was something else entirely. A pawn.

"Ironeyes?" Marasi asked. "Is . . . is Wayne *really* gone? Like . . . are we absolutely certain?"

Death smiled. "I didn't meet his soul, Marasi. I only do that some of the time, when Saze Invests me with the power. I think he likes the idea of me living up to the stories people decided to tell about me. It's . . . his way.

"Regardless, I didn't meet Wayne as he left. Harmony did that personally. Yes, your friend is gone." He nodded to the statue. "Remarkable likeness . . . It took an intervention to get Vin's right. But this is spot-on from the first try."

He nodded to the group of them, then handed a small note to Wax. From there, Death withdrew. Wax didn't buy his explanation of using emotional Allomancy to remain hidden. There was something more here.

He turned over the card that Death had given him. It was from Harmony.

I've heard distressing things, Waxillium Ladrian, that you've been worrying about. I would like to promise you something. With all the essence and axi of my being, I declare this.

  No one else moves you.

  Your life is yours.

  And you have my deepest apologies that I had a hand in teaching you otherwise.

Wax held that card for a long time. Then he tucked it into his pocket. He took Steris's hand and looked up at the statue.

Who was he? He supposed . . . well, he was whoever he wanted to be. No decision had ever forced him to choose one role over others—and being one man did not prevent him from being the others as well. He kept making that mistake, but he vowed right then to stop. To listen to his wife, to his heart, and to Harmony himself.

Father, lawman, senator. He could be all three, and more.

So long as he was helping people.

THE END OF ERA TWO OF MISTBORN

ARS ARCANUM

METALS QUICK REFERENCE CHART

METAL	ALLOMANTIC POWER	FERUCHEMICAL POWER	HEMALURGY
☾ *Iron*	Pulls on Nearby Metal	Stores Physical Weight	Steals Strength
⟠ *Steel*	Pushes on Nearby Metal	Stores Physical Speed	Steals Physical Allomancy
ⓜ Tin	Increases Senses	Stores Senses	Steals Senses
⬙ **Pewter**	Increases Physical Abilities	Stores Physical Strength	Steals Physical Feruchemy
⬠ *Zinc*	Riots Emotions	Stores Mental Speed	Steals Emotional Fortitude
⬗ *Brass*	Soothes Emotions	Stores Warmth	Steals Cognitive Feruchemy
⬡ Copper	Hides Allomantic Pulses	Stores Memories	Steals Mental Fortitude
⬢ **Bronze**	Reveals Allomantic Pulses	Stores Wakefulness	Steals Mental Allomancy
⬘ *Cadmium*	Slows Down Time	Stores Breath	Steals Temporal Allomancy
⬖ *Bendalloy*	Speeds Up Time	Stores Energy	Steals Spiritual Feruchemy
⬙ Gold	See Your Own Past	Stores Health	Steals Hybrid Feruchemy
☽ **Electrum**	See Your Own Future	Stores Determination	Steals Enhancement Allomancy
⬤ *Chromium*	Destroys Target's Allomantic Reserves	Stores Fortune	Might Steal Destiny
⬣ *Nicrosil*	Enhances Target's Next Metal Burned	Stores Investiture	Steals Investiture
⬚ Aluminum	Destroys Your Allomantic Reserves	Stores Identity	Removes All Powers
⬟ **Duralumin**	Enhances the Next Metal Burned	Stores Connection	Steals Connection & Identity

GOD METALS

METAL	ALLOMANTIC POWER	FERUCHEMICAL POWER	HEMALURGY
Atium	See Other People's Futures	Stores Youth	Steals Any Power
Lerasium	Bestows All Allomantic Abilities	Unknown	Steals All Abilities
Harmonium	Unknown	Unknown	Unknown
Trellium	Unknown	Unknown	Unknown

External metals have been *italicized*. Pushing metals have been **bolded**.

ALLOMANCY ALPHABETICAL REFERENCE

ALUMINUM: A Mistborn who burns aluminum instantly metabolizes all of their metals without giving any other effect, wiping all Allomantic reserves. Mistings who can burn aluminum are called Aluminum Gnats due to the ineffectiveness of this ability by itself. Trueself Ferrings can store their Spiritual sense of Identity in an aluminum metalmind. This is an art rarely spoken of outside of Terris communities, and even among them it is not yet well understood. Aluminum and a few of its alloys are Allomantically inert; they cannot be Pushed or Pulled and can be used to shield an individual from emotional Allomancy.

BENDALLOY: Slider Mistings burn bendalloy to compress time in a bubble around themselves, making it pass more quickly within the bubble. This causes events outside the bubble to move at a glacial pace from the point of view of the Slider. Subsumer Ferrings can store nutrition and calories in a bendalloy metalmind; they can eat large amounts of food during active storage without feeling full or gaining weight, and then can go without the need to eat while tapping the metalmind. A separate bendalloy metalmind can be used to similarly regulate fluid intake.

BRASS: Soother Mistings burn brass to Soothe (dampen) the emotions of nearby individuals. This can be directed at a single individual or across a general area, and the Soother can focus on specific emotions. Firesoul Ferrings can store warmth in a brass metalmind, cooling themselves off while actively storing. They can tap the metalmind at a later time to warm themselves.

BRONZE: Seeker Mistings burn bronze to "hear" pulses given off by other Allomancers who are burning metals. Different metals produce different pulses. Sentry Ferrings can store wakefulness in a bronze metalmind, making themselves drowsy while actively storing. They can tap the metalmind at a later time to reduce drowsiness or to heighten their awareness.

CADMIUM: Pulser Mistings burn cadmium to stretch time in a bubble around themselves, making it pass more slowly inside the bubble. This causes events outside the bubble to move at blurring speed from the point of view of the Pulser. Gasper Ferrings can store breath inside a cadmium metalmind; during active storage they must hyperventilate in order for their bodies to get enough air. The breath can be retrieved at a later time, eliminating or reducing the need to breathe using the lungs while tapping the metalmind. They can also highly oxygenate their blood.

CHROMIUM: Leecher Mistings who burn chromium while touching another Allomancer will wipe that Allomancer's metal reserves. Spinner Ferrings can store Fortune in a chromium metalmind, making themselves unlucky during active storage, and can tap it at a later time to increase their luck.

COPPER: Coppercloud Mistings (a.k.a. Smokers) burn copper to create an invisible cloud around themselves, which hides nearby Allomancers from being detected by a Seeker and which shields the Smoker from the effects of emotional Allomancy. Archivist Ferrings can store memories in a copper metalmind (coppermind); the memory is gone from their head while in storage, and can be retrieved with perfect recall at a later time.

DURALUMIN: A Mistborn who burns duralumin instantly burns away any other metals being burned at the time, releasing an enormous burst of those metals' power. Mistings who can burn duralumin are called Duralumin Gnats due to the ineffectiveness of this ability by itself. Connector Ferrings can store Spiritual Connection in a duralumin metalmind, reducing other people's awareness and friendship with them during active storage, and can tap it at a later time in order to speedily form trust relationships with others.

ELECTRUM: Oracle Mistings burn electrum to see a vision of possible paths their future could take. This is usually limited to a few seconds. Pinnacle Ferrings can store determination in an electrum metalmind, entering a depressed state during active storage, and can tap it at a later time to enter a manic phase.

GOLD: Augur Mistings burn gold to see a vision of a past self or how they would have turned out having made different choices in the past. Bloodmaker Ferrings can store health in a gold metalmind, reducing their health while actively storing, and can tap it at a later time in order to heal quickly or to heal beyond the body's usual abilities.

IRON: Lurcher Mistings who burn iron can Pull on nearby sources of metal. Pulls must be directly toward the Lurcher's center of gravity. Skimmer Ferrings can store physical weight in an iron metalmind, reducing their effective weight while actively storing, and can tap it at a later time to increase their effective weight.

NICROSIL: Nicroburst Mistings who burn nicrosil while touching another Allomancer will instantly burn away any metals being burned by that Allomancer, releasing an enormous (and perhaps unexpected) burst of those metals' power within that Allomancer. Soulbearer Ferrings can store Investiture in a nicrosil metalmind. This is a power that very few know anything about; indeed, I'm certain the people of Terris don't truly know what they are doing when they use these powers.

PEWTER: Pewterarm Mistings (a.k.a. Thugs) burn pewter to increase their physical strength, speed, and durability, also enhancing their bodies' ability to heal. Brute Ferrings can store physical strength in a pewter metalmind, reducing their strength while actively storing, and can tap it at a later time to increase their strength.

STEEL: Coinshot Mistings who burn steel can Push on nearby sources of metal. Pushes must be directly away from the Coinshot's center of gravity. Steelrunner Ferrings can store physical speed in a steel metalmind, slowing them while actively storing, and can tap it at a later time to increase their speed.

TIN: Tineye Mistings who burn tin increase the acuity of their five senses. All are increased at the same time. Windwhisperer Ferrings can store the acuity of one of the five senses into a tin metalmind; a different tin metalmind must be used for each sense. While storing, their acuity in that sense is reduced, and when the metalmind is tapped that sense is enhanced.

ZINC: Rioter Mistings burn zinc to Riot (enflame) the emotions of nearby individuals. This can be directed at a single individual or across a general area, and the Rioter can focus on specific emotions. Sparker Ferrings can store mental speed in a zinc metalmind, dulling their ability to think and reason while actively storing, and can tap it at a later time to think and reason more quickly.

ON THE THREE METALLIC ARTS

On Scadrial, there are three prime manifestations of Investiture. Locally, these are spoken of as the "Metallic Arts," though there are other names for them.

Allomancy is the most common of the three. It is end-positive, according to my terminology—meaning that the practitioner draws in power from an external source. The body then filters it into various forms. (The actual outlet of the power is not chosen by the practitioner, but instead is hardwritten into their spiritweb.) The key to drawing this power comes in the form of various types of metals, with specific compositions being required. Though the metal is consumed in the process, the power itself doesn't actually come from the metal. The metal is a catalyst, you might say, that begins an Investiture and keeps it running.

In truth, this isn't much different from the form-based Investitures one finds on Sel, where specific shape is the key—here, however, the interactions are more limited. Still, one cannot deny the raw power of Allomancy. It is instinctive and intuitive for the practitioner, as opposed to requiring a great deal of study and exactness, as one finds in the form-based Investitures of Sel.

Allomancy is brutal, raw, and powerful. There are sixteen base metals that work, though two others—named the "God Metals" locally—can be used in alloy to craft an entirely different set of sixteen each. As these God Metals are no longer commonly available, the other metals are not in wide use.

Feruchemy is still widely known and used at this point on Scadrial. Indeed, you might say that it is more present today than it has been in many eras past, when it was confined to distant Terris or hidden from sight by the Keepers.

Feruchemy is an end-neutral art, meaning that power is neither gained nor lost. The art also requires metal as a focus, but instead of being consumed, the metal acts as a medium by which abilities within the practitioner are shuttled through time. Invest that metal on one day, withdraw the power on another day. It is a well-rounded art, with some feelers in the Physical, some in the Cognitive, and even some in the Spiritual. The last powers are under heavy experimentation by the Terris community, and aren't spoken of to outsiders.

It should be noted that the interbreeding of the Feruchemists with the general population has diluted the power in some ways. It is now common for people to be born with access to only one of the sixteen Feruchemical abilities. It is hypothesized that if metalminds could be made from alloys with the God Metals, other abilities could be discovered.

Hemalurgy is less widely known in the modern world of Scadrial. Its secrets were kept close by those who survived their world's rebirth, and the only known practitioners of it now are the kandra—who for the most part serve Harmony—a few scattered koloss clans, and the Set.

Hemalurgy is an end-negative art. Some power is lost in the practice of it. Though many through history have maligned it as an "evil" art, none of the Investitures are actually evil. At its core, Hemalurgy deals with removing abilities—or attributes—from one person and bestowing them on another. It is primarily concerned with things of the Spiritual Realm, and is of the greatest interest to me. If one of these three arts is of great importance to the cosmere, it is this one. I think there are numerous possibilities for its use.

COMBINATIONS

It is possible on Scadrial to be born with ability to access both Allomancy and Feruchemy. This has been of specific interest to me lately, as the mixing of different types of Investiture has curious effects. One need look only at what has happened on Roshar to find this manifested—two powers, combined, often have an almost chemical reaction. Instead of getting out exactly what you put in, you get something new.

On Scadrial, someone with one Allomantic power and one Feruchemical power is called "Twinborn." The effects here are more subtle than they are when mixing Surges on Roshar, but I am convinced that each unique combination also creates something distinctive. Not just two powers, you could say, but two powers . . . and an effect. This demands further study.

ON SPIKES AND COMPOUNDING

Something odd is happening with the nature of spikes and Hemalurgy on Scadrial, of particular note to any arcanists who study the nature of Intent and Connection. I have, after lengthy questing, obtained an interview with Marsh, the one known as Ironeyes on Scadrial. (As a side note, it is curious how news of his nature is spreading to other worlds. Is this natural rumormongering, or something more supernatural?)

I can confirm, as best as it can be attested, that he is fully capable of Compounding to expand his life. He speaks of things of the past, like Hemalurgic decay and the toll that holding so many spikes takes upon the body. Inquisitors during his day slept for many hours; the Words of Founding say this was due to the need for storing health, but Marsh indicates there may be more subtlety to it than first understood. I'd postulate that it was in part a side effect of the incredible burden placed upon their souls by the nature of their horrific transformations.

Modern souls, however, seem to simply reject spikes of this magnitude. Further research is required, but I believe that this has something to do with the nature of Ruin's subservience to Preservation in the current dual vessel known as Harmony. The level of corruption of a soul that was possible in ancient days is no longer viable; if too many spikes are added, souls stop gaining powers. Marsh doesn't think this is a conscious decision on Harmony's part. Indeed, I think this is beyond the conscious abilities of even a Shard.

Instead, I believe this is the nature of souls (read: the Invested portion of a person's nature) and their balance with the cosmere. In the ancient days, Ruin was pushing hard on the fabric of Scadrial, leaking into spirit-webs through any method possible. Causing souls to decay faster, to accept more spikes than they should have been able to, and leaving the resulting person burdened beyond what was reasonable.

At any rate, the end result is a limit on the number of spikes a person can hold without external intervention. And, most key, Compounding seems beyond the abilities of any Hemalurgist created in this more modern era. The secret to cracking why this is, and how to circumvent it, could be of utmost importance to those watching Hemalurgy and its (presumed) danger to the cosmere as a whole.